THE PRESENCE OF LOSS

By

SUSAN TUZ

Printed in the United States of America
First edition: August 2012
Published by LuLu . www.lulu.com
ISBN: 978-1-300-03036-2

NEW AND COLLECTED POEMS AND SHORT STORIES

2012

CONTENTS

THE PRESENCE OF LOSS

The gardenias were in bloom. And Madge could see Ray, a smear of brown dirt on his brow, bending over, weeding them.

Around him, children had gathered. They smiled and waved to Madge, beckoning her to join them in the warm summer sun.

"We'll want to plant a weeping cherry next spring," Ray said, wiping his forehead with the back of his hand.

A gentle breeze blew across Madge's hair. She hadn't noticed the window was open. The smell of gardenias wafted in, sweet and inviting. The door opened and she could hear footsteps making their way across the kitchen floor. Ray would be in the dining room soon, standing beside her, his hand brushing back the hair that had blown across her face. Her senses quickened. She anticipated his touch...

Madge woke with a start. The cat had knocked a ceramic coffee mug off the kitchen table. The crash startled her. Lifting her head, she brushed a paper napkin from her cheek. The imprint of the wrinkled paper remained.

It had been a year since Ray had died but her memory created images of him in the yard, in the library and around the boathouse. They were images she welcomed and some days, lived for.

"We'll want to plant a weeping cherry next spring." She heard his words as clearly as she heard her mother's urging over the phone each day, "you have to let him go, get on with your life."

They had met in middle-age. Her years of fertility gone, there were no heirs to carry on his name -- no boy with shinning eyes and fair blonde hair reflecting his father's image. Madge envied women with sons.

When the cancer came, they'd faced it together. Sitting by his side, Madge had searched Ray's face during chemotherapy. Or they read the paper together, noting articles that amazed them. "Look," she'd said, "they're going to start taxing groceries. What next?"

Keeping a normalcy to Ray's life became her job. This tumor that lived in his brain, that was eating away the man she knew, would not take him from her. She was determined. But in the end, the tumor won.

The day Ray died, Madge walked the path in Washington Park. Tears streaming down her face, she'd repeated his name again and again. Her legs moved like lead. Lifting each foot and moving forward was an effort. It was as if an invisible force was pushing against her, taking the life force from her body. She felt spent on a level she had never experienced before.

Now -- a year later -- life pulsed within her, but at a slower pace. Grief still clouded her mind many days, a miasma that she had to fight her way through.

"When are you going to get rid of these suits?" her mother asked holding the closet door open. It was Saturday and her mother was there to take Madge out to lunch. "There are families at the church who could use these clothes."

Madge flinched. Taking the closet door from her mother's hand, she closed it. The suits would remain where they hung for now, like the sweaters shut away in the cedar chest or the shoes on the shoe rack. The thought of someone else wearing them was too painful and, standing at the closet door, her eyes running over Ray's suits, his shoes, created a sense of his presence that she still needed.

Her mother had a chastised look on her face. "I'm sorry dear," she said. "I'm just trying to help." Madge said nothing, put on her jacket, and left the room. Her mother followed. There would be no more "help" for now.

Madge knew her mother meant well, spoke out of love for her daughter. Her friends were more cautious, as if they sensed that hearing Ray's name spoken, having others suggest "moving on with life," was too painful for Madge to hear. The words of an Ezra Pound poem came to mind,,,

"You came in our of the night/And there were flowers in your hands./Now you will come out of a confusion of people/Out of a turmoil of speech about you. "I who have seen you amid the primal things/Was angry when they spoke your name/in ordinary places..."

The next morning arrived with another soft breeze. As Madge walked through the study, her eyes passed over a Meerschaum pipe in the pipe rack. A fishing crewel hung by the door. She remembered a day, a summer's day, when, the Morgan parked on the dirt road above, Ray cast his fly line out over a western river. This was how she imagined him in Heaven. Each of us has our own heaven, the one we carry in our soul and heart. She was sure of it. And this would be Ray's.

One day she would join him there. Taking the red checkered tablecloth that he had given her, she would spread it on the ground beneath a tree. She would set out a picnic lunch of popovers and jam, wild blackberries and sweet iced tea made just the way he liked it. They would bask in the sun.

But today, today she had to get on with life. There was work waiting for her at the office and a world of friends and family beckoning her to join them.

YESTERDAY

There is no evidence of yesterday

existing as a place.

Yet we go there often,

visiting old friends,

licking old wounds.

How would the road signs

to yesterday read?

Would their shape and color

be the elongated yellow

of a passing sign?

Or an inverted triangle of white

signaling a merge?

A MORNING TO SAVOR

I like the pale, cool grayness
 of this morning.

Mist veils soft green foliage
billowing against the sky.

Problems seem so far away,
shrouded by the fog.

The world is quiet
and soft,
cloistered and safe.

I savor the moment,
a neophyte ready for her oath.

MEMORIES OF YOU (FALL 2010)

We demand of others
what we have no right to ask,
And perhaps that is what makes them
love us.

You reached out to me,
And it was painful, hurtful,
left me angry,
Yet somehow touched my heart.

As I view your son years later,
I remember what you said to me
on that cold winter day four years ago:
"I don't want my son to know."

There is a pureness and sweetness
to this young man,
And I understand your urgency.

There is sadness in the air
as we stand together at your grave.
Steps fall in silent rhythm
as feet shuffle through the passageways of time.

I think of you,
of warm and tender moments
spent wrapped in your arms.

I remember your smile and your laugh,
a sweet boy who offered love and peace:

It was the '70s and we were young.

"Life is much more like a river
than a book," I read for your
eulogy,
And deeply weep.

O APPETITE

Wildmen
often chew
on the edges of books
rending their pages 'till
tattered and frayed.

Choirs of ladies
ingest
translucent,
incorporeal bonbons,
jouet jouetes,
sweet and lilting,
ephemeral and light.
Bijoux
presentations
10 cents a show.

The ardent reader
moves across the page
eyes intent
catching each allusion
savoring each construction
feeling the metaphors
Kantingly engaged.

Mrs. O'Clary
marks her page
with a bit of buttermilk.
2 tbsp. b. p.
3/4 tsp. a. p.

a dash of almond.

Little Jenny
tucks V. Rabbit
under her arm pit
sucking
her thumb
in she digs
pulling handfuls
of buggers
which stick on the page
like so many globs
of white alum paste

O appetite
thou hoary beast
ye' roam among the briars
and lead a lad and many a lass
to complicated Dryers.

SIMPLE PLEASURES

I like the concave

shape of a spoon,

it's simple symmetry

of curve and line.

"He liked to spoon,"

she said.

And I thought of you.

Curved 'gainst my back,

or I 'gainst yours,

we'd drift

eluding consciousness --

Two travelers in the

world of counterpane,

intent on hedonistic pleasures

of the gentlest kind.

THE WATERTUMBLESS OF WORDS
(thoughts on Lauren Camp)

I read her words.
Like shiny stones they
tumble from the page.

The Watertumbless of words,
she intrigues me
pulls me in,
washing along with her thoughts
and concepts that whirl
about my mind's eye.

I am lifted from my chair,
set free to blow about a
universe of possibilities.

She is the maestro
and my intellect --
her instrument of choice.

A SUDDEN MOMENT

I was thinking,

as he was talking,

And our consciousness

Clicked,

linking together,

entwining,

And I thought the thoughts he thought

as he spoke them.

It was magic, ephemeral --

And I looked away.

PERMISSION TO BE KIND

As a younger woman, I railed

'gainst my teachings to be

Sweet and Reassuring,

to make Sycophantic statements

in the wake of other's sorrow,

other's tragedy, other's travails.

But now, an older woman,

I find within me

the permission to be kind.

"It is better to be kind, than right,"

I read,

"because when you are kind,

you are always right."

I nod a hard-learned "Yes."

I am no street fighter

in the face of adversity,

Mine, or others.

As a younger woman,

I wore a sneer,

carried indifference like

a badge of honor.

But now I embrace

that we are fragile beings

in need of comfort,

of a kind word,

an understanding gesture,

Shelter from the storm.

GIFTS FOR A MOTHER

I gave you drawings, poems

and wild strawberries picked with tiny

fingers from a neighbor's field.

You gave me life,

Laid the foundation for a future,

and where there to lift me when I faltered.

I thrived in the radiance of your smile,

matured in the stern insistence of your displeasure.

You faced the disdain of a teenager,

waiting for the moment of maturity

when a grown woman would realize

your value.

You gave me gifts I can never repay,

gave me love I can only strive to match.

You are my mother, my dearest friend,

and I have the fortune to be your daughter.

SONG FOR A FATHER

Snow geese on a pale evening sky

Silhouettes against a full harvest moon.

I remember the first time I saw them,

the smell of woodsmoke, a patch of red

and you,

pointing them out to me, explaining what they were.

You seemed to have the answers to

everything in those days.

BLUE GIRAFFES

The day started with a warm breeze and Judith sensed good things to come.

From the bedroom her daughter, Angie, was groaning. In the early weeks of pregnancy, Angie was playing up the discomforts of morning sickness for maximum sympathy.

"Oh, I can't stand it." Angie's face showed from the folds of an Eideldown comforter, a tangle of brown hair falling over her forehead and into her eyes. "And why do they call it morning sickness? It comes at all times during the day."

Judith picked up a blouse and slacks from the bedroom floor and carried them to the hamper. From downstairs the notes of Cyrus Chestnut, soft and jazzy, carried upstairs. Angie's husband, Andrey, was starting the day on the right note, Judith thought.

"Would you bring me a cup of tea?" Angie asked, her voice soft and pitiable.

"It will do you good to get up," Judith replied. "You're not the first woman to have morning sickness. Why don't you go down and join Andrey in the sunroom?"

She was tired of her daughter's prima donna routine. With a husband who adored her and a mother who cared for her, Angie had it better than many women, Judith realized.

Throwing back the comforter, Angie eased her feet into pink slippers and started for the door. "It's not that I'm not happy about the pregnancy. I'm over the moon," she said. "But this morning sickness -- it's so debilitating."
"I'm excited about the baby, our little girl. For my generation, it's not like it was for women of yours. The fetus is a child already to us, a living being and we love it from inception," Angie said, pulling on her housecoat. Judith stopped tidying and looked at her daughter.

"I know your generation was fighting for the right to safe abortions. For political reasons, you spoke of the baby as a fetus, had a different view of it. For me, this child in me has a name already. She's Sarah. But she's making me suffer to get here," Angie left the room, making her way to the stairs. As she watched her daughter descend, a memory from Judith's past carried her back to 1977...

As she approached the grey cement building on Burton Street, Judith could see the protesters. Carrying a poster picture of a fetus, a woman in a camel coat yelled, "Don't kill your baby. Please, don't" at a young woman entering the clinic. Judith steeled herself and made her way through the protesters to the clinic door.

"Don't they know how hard this is?" said the young woman as she looked out of the waiting room window to the protesters below. She was one of five women already in the room when Judith entered, their faces strangely all the same hue of ashen grey.

As she'd entered the clinic, Judith had heard the receptionist saying to a nurse, "He's still going to do the procedures with the autoclave broken?" The nurse nodded. "He'll just give them stronger antibiotics. It will be fine.' Judith thought perhaps she should leave, come back another morning. But could she steel herself to face the protesters, to come again? And how, a college freshman with no degree yet, would she support a child? She owed a child more than a life of poverty and struggle.

When the procedure was over, Judith left the clinic through the back door, taking a taxi to her apartment. The cabbie was kind. "Doing this on your own? That's rough," he said. Judith said nothing.

That night, through a fog, her dreams were full of images of meat being ground, large blue giraffes and grey elephants passing by. Rough, callused hands stuffing in meat, the seams of the toys bulged nearly ripping, with blood running everywhere. It was a dream that would return...

Judith's memory fast forwarded to 1987. It was a cold November morning and she was walking to the office. She was pregnant again but under very different circumstances. She was ecstatic. "I'll take care of you. Protect you. Nothing, no one will ever hurt you," she said to the baby growing inside her.

She and Bob were two years into their relationship. Her career was on a steady track at the law firm. A pregnancy leave wouldn't put her on the fast track to a corner office, but it wouldn't derail her career either. She picked up her pace as a cold breeze blew down the sidewalk. There would be no December wedding. Bob wasn't ready to make the commitment. But a new daughter in June --- Judith felt blessed. She would name the baby Angie...

The Cyrus Chestnut CD ended. The silence brought Judith back to the present. "Mom, are you coming down for coffee?" Andrey called. "We're leaving for the doctor's soon." Judith entered the sunroom. Angie and Andrey sat in rattan chairs, their faces bathed in sunlight. Judith brushed her hand through her daughter's hair.

"Feeling better?" she asked gently. "Yes, much," Angie answered. "I don't know what I'd do without you, Mom," she added, nesting her head against Judith's hand. "Nor I without you," Judith answered, caressing her gently.

READING OVID IN NORTHEASTERN SPAIN*

*In 8th Century Spain, a myth existed among the Kabbalist that
Adam had a first wife, Lilith. She was formed from the clay of
the earth by God at the same time he formed Adam.
Lilith refused to abdicate her equality to Adam. She fought with
him about sex. She was a seducer of men. She strangled children.
One day, she uttered the four-letter word for God and flew off into
the sky never to return.*

Atalanta disrobes,

wearing little but ribbons

that flutter at her ankles

and knees.

Hippomenes' heart takes fire.

As they race,

side by side,

Atalanta sighs --

languishing on his face,

she halts

to pick up the golden apples

he lets fall,

losing the race.

I am no Atalanta,

but am I Lilith?

NEPHILIIM NO MORE

Do the children of the Nephilim

still walk the earth?

Banished from the Heavens,

their fathers defied

God's plan,

mating with mortal women.

Slain by Michael,

they came to their end.

But what of their offspring?

Are they the Yeti

said to flee from man's sight

As they wander the Himalayas,

timid, yet gigantic in size?

Would you know one

if you saw one?

Would her language be

unfathomable to human ears?

"Eiiyee,

I am the Nephilim spawn,"

she'd cry.

Her attempts to share

her loneliness

falling on deaf ears.

THE TOOTHLESS WOMAN

"--39--"

The toothless woman

peers into the lens

grimacing, growling

putting on a face

designed by another:

plastic form, rubberized mask.

"Glads ta get ta Noh U"

The photographer stoops,

placing another stem of

gladiolus in the vase.

Framed by trumpets,

an entablature of fauna

and redwood flooring

the toothless woman
howls with rage,

eyes rolling, tongue lashing,
billowing cheeks, snort froth.
--Take --

PAVEMENT HOLDS NO IMAGE

White Hair.

I remember white hair:
sublime
mixed with blonde
A strand
or two of black
but mostly white.

Legs.

I remember no legs:
a form
lithe & lilting
a quiver
singing without speaking.
His lips never moved.

Rocks are not always
what they seem.
They grow with the years.

I remember that man.
How he sat in that chair
torn blanket 'round a form
Hair spiky and short.

I remember a dog
pulling that chair,
with laughter, disturbing
        or
Laying by his side.

"They'll take that dog from him,"
her words rang
"He has to fit in
or become a fool
in a wheelchair."

"Old age in a god
is tough and greene."
I am no god,
The stone said
though once Phoebus seemed
to shine through me.

Eyes to the ground
eyes of a stone
pavement holds no image
only the rain.

THE VICTIM

Her eyes were vacant,
flat slabs of black in a swollen face
emanating hatred.

Her lips barely moved,
Her words falling flat:
The facts were wrong

She had three broken ribs
and numerous contusions.

My heart ached.
How could one human being
inflict so much distress
on another?

What would drive a person
to so completely wound
and damage this woman?

OH REALLY LAWRENCE?

I rail 'gainst Lawrence Ferlinghetti's premise:

"there is what used to be called the 'mystery of Woman,'
a romantic concept that endowed her with an illusive inscrutable
allure, both sexual and spiritual.
Then the feminist revolution brought Woman down from her
pedestal."

What pedestal? I ask.

Raped in alleys, suffering back-room abortions, or

raising children alone in ghetto apartments?

Where is the allure of a screaming child,

going without enough to eat, warm clothes to wear,

or a man to hold him and to mold his character?

No mystery in the drudgery of waitress

days, spent

Standing on swollen feet, 10, 12 hours at

a stretch.

No allure in broken bones,

swollen lips or blackened eyes

suffered by battered women.

"the feminist revolution," Lawrence,

freed women from their bondage

of male fantasy, Romantic pedagogy,

and unspoken suffering.

Take your wistfulness, Lawrence,

o're fantasy lost

And shove It.

FAT ASS MAMA

Whenever I saw it

I thought of fat ass mama

an' how she useta wauk

down the street.

Red hair shinin'

in the aftanoon sun,

broad hips swingin'

gently movin'

     right

then left

left

     then right.

That's what I thought of

when I saw that ole bus,

sittin' on the hillside

all covered in rust:

fat ass mama

that ole big bottom gal

an' i'd laugh

an' i'd wonda

just wonda

where she's waukin' now.

You see, it was somehow proper in proportion
and pleasing to the eye, yet obtrusive and
unsightly -- kinda like a fat lady's butt.

WINTER'S MORNING

Light breaks through

a winter's sky

cold and sharp

against slate grey.

Two china cups,

mauve and lilac,

orange sections

neatly cut,

and a jar of lemon curd,

These images start the morning,

one like many others.

I start the day,

cocooned in warmth,

bracing 'gainst the cold to come.

OLD MEN'S EARS

Old men's ears hang

large and lobed

'gainst grey heads filled with

life's knowledge.

The words they hear

echo past years,

bring a flood of experience,

a rush of life.

Old women's voices,

caress those ears,

accost those ears,

fill those ears

with memories of

dreams once drempt

in young men's minds.

Don't box those ears,

outfox those ears,

remember years

of sound have filled them.

A child's laugh,

a lass's gaffe:

true music to those ears.

WOMAN AS VESSEL

Some sisters hate the thought

of woman as vessel.

But if a poet is

the vessel,

And language the medium,

then Vessel Woman I gladly am.

Picasso stands beside

an urn,

back of a nude adorning it.

His look is pensive,

his pose, the same.

Woman is truly his vessel.

His medium,

canvass and paint.

The medium of language

inadequate,

He is trapped in Spanish.

Thus,

he drinks from the vessel often,

Reporting his conversations

with nature in periods.

ONE COW AT A TIME

Angie wanted to give a milk-producing waterbuffalo to a poor family.

She'd read it was the thing to do so families in developing countries could have enough milk to drink. And some to sell.

She'd read it On one of those "Save The World" websites.

But why send good American Dollars to The Sudan? Angie thought.

She saved her dimes and quarters,
And by December had enough to buy the cow.

She sent it to a family whose name she found on the web,
the address suggested a tenement apartment on the Lower East side
of Chicago.

Angie felt good about the gift.
But somehow the waterbuffalo gift Didn't turn out right.

Sure, the family had more than enough milk,
But the Housing Authority made them move.

Go Figure.

THE HOUSE OF GERANIUMS

The skinned bear looked like a human male. It's sinew exposed. It's muscles on display. It's heart was gone. No doubt pickled to be eaten with sliced onions, washed down with home-brewed beer.

Lilly looked on the bear with eyes filled with wonder. She had never seen a freshly killed animal before and was intrigued while at the same time disturbed by the scene.

Her father and the other men sharpened knives, preparing to cut up the animal to package as meat for the long winter ahead.

"Better salt the kidneys down, Bruce," one of the men said as he pulled organs from the hanging carcass.

The smell of warm blood and meat filled Lilly's nose. The 14-year-old left the basement room. She thought she might retch. Making her way upstairs she heard her mother and the other women in the kitchen.

They were canning tomatoes, making chili sauce to serve at meals with roast bear steaks.

Lilly knew this would be her life one day, canning as she cared for babies, while her husband hunted or butchered fresh-killed game with his hunting buddies in the basement below.

It was a future she accepted, uninspired, more submitted to the role she was soon to play.

The winter had been long and hard, but spring was just around the corner as Lilly walked to the school bus on a crisp April morning. She smiled as she walked past the Tanner's place. Water rushed over pebbles in the brook that hugged the bank along the dirt road where she walked. Spring brought promise and Lilly was ready for life's promises ahead.

"Hello," a woman waved from the Tanner's porch. "On your way to school?"

Lilly nodded. The woman pushed a strand of red hair from her forehead, brushed her hands across her slacks, then turned back to the pots of geraniums she was working with.

I wonder who that is? Lilly thought. Unusual to see a stranger here in Elizabethtown. When the school day ended, Lilly made her way home from the bus stop past the Tanner's place. The woman was nowhere to be seen. Lilly had hoped she'd be out on the porch again. Maybe they could talk.

"Oh hello," the woman appeared from around the side of the house. "Aren't you the Barlow girl? I'm Lilith, Lilith Adams."

All that spring Lilly looked forward to the end of the school day when she could stop by the Tanner place and visit with Lilith. Long empty, the Tanner's now bustled with life. Lilith and her husband, Seth, and their daughter, Batina, had brought the old property back to life.

Afternoons, Lily would dink lemonade and eat homemade cookies while Lilith talked to her about her former life in New York City. Lilith had been a teacher in New York when she first married Seth. The couple moved to the Adirondacks where Seth could paint plen' aire canvasses of the natural settings.

"What are your plans for college?" Lilith asked one day as she brushed crumbs from Batina's bib and lifted the 18-month-old from her highchair. "It's a bit early, but not really too soon to start thinking about where you'd like to go."

Lilly blinked. College? Nobody she knew had ever gone to college.

"Oh, I don't know," Lilly moved her toes in a circle on the stone floor. "Haven't really thought about it."

"Well if you want to go to Chicago I'm sure Seth would write a letter of recommendation for you to the school of art there." Lilith said it as easily as she might ask Lilly to hand her the butter dish.

Lilly felt uncomfortable. Here she was pretending she was someone she wasn't, pretending she belonged in a world of geraniums and paintings, with classical music playing on the record player.

"I better be getting home," Lilly gathered up her school books.

"OK, are you still on to babysit Saturday?" Lilith stood by the kitchen sink, the sun shining through the window brought out the highlights in her red hair.

That Saturday, Lilly sat in the brown leather chair at Lilith and Seth's, reading a book on the life of Jesus Christ she had come across on the bookshelf. Batina slept peacefully in the bedroom.

The work treated Christ as an historical figure. Funny, Lilly thought, I'd always thought he was a character created by whoever wrote The Bible. There really was a Jesus Christ?

Putting down the book, Lilly walked back to the bookshelf. What else is here that I never thought of? she wondered. A book of poetry by Percy Shelley caught her eye:

"Maidens and youths fling their wild arms in air;/As their feet twinkle; they recede, and now/Bending within each other's atmosphere/ Kindle invisibly"

Lilly's eyes went to a notation on the page in Lilith's handwriting "Petroarchian." What does she mean, Petroarchian? Lilly wondered.

As she walked home later that evening, Lilly fought back tears. She suddenly felt trapped, trapped in a life that promised nothing more than dull days of household drudgery. School was more boring than ever. The secretarial courses of typing, bookkeeping and shorthand worse that ever. But her family didn't have money. She had to be ready to get a job out of high school and support herself until she married.

Married -- Marriage had never been a welcomed prospect but now she thought, "Could I have a husband like Seth? An artist? Could I have a house full of geraniums in dark clay pots and shelves full of books. It seemed unlikely.

It was a life Lilly had never thought of before, still couldn't believe could ever be hers. No, that was the future for other girls, for girls like Batina with her exotic name.

Summer came and went. Lilly helped harvest the garden, picked fruit from the neighbor's orchard. As she stirred a pot of apple sauce, she hummed to herself a song Lilith sang to Batina, "Le jardin du mon pere, la lilas son fleur de lis" sang in her mind. Lilly hesitated to sing the words out loud. Her mother had ridiculed her just the other day when she put a cabbage leaf on her head and said "mon petite chou chappeau." "What's that suppose to mean? Don't babble that nonsense and take that leaf off your head," her mother's words cut deeply.

By 16, Lilly was posing for Seth. Wearing a Greek wedding dress of white cotton, she stooped from her seat in the chair, hands arranging peonies in a bowl. This was living, Lilly thought. She lived for these hours spent in the studio, classical music playing, Seth arranging fabric, flowers and china bowls -- creating a world where beauty enveloped them.

When the senior play was being planned, Lilly asked if she could draw the posters. She had finished the majority of her secretarial classes and had some down time during the school day that was otherwise spent in study hall.
"If I'd known you enjoyed doing this, we could have had you working on other projects over the years," the school counselor said as she stood watching Lilly apply pen and ink to poster board.
Sure, Lilly thought, like I could really spend my time on this when there was serious work to do. It wouldn't have been possible, she thought.

When Lilly graduated, she got a job at the money order office on Main Street. She spent her days reading through canceled money orders, checking against FBI files for forgeries. The days were long and boring and the pay was minimal, $50 a week. The year was 1967.
Her brother John, 6 years her junior, worked with her father on construction sites earning far more. "Why couldn't Dad have taught me to be a carpenter," she asked her mother one day. Her mother laughed. "I don't think you'd have the strength to swing the hammer," she replied. "Do you really want to be a carpenter?" "Well, it would pay more," Lilly said.
Elmer Bryer had started stopping by evenings on his motorcycle. Lilly would ride, sitting behind him. "I wish I could have my own bike, be the driver," she thought. Elmer's conversations were pedantic and Lilly patiently sat through Saturday afternoon at the local diner, listening to him talk about the garage of his own he would have one day. Some days she wanted to scream, "NO, my life is not going to be watching your kids, washing your clothes and cooking your meals." But she sat quietly in the booth, a smile on her lips. If she had learned anything in her 18 years, it was not to let people see what she was really thinking.

Seth and Lilith had moved to another town. They had three children now. Lilly thought of them often.

She drifted from one job to another . Was a receptionist for awhile at a stereo plant. Even tried working at the local paper mill, but the repetition of the job brought mind-numbingly agony. After six weeks, she quit.

"I don't know what's wrong with you," her mother said. "You just don't seem to be able to settle down to one thing. And Elmer, he was a nice boy and you brushed him off. Now he's married to the Lind girl. You'll be sorry you let that one go, some day."

Not bloody likely, Lilly thought.

She'd started drinking heavily on weekends. When she met Bill and he introduced her to marijuana, it set her free -- at least temporarily. High, she would write for hours or draw. Their love making took her to a place she'd never dreamt existed.

When a woman she'd met at the stereo plant asked her to go to California with her, Lilly agreed. Everyone was going to San Francisco and Monica would be her tour guide. "Why didn't you ever go to college?" Monica asked as they drove across the plains of Nebraska. "You're bright. You would have done well."

"Oh I don't know," Lilly was hesitant to admit her family's financial situation. "Just didn't." When they arrived in San Francisco, the two women stayed with a friend of Monica's, a flamenco guitar player who worked days as a seller in an art gallery. This was life, Lilly thought.

The month went by too fast. As they drove back across the country, Lilly found the long drive boring and dreaded the arrival back in New York state. Within a year, she was back on the road, this time driving her own Volkswagen, headed west.

"All of that seems so long ago," Lilly thought, as she sat in her office in Seattle. The San Juan Islands had become her home. The year was 2002. The 1970s, 80s and 90s were behind her. They were years of exploration, study and a degree earned at Berkeley. She'd kept in touch with Lilith and Seth. They had divorced. Lilith lived in Florida. Seth was back in Chicago, teaching and taking groups of students on painting tours of Europe.

Lilly often thought of them warmly. Grateful for the world of art and literature and possibilities they had shown her, opened for her. She'd never married. There had been relationships but nothing permanent.

What would my life had been if I'd never met Lilith Adams? If the feminist movement of the 1970s hadn't occurred? She shuddered at the thought.

That night, she met friends at a new wild game restaurant on The Sound. As she watched the ferries making their way across the water, Lilly's eyes ran over the menu. "Ill have the venison stew," she said to the waiter. Lifting her glass of chardonnay, she smiled across the table to her friends. "Bon appetit," she said, her thoughts going back to a young girl of 14 standing on the cellar stairs, in limbo between two worlds.

A poet once wrote, "I learned life is not personal." He was wrong. Life is nothing if not personal. We go to colleges of some prestige to learn to distance ourselves from the all-too-personal aspect of life. We come away somewhat shielded, perhaps with veneration for those who went before us into that good night untouched, unfettered by the insatiable personal-ness of it all.

Susan

Susan Tuz holds a bachelor of arts in English Literature. She attended college at Reed College and Western Connecticut State University. She is a staff writer for two newspapers in Connecticut.

TECHNOLOGY
AND
EMPLOYMENT

Innovation and Growth
in the U.S. Economy

Richard M. Cyert and David C. Mowery, Editors

Panel on Technology and Employment
Committee on Science, Engineering, and Public Policy

National Academy of Sciences
National Academy of Engineering
Institute of Medicine

NATIONAL ACADEMY PRESS
Washington, D.C. 1987

NATIONAL ACADEMY PRESS • 2101 Constitution Avenue, NW • Washington, DC 20418

The National Academy of Sciences (NAS) is a private, self-perpetuating society of distinguished scholars in scientific and engineering research, dedicated to the furtherance of science and technology and their use for the general welfare. Under the authority of its congressional charter of 1863, the Academy has a working mandate that calls upon it to advise the federal government on scientific and technical matters. The Academy carries out this mandate primarily through the National Research Council, which it jointly administers with the National Academy of Engineering and the Institute of Medicine. Dr. Frank Press is President of the NAS.

The National Academy of Engineering (NAE) was established in 1964, under the charter of the NAS, as a parallel organization of distinguished engineers, autonomous in its administration and in the selection of members, sharing with the NAS its responsibilities for advising the federal government. Dr. Robert M. White is President of the NAE.

The Institute of Medicine (IOM) was chartered in 1970 by the NAS to enlist distinguished members of appropriate professions in the examination of policy matters pertaining to the health of the public. In this, the Institute acts under both the Academy's 1863 congressional charter responsibility to be an adviser to the federal government and its own initiative in identifying issues of medical care, research, and education. Dr. Samuel O. Thier is President of the IOM.

The Committee on Science, Engineering, and Public Policy is a joint committee of the National Academy of Sciences, the National Academy of Engineering, and the Institute of Medicine. It includes members of the councils of all three bodies.

ISBN 0-309-03782-4, hard cover
ISBN 0-309-03744-1, soft cover

Library of Congress Catalog Card Number 87-42807

This publication was prepared by the Panel on Technology and Employment of the Committee on Science, Engineering, and Public Policy. The statements, findings, conclusions, and recommendations are those of the authors and do not necessarily reflect the views of the Economic Development Administration or other sponsors.

Cover photographs: (top) chip for echo-free conversations (Photomacrograph, fiber optic illumination) © AT&T MicroScapes; (left) UNIPHOTO; (right) FourByFive.

Printed in the United States of America

Panel on Technology and Employment

Committee on Science, Engineering, and Public Policy

Sponsors

This project was undertaken with both public and private support. Within the federal government, support was provided by the U.S. Department of Labor (the Assistant Secretary for Policy), the U.S. Department of Commerce (the Economic Development Administration), and the Army Recruiting Command. The following private organizations provided support for the study: the AT&T Foundation, the American Federation of Labor and Congress of Industrial Organizations, Citicorp, the Computer and Business Equipment Manufacturers Association, the General Motors Foundation, IBM Corporation, and the Xerox Foundation.

The project also received support from the Thomas L. Casey Fund of the National Academy of Sciences and the National Research Council (NRC) Fund. The NRC Fund, a pool of private, discretionary, nonfederal funds, is used to support a program of Academy-initiated studies of national issues in which science and technology figure significantly. The fund consists of contributions from a consortium of private foundations including the Carnegie Corporation of New York, the Charles E. Culpeper Foundation, the William and Flora Hewlett Foundation, the John D. and Catherine T. MacArthur Foundation, the Andrew W. Mellon Foundation, the Rockefeller Foundation, and the Alfred P. Sloan Foundation; the Academy Industry Program, which seeks annual contributions from companies that are concerned with the health of U.S. science and technology and with public policy issues that have technology content; and the National Academy of Sciences and the National Academy of Engineering endowments.

Preface

In recent years, concern over the effects of technological change has led many Americans to ask whether the development and application of new technologies within the U.S. economy will create new employment or contribute to higher unemployment. Many Americans appear to be pessimistic about the answer to this question, an attitude that, if anything, has become more widespread, despite the nation's recovery from the 1981–1982 recession. The relationship of technology to employment and the effects of technological change on the workplace and on U.S. productivity have become topics of national debate in the face of slow economic growth, high unemployment, and stagnation or decline in the real (inflation-adjusted) earnings of workers since 1970. The importance of these issues to the economic welfare of all Americans, coupled with the impetus of a 1983 National Academy of Engineering symposium that revealed a range of conflicting opinions on the long-term implications of technological change for employment and a request from the Council of the National Academy of Engineering, prompted the Committee on Science, Engineering, and Public Policy (COSEPUP)[1] to initiate the current study following consultation with scholars, government officials, and business, labor, and civic leaders familiar with the employment-related effects of technology. Thus, in 1985 COSEPUP created the Panel

---

[1]COSEPUP is a joint committee of the National Academy of Sciences, the National Academy of Engineering, and the Institute of Medicine.

vii

on Technology and Employment to carry out a new inquiry into the impact of technological change on employment opportunities, productivity, and the quality of work life (COSEPUP's charge to the panel is Appendix A).

The Panel on Technology and Employment first met in September 1985 and continued to meet at regular intervals during the next 18 months. This report incorporates the results of our discussions in panel meetings, the expertise of individual panel members, staff research and analysis, briefings from experts in industry, academia, and labor (Appendix B is a list of individuals who presented briefings to the panel or served as consultants), and the findings of the research papers commissioned by the panel (see Appendix C). A selection of these papers will be published separately in *Studies in Technological Change, Employment, and Policy* in late 1987. To disseminate our analysis and findings as widely as possible, we will also publish a summary of our report, entitled *Technology and Work in America: A Critical Challenge.*

This report addresses a number of issues that have surfaced in the debates over the employment impacts of technological change. These issues include the effects of technological change on levels of employment and unemployment within the economy; on the displacement of workers in specific industries or sectors of the economy; on skill requirements; on the welfare of women, minorities, and labor force entrants in a technologically transformed economy; and on the organization of the firm and the workplace. We have concluded that technological change will contribute significantly to growth in employment opportunities and wages, although workers in specific occupations and industries may have to move among jobs and careers. Included among our policy recommendations, therefore, are initiatives and options that can assist workers in preparing for and making such transitions.

In part because of the increased importance of international trade and competition within this economy, technological change has become essential to the preservation and expansion of U.S. employment and wages. The employment losses that result from a decline in U.S. international competitiveness are likely to outweigh any that might result from rapid technological change. Accordingly, we have developed policy recommendations to aid firms in the development and adoption of new technologies, so as to enhance their international competitiveness.

Technological and structural change pervade the U.S. economy, as they do any dynamic economic system. To ensure growth in economic opportunities for U.S. workers, technology should be viewed not as the problem but rather as a key component of the solution. With the development of policies that support investment in the human resources of this nation, as well as policies that deal with the consequences of technological change in an equitable and humane fashion, we believe that this latest in a series of transitions to new structures of work and employment can be accomplished efficiently and fairly. In the modern world economy, there is little choice—the United States must remain at the leading edge of technology in order to preserve and improve the economic welfare of all Americans.

On behalf of the panel, I would like to thank the numerous individuals who met with us in the course of our deliberations to provide briefings and other assistance and information. We also wish to express our appreciation for the work of the panel's professional staff: Dr. David Mowery, the study director; Dennis Houlihan; Nina Halm; Sara Collins; Leah Mazade, who worked with the staff in editing the report for publication; and Dr. Leonard Rapping, the panel's study director from June 1985 through March 1986. In addition, the panel is indebted to Dr. Allan Hoffman, executive director of COSEPUP, for his unflagging support of this study since its inception and to the reviewers of our report, including the members of COSEPUP. Finally, I extend my personal thanks to the members of the panel, who served with dedication and good humor throughout this study of a difficult and extensive set of problems and issues.

Richard M. Cyert
Chairman

Contents

Executive Summary

TECHNOLOGY AND AMERICAN ECONOMIC WELFARE

Technological change transforms the production of goods and services and improves the efficiency of production processes. It also allows the production of entirely new goods and services. Since the beginnings of American industrialization, such change has been a central component of U.S. economic growth, growth that has been characterized by the creation of new industries and the transformation of older ones as a result of innovations in products and processes. Technological advance has also played an increasingly important role in the growth of income per person during the past 100 years; its contribution to that area and to economic growth is likely to increase still further as the United States becomes more closely linked to the global economy.

The use of new technologies in production processes frequently reduces the labor and other resources needed to produce a unit of output; these reductions in turn lower the costs of production and the employment requirements for a fixed output level. If reductions in the demand for labor were the only effect of technological change on employment, policymakers addressing the problem of maintaining U.S. economic welfare would only have to balance the contributions of technological change against the costs of higher unemployment.

However, technological change has other important effects that historically have enabled society to achieve greater prosperity without sacrificing employment. By reducing the costs of production and thereby

1

lowering the price of a particular good in a competitive market, technological change frequently leads to increases in output demand; greater output demand results in increased production, which requires more labor, offsetting the employment impacts of reductions in labor requirements per unit of output stemming from technological change. Even if the demand for a good whose production process has been transformed does not increase significantly when its price is lowered, benefits still accrue because consumers can use the savings from these price reductions to purchase other goods and services. In the aggregate, therefore, employment often expands. Moreover, when technological change results in the development and production of entirely new products, employment grows in the industries producing these new goods. Historically and, we believe, for the foreseeable future, reductions in labor requirements per unit of output resulting from new process technologies have been and will continue to be outweighed by the beneficial employment effects of the expansion in total output that generally occurs. Indeed, the new realities of the U.S. economy of the 1980s and 1990s will make rapid development and adoption of new technologies imperative to achieving growth in U.S. employment and wages.

One crucial new reality of the U.S. economy of the 1980s is that it is more "open" to international trade than was the American economy of the 1950s and 1960s. The increased importance of trade means that higher productivity growth, which is supported by technological change, is essential to the maintenance of higher real earnings and the preservation of U.S. jobs. Moreover, the more rapid rates of international technology transfer characteristic of the modern economic environment mean that the knowledge forming the basis for commercial innovations need not be domestic in origin, just as U.S. basic research has underpinned the technological advances of firms in other nations.

The relative rates of development and adoption by U.S. and foreign industries of new process technologies affect the rates of growth in labor productivity (output per worker) in those industries and therefore can produce differences in labor costs among U.S. and foreign firms. To the extent that foreign firms develop and adopt new technologies faster than U.S. firms, the production costs of foreign producers will fall more rapidly. Barring shifts in U.S. and foreign currency exchange rates, declines in the wages of U.S. workers, or comparable technological advances by U.S. firms, these reductions in foreign producers' costs will decrease markets for U.S. firms and ultimately reduce jobs for American workers within the affected industries. To remain competitive in the absence of technological change and labor productivity growth in these industries, U.S. labor costs, relative to those of foreign producers, must be lowered, either by direct reductions in wages or through government policies that support devaluation of the dollar. Either of these methods decreases U.S. workers' incomes relative to those of foreign workers. Thus, if U.S. firms fall behind foreign firms in developing and adopting new technologies, the alternatives are not attractive—U.S. workers must accept fewer jobs or lower earnings.

Yet, if U.S. firms consistently develop and adopt new technologies more rapidly than foreign producers, the picture is quite different. The resultant higher productivity growth in U.S. industries will support reductions in production costs, which will enable U.S. workers to retain higher-wage jobs. Because new knowledge and technologies developed in the United States now are transferred to foreign competitors more rapidly than they were in the past, however, any technology-based advantages held by U.S. firms and workers over foreign firms and workers are likely to be more fleeting in the future. A key factor in sustaining American living standards and employment thus is continued public and private investment in the generation of new knowledge. Of equal importance, however, is the need for U.S. firms to advance from fundamental knowledge to commercial innovations more rapidly than in the past.

We have defined our task in this study as that of analyzing the contribution of technological change to employment and unemployment. Because technological change plays a limited role in determining total employment, its impacts in this area are primarily sectoral in nature, and those impacts are affected only indirectly by aggregate economic conditions. We therefore regard the design of macroeconomic policies aimed at achieving high levels of aggregate demand and employment as outside this panel's charge. Despite the increased importance of international trade for this economy and the role of technological change within it, a discussion of trade policies also would have taken this panel far beyond its charge; trade policy therefore was not considered in detail by the panel.

Our principal finding may be succinctly stated:

Technological change is an essential component of a dynamic, expanding economy. Recent and prospective levels of technological change will not produce significant increases in total unemployment, although individuals will face painful and costly adjustments. The modern U.S. economy, in which international trade plays an increasingly important role, must generate and adopt advanced technologies rapidly in both the manufacturing and nonmanufacturing sectors if growth in U.S. employment and wages is to be maintained. Rather than producing mass unemployment, technological change will make its maximum contribution to higher living standards, wages, and employment levels if appropriate public and private policies are adopted to support the adjustment to new technologies.

Technological change often involves difficult adjustments for firms and individuals. Workers must develop new skills and may be required to seek employment in different industries or locations. In many cases, workers suffer severe financial losses as a result of permanent layoffs or plant closings. Managers also face serious challenges in evaluating and adopting new manufacturing and office technologies in an increasingly competitive global economy.

Given these realities, we recommend policies to help workers adjust to technological change. Our recommendations propose initiatives to aid displaced workers through job search assistance, basic skills training, training in new job-related skills, and advance notice of plant shutdowns and large-scale permanent layoffs. Through these initiatives we focus on the need to assist individuals who experience hardship as a result of technological change and to aid them in securing new employment. We also offer recommendations that call on U.S. firms to develop and adopt new technologies more rapidly and suggest policies—both public and private—that might encourage them to do so.

The technological revitalization of American industry that is the goal of these recommendations is essential to the national welfare. The alternative to rapid rates of technological change is stagnation in U.S. wages and employment. In the end, no trade-off need be made between the goals of high levels of employment and rapid technological change. Policies that help workers and managers adjust to technological change can aid and encourage the adoption of productivity-enhancing technologies.

Technological change poses significant challenges to government policymakers, business, and labor, as well as to individual workers. Although the United States remains a technological and economic leader, the performance of this economy in adopting new technologies, achieving higher levels of productivity, and dealing with the adjustment of workers to new technologies leaves a great deal to be desired. If business, labor, and government fail to develop appropriate adjustment policies, the eventual price may be reduced technological dynamism and a decline in the international competitiveness of the U.S. economic system.

CENTRAL FINDINGS

In addition to the principal finding already stated, the central findings of this panel cover a number of dimensions of the employment impacts of technological change and form the basis for our policy recommendations, summarized below and discussed in greater detail in Chapter 10 of our full report. The complete set of findings for this study is compiled in Chapter 9.

**Employment and Wage Impacts of Technological
Change in an Open Economy**

• *Historically, technological change and productivity growth have
been associated with expanding rather than contracting total employment and rising earnings. The future will see little change in this pattern.*
As in the past, however, there will be declines in specific industries and
growth in others, and some individuals will be displaced. Technological
change in the U.S. economy is not the sole or even the most important
cause of these dislocations (see Chapters 2 and 3).

• *The adoption of new technologies generally is gradual rather than
sudden.* The employment impacts of new technologies are realized through
the diffusion and adoption of technology, which typically take a considerable
amount of time. The employment impacts of new technologies therefore are
likely to be felt more gradually than the employment impacts of other factors,
such as changes in exchange rates. The gradual pace of technological change
should simplify somewhat the development and implementation of adjustment policies to help affected workers (see Chapter 2).

• *Within today's international economic environment, slow adoption
by U.S. firms (relative to other industrial nations) of productivity-
increasing technologies is likely to cause more job displacement than the
rapid adoption of such technologies.* Much of the job displacement of the
past 7 years does not reflect a sudden increase in the adoption of
laborsaving innovations but instead is due in part to increased U.S.
imports and sluggish exports, which in turn reflect macroeconomic forces
(the large U.S. budget deficit and the high foreign exchange value of the
dollar during 1980–1985), slow adoption of some technologies in U.S.
manufacturing, and other factors (see Chapters 2 and 3).

• *The rate of technology transfer across national boundaries has grown;
for the United States, this transfer increasingly incorporates significant
inflows of technology from foreign sources, as well as outflows of U.S.
research findings and innovations.* In many technologies, the United States
no longer commands a significant lead over industrial competitor nations.
Moreover, technology "gaps" (the time it takes another country to become
competitive with U.S. industry or for U.S. firms to absorb foreign technologies) are likely to be shorter in the future (see Chapter 3).

**Technology and the Characteristics
of Tomorrow's Jobs**

• *New technologies by themselves are not likely to change the level of
job-related skills required for the labor force as a whole.* We do not
project a uniform upgrading or downgrading of job skill requirements in the

U.S. economy as a result of technological change. This does not deny the need, however, for continued investment and improvement in the job-related skills of the U.S. work force to support the rapid adoption of new technologies that will contribute to U.S. competitiveness (see Chapter 4).

• *Technological change will not limit employment opportunities for individuals entering the labor force with strong basic skills.* The most reliable projections of future job growth suggest that the number of jobs in the broad occupational categories accounting for the majority of entrant employment will continue to expand. Combined with a projected lower rate of growth in the entrant pool, this conclusion suggests that labor force entrants with strong basic skills (numerical reasoning, problem solving, literacy, and written communication) will fare well in the job markets of the future (see Chapter 5).

Technology and Work Force Adjustment

• *A substantial portion—from 20 to 30 percent—of displaced workers lack basic skills.* These workers often remain unemployed longer and have difficulty finding new jobs without incurring significant wage reductions. In view of the fact that technological and structural change in this economy will place increasing demands on the ability of workers to adjust, experienced workers who lack basic skills will face even greater difficulties in future job markets (see Chapter 3).

• *The evidence suggests that displaced workers who receive substantial advance notice of permanent job loss experience shorter periods of unemployment than workers who do not receive such notice.* Substantial advance notice (several months) of permanent layoffs or plant shutdowns appears to reduce the severity of worker displacement. Moreover, such a policy can improve the effectiveness of job search assistance, counseling, and retraining programs, thereby reducing the public costs of unemployment (see Chapter 7).

• *The primary federal program for displaced workers, Title III of the Job Training Partnership Act (JTPA), emphasizes the rapid placement of workers in new jobs. It does not appear to serve the needs of many displaced workers.* JTPA provides little training for the substantial number of displaced workers who need better basic skills; it also provides little extended training in job-related skills for other workers (see Chapter 7).

• *Displaced worker adjustment assistance programs reduce the duration of unemployment after displacement and result in higher wages in new jobs obtained immediately after participation in such programs.* There is limited evidence on the specific contribution of retraining in basic and job-related skills (a component of many such programs) to the employment and earnings prospects of displaced workers. Nevertheless, it would be wrong to conclude from this that retraining is ineffective or that it has a negative impact on earnings or reemployment prospects. Too little is known about the components of effective adjustment programs for displaced worker populations with different characteristics because of the paucity of rigorous evaluations of such programs. Additional policy experiments and evaluations are badly needed to improve these programs (see Chapters 7 and 8).

POLICY OPTIONS AND RECOMMENDATIONS

Our policy options and recommendations are based on the conclusion that, with an appropriate policy structure, technological change can support growth in U.S. employment and living standards. Toward that end, we have developed options and recommendations for the public and private sectors that emphasize three broad initiatives in public and private sector policies: (1) public policies to aid worker adjustment to technological change; (2) public policies to support the development and application of advanced technologies; and (3) improvements in labor–management cooperation in the adoption of new technologies, as well as improvements in private managers' expertise in evaluating and implementing new technologies.

Although the overall U.S. standard of living and average real (inflation-adjusted) wages generally increase as a result of technological change, individuals suffer losses. Many of our public policy recommendations stem from the belief that a portion of the affluence created by technological change should be used to assist those suffering losses as a result of it. In addition, public policies that deal with the equitable distribution of gains and losses from technological change can facilitate such change by reducing the resistance of potential losers to new technologies in the workplace. Just as management policies to support adoption of new technologies within the firm must address worker concerns about adjustment and employment security (see Chapter 7 of our full report), public policies that aid adjustment can reduce potential resistance to new technologies and support their more rapid adoption. On balance, if policies are developed that will ease the burden of adjustment for those individuals faced with job loss and thereby facilitate the adoption of new technologies, all members of our society can benefit.

Recommendations for the Public Sector

POLICIES FOR WORKER ADJUSTMENT

Our options and recommendations for assisting worker adjustment to technological change focus on the two groups that may be affected adversely by such change: experienced workers who may lose their jobs as a result of the adoption of technology, and labor force entrants, whose employment prospects may be reduced by technological change. Our options and recommendations to assist experienced displaced workers focus primarily on modifications in the primary federal program for which technologically displaced workers, as well as workers displaced by other causes, are eligible, Title III of JTPA. We also suggest other policies (advance notification of plant shutdowns and large-scale layoffs) to enhance the effectiveness of Title III. Our recommendations to aid labor force entrants focus on the need for additional research and actions based on the reports of other expert groups, a decision that reflects the fact that a complete evaluation of policies affecting the educational attainment and basic skills preparation of entrants is beyond the scope of this report. Our public policy recommendations also address the impacts of technological change on the employment prospects for minority and female members of the labor force.

Options for Adjustment Assistance for Displaced Workers

We recommend that action be taken to improve existing JTPA Title III programs of job search and placement assistance and training in both basic and job-related skills for displaced workers. We recommend that some or all of the following options be implemented:

- *broadening the range of employment services provided to displaced workers and those facing imminent displacement, including job counseling, skills diagnosis, job search assistance, and placement services;*
- *increasing the share of Title III funds devoted to training in basic and job-related skills;*
- *broadening income support for displaced workers engaged in training;*
- *instituting a program of federally provided direct loans or loan guarantees, administered by state or local authorities, to workers displaced by technological change, plant shutdowns, or large-scale layoffs (these loans could be used by displaced workers to finance retraining or relocation or to establish new businesses); and*
- *establishing a program for demonstrations and experiments with rigorous evaluation requirements to test and compare specific program designs.*

In addition to these modifications to JTPA, we recommend revising state unemployment compensation laws to guarantee explicitly that displaced workers who are eligible for unemployment compensation can continue to receive benefits while undertaking retraining.

We have concluded that the federal government should be the primary source of funding for the abovementioned policy options. Federal financing is preferable to state funding because of the inequities created by differences in the level of state resources for such programs. Indeed, states that are experiencing severe economic dislocations are likely to face serious problems in funding significant displaced worker programs. In view of the fact that one of the central motives for worker adjustment programs is the equitable distribution of the costs and benefits of new technology adoption among the U.S. population, the avoidance of regional inequities is an important consideration. One option for financing the economic adjustment loans, like the arrangements for other federal loan programs, would employ the Federal Financing Bank and therefore would not require federal funds from general revenues.

Estimates of the costs of these adjustment assistance options for displaced workers depend on estimates of the population of displaced workers. In Chapter 3, we note that estimates of the number of workers displaced annually range from 1 million, if displaced workers are defined as individuals with 3 years' employment in their jobs prior to layoff, to 2.3 million. Cost estimates also depend on assumptions about the rates of worker participation in such programs, an area in which reliable data are scarce. Existing programs that combine income support with retraining for displaced workers, such as the UAW-Ford program, have enrolled 10–15 percent of the eligible population (see Chapter 7). Although we lack conclusive evidence on this point, it may be that participation rates would be higher in programs involving displaced workers from industries that pay lower wages than the automotive industry.[1]

We have compiled estimates of the costs to the federal government of job search assistance, training, and extended unemployment compensation for two values of the annual flow of displaced workers (the two values are drawn from the 1984 survey of displaced workers conducted by the U.S. Bureau of Labor Statistics): 1 million workers, which is the estimated number of displaced workers who had been employed for 3 or more years in the job from which they were displaced; and 2.3 million, which is the estimated total number of workers suffering permanent job loss. As estimated rates of participation in these programs range from 5 to 30 percent of the displaced worker population, the estimated costs of these policy options range from $131 million (5 percent participation rate)

---

[1]Participation rates also will be affected by the policies and guidelines adopted by states in administering any system of training, job search assistance, and income support.

to $786 million (30 percent) for an annual flow of 1 million displaced workers. It is important to note that the highest estimated participation rate exceeds any observed thus far in a displaced worker training program in the United States. If we assume that the flow of eligible displaced workers is 2.3 million annually, the estimated costs of the program range from $301 million (5 percent participation rate) to about $1.8 billion (30 percent).[2] JTPA Title III outlays for fiscal year 1987 are roughly $200 million, although a significant expansion has been proposed in the President's budget for fiscal year 1988.

How could these policy options be financed? The panel discussed revenue alternatives and found no single method that was preferable to all others on equity and other grounds. In the absence of evidence suggesting that one alternative is superior to all others, the decision on funding sources and budgetary reallocations is properly political, involving considerations that extend well beyond this panel's charge.

Advance Notice of Plant Closures and Large Permanent Layoffs[3]

We have concluded that substantial (a minimum of 2–3 months) advance notice of permanent plant shutdowns and large permanent layoffs offers significant benefits to the workers who are displaced and to the nation by reducing the average duration of the workers' unemployment and lessening the public costs of such unemployment. The current system of voluntary advance notice, however, fails to provide sufficient advance notice to many U.S. workers. We therefore recommend that federal action be taken to ensure that substantial advance notice is provided to all workers. Although the panel agreed on the need for federal action to broaden the coverage of advance notice within the U.S. work force, panel members were not unanimous in their support of a specific legislative or administrative mechanism to achieve this goal. The panel believes that the following alternatives are viable options to achieve broader advance notice, with appropriate provisions to reduce the burden on small business and provide for unforeseen circumstances:

*   *federal action to require employers to provide substantial advance notice of permanent plant shutdowns and large permanent layoffs; or*

---

[2]If the annual flow of displaced workers is estimated to amount to 1.2 million workers (the estimate used by the Secretary of Labor's Task Force on Economic Change and Dislocation, 1986), the estimated costs of these options range from $157 million to $943 million.

[3]Panel member Anne O. Krueger dissents from this recommendation. Her statement appears in Appendix D.

• *federal action to provide tax incentives for employers to give such notice.*

The current system of voluntary advance notice does not provide workers with the "best-practice" amount of advance notice (a minimum of 2–3 months)—as Chapter 7 notes, too few workers are notified in advance of permanent plant closures or large permanent layoffs, thus hampering their adjustment. When workers receive sufficient advance notice, the evidence suggests that they adjust more rapidly and more successfully to job loss, which reduces the costs of displacement to them and to the public sector. We believe that the benefits of advance notice more than outweigh the costs of such a policy—costs that exist, but that are distributed differently, when no advance notice is provided. When advance notice is given, the costs of worker displacement are shared by taxpayers, by the displaced workers, and by the firms closing plants or permanently discharging workers, rather than being borne primarily by taxpayers and the workers being laid off.

Through its public policies, this society has made a judgment that the costs of many regulations (e.g., those covering health and safety, consumer protection, or securities markets) that enhance the flow of information to workers and consumers and distribute costs more equitably among workers, consumers, and firms are more than offset by the benefits of such policies. We believe that advance notice falls into the same category of public policy and that steps to mandate this practice should be taken by the federal government.

Training for Labor Market Entrants

We share the concerns of other studies, set forth in the reports of the COSEPUP Panel on Secondary School Education for the Changing Workplace ("High Schools and the Changing Workplace: The Employers' View," 1984), the Task Force on Teaching as a Profession, of the Carnegie Forum on Education and the Economy ("A Nation Prepared: Teachers for the 21st Century," 1986), and the U.S. Department of Education ("A Nation at Risk: The Imperative for Educational Reform," 1983), regarding the amount and quality of basic skills preparation provided to labor force entrants by U.S. public schools. Improvement in the basic literacy, problem-solving, numerical reasoning, and written communication skills of labor force entrants is essential. We endorse additional public support for research on strategies to achieve this goal, as well as financial support for the implementation of programs that improve the basic skills of labor force entrants and of those already in the labor force who lack these skills.

Equal Employment Opportunity

We recommend more vigorous enforcement of policies to combat racial and sexual discrimination in the labor market as a means of improving the ability of minority and female workers, as well as minority and female labor force entrants, to adjust to the demands of technological change.

SCIENCE AND TECHNOLOGY POLICY TO SUPPORT THE ADOPTION OF NEW TECHNOLOGIES

We support continued high levels of investment by industry and the federal government in basic and applied research—this is the essential "seed corn" of innovation, and such investments play a significant role in the education of scientists and engineers. Federal support for nondefense R&D is particularly important, in view of the limited commercial payoffs from the high historical levels of defense R&D in this country (there are important but limited exceptions to this generalization, as noted in Chapter 2). The foreseeable contribution of defense R&D to the civilian U.S. technology base appears to be limited at best.

In addition to a strong research base, however, public policies to support more rapid adoption of new technologies within this economy deserve consideration. The historic focus of post-World War II science and technology policy on the generation rather than the adoption of new civilian technologies (once again, a generalization with several important exceptions) contrasts with the orientation of public science and technology policy in several other industrial nations (e.g., Japan, Sweden, and West Germany) and may have contributed to more rapid adoption of manufacturing process innovations and more rapid commercialization of new product technologies in those nations. We therefore support the development and evaluation of additional public policies to encourage the more rapid adoption of new technologies within the United States.

We recommend increased federal support for activities and research to encourage more rapid adoption of new technologies. Although the achievement of this goal requires actions in a number of areas not considered by this panel, our review of policies leads us to recommend the following options for consideration:

• *Strengthen research on technical standards by public agencies (primarily the National Bureau of Standards) to support, where appropriate, private standard-setting efforts.*

• *Strengthen research programs supporting cooperative research be-*

tween industry and the federal government in the development and application of technologies.

• *Increase support for federal programs to improve U.S. firms' access to foreign science and engineering developments and innovations.*

THE ADEQUACY OF THE DATA

In the course of this study, the panel has found that the data available from public sources are barely sufficient to analyze the impacts of technology on employment. In some cases this data problem reflects the rapid expansion of new sectors of the economy, such as services, for which federal agencies have been hard-pressed to monitor and collect data comparable in quality and quantity to those available for manufacturing. In other cases these data have declined in quality during the past decade as a result of reductions in data collection budgets. The amount and quality of data on evaluations of worker adjustment assistance programs also must be improved.

• *We recommend that post-fiscal year 1980 reductions in key federal data collection and analysis budgets be reversed and that (at a minimum) these budgets be stabilized in real terms for the next decade in recognition of the important "infrastructural" role data bases play within research and policymaking. We urge that a portion of these budgets be devoted to improvements in the collection and analysis of employment, productivity, and output data on the nonmanufacturing sector of this economy.*

• *We recommend that a new panel study or a supplement and follow-up to the Current Population Survey be undertaken by the Bureau of Labor Statistics to examine the effects of technological change on the skill requirements, employment, and working conditions of individuals of working age. We also support the development by the Census Bureau of better data on technology adoption by firms.*

• *We recommend that the Bureau of Labor Statistics expand its survey of displaced workers (the special supplement to the Current Population Survey) to allow annual data collection and that this survey improve its question on the nature and effect of advance notice of layoffs.*

• *We recommend that any expansion of adjustment assistance services for displaced workers be accompanied by rigorous evaluations of these programs to provide information on the long-term effectiveness of different program designs and strategies.*

To reduce the potential for conflicts of interest that may arise when an organization charged with operating adjustment assistance programs has sole responsibility for the design and administration of evaluations of these programs, we recommend that federal or state agencies responsible for the operation of such programs share with other agencies the responsibility for evaluating them, or conduct such evaluations with the advice of independent expert panels.

• *We recommend that evaluations be undertaken of the implementation of the provisions of the Perkins Vocational Education Act of 1984 that allow federal and state funds to be used for improving the skills of the employed work force. In addition, a federally sponsored evaluation of a sample of state-level programs in upgrade training should be undertaken to determine the overall effectiveness of such programs and the specific design features that contribute to success.*

HEALTH AND SAFETY IMPACTS OF TECHNOLOGICAL CHANGE

We recommend a major interdisciplinary study of the consequences of technological change for workplace health and safety and the regulatory structure designed to ensure that worker health and safety are protected. These areas also should be monitored carefully by federal and state agencies.

Recommendations for the Private Sector

LABOR–MANAGEMENT COLLABORATION IN TECHNOLOGY ADOPTION

Rates of adoption of new technologies, as well as the exploitation of computer-based manufacturing and office automation technologies to increase worker productivity, satisfaction, and safety, are affected significantly by the management of the adoption process. If the process proceeds smoothly, both workers and management can benefit from these technologies, which have the potential to enrich work as well as to enhance its efficiency. The potential payoffs from cooperation between labor and management in technology adoption are high, but such cooperation has been lacking in some U.S. industries. Our recommendations in this area highlight some key components of successful adoption strategies.

Elements of "Best-Practice" Strategies for Technology Adoption

• *We recommend that management give advance notice of and consult with workers about job redesign and technological change.*

- *We recommend that the adoption of new workplace technologies be accompanied by employment policies that strengthen employment security; such policies include retraining of affected workers for other jobs and a reliance on attrition rather than on permanent layoffs wherever possible. At the same time, workers and unions must recognize their stake in a more productive workplace and consider modifications of work rules and job classifications in exchange for such employment security policies.*

Protection from the Costs of Displacement

We recommend that management and labor explore the use of severance payments for permanent layoffs of experienced workers. To preserve such benefits in the event of a firm's bankruptcy, we also recommend that employers and workers consider establishing a joint insurance fund.

EDUCATION FOR MANAGERS

We recommend that the current efforts to strengthen the quality of managerial education in the management, adoption, and evaluation of advanced manufacturing and service production processes be continued, both within business schools and through other institutions. Additional research on this topic is needed and could be funded through university industry research collaboration, among other possibilities. Education for those currently employed as managers also must be strengthened to incorporate instruction in the adoption of new technologies and in strategies for helping the work force adjust to technological change.

1

Introduction

TECHNOLOGY AND AMERICAN ECONOMIC WELFARE

Technological change transforms the production of goods and services and improves the efficiency of production processes. It also allows the production of entirely new goods and services. Since the beginnings of American industrialization, such change has been a central component of U.S. economic growth, growth characterized by the creation of new industries and the transformation of older ones through innovations in products and processes. One of the results of these innovations has been increased productivity—that is, greater output per unit of input—which has been largely responsible for growth in U.S. income per person during most of this century. Such growth in turn has contributed to higher living standards for Americans and shorter workweeks (Abramovitz, 1956; Denison, 1962; Solow, 1957). The contribution made by technological advances to growth in income per person has increased during the past 100 years (Abramovitz and David, 1973; Temin, 1975); that contribution, as well as the contribution of new technology to overall U.S. economic advance, is likely to increase still further as the United States becomes more closely linked to the global economy.

Technological change in production processes frequently reduces the amount of labor and other resources needed to produce a unit of output; these reductions lower both the costs of production and the labor requirements for a fixed output level. If a reduced demand for labor were the only effect of technological change on employment, policymakers addressing the problem of maintaining U.S. economic welfare would simply have to balance the contributions of technological change against the costs of higher unemployment.

Yet technological change has other important effects that historically have enabled society to achieve greater prosperity without sacrificing employment. By reducing the costs of production and thereby lowering the price of a particular good in a competitive market, technological change in production processes frequently leads to increased demand for that good; greater output demand results in increased production, which requires more labor, and offsets the effects of reductions in the amount of labor required per unit of output. Even if the demand for a good whose production process has been transformed does not increase significantly when the price of the good is lowered, benefits still accrue because consumers can use the savings from price reductions to purchase other goods and services. In the aggregate, therefore, employment often expands. Moreover, when technological change results in the development and production of new products, employment grows in the industries that serve the markets for these goods, as well as in the industries supplying inputs to them. Historically and, we believe, for the foreseeable future, any laborsaving impact of technological change on aggregate employment has been and will continue to be outweighed by the beneficial employment effects of the expansion in total output that generally occurs.

Total employment within an economy is determined by a great many influences, of which technological change is only one—and far from the most important. The level of total employment is influenced by the rate of economic growth, operating in conjunction with growth in the labor supply; by the level of real (inflation-adjusted) wages; by business cycle fluctuations; and by occasional "shocks" to the economic system—for example, the massive oil price increases of 1973 and 1979. We have defined our task as that of analyzing the contribution of technological change to employment and unemployment. Because technological change plays such a limited role in determining total employment, its employment impacts in this area are primarily sectoral, and those impacts are affected only indirectly by aggregate economic conditions. We therefore regard the design of macroeconomic policies aimed at achieving high levels of aggregate demand and employment as outside the panel's charge.

In recent years, international trade has become an important force within the U.S. economy. Consequently, international trade flows interact with technological change to affect U.S. employment. Some of the implications of this interaction for economic policy and employment in the U.S. economy are discussed later in this report (see Chapters 2 and 3). A detailed analysis of international trade issues and recommendations for international trade policy, however, would have drawn us far from our primary focus—the impact of technological change on employment. We therefore devote little attention to international trade policies.

Much of our analysis focuses on the employment effects of technological change in particular industries or sectors. As technological change and other factors alter the structure of the economy, unemployment can and will result in some areas, while expanding employment opportunities appear elsewhere. Our analysis and policy prescriptions highlight ways of facilitating the movement of workers from sectors or occupations in which labor demand is declining to areas in which it is growing.

Our principal finding may be succinctly stated:

Technological change is an essential component of a dynamic, expanding economy. The modern U.S. economic system, in which international trade plays an increasingly important role, must generate and adopt advanced technologies rapidly in both the manufacturing and nonmanufacturing sectors if growth in employment and wages is to be maintained. Recent and prospective levels of technological change will not produce significant increases in total unemployment, although individuals will face painful and costly adjustments. Rather than producing mass unemployment, technological change will make its maximum contribution to higher living standards, wages, and employment levels if appropriate public and private policies are adopted to support the adjustment to new technologies.

Technological change often involves difficult adjustments for firms and individuals. Workers must develop new skills and may be required to seek employment in different industries, occupations, or locations. In many cases, workers suffer severe financial losses as a result of permanent layoffs or plant closings. Managers also face serious challenges in evaluating and adopting new manufacturing and office technologies in an increasingly competitive global economy.

In light of these realities, we recommend policies to help workers and firms adjust to technological change. Our recommendations propose new initiatives to aid displaced workers through job search assistance, basic skills training, retraining, and advance notice of plant shutdowns and large-scale permanent layoffs. These initiatives focus on the need for society as a whole, which benefits from technological change, to assist individuals who experience hardship as a result of it and to help them secure new jobs. We also discuss strategies to help firms adopt new technologies more rapidly.

The alternative to rapid rates of technological change is stagnation in productivity growth and real wages. In foreign economies, technological change will be rapid for the foreseeable future; if the United States is to remain an industrial power capable of generating high-wage employment, such change is indispensable (although other factors, e.g., capital formation, also affect the international competitiveness of U.S. industry). In the end, the goals of increased high-wage employment and rapid rates of technological change are more than compatible; achieving the first goal depends on accomplishing the second.

Technological change poses significant challenges to government policymakers, business, and labor, as well as to individual workers and managers. Although the United States remains a technological and economic leader, the performance of this economy in adopting new technologies, achieving higher levels of productivity, and dealing with the adjustment of workers to technological change leaves much to be desired. The costs of continued suboptimal performance in these areas are not inconsequential: if business, labor, and government fail to develop appropriate adjustment policies, the technological dynamism and international competitiveness of the U.S. economy will decline.

WHOSE JOBS ARE AFFECTED BY TECHNOLOGICAL CHANGE?

Total employment depends on the supply of and demand for labor. The labor supply is determined by demographic factors, which affect the number of entrants to the labor force each year, and by changes in the proportion of different population groups seeking employment (labor force participation rates). The demand for labor depends primarily on the rate of growth in total output and real wages, both of which can be affected by cyclical fluctuations, and on numerous other factors.

Although technological change is of secondary importance in determining total employment, it does affect one component of aggregate *unemployment*. "Structural" unemployment is unemployment of long duration that persists in the face of economic expansions. It stems from the dynamism of the economic system in which jobs are created and eliminated constantly, regardless of the state of aggregate or total demand (Leonard, 1986). Although the duration of either unemployment after job loss or job search after entry into the labor force is relatively short for most workers, others have great difficulty finding new jobs and thus may be unemployed for much longer periods.

Our discussion of technological change and employment focuses on the effects of new technology on the employment of experienced workers and on job openings for those entering the labor force. For example, technological change may contribute to unemployment among experienced workers because the jobs created by new technology are located far away from the areas with significant job losses; in addition, the new jobs that result from technological change may require skills that make them difficult for displaced workers to fill. The evidence suggests that the adoption of new technologies by U.S. firms is a relatively modest contributor to permanent job loss in this economy, although precise distinctions among the causes of displacement are virtually impossible to make. There is, however, some reason to believe that technological change may play a role in other causes of experienced worker displacement. As we discuss later (see Chapters 2 and 3), much of the displacement of U.S. workers resulting from import competition reflects more rapid technological progress in other nations.

Programs such as job search assistance and counseling, as well as retraining, are designed to help experienced displaced workers adjust to technological change and are potential means of reducing structural unemployment. Because there have been few evaluations of such programs, however, there is little guidance for successful program planning and design. New initiatives in this area must incorporate substantial resources for experimentation and evaluation, as discussed in Chapters 7 and 8.

As for labor force entrants (discussed in Chapters 3 and 5), our review of the evidence suggests that a strong foundation in basic skills will be indispensable to finding good jobs in the workplace of the future (see also the report of the COSEPUP Panel on Secondary School Education for the Changing Workplace, 1984). Job openings for well-prepared entrants to the labor force should remain sufficient to absorb the projected smaller population of entrants in the future.

TECHNOLOGICAL CHANGE AND EMPLOYMENT IN AN "OPEN" ECONOMY

The U.S. economy of the 1980s is more "open" to international trade than the U.S. economy of the 1950s and 1960s; imports and exports affect a larger share of economic activity and employment. In such an environment, productivity growth, which is influenced by technological change, is essential to maintaining higher real earnings and preserving U.S. jobs. Our discussion of the employment impacts of technological change is influenced by our recognition that *within an open economy, growth in output and employment depends on productivity growth.*

How does technological change support growth in productivity, employment, and output within an economy that is open to international trade? The answer lies in the interdependence of these factors, a key concept in explaining the analysis in this report. The process of technological change, which is discussed in greater detail in Chapter 2, involves exploiting scientific and technical knowledge in the invention and innovation stages. Within the modern economic environment, the knowledge that is the basis for commercial innovations need not be domestic in origin. U.S. firms have relied on discoveries made elsewhere in the world in developing new technologies, and U.S. basic research may underpin (and has underpinned) the technological advances of firms in other nations.

The relative rates of development and adoption by U.S. and foreign industries of new process technologies affect the rates of growth in labor productivity in those industries and therefore can produce differences in labor costs among U.S. and foreign firms. To the extent that foreign firms develop and adopt new technologies more quickly than U.S. firms, the production costs of foreign producers will fall more rapidly. In the absence of other adjustments, these reductions in the production costs of foreign producers will decrease markets for U.S. firms and ultimately reduce jobs for U.S. workers within the affected industries.

To remain competitive in the absence of technological advance and productivity growth in these industries, U.S. labor costs must be lowered relative to those of foreign producers. This can occur through direct reductions in wages or through reductions in the foreign exchange price of the U.S. dollar. Both of these alternatives shrink U.S. workers' incomes, relative to those of workers in other nations, and thereby contribute to stagnation in U.S. living standards. Thus, if U.S. firms fall behind foreign firms in rates of development and adoption of new technologies, the alternatives are not attractive—U.S. workers must accept fewer jobs or lower earnings.

Yet, if U.S. firms can consistently develop and adopt new technologies more rapidly than foreign producers, the picture is quite different. The resultant higher productivity growth in U.S. industries will support lower production costs, which will enable U.S. workers to retain higher-wage jobs. Within the modern world economy, however, new knowledge and technologies developed within the United States are transferred to foreign competitors more quickly than they were in the past. Therefore, any technology-based advantages held by U.S. firms and workers over foreign firms and workers are likely to be more fleeting in the future. One key factor in sustaining American living standards, wages, and employment is continued public and private investment in the generation of new knowledge. U.S. firms also must advance from fundamental knowledge to commercial innovations more rapidly than in the past.

The open character of the U.S. economy of the 1980s and 1990s means that the link between productivity and output growth will play a central role in determining wages and employment in U.S. manufacturing (and eventually in portions of the U.S. services sector, as this sector becomes increasingly involved in international trade). The changing nature of international competition has enhanced the importance of higher levels of skills within the employed work force. More highly skilled workers can adopt new technologies more quickly and adapt more easily to changing markets and competitive conditions. We see improvements in the skills of the employed work force as a major factor in preserving and strengthening high-skill, high-wage employment in the U.S. economy.

ORGANIZATION OF THE REPORT

Our report contains nine additional chapters. Chapter 2 describes the process of technological change, devoting particular attention to the adoption of new technologies and to the special problems of small firms in managing technological change and adoption. Chapter 3 discusses how technology, labor supply, and labor demand affect the impact of technological change on employment in an open economy. Chapter 4 considers the impact of technological change on employment and wages, focusing on empirical studies of the sectoral employment effects of such change, and also discusses the impact of new technologies on job skill requirements. The employment and economic status of entrants to the labor force and the employment prospects of women and minorities are discussed in Chapter 5.

Chapter 6 examines the impacts of technology on the workplace, exploring the effects of technological change on the structure of the firm, the role of labor–management relations in managing these changes in the workplace and the challenges and opportunities in occupational health and safety that result from technological innovations. Chapter 7 discusses public and private policies that affect the adjustment of the economy and the labor force to technological change. Chapter 8 proposes several strategies for further research on technology, employment, and worker adjustment assistance programs and stresses the need to collect data on the diffusion of innovations and their effects on workers and the workplace. Chapter 9 contains the panel's findings, and Chapter 10 presents our policy recommendations.

The panel did not reach definitive conclusions or findings in some areas of its charge. Because of a lack of data, for example, as well as our conclusion that technological change will have only a limited effect on regional growth in the future, we did not analyze in detail the regional economic impacts of technological change. Analysis of the effects of technology on the length of the working day was not pursued for similar reasons. *The absence of a panel finding or policy recommendation should not be taken as evidence that the issue in question is unimportant or that it does not require further research and monitoring.* In those cases in which an important issue could not be addressed—for whatever reasons—we have noted the need for additional work. In other areas— for example, the evaluation of the effectiveness of retraining for displaced workers—there is insufficient quantitative evidence for a factual finding. In these instances, we have provided a statement of our collective judgment based on the expertise of our panel members and on the research and analysis carried out by panel members, staff, and authors of commissioned papers during the past 18 months.

2

The Sources and Rate of Technological Change in the U.S. Economy

Technological change is often difficult to predict, and its employment and productivity consequences usually are felt gradually rather than suddenly. Although the pace of technological change affects employment and productivity growth, the impact of new technologies also is affected heavily by organizational, institutional, and social factors. A central reason for the complex, gradual character of the employment, productivity, and other economic effects of such change is that these impacts are felt only through the adoption of new technologies by individuals and firms. In light of this fact, we devote considerable attention in this chapter to the process of adopting new technologies.

DEFINING TECHNOLOGICAL CHANGE

Technological change has two major effects: (1) it transforms the processes by which inputs (including labor and materials) are converted into goods and services, and (2) it enables the production of entirely new goods and services. *Process innovation* is technological change that improves the efficiency with which inputs are transformed into outputs; *product innovation* results in the production of new goods. The distinction between process and product innovation often is hazy. New products, such as the transistor, frequently require significant process innovations before they can be produced economically. Conversely, the potential cost reductions offered by many new manufacturing processes may be realized only after the products to which they are applied have been redesigned. In addition, an innovative product developed by one firm—for example, computer numerically controlled machine tools—may be transformed into a process innovation when it is adopted by another firm.

Product innovations may serve entirely new markets; consequently, their effects are notoriously unpredictable. (Chapter 4 explores the uncertainty surrounding predictions of the employment consequences of process innovations.) Repeatedly, technological forecasts have failed to foresee the size and nature of the markets for new products. Computers are a classic example. Howard Aiken, one of the developers of the electronic computer in the 1940s, was skeptical about the plans of J. Presper Eckert and John Mauchly to launch commercial computer production; Aiken predicted that the total U.S. market would be no more than four or five machines. Internal IBM studies conducted prior to the firm's decision to begin computer production were equally pessimistic; according to the studies, the market for the "tape processing machine" would amount to roughly 25 units (Ceruzzi, 1986). The record of technological advance contains many such examples (Rosenberg, 1983).

Invention, Innovation, and Diffusion

The history of scientific discoveries like penicillin or x rays contributes to a popular perception that technological change is a process of dramatic breakthroughs. In fact, it might better be described as incremental and consisting of several stages, extending well beyond the moment of scientific discovery. The *invention* stage includes the discovery of a scientific or technological advance and its translation into a prototype—for example, a working model. Invention, which subsumes basic research, must be distinguished from *innovation*, which includes the processes of advanced development (e.g., "scaling up" a pilot plant for commercial-volume production). In the case of the transistor, an important product innovation that has been fundamental to modern technological advance, invention spanned the period from the late 1930s, when Bell Telephone Laboratories inaugurated its program of basic research in solid-state physics, through 1947, when the first model of a point-contact transistor was produced by Bardeen, Brattain, and Schockley (see Braun and MacDonald, 1978; Mowery, 1983; Nelson, 1962; Tilton, 1971). The innovation stage that saw the translation of this crude invention into a commercially marketable product occurred during 1947–1954. This stage included significant advances in the theory of semiconductors and in materials refining and processing. Advances in both the theory of materials and in production techniques for making pure silicon crystals contributed to the introduction by Texas Instruments of the silicon junction transistor in 1954.

The *diffusion* of an innovation (discussed in detail later in this chapter) refers to the period of its adoption by users. Once again using transistors as an example, the diffusion that began once the product was introduced commercially in 1954 has continued to the present day; moreover, during this period, transistors have undergone considerable modification in design and production. Chaudhari (1986) described the dramatic advances since 1960 in the miniaturization of transistor components, focusing on the shrinkage in the width of "lines" that connect the transistor to other electronic components: "A typical line width in 1960 was 30 micrometers. . . . Today line widths are commonly on the order of one micrometer. . ." (p. 137). Among other significant advances during the diffusion stage was the development of the planar process for manufacturing integrated circuits and other solid-state components.

Each of these stages—invention, innovation, and diffusion—consists of a series of interacting phases; within the invention stage, for example, basic research often is heavily influenced by applied research findings (see Kline and Rosenberg, 1986; Rosenberg, 1983). Moreover, the invention, innovation, and diffusion processes themselves are linked in a complex fashion, which can be seen in the extensive modifications that are often made to an innovation during its diffusion. In the case of the transistor, the innovation stage of its development required fundamental research, just as its application to new uses during the diffusion stage has required investments in applications engineering and fundamental research.

Influences on Invention, Innovation, and Diffusion

Despite the close links among them, the invention, innovation, and diffusion stages of a technology appear to respond to different influences that are not always easy to distinguish. In the case of invention, for example, the factors affecting individual genius simply are not well understood. These stages also may be carried out by different individuals or organizations. In many instances, the inventor of a new product or process does not develop and market it. The original inventors of the computer, for example, were not employees of the firm that proved most successful at developing, improving, and marketing the device. Another case is that of DuPont. Many of the most significant innovations commercialized by DuPont prior to the invention of nylon during the 1920s and 1930s were based on patents purchased from other firms and individuals, rather than on the inventions of its employees.

Compared with invention, innovation is a far more costly stage of technological change.[1] It is likely therefore to be affected by such economic factors as the investment climate, rates of capital formation, or expectations of the location and size of future markets. The diffusion of innovations, which is discussed later in this chapter, appears to be influenced by cost considerations, uncertainty, and other factors unique to specific markets, such as regulations that affect the structure of the market for an innovation. For example, the regulation of pharmaceuticals and air transportation and the availability of third-party payments for medical services have affected the speed and the extent of new technology diffusion in those industries. Moreover, inasmuch as the diffusion of new technology is the result of decisions to invest in machinery or products that embody a technology, the rate of diffusion of innovations is affected by factors that determine the rates of net investment within an economy, including the domestic savings rate, the cost of capital, depreciation practices, and price stability.

The Interaction of Technological and Organizational Change

Technological change creates new options for the performance of specific functions. Yet the precise organization of these functions or the skill requirements associated with them are seldom determined solely by the characteristics of the technology. Organizational factors strongly influence the implementation of new technologies and their effects on skill requirements, quality of worklife, productivity, and profitability. Indeed, the potential improvements offered by many innovations often can be realized only if there are complementary organizational changes.

For example, redesigning products often allows more profitable use of many new computer-based manufacturing technologies. After installing equipment for computer-integrated production of lawn and garden tractors, Deere and Company realized substantial savings by redesigning its products to allow a single component design to be used in eight different tractors.[2] Other firms have redesigned their products for easier automated assembly; a recent IBM desktop printer has been so simplified for automated assembly that it can be manually assembled in minutes.

---

[1] "Development" alone, which is the portion of innovation incorporating most of the activities of production engineering and tooling, typically accounted for more than 65 percent of privately financed U.S. R&D investments annually during 1960–1985 (National Science Foundation, 1985, Appendix Tables 2-3 and 2-9).

[2] Remarks by G. R. Sutherland of Deere and Company at a meeting of the Panel on Technology and Employment, April 25, 1986.

(Lehnerd, 1987, discusses similar changes in the design of Black and Decker power tools.)

Such integration of production engineering and product design often demands extensive organizational change. The National Research Council's Committee on the Effective Implementation of Advanced Manufacturing Technology (1986) noted in its report that computer-integrated manufacturing (CIM) requires that "[d]ecisions once made by people in functions that were relatively independent must now be made jointly. Efforts to design the product and process simultaneously, for example, require product engineering and manufacturing engineering to work closely together" (p. 29). Although CIM has not yet been widely adopted in U.S. manufacturing, its requirements for organizational adaptation are by no means unique. A number of other computer-aided manufacturing technologies impose similar organizational demands.

In many cases, once a new technology has been adopted, the resulting improvements in the quality of a firm's manufactures and its productivity come as much from the reorganization of production and other activities required by the adoption as they do from the technologies themselves. For example, management personnel interviewed by panel members and staff in the course of this study argued that the organizational changes necessary to adopt computer-aided manufacturing processes yielded savings as great as those realized from this new production technology itself (the IBM printer described previously is one example). In most cases, these organizational changes were necessary to introduce computer-aided technologies. The converse was not true, however—the reorganization of design, engineering, and production processes did not require new technologies.

The value and importance of attention to the organizational dimensions of technological change, then, cannot be overstated. Indeed, without such attention, the potential profitability or product quality benefits of new technology may not be realized. Prior to the extensive use of advanced computer-aided or computer-integrated manufacturing technologies, Japanese automotive firms, for example, achieved great advances in productivity and product quality mainly through organizational techniques. The best-known of these successes, the Toyota production system, was developed during the 1960s and 1970s, prior to the development of CIM and robotics; it used production technologies that did not differ significantly from those of U.S. automobile manufacturers at the time (Abegglen and Stalk, 1986).

Within the U.S. automotive industry, General Motors (GM) offers dramatic plant-level contrasts in productivity and product quality that illustrate the importance of organizational factors in realizing the potential of new technology. In Fremont, California, the joint venture between GM and Toyota (known as New United Motor Manufacturing, Inc.—NUMMI) uses modest levels of factory automation that are embedded in the Toyota production system manned by a unionized work force; thus far, NUMMI has been extraordinarily successful in meeting production and quality targets. By contrast, GM's factory in Hamtramck, Michigan, which uses advanced factory automation technologies, operates at roughly 50 percent of its planned capacity and has experienced serious quality problems (Nag, 1986; Womack, in press).

Qualitative and anecdotal evidence suggests that, in the past, U.S. management and labor have been insufficiently attentive to the need to reorganize design and work processes to support technological change. Jaikumar (1986) presented data that illustrate this point in his analysis of 35 "flexible" manufacturing systems (i.e., systems that use computer-aided machinery and "work cells" to produce a wide variety of products at low cost) in the United States and 60 such installations in Japan. He concluded that:

Rather than narrowing the competitive gap with Japan, the technology of automation is widening it further. . . .

With few exceptions, the flexible manufacturing systems installed in the United States show an astonishing lack of flexibility. In many cases, they perform worse than the conventional technology they replace. The technology itself is not to blame; it is management that makes the difference. Compared with Japanese systems, those in the U.S. plants produce an order-of-magnitude less variety of parts. Furthermore, they cannot run untended for a whole shift, are not integrated with the rest of their factories, and are less reliable. Even the good ones form, at best, a small oasis in a desert of mediocrity. (p. 69)

U.S. managers and workers must understand that the "rules of the game" of international competition and technology's role within that competition have changed. Automation and firm and factory reorganization are means to the end of higher-quality, lower-cost products. Achieving this goal requires attention to production technology, product design, and work organization. Without such attention, the payoffs from the adoption of new technologies will be realized slowly or not at all.

Measuring Technological Change

If we could measure the rates of invention, innovation, and diffusion in the U.S. economy, we could simplify greatly the analysis of technology's impact on employment. Such measurements, however, are far from simple. The United States and most other industrial nations do not collect systematic time series data on the rates of diffusion of specific new technologies. As a result, there are few reliable data or indices with which to measure such rates. Measuring the rates of invention or innovation also is hampered by the fact that the outputs of these stages are extraordinarily difficult to measure. Those indices that have been used—the number of patents, publications, or expert tabulations of technologically and commercially significant innovations—have serious shortcomings. For example, a widely used gauge of inventive or innovative activity, R&D investment, measures only inputs into invention and innovation, rather than outputs. Without output measures, we cannot assess the efficiency with which investments in science and technology are translated into inventions or innovations. A further inadequacy of R&D investment as a measure is that it includes development expenditures; such expenditures affect both invention and innovation, as well as diffusion, and thus do not allow for separate measurement of these stages.

Other commonly used proxies for the rate of technological change include increases in the joint productivity of capital and labor—that is, "total" or "multifactor" productivity growth. Multifactor productivity growth measures improvements in the efficiency with which inputs are translated into outputs and thus should be responsive to changes in the rates of new technology generation and adoption. As a gauge of technological change, however, this index has several defects. Empirically, multifactor productivity growth is derived as a residual—that is, after adjusting for contributions made to greater output by increases in the quality and quantity of capital and labor. As a residual, it is a measure of ignorance, an index of the contributions to output growth of unmeasured influences rather than a direct measure of technological change. In addition, like all productivity indexes, measures of multifactor productivity are sensitive to fluctuations in the level of economic activity. To reduce the influence of such fluctuations, multifactor productivity growth typically is measured across business cycles. An alternative productivity measure that does not account for improvements in the productivity of capital inputs is labor productivity growth, measured as growth in output per hour. During most of the postwar period, these two measures have exhibited similar trends; since 1973 rates of growth in both labor and multifactor productivity have been much lower than in the 1950s and 1960s (Gullickson and Harper, 1986).

Using productivity growth as an index of the rate of technological change has other drawbacks. Many factors other than technology influence investment and diffusion, the processes that underpin productivity advance. The low savings rate in the United States, for example, may increase the cost of capital to private firms, thus lowering net investment and impeding diffusion and productivity growth. Furthermore, in measuring productivity change, it is often difficult to adjust measures of physical output for changes in the quality of products. Should a modern computer be treated as identical in quality to the machines of the mid-1950s? In theory, quality adjustments should be made frequently, but the data requirements for such a task are so great that until recently, the output data compiled by the Bureau of Economic Analysis (BEA) of the U.S. Department of Commerce, which historically have been used by the Bureau of Labor Statistics (BLS) for productivity measurement, did not incorporate adjustments for improvements in product quality. In 1985 BEA developed a computer price index that adjusted computers for quality; the new index resulted in dramatic declines in the estimated costs of such equipment after 1972, and it also will affect measured productivity growth for this period (Cole et al., 1986; Slater, 1986). This is merely one example of the complexity involved in analyzing and measuring the relationship between technological change and productivity growth.

Much of the current concern over the effects of technological change on employment is based on the belief that the rate of such change—whether it is defined as innovation or diffusion—has increased in recent years. Although specific technologies (e.g., office automation) may be experiencing more rapid change or diffusion now than in the past, aggregate indicators suggest that there has been no across-the-board increase in the rates of innovation or diffusion of technologies. The rate of growth in the number of patents granted within the United States (i.e., the number of inventions deemed novel and therefore patentable by the U.S. Patent Office) was lower during the early 1980s than during the late 1960s.[3] The average annual rate of growth in patent grants was 3.7 percent during 1965–1970, −0.1 percent during 1970–1975, 0.1 percent during 1975–1980, and 1 percent during 1980–1984 (National Science Foundation, 1985, Table 4-8). In another study, Baily (1986) examined technological change in several industries, including the research-intensive chemicals industry, and concluded that innovation actually may have slowed in these industries in the past decade, resulting in lower rates of productivity growth.

Measures of diffusion rates are, if anything, even more difficult to obtain than measures of the rates of invention or innovation. What work there has been in this area lends support to the conclusion that diffusion rates are not increasing. Mansfield (1966), for example, found little or no support for the hypothesis that the rate of diffusion had increased during the post-World War II period. The National Research Council's Panel on Technology and Women's Employment (1986) also expressed skepticism about the claim that diffusion rates of information technologies are likely to increase: "In the panel's judgment, diffusion will not accelerate over

---

[3]To avoid deceptive, short-run fluctuations as a result of changes in the length of time required to process patent applications, patents were dated by the year in which they were applied for rather than the year in which they were granted.

the next ten years: deliberate rather than headlong speed seems likely'' (p. 64). As noted previously, measures of multifactor or labor productivity growth, which incorporate the impacts of changes in rates of innovation and diffusion, also have been lower since 1973. (See Chapter 3 for an extended discussion of productivity.)

The rates of invention, innovation, and diffusion within the U.S. economy thus do not appear to have increased during the past two decades. Nevertheless, the widely perceived increases in the employment-displacing effects of technological change on the U.S. economy, which have generated increased concern over the employment impacts of technological change, may reflect shifts in the geographic location of innovative activity.

For much of the 1950s and 1960s, the United States commanded a considerable technological lead over European industrial nations and Japan. Since then, the technological dominance of the United States has declined somewhat (see "The Diffusion of Technology" later in this chapter). Foreign governments and enterprises now are important sources of new technology as well as leaders in its adoption (see the next section). As a result, there is an increased likelihood that innovation and diffusion will occur either initially or more rapidly in other countries, enhancing the competitiveness of foreign producers. As the sources of new technologies and the location of their initial application continue to broaden internationally, the displacement of U.S. workers due to more rapid foreign technology adoption or innovation may occur more frequently and more quickly—although there may be no change in the underlying worldwide rate of innovation. Moreover, the pace at which technologies are transferred within the international economy and thus become available to foreign firms now appears to be more rapid than in previous decades (Abramovitz, 1986; Baumol, 1986; Mansfield and Romeo, 1980; Organisation for Economic Co-operation and Development, 1979). Indeed, Baumol suggests that the increased speed of international technology transfer is partly responsible for convergence in productivity growth rates among industrialized nations.

SOURCES OF TECHNOLOGICAL CHANGE

Although individual inventors continue to play a role in the U.S. innovation system, their importance as a source of new technology has declined considerably over the course of this century (Schmookler, 1957). Broadly speaking, there are now three main sources of U.S. technological change—that is, three sources of financial support for the development and application of new technologies within the U.S. economy: (1) industrially financed R&D; (2) R&D financed by the federal government and performed in industry, university, and government laboratories; and (3)

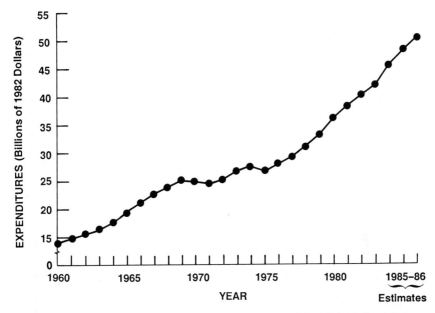

FIGURE 2-1   Industry expenditures on R&D, 1960–1986. SOURCE: National Science Foundation (1985, 1986a).

foreign R&D, both privately and publicly funded. The relative importance of these three sources has shifted over time and changed substantially during the postwar period. Two significant changes since the 1960s include reductions in the importance of federally financed defense R&D for commercial innovation and an increase in the amount of foreign R&D.

Industrially Funded Research and Development in the United States

A large share (30–50 percent during the postwar period) of the total U.S. R&D investment is industrial research expenditures (National Science Foundation, 1985). Figure 2-1 depicts trends (in 1982 dollars) during 1960–1986 in industrially funded R&D. After growing throughout the 1960s at an annual rate of more than 6 percent, industrial R&D spending scarcely grew at all during the early 1970s; after 1975 it began to climb again.[4]

---

[4]The deflator (i.e., the index used to convert these figures into 1982 dollars, which is the implicit gross national product deflator) used in Figure 2-1 may understate growth in the costs of R&D somewhat (Mansfield, 1984). This means that some of the apparent rebound in real R&D spending after 1974 may be illusory. In addition, as Cordes (1986) notes, industrial R&D spending as a share of sales declined from 1970 to 1978; after 1978, growth resumed.

Empirical research suggests that industrially funded R&D yields significant improvements in productivity. Mansfield's (1972) summary of a number of industry studies concluded that productivity growth was directly related to the level of R&D investment. Griliches (1985) conducted a statistical analysis of a large sample of firms, concluding that higher levels of privately financed R&D were associated with higher rates of productivity growth. Mansfield (1980b) found that the share of "long-term" or basic R&D within privately financed R&D was associated positively with productivity growth within both industries and firms. (See also Mansfield, 1980a, for a summary of this research.) These and other studies suggest that the benefits of R&D investment are realized only after a lag of 3–6 years (the lag is greater for basic research investments), which reflects the length of time needed to embody R&D results in innovations and market or adopt the innovations. Thus, the detrimental effects of the slowdown in industrial R&D spending during the early 1970s have been felt within the past 5–10 years; the benefits of the renewed growth in R&D investment after 1975 have probably been realized only since 1980.

Neither the slowdown in industrial R&D investment during the early 1970s nor its resurgence in the late 1970s and early 1980s have been satisfactorily explained. For example, there is little evidence that the lower U.S. R&D investment of the early 1970s was the result of less favorable tax treatment. Neither can we explain the recent resurgence of growth in R&D investment by the more lenient treatment of R&D under the tax code; the resurgence in R&D investment substantially predates the passage of the R&D tax credit in 1981. (See Cordes, 1986, for a summary of the evidence for these conclusions.)

Clearly, the recent recovery in U.S. R&D growth is a positive economic development, but when measured as a share of the gross national product (GNP), privately financed U.S. R&D lags behind that of such nations as Japan and West Germany. In 1984, the last year for which comparable data are available, the GNP shares for industry-financed R&D were 1.3, 1.5, and 1.7 percent, respectively, in the United States, West Germany, and Japan. For the GNP share of privately financed U.S. R&D to match the GNP share of privately financed Japanese R&D investment, U.S. industry would have to increase its 1984 R&D spending (roughly $49 billion) by approximately $15 billion—more than 30 percent of privately financed U.S. R&D in 1984 (National Science Foundation, 1986a). Although some scholars (e.g., Brooks, 1985) have criticized the use of GNP shares as a basis for comparing national R&D investments, this measure captures the concept of R&D investment as a necessary cost of competing in the modern world economy as a developer or adopter of new technologies. In contrast to its competitors, U.S. industry appears to

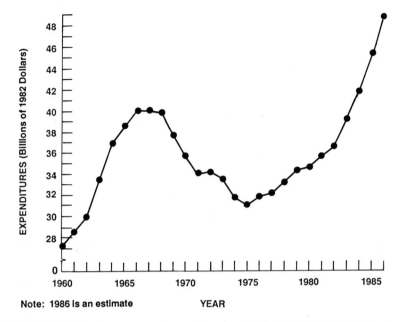

Note: 1986 is an estimate   YEAR

FIGURE 2-2   Federal government expenditures on R&D, 1960–1986. SOURCE: Budget authority data from the National Science Foundation (1985, 1986b).

invest less in this activity, relative to the level of American economic activity.

Industrial R&D expenditures are dominated by applied and development activities rather than by basic research. With some exceptions (e.g., IBM, DuPont, and Bell Laboratories, all of which pursue large basic research programs), industry devotes a small share of its R&D investment to basic research. The share of total industrial R&D accounted for by development has fluctuated between 65 and 74 percent since 1960; the basic research share of this investment has declined from 7.6 percent in 1960 to 5 percent in 1985, an estimate that represents a slight recovery from the low point of 4.1 percent reached in 1980 (National Science Foundation, 1986b, Appendix Tables 5, 7, and 9).

Federally Funded Research and Development

The federal share of total U.S. R&D spending since 1960 has varied between 47 and 66 percent, which is matched or exceeded among industrial nations only by French and British publicly financed R&D. Figures 2-2 and 2-3, respectively, depict the inflation-adjusted level of federal spending on R&D during 1960–1986 and the share of total U.S.

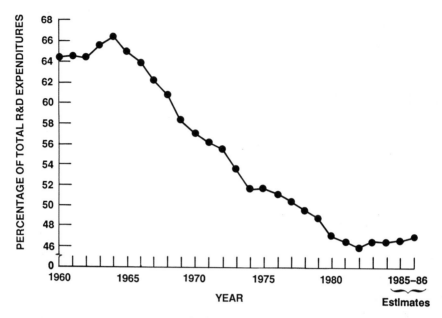

FIGURE 2-3   Federal government expenditures on R&D, 1960–1986, as a percentage of total R&D expenditures. SOURCE: National Science Foundation (1985, 1986b).

R&D supported by federal funding. The federal share of total R&D spending has declined from a 1964 peak of 66 percent to 47 percent in 1985 (National Science Foundation, 1985, 1986b).

Federal government R&D expenditures primarily support the activities of federal agencies (mainly in the areas of defense and space) rather than supporting growth in fundamental knowledge or the development of industrial applications of such knowledge. Brooks (1985) among others has noted that:

... it is striking that the United States admits to such a small fraction of its R&D effort as being applicable explicitly to industrial development. . . .

Another interesting difference between the United States and other countries is the smaller proportion of [government-funded] R&D devoted nominally to the "advancement of knowledge". . . it reflects strongly the pragmatic rationale historically underlying U.S. science policy, that most research aimed at the advancement of knowledge is supported by mission-oriented agencies and is justified politically as furthering some societal purpose outside of science itself. Recognition of a federal responsibility to foster the advancement of knowledge for nonspecific social purposes has come much more slowly in the United States than in other countries. (p. 3)

Defense-related R&D in the United States has accounted for 50–60 percent of total federal R&D expenditures (measured in terms of budget authority) during most of the postwar period and recently has increased dramatically—from 50 percent of federal R&D in 1980 to more than 70 percent in 1986. Federal defense-related R&D investment is devoted largely to applications rather than to fundamental research, a focus that tends to limit the commercial applicability of its results.[5] Although defense-related R&D has yielded important civilian "spillovers"—that is, commercially applicable technologies—in the microelectronics, computer, and commercial aircraft industries, such spillovers generally occur only in the early stages of development when technologies appear to display greater commonality between military and civilian design and performance characteristics. Over time, military and civilian requirements typically diverge, resulting in declining commercial payoffs from military R&D (Nelson and Langlois, 1983).

Brueckner and Borrus (1984) argue that commercial spillovers from defense R&D may be increasingly negative, suggesting that defense-related R&D may actually impair the competitive abilities of firms that rely heavily on it. They cite as examples the imposition of export controls on civilian technologies developed from military antecedents and the erosion of some firms' cost discipline as a result of operating in the more insulated competitive environment of military procurement. Lichtenberg (1985) concluded that few of the patented inventions to which government contractors are granted title by the military are exploited commercially.

The increasing divergence among military technological and procurement needs and civilian technologies in most areas suggests that future commercial spillovers of military R&D are likely to be modest, with the possible exceptions of defense-related R&D in artificial intelligence and computer science. Indeed, according to a report in *Aviation Week and Space Technology* ("Executives Cite Erosion of Defense Industry Base," November 24, 1986) quoting members of the Department of Defense's Public Advisory Committee on Trade (DPACT), the direction of technological spillovers recently has been reversed: " 'This marks a new era, when civil technology spins off military applications,' one of the DPACT executives' staff members said. Military aircraft and weapons programs used to lead to civil versions, but the trend is shifting in the opposite direction" (p. 69). COSEPUP's Panel on the Impact of National Security Controls on International Technology Transfer (1987) also noted that civilian technology is leading military applications in many areas. The panel's analysis agreed with that of Brueckner and Borrus, concluding

---

[5]Rosenberg (1986) argues that this tendency also characterizes research for the Strategic Defense Initiative.

that excessive restrictions on the export of technologies with military and civilian applications may reduce the commercial viability of these technologies. This outcome ultimately could undermine the commercial health of the producers of these technologies, thereby impairing the development of military applications as well.

As the share of federal defense-related research has grown in recent years, the proportion of federal nondefense research outlays has declined to approximately 30 percent of all federally supported R&D (National Science Foundation, 1985, Appendix Table 2-11). An important aspect of federally funded R&D that has implications for technological change is the allocation of these nondefense research funds between basic and more applied research. With the significant exceptions of portions of the National Aeronautics and Space Administration's aeronautics research program and the research programs of the U.S. Department of Agriculture and the National Institutes of Health, federally funded nondefense research (outside of energy during the 1970s) has focused largely on basic research; there has been little funding for research activities supporting the adoption of new technologies. This focus of U.S. public research support contrasts with publicly funded research programs in Sweden, West Germany, and (to some extent) Japan; in those programs, greater emphasis is placed on support for both applied and adoption-related research (Ergas, 1987; Mowery, 1984). Such differences in national science and technology policies may contribute to the more rapid diffusion of advanced manufacturing technologies in other nations (see the next section for a comparison of rates of utilization of advanced manufacturing technologies in different countries). In addition to supporting long-term research relevant to the generation of new technologies, then, public financial resources may also be important for the support of technology adoption. The U.S. public research budget currently provides little if any support for the adoption of new technologies.

Foreign Research and Development

The increasingly sophisticated technological capabilities of foreign firms noted earlier are due in large part to increased R&D investment by both the public and private sectors of other industrial nations. Figure 2-4 shows the convergence in the shares of GNP devoted to R&D investment by industrial nations during 1961–1985. When defense-related, publicly funded research is excluded from these data (Figure 2-5, which covers only 1971–1986), France, Japan, and West Germany are seen to devote a larger share of their GNP to R&D investment than the United States.

One result of this investment has been the narrowing of technological gaps between the United States and many of its industrial competitors, a trend that also reflects the recovery of other nations from the physical and eco-

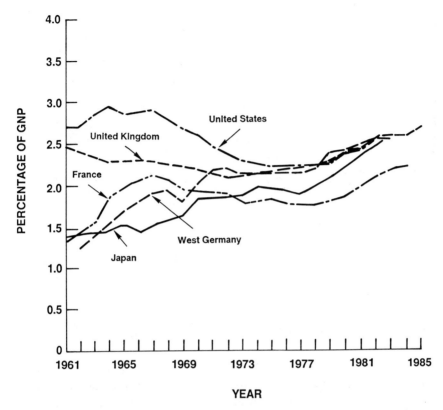

FIGURE 2-4 National expenditures for performance of R&D* as a percentage of gross national product (GNP) by country. SOURCE: National Science Foundation (1985).
*These are gross expenditures for performance of R&D including associated capital expenditures (except for the United States, where total capital expenditure data are not available). Estimates for 1972–1980 show that the inclusion of capital expenditures for the United States would have an impact of less than 0.1 percent per year.

nomic devastation of 1914–1945. In fact, some of the technologies that are of interest in this report, including telecommunications and digital information transmission, have contributed to higher rates of international technology transfer. U.S. and Japanese firms, for example, have relied on these technologies to collaborate in the development of advanced passenger aircraft and engines (Mowery, 1987). The growing technological pluralism in the modern world economy makes it imperative that U.S. firms emulate those of other nations, such as Sweden and Japan, and monitor the international technological environment assiduously to remain abreast of new developments and research. Neglecting such monitoring or performing it less effectively than foreign competitors reduces the ability of U.S. firms to develop technologies rapidly and compete successfully in the world economy.

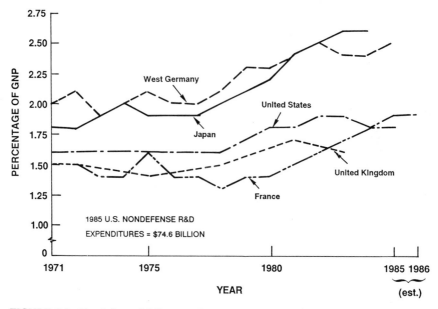

FIGURE 2-5   Nondefense R&D expenditures as a percentage of gross national product (GNP) by country. SOURCE: National Science Foundation (1987).

Although R&D investment is an important source of technological innovation, as the previous discussion noted, the firm or nation undertaking such investment does not always receive a majority or (in some cases) any of the profits from its investment. As scientific and technical data and research results spread throughout the world more quickly, the ability of a single firm or nation to "appropriate" all the financial or competitive fruits of its R&D investment has declined. Sustained support for the generation of new knowledge remains critically important in the current world economic environment. What is now of equal importance, however, is the ability of a firm to move rapidly from invention to commercial application and the ability of a national economy to adopt new technologies quickly, thus narrowing the gap between current and "best" practices. R&D investment positively influences the adoption and rapid exploitation of new technologies; these activities are discussed in the next section.

THE DIFFUSION OF TECHNOLOGY

The economic effects of new technology, whether revealed in productivity growth, creation or loss of jobs, or changes in wages and profits, are realized only through its adoption. Therefore, no analysis of the effects of new manufacturing and office technologies on U.S. economic performance and employment is complete without considering technology diffusion—that is, the factors that affect the speed and extent of adoption of innovations.

Perhaps the most striking aspect of diffusion, and the factor that most complicates the task of forecasting the employment and economic impacts of new technologies, is its gradualness.[6] It can take decades for all of the members of a given industry, firm, or sector to adopt an innovation. Enos (1962) found that the period between the invention of a new process or product and its *initial* application (in other words, substantially prior to its extensive utilization) averaged 14 years for one sample of inventions; in another study, Mansfield (1961) found that, for 9 of 12 innovations, adoption by all of the large firms in the coal mining, railroad, brewing, and iron and steel industries took more than 10 years.

There are several reasons why diffusion is such a lengthy process. Prospective adopters often find it difficult to evaluate new technologies; as a result, they are uncertain about the benefits and costs involved and may be reluctant to adopt a new technology rapidly. Moreover, the transmission and absorption of the information necessary to adopt an innovation require considerable time. Adopting a specific innovation may also demand extensive complementary investments in new plants and equipment and in work force training and retraining. Finally, the age and other characteristics of the existing capital stock in potential adopter firms affect the attractiveness of investing in a new technology.

Factors Affecting the Diffusion of Technology

Theoretical and empirical studies of technology diffusion suggest that two broad factors influence the rate of diffusion of technologies: (1) uncertainty surrounding the characteristics of a new technology and the payoffs from adopting it, and (2) the actual profitability of its adoption.

Sociologists such as Rogers (1983) and economists such as Griliches (1957, 1960) and Mansfield (1961, 1963b, 1966) have defined the characteristic s-shaped curve describing the diffusion of an innovation: plotted against time, the proportion of adopters within a population increases slowly, then accelerates, and finally levels off (Figure 2-6). These researchers suggest that the adoption of a technology by a growing number of firms or individuals progressively reduces uncertainty and increases

---

[6]The fact that the economic and employment consequences of new technologies frequently are felt more gradually than economic change induced by other causes, such as currency fluctuations or natural disasters, should simplify the development of policies to aid worker adjustment (see Chapter 7).

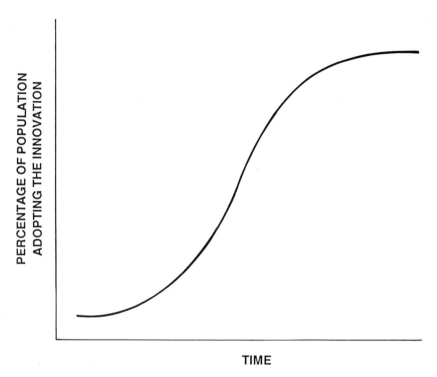

FIGURE 2-6   Time path of the diffusion of a "typical" innovation.

the amount of information available to potential adopters, thereby accelerating adoption, until a large fraction of the relevant population has adopted the innovation. Firm size also affects the speed with which an innovation is adopted. Mansfield (1963a) found that large firms adopted innovations more rapidly than small firms and attributed this difference to the larger in-house engineering and scientific staff and financial resources of the bigger firms, among other factors.

Diffusion rates vary across industries and technologies as a result of structural and other factors that affect the profitability of adoption and the level of uncertainty about such profitability. For example, government regulation can play a role either in increasing or slowing diffusion. Regulation of U.S. commercial air transportation prior to 1978 supported rapid diffusion of new commercial aircraft among the passenger airlines by encouraging competition based on service quality rather than on price (Jordan, 1970; Mowery, 1985); in another case, more stringent regulation since 1962 appears to have slowed the introduction and diffusion of new pharmaceuticals in the United States (Schwartzman, 1976). There are limits, however, to what can be determined about technology diffusion from the available data. Most empirical studies of diffusion focus on cross-sectional differences in the adoption of a single innovation, which restricts the ability to predict diffusion rates for multiple innovations over time. Thus, little is known about the determinants of aggregate trends in diffusion rates within an economy.

Any analysis of the diffusion of innovations is further complicated by the fact that an innovation often is greatly modified in the course of its diffusion (Rosenberg, 1976). Examining the diffusion of computers during the past four decades, for example, involves analyzing the diffusion of a number of very different products, each of which has been modified drastically since its introduction—the capabilities of the original personal computers differed greatly from those of subsequent microcomputers, and these products bear little if any resemblance to the mainframe behemoths of the 1950s and 1960s.

Another limitation in any analysis of diffusion rates is that empirical studies have focused on manufacturing, health care, or agriculture—there are few studies of the diffusion of innovations within the services sector outside of health care. The service industry diffusion studies that have been performed (e.g., Stoneman, 1976, who considered the diffusion of computers within British banks) confirm the importance of profitability and information as key determinants of the rate at which productivity-enhancing innovations are adopted. Although the specific impediments to diffusion within the service industries may differ somewhat from those observed within manufacturing, the general determinants of the rate of diffusion appear to be quite similar across the two sectors.

How do the diffusion rates of specific technologies in manufacturing and services compare? U.S. industry's use of advanced manufacturing technologies, including robotics and computer numerically controlled machine tools, seems to be increasing at a rate comparable to the rates of diffusion of earlier process innovations such as mainframe computers. The number of robots in U.S. industry, for example, grew at an average rate of roughly 40 percent per year during 1981–1985, although this growth appears to have slowed recently.[7] The number of robots per 1,000 manufacturing employees (a figure including white-collar workers) grew from 0.1 in 1976 to 1.3 in 1986 (J. Bernstein, Robotic Industries Association, personal communication, 1987; Flamm, 1986). Moreover, and of greater significance for the long-run employment impacts of technological

---

[7]Flamm (1986); see also "GM Throws a Monkey Wrench Into the Robot Market," *Business Week,* August 25, 1986.

change in U.S. manufacturing, both the level of use and the rate of adoption of such productivity-enhancing innovations as robotics and computer numerically controlled machine tools within U.S. industry appear to be lagging behind those of many industrial competitors, notably Japan, Sweden, and West Germany (Flamm, 1986; Mowery, 1986; Technology Management Center, 1985). Jaikumar (1986) estimates that "[i]n the last five years, Japan has outspent the United States two to one in automation. During that time, 55% of the machine tools introduced in Japan were computer numerically controlled (CNC) machines, key parts of FMSs [flexible manufacturing systems]. In the United States, the figure was only 18%" (p. 70).

The differences that can be observed among the United States and other nations in the rates of diffusion and use of robotics are not well explained by differences in wage rates, capital costs, or industry mix in U.S. and foreign economies (Flamm, 1986). The empirical evidence on rates of adoption (Mansfield, 1963b) also suggests that small U.S. firms are likely to be even further behind the technological "frontier" than large firms. This is a matter of some concern; the competitive and technological vitality of smaller firms is important for overall U.S. employment and competitiveness because of the roles such firms play as employers (see Chapter 6) and as suppliers to larger manufacturing firms.

Data on rates of investment by U.S. firms in office automation and information technologies suggest that diffusion of these technologies may be occurring somewhat more rapidly than the diffusion of some new manufacturing technologies. In the early 1980s, the rate of growth in the use of computer workstations (on-line terminals and workplace personal computers), which are predominantly found in nonmanufacturing settings (Harris, 1983), was higher than that for robots. As Figure 2-7 indicates, the number of U.S. workstations has increased from approximately 675,000 in 1976 to roughly 28 million in 1986, an average growth rate of 47 percent per year.[8] The number of workstations has grown from 15.4 for every 1,000 white-collar employees in 1976 to 450 per 1,000 white-collar workers in 1986.

Obstacles to the Diffusion of Technology

Before a firm can adopt many of the computer-based office and manufacturing technologies of interest to this panel, it must overcome a number of obstacles, which reflect the factors mentioned earlier as important influences on the diffusion of technology. The obstacles a firm

---

[8]Letter of January 8, 1987, to Dennis Houlihan from Donald C. Bellomy, editor of International Data Corporation's computer industry report *The Gray Sheet.*

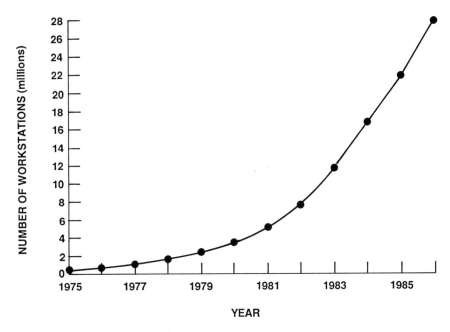

FIGURE 2-7   Growth in the number of U.S. workstations (on-line terminals and nonhome personal computers), 1975–1986. SOURCE: Donald C. Bellomy, International Data Corporation, personal communication, January 8, 1987.

faces can be grouped into three broad and overlapping categories: (1) adoption costs, (2) product standards, and (3) the availability and evaluation of relevant information.

The adoption costs associated with computer-based technologies that integrate numerous separate operations are in many cases greater than those associated with discrete innovations with less demanding integration requirements. Often, the technologies that underpin many of these computer-based innovations are new to the industries and firms faced with an adoption decision—a factor that heightens the uncertainties about the technology and increases the costs of acquiring the necessary expertise for its evaluation and operation. Uncertainty—and hence costs—are also increased by rapid changes in these technologies. The substantial costs of the applications engineering necessary for adoption are likely to be particularly onerous for smaller firms, which may have few or no specialized technical personnel on their payrolls.

A related impediment contributing to higher adoption costs stems from the fact that higher-level skills are often required for successful adoption in the early stages of the introduction of new technologies. A number of scholars (Bartel and Lichtenberg, 1987; Nelson and Phelps,

1966; Nelson et al., 1967) argue that the installation and "debugging" of complex machinery for which little operating experience has been compiled are frequently lengthy processes, requiring specialized skills and in many cases extensive scientific or technical training:

> The observers of the early production of transistors remarked on the high percentage of physicists and engineers required to control the processes. As experience accumulated, however, it became possible to design machines to do some of the jobs formerly requiring highly educated talent, and to develop training programs to teach less educated workers the special things that they needed to know to be effective workers. (Nelson et al., 1967, p. 106)

A highly skilled work force can adopt new technologies more rapidly. Nonetheless, the high costs of training may impede the diffusion of technologies in the United States; this is especially true if firms and workers are unable to develop contractual agreements to share the costs and benefits (in terms of higher productivity, higher wages, or product quality) of retraining investments (Bendick and Egan, 1982). Moreover, these retraining costs may place heavy burdens on small firms. Sweden and Japan have been leaders in the adoption of computer-based manufacturing technologies and robotics, and both have labor market institutions and practices that may support higher levels of investment in training for their blue-collar work forces (see Chapter 7). Such investments may aid the faster adoption of some key manufacturing technologies in these nations.

Product standards play a central role in the development and adoption of information and computer technologies. Within the United States, standards in information technologies historically have been set by market forces rather than by a governmental or industry-wide group. For example, standards for computers were largely established by IBM, reflecting its dominance of the market. For other technologies (e.g., office automation or computer-based manufacturing), no single vendor dominates the market; as a result, standards have been slower to emerge, despite the activities of the Corporation for Open Systems and the American National Standards Institute.

Because standards lessen the need for large investments in applications engineering to modify interfaces among incompatible pieces of hardware or software, they lower adoption costs and aid the adoption of new technologies. In view of the salience of these costs for small firms, standards are likely to be particularly useful in helping small firms adopt new technologies. Once established, however, a product or process standard may have an extremely powerful influence over the future direction of technological change. Uninformed or hasty standardization may effectively "lock in" an inefficient technology (David, 1985). The lack of standards thus retards diffusion, whereas their premature or ill-informed establishment increases the risks of technological suboptimization.

Prospective adopters of computer-based technologies in manufacturing and services often face problems in evaluating the cost consequences of adoption. Many of the essential areas in which these process technologies yield significant cost savings are not incorporated in conventional investment analyses because of conceptual flaws in these analytic frameworks. For example, reductions in inventory or work in progress have been singled out by several researchers as important dimensions of resource savings that are ignored by accounting systems developed for the evaluation of discrete investment decisions (see Ettlie, 1985, 1986; Kaplan, 1986; Technology Management Center, 1985). In some instances, U.S. managers are not sufficiently familiar with a new technology to evaluate its performance effectively. Improving management education may be one way to provide the familiarity and analytic skills necessary for informed evaluations of new technologies.

KEY TECHNOLOGY "CLUSTERS"

The preceding sections of this chapter have discussed technology in general terms. What specific technologies will affect employment and the workplace in the next 10–15 years? Brief descriptions of several salient technologies follow; our discussion of them focuses on trends in technological development and adoption and their employment implications. Four technology "clusters" are considered: information technologies; computer-aided manufacturing technologies (robotics, CIM, and flexible manufacturing systems); materials; and biotechnology. Many of the important innovations in all four of these technology clusters are well beyond the invention stage and are now undergoing development for commercial applications. This list is not comprehensive, nor are the items on the list mutually exclusive—information technologies, for example, are critical to CIM, and innovations in materials underpin both information technologies and computer-aided manufacturing processes. The panel considered these technologies to be worthy of particular attention because of the widespread notice each has received as well as their potential for widespread application within the U.S. economy in the near future.

Information Technologies

One of the most important structural changes in the U.S. economy, a change that affects both the manufacturing and services sectors, has been the rapid development and application of information technologies (i.e., technologies that store, retrieve, analyze, or transmit information). Computers, telecommunications equipment, and the microelectronic components on which they rely are included in this cluster. Within many sectors of the modern economy, information is an increasingly important input to the production of goods and often reduces the amount of labor and the quantity of other inputs required per unit of output.[9] Information has also become an increasingly valuable commodity in its own right. The evidence (e.g., U.S. Bureau of Labor Statistics, 1986b) suggests that the development of these technologies should enhance the demand for workers who manipulate and analyze information, relative to the demand for workers who enter and collate data.

Computer-Aided Manufacturing Technologies

The incorporation of computer- and microelectronics-based technologies within manufacturing has transformed the work environment in some industries and firms while simultaneously contributing to public concern over job displacement. These technologies include robotics, computer-aided design and manufacturing, and microelectronics-based, machine-controlled technologies such as computer numerically controlled machine tools.

Current estimates of the rates of development and diffusion of these technologies in a wide range of functions suggest that they are unlikely to produce mass displacement of workers during the next decade or two. Moreover, according to some analysts (Cyert, 1985; Sanderson, 1987), computer-aided technologies could support growth rather than reductions in U.S. manufacturing employment: the reduced direct labor costs made possible by these technologies may allow some U.S. firms to move assembly and fabrication operations back to the United States from low-wage areas of the world. Most public concern about these technologies focuses on the displacement of production workers. Widespread adoption of computer-aided manufacturing technologies, however, is also affecting middle-level engineers and managers, as Chapter 6 notes.

Advanced Materials

Fundamental to progress in microelectronics and information technologies, as well as to many areas of manufacturing and the services sector, are advances in such materials as ceramics (including high-temperature

---

[9]Freeman and Soete (1985) argue that "it is this feature which distinguishes IT [information technology] so clearly from 'old-fashioned' automation. Some of the most significant productivity gains linked to the introduction of IT relate to more efficient inventory control, as well as significant energy, materials, and capital savings" (p. 55).

superconducting materials), nonmetallic composites, and polymers. Innovations in materials technology affect employment in several ways. First, they may reduce markets for the materials they replace. On the other hand, markets for the new materials may expand and create new employment. The net employment effect of such a substitution is determined by the comparative labor requirements per unit of output for the two materials, as well as the relative size and rates of growth in the respective markets. Materials innovations also may affect labor requirements for processing and fabricating materials. Currently, however, the magnitude and even the direction of these employment effects are uncertain.

Biotechnology

The U.S. Congress's Office of Technology Assessment (1984) defines biotechnologies as technologies that use living organisms to modify plants or animals and develop microorganisms for specific purposes.[10] Biotechnology arguably is the least advanced of the four clusters, reflecting its recent development and the impediments to its rapid diffusion. The sectors in which these technologies initially will be introduced—the pharmaceutical and chemical industries, agriculture, and environmental protection—do not employ large numbers of people, leading us to conclude that the near-term aggregate employment impacts of biotechnologies will be modest and will primarily influence shifts within professional and technical occupations.

SUMMARY

The pace of technology diffusion governs the rate at which the economic and employment effects of new technologies are realized. The data discussed in this chapter suggest that within the U.S. manufacturing sector, the pace of adoption of some new technologies is slower and the levels of utilization lower than in some other industrial nations. This slower rate of adoption within U.S. manufacturing may allay concerns over the job-displacing impacts of rapid technological change, but it actually carries a false assurance. Because foreign firms are adopting

---

[10]This definition is by no means universally accepted. The National Research Council's Board on Agriculture (1987) defines biotechnology as "the use of technologies based on living systems to develop commercial processes and products . . . [including] the techniques of recombinant DNA, gene transfer, embryo manipulation and transfer, plant regeneration, cell culture, monoclonal antibodies, and bioprocess engineering" (p. 3). Other analysts (Miller and Young, 1987) reject any effort to develop a definition of biotechnology.

these technologies more rapidly than U.S. firms and are expanding their shares of the U.S. and world markets, job displacement from the slow adoption by U.S. firms of these productivity-increasing manufacturing technologies is likely to be more serious than any displacement resulting from rapid adoption; the recent surge in import penetration of many U.S. manufacturing industries provides support for this assertion (see Chapter 3 for additional discussion). U.S. industry must operate closer to the technological frontier if this nation is to maintain high employment levels and living standards.

3

Labor Supply and Demand Within the U.S. Economy

As we noted in Chapter 1, the level of total employment within the U.S. economy is determined primarily by nontechnological factors. Technological change can, however, affect the demand of individual sectors or industries for labor. Process innovations that increase labor productivity reduce the amount of labor (and potentially the amount of other inputs) required *per unit of output*. But this reduction need not and in fact has not translated into increased total unemployment in the United States. Instead, the employment impacts of any reductions in the amount of labor required for each unit of a product typically are offset by increases in demand for the product—in response to lower prices—or increases in the demand for other commodities. In addition, product innovations can create jobs in entirely new industries. To maximize the employment-expanding influence of technological change within the economy, workers must be able to move from sectors of declining labor demand to those in which employment opportunities are expanding. Indeed, the technological and other factors that have altered the structure of the U.S. economy and the demand for different types of labor during the past two decades appear to have increased the need for such movement.

THE U.S. ECONOMY: CHANGES IN STRUCTURE AND PERFORMANCE SINCE THE 1960s

Both the structure and performance of the U.S. economy have changed greatly since the 1960s. The share of private nonagricultural employment

51

accounted for by manufacturing, which stood at roughly 36 percent in 1966, has continued to decline, to roughly 24 percent in 1985 (U.S. Bureau of Labor Statistics, 1985a, 1986a). At the same time, international trade has expanded and now plays a much more significant role within the economy. Imports were 5.1 percent of GNP in 1966 and 11.4 percent in 1986; the share of GNP represented by exports expanded from 6 percent in 1966 to 8.9 percent in 1986 (President's Council of Economic Advisers, 1987, Tables B-1 and B-99).[1]

Sales in the industries associated with (as it was known in the 1960s) "automation"—that is, instruments, office equipment, computers, and electronic components—have more than doubled, growing from $53.4 billion (in 1986 dollars) in 1967 to more than $114 billion in 1985 (U.S. Bureau of the Census, 1982b, 1985a, 1985b).[2] Although the pace of technological change may not have increased greatly since the 1960s, "automation" technologies now are applied more widely. Twenty years ago, automation was viewed as applicable mainly in the manufacturing sector; now, both the manufacturing and nonmanufacturing sectors make extensive use of information and computer-based technologies.

As we noted in Chapter 2, changes in the international economic environment since the mid-1960s have narrowed the technological "gap" between the United States and other industrial economies. The dwindling technological lead of the United States, along with many other factors (e.g., the Vietnam war, oil price increases by the Organization of Petroleum Exporting Countries), has contributed to a deterioration in the performance of the U.S. economy. Unemployment levels throughout the 1970s and 1980s have remained well above those of the 1960s (Podgursky, 1984).[3] The average annual rate of growth in real average hourly earnings during 1970–1986 was −0.4 percent, following average annual growth rates of 2.7 and 1.7 percent, respectively, during the 1950s and 1960s (President's Council of Economic Advisers, 1987, Table B-41). Finally, labor productivity growth in the U.S. nonfarm sector has declined since the 1960s, reaching an average annual rate of less than 1 percent during 1973–1986 (President's Council of Economic Advisers, 1987, Table B-44).

---

[1]Growth in imports and exports of goods relative to total U.S. production of goods during this period is even more dramatic. "Merchandise" imports and exports, which include agricultural products, automotive goods, petroleum products, and industrial supplies and materials, respectively, grew from 6.6 and 7.6 percent of U.S. goods production in 1966 to 20.2 and 12.8 percent in 1985 (President's Council of Economic Advisers, 1987, Tables B-6 and B-99).

[2]This calculation does not include telecommunications equipment sales, which have also grown rapidly since the mid-1960s.

[3]Podgursky noted that unemployment rates at the business cycle quarterly peaks in 1969, 1973, 1979, and 1981 were 3.6, 4.8, 6.0, and 7.4 percent, respectively.

TABLE 3-1 Sectoral Composition (percent) of New Jobs in the U.S. Economy, 1955–1965, 1965–1975, and 1975–1985

	Period		
Sector	1955–1965	1965–1975	1975–1985
Manufacturing	11.9	1.9	4.8
Mining and construction	2.0	2.5	6.3
Transportation and utilities	−1.0	3.1	3.4
Wholesale and retail trade	21.8	26.5	29.0
Finance, insurance, and real estate	6.9	7.4	8.7
Services	27.7	30.2	39.1
Government	31.7	28.4	8.2

NOTE: There were 10.1 million new jobs created during 1955–1965, 16.2 million during 1965–1975, and 20.7 million during 1975–1985. Percentages may not total 100 due to rounding.

SOURCE: U.S. Department of Commerce, International Trade Administration (1987), Table 9, p. 12.

Despite its disappointing performance in these areas, the U.S. economy expanded employment opportunities rapidly during 1975–1985. Indeed, more than 20 million jobs were created during the 1975–1985 decade, an expansion that allowed the labor force to absorb both the "baby boom" cohort and greater numbers of women seeking employment. The share of the 20.7 million new jobs created during 1975–1985 accounted for by the private nonmanufacturing sector was greater than in previous decades of the post-World War II period (Table 3-1). Four industry groups (wholesale and retail trade; transportation and utilities; finance, insurance, and real estate; and services) collectively accounted for approximately 80 percent of the new jobs created during 1975–1985, a substantial increase from these groups' shares of roughly 55 percent during 1955–1965 and 67 percent during 1965–1975. Although the manufacturing sector's share of the jobs created during 1975–1985 (4.8 percent) was well below its share during 1955–1965 (11.9 percent), the 1975–1985 share was higher than that of 1965–1975 (1.9 percent). Many more jobs were created in manufacturing during 1975–1985 than during 1965–1975.

Several studies (e.g., Bluestone and Harrison, 1986) have noted that many of the jobs created during 1979–1984 paid relatively low wages. Bluestone and Harrison's empirical results, however, are sensitive to the temporal end point of their analysis. Extending their analysis beyond 1984 to cover 1985 substantially increases the share of high-wage jobs that were created during the entire period because 1981 and 1982, years that include a severe recession, receive less weight in the longer time series.

Other evidence suggests that the jobs created during 1975–1985 were not uniformly "low-quality" jobs (i.e., low-wage jobs with minimal skill requirements and prospects for advancement). Leon's (1982) study of the occupational structure of the jobs created during 1972–1980 indicates that, during most of this period, the occupations exhibiting the highest rates of growth were professional, technical, and managerial positions. Moreover, according to Rosenthal (1985), the distribution of weekly earnings within the overall occupational structure in 1982 was slightly less skewed toward low-wage occupations than in earlier years. Nonetheless, McMahon and Tschetter (1986) argue that, within the high-wage occupations whose growth has been rapid, there is a tendency for the jobs created since 1973 to occupy a relatively low position in the intraoccupational earnings distribution.

The facts of job expansion, earnings growth, and occupational shifts are less in dispute than the interpretation of the various trends. Some analysts (e.g., Bluestone and Harrison, 1986) view recent trends as evidence that equality of economic opportunity has declined because of technological or structural change—for example, increased international competition or the growth of service sector employment. Others (e.g., Blackburn and Bloom, 1987; Kosters and Ross, 1987; Lawrence, 1984; Levy, 1987; McMahon and Tschetter, 1986; Rosenthal, 1985) see these trends as the result of demographic factors, combined with the severe recession of the early 1980s, slow growth in the overall economy, and low productivity growth. These researchers suggest that rapid growth in the U.S. labor supply coincided with slow (or negative, during 1981–1982) economic growth, expanding the supply of job seekers relative to the number of openings and placing downward pressure on wages. Although the various trends require continued monitoring and assessment, slow economic growth and low rates of productivity increase, rather than technological change in the U.S. economy, appear to be the key factors in explaining these shifts.

The causes of the slow economic growth, high unemployment, and declining productivity growth rates that have afflicted the United States as well as other industrial nations since the 1960s are not well understood. Some portion of these developments can be ascribed to the disruptions in the global economy that occurred when oil prices rose in 1973 and 1979. But even when the effects of these disruptions are discounted, the record of U.S. demand management policies (i.e., fiscal and monetary policies) since the mid-1960s has been disappointing. Many economists and policy analysts now are more skeptical about the theory and practice of macroeconomic policy than they were in the 1960s. The ability of policymakers to reduce or eliminate unemployment through careful fiscal and monetary policies appears to be more limited than originally suspected, due in part to the structural changes that have occurred in the U.S. and global economic systems.

TRENDS IN U.S. UNEMPLOYMENT

Aggregate Unemployment

One of the most important factors contributing to public concern over the effects of technological change in the U.S. economy is the growth, noted earlier, in aggregate unemployment above the average levels of the 1950s and 1960s. There are no widely accepted explanations of the post-1973 growth in unemployment, although slow economic growth and frequent recessions (there have been four during this period) have contributed to it. Two of the recessions (1974–1975 and 1981–1982) were the most severe economic downturns the country has experienced since the Great Depression. In addition, the 1970s and 1980s saw no lengthy economic expansion comparable to that of the 1960s, although the current growth cycle may yet prove equally durable. Economic growth during 1966–1985 was much lower than that during 1948–1966 (a more detailed discussion of slower output growth follows). The frequently recessionary condition and slow growth of the U.S. economy since 1970, as well as the "oil shocks" of 1973 and 1979, all reduced the demand for labor, placing stronger upward pressure on aggregate unemployment rates than during the 1960s.

Has the entry into the labor force of the huge baby boom cohort and a growing number of women, which increased the labor supply, contributed to higher aggregate unemployment during the 1970s and 1980s? According to Podgursky (1984), the baby boom cohort contributed significantly to aggregate unemployment in the early and mid-1970s, but its contribution has since declined. Instead, higher unemployment in the early 1980s resulted in large part from permanent job losses, which were concentrated among workers in manufacturing, mining, and construction. The higher unemployment rates of the 1980s appear to reflect longer spells of unemployment for a relatively small portion of the work force, rather than an increase in the share of the work force experiencing short spells of unemployment (Podgursky, 1984).[4]

A portion of the higher post-1973 unemployment, especially the unemployment of the 1980s, appears therefore to be structural; that is, it reflects mismatches between worker skills or worker locations and job

---

[4]Average unemployment duration increased from 9.3 weeks in 1970 to 17.5 weeks in 1982 (Podgursky, 1984).

openings for a relatively small group of unemployed workers who experience lengthy spells of unemployment, rather than a cyclical downturn in the overall economy that results in short spells of joblessness for a very large number of workers (Summers, 1986). Such mismatches may come from technological change, but they also reflect rapid structural change of all types within this economy since 1970, including dramatic increases in international trade and recent significant import penetration in numerous manufacturing industries.[5]

Although aggregate unemployment has been high, relative to post-1945 averages, during the 1970s and 1980s, U.S. unemployment rates recently have fallen below those of many Western European nations, including West Germany, France, and Great Britain. Moreover, the average duration of U.S. unemployment now is shorter than that observed in a number of Western European nations. In 1985 slightly more than 15 percent of the unemployed population in the United States had been out of work for more than 6 months; in Great Britain, 60 percent of those unemployed had been out of work that long, whereas in West Germany this figure stood at 55 percent.[6]

The lower average rate and shorter duration of U.S. unemployment reflect the high rate of job creation and loss in the U.S. economy, as well as the relatively high geographic mobility of U.S. workers. Leonard (1986), in his study of Wisconsin, estimated that, each year, the jobs created and lost equaled nearly 14 percent and 11 percent, respectively, of the previous year's jobs.[7] The U.S. labor market thus is extremely fluid and dynamic, attributes that should ease the adjustment of workers to new technology.

How does high or low aggregate unemployment affect unemployment within different groups of U.S. workers? Blue-collar workers accounted for a disproportionate share of the growth in U.S. unemployment during 1970–1982. With 31 percent of the 1982 labor force, their share of the

---

[5]Costrell's (1987) measure of structural change, which is based on changes in the employment shares of the 12 economic sectors discussed in greater detail later in this chapter, suggests that such change has accelerated during 1979–1985, compared with 1973–1979 and 1966–1973. Rissman (1986) obtained similar results.

[6]See "The Supple Rigidity of America's Job Machine," *The Economist* 302 (February 7, 1987):28–29. The entry into the labor force of the baby boom cohort is partly responsible for recent high European unemployment rates. The European baby boom postdates that of the United States by 5–10 years; Western European economies now are absorbing large increases in their labor forces that exert upward pressure on unemployment rates (Norwood, 1983).

[7]Leonard's study examined the 1977–1982 period, which covers years of both economic expansion and of recession. His results therefore should not be biased by the state of the business cycle.

1970–1982 increase in the unemployment rate was 47 percent (Podgursky, 1984). Unemployment is substantially lower among whites than among blacks; black male unemployment rates are from two to three times higher than those of white men (President's Council of Economic Advisers, 1987, Table B-38; U.S. Bureau of the Census, 1986, Table 662). In general, young people and minorities bear the brunt of cyclical downturns in the economy because of labor market imperfections (e.g., discrimination) and skill differentials. Conversely, a full-employment economy (in which unemployment is restricted largely to those individuals voluntarily engaged in job search) particularly benefits disadvantaged workers (see Chapter 5).

Displacement

One group of the unemployed whose situation has attracted considerable attention and concern (Flaim and Sehgal, 1985; Podgursky, 1987; Secretary of Labor's Task Force on Economic Adjustment and Worker Dislocation, 1986; U.S. Congress, Office of Technology Assessment, 1986a, 1986b) comprises experienced workers who suffer permanent job loss or "displacement." The U.S. Bureau of Labor Statistics (BLS) 1984 survey of displaced workers[8] focused on workers who had lost jobs because of plant shutdowns, an employer going out of business, or permanent layoffs resulting from other factors (Flaim and Sehgal, 1985).[9] Displaced workers are widely cited (U.S. Congress, Office of Technology Assessment, 1986b) as victims of technological change.

How large a share of the unemployed population comprises displaced or dislocated workers? Any estimate of this share depends on the definition of dislocation used. Counting all workers suffering from permanent job loss as displaced, BLS estimated that 11.5 million workers were displaced during 1979–1983, yielding an average annual flow of 2.3 million workers. (Unpublished BLS data cited in U.S. Congress, Office of Technology Assessment, 1986a, suggest that the flow ranged from 1.2 million workers in 1979 to 3.3 million workers in 1983.) When the definition of a displaced worker is restricted to "experienced" workers—

---

[8]The BLS administers the quarterly Current Population Survey (CPS), gathering data on the employment and earnings of respondents. In January 1984 and January 1986, BLS added a special supplement to the CPS to obtain data on the former earnings and employment status of workers (20 years of age or older) who had lost their jobs. These data are the basis of the analyses by Flaim and Sehgal (1985), Podgursky (1986), and others.

[9]Estimating the size of the displaced worker population is a complex problem. The Secretary of Labor's Task Force on Economic Adjustment and Worker Dislocation (1986) developed seven definitions of displaced workers, each of which yielded a different estimate of the displaced worker population.

workers with at least 3 years' experience in the job from which they were laid off—the BLS survey data suggest that a total of 5.1 million workers were displaced during 1979–1983 (Flaim and Sehgal, 1985), which implies an annual average flow of slightly more than 1 million workers. (BLS data cited in U.S. Congress, Office of Technology Assessment, 1986a, estimate that this flow ranged from 0.6 million workers in 1979 to 1.4 million workers in 1983.) Podgursky (1987) also analyzed the number and characteristics of workers displaced during 1979–1982, restricting his population to full-time nonagricultural workers. He estimated that 6.4 million workers were displaced during this period, yielding an average annual flow of 1.6 million displaced workers.[10] Significantly, Podgursky's comparative analysis of data from the 1984 and 1986 displaced worker surveys revealed little decline in the average rate of displacement—1.5 million workers per year during 1981–1984.

Although the BLS estimate of the number of experienced workers displaced annually (regardless of the causes of displacement) is no more than 10–13 percent of the total unemployed population at any point in time, if one considers the share of unemployment accounted for by all displaced workers, the annual flow of such workers increases to 20–31 percent. Moreover, the contribution of displaced workers to increases in unemployment since 1980 has been unusually high (Summers, 1986). The Secretary of Labor's Task Force on Economic Adjustment and Worker Dislocation (1986) estimated that more than 50 percent of the increase in unemployment during the 1981–1982 recession resulted from permanent job loss—a substantially higher figure than the permanent job loss share of the unemployment increase (roughly 37 percent) in the three prior recessions.

Once displaced, how long are workers unemployed? According to the 1984 BLS survey, nearly 25 percent (1.3 million) of the 5.1 million workers displaced during 1979–1983 were still unemployed in January 1984, and more than 13 percent (700,000) of those 5.1 million had left the labor force during 1979–1983 (Flaim and Sehgal, 1985). As of January 1984, 60 percent of the experienced workers displaced during the previous 5 years had found employment, albeit at wages that may have been lower than those of their previous jobs; 67 percent of the displaced workers surveyed in January 1986 had found jobs (Flaim and Sehgal, 1985; U.S. Bureau of Labor Statistics, 1986d). Podgursky's analysis (1987) revealed

---

[10]Unlike BLS, however, Podgursky did not use job tenure to further restrict his population of displaced workers. He did restrict his analysis to workers who had lost their jobs at least 12 months prior to the date of the 1984 and 1986 BLS surveys in order to better assess the postdisplacement unemployment history of survey respondents and minimize the share of workers who were in fact laid off temporarily.

little if any change in the median duration of unemployment following displacement in his samples of the displaced worker populations from the 1984 and 1986 surveys; median weeks of unemployment for blue-collar males fell from 26 weeks (in the 1984 survey, based on 1979–1982) to 20 weeks (from the 1986 survey, covering 1981–1984), whereas median female blue-collar unemployment increased from 40 to nearly 48 weeks. The median duration of white-collar workers' unemployment following displacement fell from 14 weeks to 12 weeks during this period.

Bendick and Devine (1981) found that the geographic region within which displacement occurred was more significant in explaining the duration of unemployment than the industry from which workers were displaced. Indeed, according to the Secretary of Labor's Task Force on Economic Adjustment and Worker Dislocation (1986), each additional percentage point in the regional unemployment rate added 1–4 weeks to the average duration of unemployment for displaced workers in that area. Other analyses of displaced workers (Flaim and Sehgal, 1985) found that the earnings losses associated with reemployment after displacement were largest in areas of high unemployment.

What are the financial consequences of displacement? Of the 5.1 million experienced workers identified as displaced in the January 1984 BLS survey, a sizable portion—1.6 million—did not receive unemployment benefits. Moreover, nearly 50 percent of the 3.5 million experienced workers who received benefits had exhausted them by January 1984. About 60 percent of the workers still unemployed in January 1984 who were covered by health insurance in their previous jobs (a total of 1 million) had lost health insurance coverage.

The median ratio of earnings in new jobs to earnings in previous jobs for displaced workers who previously were full-time workers and eventually found other full-time employment (59 percent of blue-collar and 65 percent of white-collar workers in the 1984 survey) in Podgursky's sample was 93 percent for blue-collar workers and 99 percent for white-collar workers (Podgursky, 1987). This median disguises considerable variance, however, as 30 percent of blue-collar workers and 24 percent of white-collar workers found jobs that paid less than 75 percent of the wages they received in their previous jobs. For experienced workers previously employed in durables manufacturing who were displaced during 1979–1983, median weekly earnings declined by more than 20 percent, from $344 to $273 (Flaim and Sehgal, 1985). Many displaced workers thus face considerable income losses as a result of layoffs, although they may own substantial assets (primarily homes).

Data from the 1984 BLS survey (Flaim and Sehgal, 1985) suggest that the goods-producing sector accounted for the majority of displacements (60 percent), although it employed less than one-third of the total U.S.

work force. Durables manufacturing, with 12 percent of nonfarm employment, accounted for 33 percent of total displacements.

The majority of displacements during 1979–1983 occurred in blue-collar occupations—specifically, among operators, fabricators, and laborers (Flaim and Sehgal, 1985; Podgursky, 1987).[11] Displaced workers tended to be younger and were more likely to be female or black than employed workers. The duration of unemployment was positively associated with age: older displaced workers experienced longer periods of unemployment. Race was the single most significant characteristic in explaining the duration of displacement; displaced black workers endured significantly longer periods of unemployment (Podgursky, 1987).

Few studies of displaced workers analyze the relationship between education and displacement. Those that do (e.g., Flaim and Sehgal, 1985) have found that better-educated workers fare better after layoffs. According to Flaim and Sehgal (1985), "about 75 percent of those who had been in managerial and professional jobs were back at work when interviewed [in the BLS survey of January 1984]. In contrast, among the workers who had lost low-skill jobs as handlers, equipment cleaners, helpers, and laborers, less than one-half were working in January 1984" (p. 6). Podgursky (1987) also found that higher educational attainment was associated with shorter spells of unemployment after displacement.

The evidence that higher levels of skill are associated with shorter unemployment is significant in view of the fact that many displaced workers have serious deficiencies in basic skills. Bendick (1982) found that 34 percent of those workers from declining industries who were unemployed for 8 weeks or more did not have high school diplomas. Moreover, 49 percent of workers with such limited educational attainment were functionally illiterate. The U.S. General Accounting Office (1987a), citing unpublished data from the January 1984 BLS survey, reported that 32 percent of the dislocated workers unemployed as of January 1984 were high school dropouts and thus may have had serious basic skills deficiencies.

Among the causes of recent worker displacement, domestic technological change appears to be a relatively minor factor. Although the 1984 and 1986 surveys of displaced workers did not determine the causes of worker displacement, a 1986 U.S. General Accounting Office (GAO) study did pursue this question. GAO surveyed approximately 400 establishments to assess the reasons for plant closures and permanent layoffs, the events

----

[11]The census category of "operators, fabricators, and laborers" includes machine operators; assemblers; inspectors; welders; motor vehicle operators; operating engineers; freight, stock, and equipment movers; and general laborers. For a complete list of the detailed occupational categories included in blue-collar employment, see U.S. Bureau of the Census, 1980, pp. xvi–xviii.

responsible for most worker displacement. The most significant cause of these events, cited by 70 percent of the respondents, was reduced product demand. Increased competition, high labor costs, and the high value of the U.S. dollar accounted for 69, 57, and 32 percent, respectively, of the responses. Those causes of displacement that appeared to be directly related to technological change—facility obsolescence and production automation—accounted for 23 percent (10th out of 14 causes) and 16 percent (12th out of 14), respectively, of the responses.

Although these GAO data are subject to recall bias and differing interpretations of the meaning of the various causes of layoffs and closures, they suggest that technological change is not one of the primary causes of worker displacement. Nonetheless, technological change in foreign firms or nations often underpins trade-related displacement. When we view the issue in such global terms, it increases the likelihood that technological change *in other nations* may play a significant role in the displacement of American workers.

Although technological displacement is not a large problem for the U.S. economy in the aggregate, for those workers experiencing prolonged unemployment, the financial and emotional costs of technological displacement are enormous. We believe that the costs of displacement, regardless of its cause, are often so high that ameliorative policies are needed. (See Chapter 7 for a discussion and critique of current public policies for displaced workers; Chapter 10 presents policy recommendations and options for adjustment assistance for displaced workers.)

TRENDS IN LABOR SUPPLY

Long-Term Growth

LABOR FORCE GROWTH, 1947–1986

The supply of labor in the economy is an important influence on aggregate unemployment. Periods of rapid growth in the labor supply, other things being equal, will exhibit higher rates of unemployment.[12] The level of aggregate unemployment in turn strongly affects the ease with which displaced workers find new jobs, which influences the duration of unemployment they face and the level of wages associated

---

[12]Leonard (1986) notes that during a period of rapid growth in the labor force (1979–1982) in Wisconsin, an average annual rate of decline in employment of less than 1.2 percent doubled the state's unemployment rate in 3 years, from 5 percent in 1979 to 10 percent in 1982.

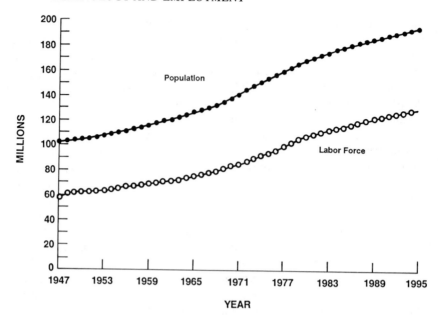

FIGURE 3-1   U.S. noninstitutional population 16 years of age and older and the civilian labor force, 1947–1995. SOURCE: President's Council of Economic Advisers (1987) and U.S. Bureau of Labor Statistics (1986b).

with reemployment. The employment prospects of labor force entrants also are affected by conditions of labor supply and demand. Trends in labor supply thus are important to predicting the ease with which labor markets adjust to the adoption of new technologies.

The U.S. civilian labor force[13] grew at an average rate of 1.9 percent per year during 1947–1986, whereas the civilian noninstitutional U.S. population 16 years of age and older[14] grew 1.6 percent per year (Figure 3-1). Labor force growth was higher than the rate of growth of the U.S. population during this period due to the entry of the baby boom cohort into the labor force, as well as to increases in the proportion of the female population active in the labor force. During 1970–1986, the U.S. civilian labor force grew by 2.3 percent per year on average, compared with a growth rate of 1.7 percent per year for the civilian noninstitutional population (President's Council of Economic Advisers, 1987).

---

[13]The civilian labor force consists of individuals, excluding members of the active-duty armed forces, 16 years of age and older who are employed or seeking employment.

[14]This population excludes individuals in prisons, hospitals, and mental institutions.

PROJECTED GROWTH, 1984–1995[15]

The U.S. Bureau of Labor Statistics (1986b) computes projections of labor force growth by forecasting labor force participation rates and applying those rates to the Census Bureau's population projections. BLS's projections for "low," "moderate," and "high" rates of labor force growth are based on different assumptions about the characteristics of the population and the labor force. The "moderate" projections indicate that the total civilian labor force will grow much more slowly in the future by comparison with 1970–1984. Projected average annual growth rates in the labor force—that is, rates of growth in the supply of labor—are 1.3 percent during 1984–1990 and 1 percent during 1990–1995, substantially below the rate during 1970–1984. The corresponding projected annual growth rates for the civilian population are 0.9 percent for 1984–1990 and 0.8 percent for 1990–1995. Labor force growth rates are projected to remain higher than population growth rates because of continued growth in labor force participation.

The most dramatic change forecast for 1984–1995 is the 16 percent reduction in the size of the 16- to 24-year-old entrant cohort, from 24 million in 1984 to 20.2 million in 1995 (U.S. Bureau of Labor Statistics, 1986b).[16] This cohort also will experience minimal change in gender and racial composition between 1984 and 1995. Although women and minorities account for approximately 75 percent of the projected growth in the labor force through 1995 (Figure 3-2), the total projected growth in the labor force during 1984–1995 of approximately 14 percent is not large enough to cause significant changes in the gender or racial composition of the overall work

---

[15]The most recent detailed 1995 labor force projections of the U.S. Bureau of Labor Statistics (1986b) use 1984 as the base year.

[16]The projected declines in the pool of labor force entrants have raised concerns about the adequacy of the future supply of scientists and engineers to meet the economic and technological challenges faced by this nation. Both the supply of and demand for scientists and engineers are influenced by a wide range of variables, however; consequently, they exhibit considerable flexibility and responsiveness. It is therefore not clear that a reduction in the number of 18- to 24-year-olds will result in a decline in the number of engineers and scientists. Immigration flows, increases in college enrollments among older members of the population, and changes in the share of the population with science and engineering undergraduate degrees that become practicing members of these professions (a decision influenced heavily by salary outlooks) can all offset the impact of declines in the size of the entrant pool (U.S. Congress, Office of Technology Assessment, 1985a). In addition, as the National Research Council's Panel on Engineering Labor Markets (1986) noted, employers can adjust to changes in the supply of scientific personnel in many ways, thus enhancing the flexibility of the overall system.

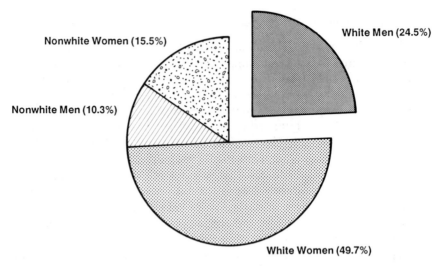

FIGURE 3-2   Composition of 1984–1995 labor force growth. SOURCE: U.S. Bureau of Labor Statistics (1986b).

force.[17] Overall, the gender and racial composition of the 1995 labor force will closely resemble that of the 1984 labor force (Table 3-2). In 1995, BLS projects that nonwhites (a category that includes blacks, Asians, and nonwhite Hispanics) will account for roughly 15 percent of the labor force, a modest increase from their current share of 13 percent.

The BLS projections incorporate very conservative estimates of the annual flow of illegal immigrants. If this source of labor continues to grow, the BLS projections of labor force growth may be low; however, the labor market impacts of such immigration should be significant in a few regions, rather than nationally. The reductions in labor force growth projected by BLS should lessen the labor market pressures that have been partly responsible for high rates of aggregate unemployment during the past decade. Structural and cyclical unemployment, however, will not vanish; as we note in Chapters 4 and 5, those workers who lack basic skills—whether they are labor force entrants or experienced workers who have been displaced—are likely to face employment problems in the future. One indicator of basic skills preparation is educational attainment.

[17]The share of 1984–1995 labor force growth accounted for by women and minorities (75 percent) is an increase over 1970–1980, when women and minorities accounted for approximately 65 percent of labor force growth (U.S. Bureau of the Census, 1987, Table 639). The projected change is largely due to an increase in the share of nonwhite men and women, accompanied by a decrease in the share of white men.

TABLE 3-2 Composition of Labor Force by Gender and
Race (percent), 1984 and 1995

Civilian Labor Force	Year 1984	1995[a]	Change in Share
Men	56.2	53.6	−2.6
Women	43.8	46.4	2.6
White	86.7	85.2	−1.5
Men	49.4	46.4	−3.0
Women	37.4	38.9	1.5
Nonwhite	13.3	14.8	1.5
Men	6.8	7.3	0.5
Women	6.4	7.5	1.1

NOTE: Percentages may not total 100 due to rounding.

[a]Projected values.

SOURCE: U.S. Bureau of Labor Statistics (1986b).

We discuss current levels of attainment in the U.S. work force and projected future trends next.

Educational Attainment of the U.S. Labor Force, 1959–1990

Table 3-3 depicts changes in the educational attainment of the civilian labor force since 1959. The median number of school years completed has increased only slightly: from 12 years in 1959 to 12.8 years in 1986.

TABLE 3-3 Educational Attainment (percent) of the Civilian Labor
Force for Selected Years, 1959–1986

Year	Total No. of Workers	Less Than High School Graduate	High School (4 Years)	College		Median No. of School Years Completed
				1–3 Years	4+ Years	
1959	65,842	50.3	30.7	9.3	9.6	12.0
1970	78,955	34.8	39.0	13.3	12.9	12.4
1975	92,328	29.3	39.6	15.5	15.7	12.5
1980	105,449	23.8	40.1	17.9	18.2	12.7
1984	111,943	19.5	40.7	19.0	20.9	12.8
1985	114,256	19.2	40.2	19.5	21.1	12.8
1986	116,087	18.5	40.4	19.9	21.3	12.8

NOTE: These data include members of the labor force who are enrolled in school.

SOURCE: U.S. Bureau of Labor Statistics (1985b, Table 61); U.S. Bureau of Labor Statistics, Office of Employment and Unemployment Statistics (1985, 1986).

The data, however, suggest considerable shifts during this period in the distribution of educational attainment within the work force. The share of the labor force without a high school degree declined from 50.3 percent in 1959 to 18.5 percent in 1986; the share with at least a college degree more than doubled. These changes are particularly noteworthy in view of the dramatic growth in the labor force during 1959–1986. Much of the increase in median educational attainment reflects the entry into the work force of younger, more highly educated individuals combined with the retirement of older workers with lower levels of educational attainment (Barnow, 1985). In view of the evidence cited earlier in this chapter suggesting that better-educated workers experience shorter periods of unemployment after job loss, these data support guarded optimism about the ability of the U.S. labor force to adjust to future technological change.

Other data reveal significant gender-based and racial differences in educational attainment. According to BLS, 20.3 percent of the male labor force had not completed high school as of 1986, a proportion slightly larger than the 16.1 percent of the female labor force lacking a diploma. Men exhibited higher levels of postsecondary educational attainment in 1986; 42 percent of men had attended college for at least 1 year, versus 40.2 percent of women in the labor force. Blacks and Hispanics continued to lag behind whites in educational attainment. In 1986, 73.9 percent of the black members of the labor force and 56.8 percent of Hispanics had high school diplomas; both of these figures are substantially lower than the 82.4 percent of white members of the labor force with diplomas. In addition although 22 percent of white labor force members had completed at least 4 years of college, only 12.3 percent of blacks and 8.9 percent of Hispanics had done so. Nonetheless, the educational gap between black and white members of the labor force has narrowed significantly since 1959; in that year only 25.5 percent of blacks in the labor force had completed high school, a figure well below the 52.6 percent of white workers with high school degrees (U.S. Bureau of Labor Statistics, Office of Employment and Unemployment Statistics, 1986; U.S. Bureau of Labor Statistics, 1985b).

Projections of future levels of educational attainment are subject to considerable uncertainty and are heavily influenced by gender-based, racial, and ethnic differences in educational attainment and by changes in these attainment levels. Barnow (1985) used the BLS labor force projections for 1990 to forecast changes in the educational attainment of different groups within the labor force through that year. Barnow, whose projections incorporated changes in educational attainment levels in male and female workers, forecast that in 1990 86.2 percent of adult (25–64 years old) male workers would have a high school diploma, slightly lower than the 89.5 percent of female workers with diplomas. As in 1984, the postsecondary educational attainment levels of male workers were projected to exceed those of female workers, with 26.7 percent of adult male workers and 22.8 percent of female workers having college degrees.

It is difficult to extend this analysis of educational attainment to 1995 and broaden it to incorporate changes in the racial composition of the work force because of the lack of data to support projections of changes through 1995 in the educational attainment levels of white and nonwhite workers or of men and women. (Barnow's projections end in 1990 and are not broken down by race.) However, projections of the 1995 educational attainment of the U.S. labor force that hold current levels of attainment constant among men and women and white and nonwhite workers suggest that changes in the racial or gender composition of the future U.S. work force will have a minimal impact on aggregate levels of secondary or postsecondary educational attainment.[18] The changes in aggregate attainment levels due to changes in labor force composition are modest because the U.S. labor force is projected to grow relatively slowly through 1995. Although the 1984–1995 cohort of labor force entrants is projected to include a larger share of women and minorities than did the 1970–1980 cohort, as was noted above, these projected changes in the composition of the entrant cohort imply minimal change in educational attainment levels for labor force entrants through 1995.

Although average levels of educational attainment in the U.S. labor force are not likely to change dramatically in the near future, educational attainment appears to be increasingly significant to the economic welfare of an individual. Census data on individual incomes (Table 3-4) reveal that the economic returns from schooling, measured as the differences in median annual incomes for individuals with different educational attainment levels, increased during 1973–1984, especially for men and women between the ages of 25 and 34 (these data are discussed in greater detail by Levy, 1987).[19] Measured in constant dollars, the ratio of the median annual income for males between 25 and 34 who completed high school to the median annual income of males who completed only 1–3 years of high school grew by more than 25 percent during 1973–1984 and registered a comparable gain for women. With the exception of high school completion for women over 25 years of age, large increases are apparent between

[18]These projections combine data from BLS on forecast labor force growth and composition with data from the CPS on current educational attainment rates.

[19]The effects on incomes of slow economic growth, high inflation, and a rapidly expanding labor force are also revealed in the consistent declines in median annual earnings during 1973–1984 in all groups in Table 3-4.

TABLE 3-4   Education and Median Individual Total Money
Income, 1973 and 1984 (in 1982 dollars)

Group	1–3 Years of High School (A)	4 Years of High School (B)	4 Years of College (C)	Ratio (B/A)	Ratio (C/A)	Ratio (C/B)
Men 25+ years old						
1973	17,383	21,839	28,103	1.26	1.62	1.29
1984	11,590	17,414	26,093	1.50	2.25	1.50
Women 25+ years old						
1973	5,718	8,004	12,528	1.40	2.19	1.57
1984	5,142	7,252	12,622	1.41	2.45	1.74
Men 25–34 years old						
1973	17,032	20,470	23,681	1.20	1.39	1.16
1984	10,081	15,754	21,759	1.56	2.16	1.38
Women 25–34 years old						
1973	6,270	7,954	13,196	1.27	2.10	1.66
1984	4,526	7,375	13,228	1.63	2.92	1.79

NOTE: Dollar amounts were adjusted using the implicit price deflators for personal consumption expenditures (President's Council of Economic Advisers, 1987, Table B-3).

SOURCE: U.S. Bureau of the Census (1975, Table 58; 1986, Table 33).

1973 and 1984 in the income effects of greater educational attainment in all of the comparisons in Table 3-4.[20] These increases reflect the fact that changes in the structure of the economy, new technology, and increased international competition have expanded the returns to individuals (in terms of income) from higher educational attainment, especially within the cohort that entered the labor force during the 1970s. Such gains, however, also mean that continuing racial or ethnic differences in educational attainment will widen the economic gaps among these groups in the U.S. economy.

Comparing the Educational Attainment of U.S. Labor Market Entrants with Those of Other Nations

The importance of international trade and competitiveness to U.S. living standards, as well as the evidence that other nations may be developing and adopting some new technologies more rapidly than U.S. firms, draws attention to the relative levels of educational attainment of the U.S. and foreign labor forces. How does the educational attainment of

---

[20]Increases in the returns from college education during this period were partially offset by increases in the direct costs of a college education.

the U.S. labor force compare with that of the labor forces of other industrial nations? There are few reliable data on the educational attainment of the overall labor force in other industrial nations. For this reason, as well as the importance of labor force entrants' attainment for the projection of future trends in attainment levels, we present comparative data only on entrants in seven other industrial nations.

It is difficult to develop international comparisons of levels and trends in educational attainment because educational systems and policies differ markedly across nations. Consider the provision of education and training after the completion of compulsory schooling. Higher education and training in countries such as Japan, the United States, and Canada follow the "schooling model" in which such offerings are integrated into the formal educational system. Other countries—for example, West Germany—follow the "dual model," which is characterized by a strong and highly developed apprenticeship sector. The "mixed model," found in the United Kingdom, places greater emphasis on the informal sector (on-the-job training outside of an apprenticeship system) for education and training beyond the compulsory level.

Table 3-5 shows the rates of enrollment in education and training by age (ages 16–19) for several countries. To minimize the differences across the various models, both full-time and part-time participants are included. In all of the countries included in the table, more than two-thirds of the 16-year-olds are in some form of secondary or postsecondary education and training; in four countries the proportion is above 90 percent. For those countries following the schooling model (e.g., the United States), the sharpest drop in participation rates occurs between the ages of 17 and 18, corresponding to the change from secondary to postsecondary education. For countries following the dual model (e.g., West Germany), the distinction between full-time and part-time participants becomes particularly important, depending on the weight assigned to apprenticeship programs. In such countries the bulk of the 16- to 19-year-old age group attends school on a part-time basis.

The United States has the largest percentage of 16- and 19-year-olds enrolled in full-time education; the rates for 17- and 18-year-olds are second only to Japan and the Netherlands, respectively. Individuals entering higher education both within and outside of the formal university structure account for a larger share of the relevant cohort in the United States (60 percent) than in any other nation for which data are available (Organisation for Economic Co-operation and Development, 1984).

Although certain educational gaps between the United States and other nations have narrowed in recent years, the United States remains among those countries with the highest levels of participation in secondary and postsecondary education and training. There are only limited data to

TABLE 3-5   Enrollment Rates (percent) in Education and Training, 16- to 19-Year-Olds, for Eight Industrial Nations

Country	16-year-olds PT	16-year-olds FT	17-year-olds PT	17-year-olds FT	18-year-olds PT	18-year-olds FT	19-year-olds PT	19-year-olds FT
France[a]	83.9	73.3	68.9	60.0	45.2	42.2	30.0	29.4
West Germany[a]	92.1	57.3	89.3	38.9	71.5	29.6	41.8	21.3
Italy[b]	69.1	54.5	70.3	47.4	51.3	36.2	29.4	18.5
Japan[c]	94.0	94.0	94.0	94.0	n.a.	n.a.	n.a.	n.a.
The Netherlands[d]	97.8	92.0	84.7	74.8	62.8	53.4	43.9	34.6
Sweden[e]	87.4	86.7	78.4	76.7	44.7	40.3	23.5	16.9
United Kingdom[a]	68.0	48.3	52.8	30.2	37.0	16.5	28.5[f]	13.4
United States[g]	94.3	94.3	87.1	86.6	54.7	51.2	40.9	37.3

NOTE: FT = full-time enrollment; PT = part-time enrollment; n.a. = not available.

SOURCE: Organisation for Economic Co-operation and Development (1985).

[a]The last year for which data are available is 1981.

[b]Higher education is not included, but regional vocational training is included. The last year for which data are available is 1981.

[c]Statistics are from the Ministry of Education; data are for 1980. Figures refer to the proportion of young people completing lower secondary education (approximately 99 percent of the cohort) who continue at the upper secondary level. Participation rates for 17-year-olds are similar to those of the 16-year-old group given the very low dropout rate in Japan.

[d]Data are for 1982.

[e]These figures include the different types of adult education; data are for 1980.

[f]The figure includes both 19- and 20-year-olds.

[g]Data are for 1982.

support assessments of the quality of the education received by U.S. labor force entrants. Recent time series evidence, in the form of scores on standardized tests, suggests that the quality of the educational preparation of entrants may increase in coming years. Since the 1970s successive cohorts of children entering school have scored higher on standardized tests. By some measures, achievement in elementary grades is at its highest level in three decades.[21] In addition, although the gaps in test scores between minority and nonminority groups remain large, they are narrowing. College test scores remain low, but they may

[21]Test score data for the state of Iowa provide annually standardized data extending over three decades. Data from 1984 suggest that the median 3rd grader (the 50th percentile) scored better than roughly 68 percent of his or her counterparts in 1954 (Congressional Budget Office, 1986). Although Iowa is not representative of the nation as a whole, these state-level findings are corroborated by the results of the Congressional Budget Office's analysis of a much wider range of tests.

also increase as the cohorts with higher test scores move through high school (Congressional Budget Office, 1986). Nevertheless, although this evidence suggests that future U.S. entrants to the labor force may have better basic skills than those who are currently seeking employment, other evidence indicates that other nations' labor force entrants currently are better prepared in such skills. McKnight et al. (1987) and Lee et al. (1987) suggest that the quality of basic skills training in the United States lags behind that of other industrial nations such as Japan.

LABOR DEMAND

The level of demand for labor in the United States is determined primarily by the rate of growth of the entire economy, which in turn is affected by a wide range of influences including government policy, external "shocks" (e.g., the oil price increases of 1973 and 1979), and business cycle fluctuations. Technological change has little impact on aggregate labor demand. At the level of individual sectors or industries, however, the demand for labor is affected by the rate of growth in output and the level of wages, both of which may be influenced by technological change. As was noted previously, by reducing the cost of output, domestic technological change often contributes to increased domestic and international demand for output, offsetting all or much of the impact on labor demand of any reductions in the amount of labor required per unit of output that result from the use of new technology. In some cases, however, technological change may reduce U.S. employment. U.S. industries in which rates of technological change, productivity growth, and output cost reduction lag behind those of foreign firms may experience employment losses as U.S. firms lose export markets and domestic sales to the products of foreign, technologically superior competitors. Significant lags in U.S. technological performance therefore may contribute to erosion in employment and wages.

As we noted in Chapter 1, an alternative means of reducing the cost and price of U.S. goods is reductions in U.S. wages, which can occur through cuts in the dollar value of U.S. real wages or by reductions in the value of the dollar in relation to foreign currencies. These alternatives, of course, may reduce the standard of living in the United States. Moreover, as rapid rates of international technology transfer continue, the level of technological sophistication within relatively low-wage nations will increase— which means that, in the absence of technological change, U.S. wage cuts or dollar devaluations will have to be significant for this nation to compete successfully with other countries.

TABLE 3-6   U.S. Postwar Productivity Growth (percent) in the
Nonfarm Business Sector (average annual growth rates in output/hour)

Sector	1948–1985	1948–1957	1957–1966	1966–1973	1973–1979	1979–1985
Nonfarm business	1.8	2.5	2.8	1.8	0.5	0.8
Manufacturing	2.6	2.7	2.9	2.7	1.4	3.1
Nonfarm, nonmanufacturing	1.5	2.3	2.7	1.3	−0.1	−0.1

SOURCE: Calculated from unpublished data, U.S. Bureau of Labor Statistics, Office of
Productivity and Technology.

Growth in Labor Productivity and Output

Labor productivity growth provides one index of the rate of technological change within an economy. This measure admittedly is imperfect, as Chapter 2 noted; technological change need not be laborsaving in character (and thus an agent of labor productivity enhancement), and other important nontechnological influences (e.g., changes in the scale of production establishments, the rate of capital formation, improvements in the education of the work force) also affect the rate of advance in labor productivity. Nevertheless, this datum provides a crude index of the rate at which technological change is spreading throughout the economy. As the summary of this chapter and Chapter 4 discuss at greater length, growth in labor productivity, which frequently results from technological change, supports growth in real wages and international competitiveness.

Aggregate productivity growth, which is the weighted average of labor productivity growth in different sectors of the economy (weighted by the sectors' shares of total output), has remained below the average rates of the 1950s and 1960s during most of the 1970s and 1980s. Table 3-6 presents growth rates in nonfarm labor productivity over five postwar intervals, beginning and ending at comparable points in the business cycle. These figures show high rates of productivity growth during 1948–1966, which were followed by a decline during 1966–1973, further serious deterioration during 1973–1979, and a modest recovery during the most recent business cycle (1979–1985).

Consistent with the discussion in Chapter 2, recent productivity growth trends do not support the hypothesis that domestic technological change has accelerated in the overall economy. Moreover, trends in labor productivity growth and unemployment strongly suggest that, consistent with the previous discussion of the effects of technological change on employment, productivity growth is not associated with higher aggregate unemployment. Figure 3-3 displays annual rates of productivity growth in

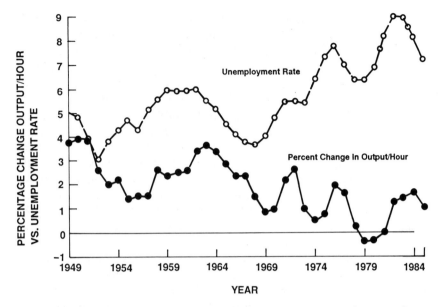

FIGURE 3-3 Percentage change in output per hour (labor productivity growth) and the annual unemployment rate, 3-year moving averages, 1949–1985. SOURCE: President's Council of Economic Advisers (1986).

the nonfarm business sector, along with annual unemployment rates, in 3-year moving averages (to reduce the effects of business cycles on long-run trends) for 1949–1985. Throughout the post-1949 period, but especially after 1973, the trends in these two series diverge—unemployment has climbed, whereas productivity growth has declined. Baumol (1986) presents similar data for longer time periods.

Table 3-6 also distinguishes trends in manufacturing labor productivity from those in nonmanufacturing and shows that rates of labor productivity growth in manufacturing and in nonmanufacturing have behaved quite differently in recent years. U.S. productivity in the nonmanufacturing sector began to decrease during 1966–1973; during the 1973–1979 business cycle, deterioration in productivity growth occurred within both sectors. During the most recent business cycle (1979–1985), productivity growth rates have increased only in manufacturing. Thus, much of the slowdown in measured U.S. productivity growth that has occurred during the last two decades is located within nonmanufacturing industry.

Two important points must be noted in any discussion of productivity trends. The first concerns the difficulty of measuring productivity in the nonmanufacturing sector of the economy. The data in Table 3-6, which suggest that productivity growth in the nonmanufacturing sector has been low, conflict with anecdotal evidence from industries such as financial services in which product innovation and productivity growth, much of which are based on information and computer technologies, appear to be considerable. If product innovation has in fact been particularly rapid in financial services, telecommunications, and other nonmanufacturing industries in recent years, the quality of productivity data for these industries may have declined because of the problems posed by product innovation for the measurement of output and productivity (see Chapter 2). An unknown portion of the low productivity growth measured in nonmanufacturing industry also may reflect problems of measuring inputs and outputs in this sector. Finally, the quality of employment and output data for the service industries is impaired by the classification schema used for these data (Kendrick, 1986; Marimont and Slater, 1986; see also Chapter 8). Rates of productivity growth in the nonmanufacturing sector thus may be understated in the available public data.

A second important point concerns the lack of explanations for the general decline of productivity growth rates in the United States and in other industrial nations since the early 1970s. Despite extensive research (summarized in Baily, 1986, and Wolff, 1985), there is no widely accepted explanation for the post-1973 decline. Studies have considered lower investments in R&D or physical capital, intersectoral shifts in labor between manufacturing and nonmanufacturing, government regulation, and lower labor force quality as contributors to changing productivity growth rates, but most analysts have yet to accept any one factor or combination of factors as a satisfactory explanation. In addition, although foreign productivity growth rates typically have exceeded U.S. performance, all industrial nations have experienced declines in productivity growth rates since 1973 (U.S. Bureau of Labor Statistics, 1986c). Many of the causes of slower productivity growth therefore are not unique to the United States but have affected all industrial nations.

Changes in the Sectoral Composition
of Output and Employment

The top portion of Table 3-7 gives the share of total private nonfarm business output accounted for by each of 12 major U.S. economic groups during 1948–1985. The manufacturing sector's share ("Durables" and "Nondurables") of total output has been remarkably constant throughout this period—in 1948, it was 27.9 percent; in 1985, it stood at 28 percent. The table also highlights the growth during this period in the shares of total output for the finance, insurance, and real estate group, which increased from 9.5 to 11.3 percent; for the services group (including business and health services), which increased from 10.7 to 15 percent;

TABLE 3-7 Percentage of U.S. Gross Domestic Product Originating in Industry Group

Group	1948	1957	1966	1973	1979	1985
Durables	17.0	17.8	18.5	17.8	17.2	17.2
Nondurables	10.9	10.6	11.0	11.5	11.1	10.8
Mining	8.5	8.2	6.8	6.3	5.3	4.7
Construction	10.6	12.2	11.5	8.0	7.0	5.8
Transportation	9.0	6.4	5.8	5.6	5.6	4.5
Communications	1.1	1.4	1.7	2.4	2.9	3.5
Utilities	1.6	2.4	2.8	3.5	3.4	3.7
Wholesale trade	6.5	6.9	7.6	8.6	8.8	9.6
Retail trade	12.4	12.3	11.8	12.1	11.9	12.3
FIRE	9.5	10.2	10.1	10.9	11.8	11.3
Services	10.7	9.7	10.5	11.8	13.3	15.0
Gov't. enterprises	2.3	1.8	1.8	1.6	1.6	1.6

	Growth Rates (percent) of Gross Domestic Product Originating in Group							
Group	1948– 1957	1957– 1966	1966– 1973	1973– 1979	1979– 1985	1948– 1966	1966– 1985	1948– 1985
Durables	4.0	4.5	2.7	1.9	2.1	4.3	2.3	3.2
Nondurables	3.2	4.5	3.9	1.9	1.6	3.8	2.6	3.2
Mining	3.2	2.0	2.1	−0.4	0.1	2.6	0.7	1.6
Construction	5.1	3.5	−1.9	0.3	−1.3	4.3	−1.0	1.6
Transportation	−0.2	2.9	2.8	2.6	−1.4	1.3	1.4	1.4
Communications	6.8	6.3	7.8	6.0	5.0	6.5	6.3	6.4
Utilities	8.5	5.8	6.4	1.8	3.5	7.2	4.0	5.5
Wholesale trade	4.1	5.1	5.1	3.0	3.4	4.6	3.9	4.2
Retail trade	3.4	3.6	3.6	2.4	2.6	3.5	2.9	3.2
FIRE	4.4	3.9	4.4	3.8	1.4	4.1	3.3	3.7
Services	2.5	4.9	4.9	4.6	4.0	3.7	4.5	4.1
Gov't. enterprises	0.8	4.1	1.6	2.5	1.7	2.4	1.9	2.2
Total	3.5	4.0	3.3	2.5	2.0	3.8	2.7	3.2

NOTE: Gross domestic product calculations based on constant 1982 dollars. FIRE = Finance, insurance, and real estate.

SOURCE: Calculated from U.S. Bureau of Labor Statistics, Office of Productivity and Technology, unpublished data developed by BLS from Department of Commerce (Bureau of Economic Analysis national income and product account data and the Federal Reserve) Index of Industrial Productivity for Durable and Nondurable Manufacturing.

and for the communication services group, which grew from 1.1 to 3.5 percent.

The bottom portion of the table shows the rates of growth in the output of each of these groups. Two conclusions are obvious. Output growth rates in most groups were higher during 1948–1966 than during 1966–1985. Slower aggregate output growth during 1966–1985, combined with rapid growth in the labor supply, contributed to higher aggregate unemployment during this period. The second conclusion concerns the relative rates of output growth in the manufacturing and nonmanufacturing sectors. During 1948–1966, the rate of growth of output for manufacturing was above the economy-wide average; it fell below the average during 1966–1985. Output growth in most nonmanufacturing industries (with the exception of mining, construction, and transportation), on the other hand, remained strong after 1966.

Intersectoral differences in productivity growth, combined with intersectoral differences in output growth, have affected the level of demand for labor in the manufacturing and nonmanufacturing sectors of the U.S. economy. Because sectoral employment growth is the difference between growth in sectoral output and growth in sectoral productivity, these differences affect the level of labor demand. Within the nonmanufacturing sector, low productivity growth and rapid output growth (outside of mining, transportation, and construction) have resulted in a strong demand for labor.

The manufacturing sector, on the other hand, has experienced a resurgence of productivity growth since 1979 to levels comparable to or greater than those of the 1950s and early 1960s. Slow growth in output, however, also has characterized this sector since 1979 because of import penetration of U.S. markets for manufactured goods and the slow growth or collapse of foreign markets for U.S. manufactured exports. During 1980–1984 alone, Davis (1986) estimated that declines in U.S. merchandise exports resulted in the loss of as many as 1.8 million jobs, many of which were in manufacturing. According to Davis (1986), "[E]xport-related jobs accounted for 80 percent of the total 1980–1984 decrease in manufacturing employment [from 20.3 million in 1980 to 19.4 million in 1984]" (p. 92).[22] Hight (1986) estimated that increased imports during 1982–1984 cost nearly 800,000 U.S. jobs in mining and manufacturing, 77 percent of which were in 14 (out of a total of 80) manufacturing industries.[23] Growth in demand for the output of U.S. manufacturing from both domestic and foreign markets supported employment growth during

---

[22]Pollock and Almon (1986) also present data suggesting that the negative employment impacts of increased imports and declining exports during 1980–1985 substantially exceeded those of technological change in all 35 of the manufacturing industries they examined.

[23]Apparel, motor vehicles, computers and office equipment, electronic components, leather products, radio and television receivers, primary metals, radio and communications equipment, industrial chemicals, furniture and fixtures, general industrial machinery, electrical machinery, sawmills and planing, and basic steel.

the 1970s, but the collapse of export markets and surging imports contributed to declines in the rate of growth or reductions in the level of employment in many manufacturing industries in the 1980s.

Manufacturing's share of U.S. private nonfarm employment has been declining gradually since 1919. As U.S. Bureau of Labor Statistics (1985a) figures show, during 1919–1948, this share declined from 44 percent to 40 percent; since 1948, the rate of decline has increased, particularly since 1966. The rate of decline in employment within manufacturing, relative to the rest of the private nonfarm economy, reached an average annual rate of 2 percent after 1966 and then increased to 3 percent per year during 1979–1985. Thus, the share of private nonfarm employment accounted for by manufacturing stood at 36, 28, and 24 percent, respectively, in 1966, 1979, and 1985. Groups registering the most dramatic gains in their shares of employment since 1966 include wholesale and retail trade, services, and finance, insurance, and real estate. Despite these declines in its share of employment, manufacturing had 19.3 million employees in 1985, versus 19.2 million in 1966 (President's Council of Economic Advisers, 1987, Table B-40). Growth in the nonmanufacturing share of total employment since 1966 reflects more rapid growth in this sector, rather than absolute declines in manufacturing employment.

Since 1979 resurgent productivity growth and stagnant output growth in manufacturing, combined with rapid output growth and stagnant productivity growth in nonmanufacturing industry, have accelerated longstanding trends of decline in the manufacturing sector's share of total employment. What role has domestic technological change played in these trends? Certainly, the resurgence in productivity growth within manufacturing must be taken as a partial indicator of improved domestic technological performance. The reasons for this resurgence, however, are no better understood than the reasons for the decline in manufacturing productivity growth during 1973–1979. Moreover, improved domestic productivity growth during 1979–1985 did not translate into growth in manufactured exports and employment. In assessing the effect of productivity growth on employment, we must also consider the reasons for the decline in manufactured exports and growth in imports after 1980.

INTERNATIONAL TRADE, TECHNOLOGICAL CHANGE, AND U.S. EMPLOYMENT

International Trade and Employment

Manufacturing industry is more exposed to international competition than most other nonagricultural industries by virtue of the internationally "tradeable" character of its outputs.[24] Manufactured exports currently dominate U.S. nonagricultural exports, accounting for nearly $182 billion in 1984 (nonagricultural merchandise exports) and substantially exceeding total services exports of $69 billion–$91 billion (President's Council of Economic Advisers, 1987, Table B-100; U.S. Congress, Office of Technology Assessment, 1986c).

Exports of manufactured goods also support numerous nonmanufacturing jobs. The U.S. Department of Commerce's International Trade Administration (1983) estimated that merchandise exports in 1982 (totaling $211 billion) supported nearly 5 million jobs, of which more than 4 million depended on the export of manufactured goods. Of these 4 million jobs, slightly more than one-half, or 2.3 million, were located in manufacturing; 1.7 million jobs were in the nonmanufacturing sector of the economy.

During 1979–1985, a number of factors were responsible for reduced U.S. manufactured exports and increased U.S. imports of manufactured goods. These influences included the appreciation of the U.S. dollar, which was associated with the combination of large federal budget deficits and tight monetary policy that characterized the U.S. economy in the early 1980s (Fieleke, 1984). Appreciation of the dollar depressed the U.S. price of imports of foreign goods while increasing the price of U.S. exports, all of which had a considerable effect on the U.S. trade balance (Figure 3-4). Imports increased from $332 billion[25] in 1980 to more than $521 billion in 1986; U.S. exports declined from $389 billion in 1980 to $371 billion in 1986 (President's Council of Economic Advisers, 1987, Table B-20). Economic growth also was weak during the early 1980s in many of the countries that are important U.S. export markets, thereby reducing the possibilities for increased exports. Furthermore, the underlying competitiveness of U.S. manufactured products, which is revealed in product quality and price/performance characteristics, may have declined during the past decade, as suggested in a number of studies (Finan et al., 1986; President's Commission on Industrial Competitiveness, 1985); this issue is discussed in greater detail below.

Technological Change and U.S. Exports

U.S. exports since 1945 from the manufacturing and nonmanufacturing sectors alike have been goods whose production depended on large

---

[24]Widespread application of information and other computer-based technologies, however, is gradually changing the extent to which services—for example, business, financial, and communications—can also be traded internationally.

[25]All figures are in 1982 dollars.

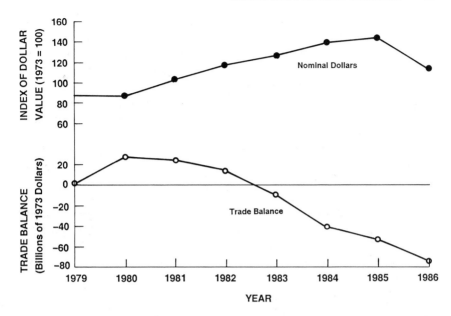

FIGURE 3-4   Changes in the U.S. trade balance and the value of the dollar, 1979–1986. SOURCE: President's Council of Economic Advisers (1987).

investments in R&D and on skilled, relatively high-wage labor. Numerous studies have documented a significant relationship between the high skill or R&D content of manufactured products and the role of those products in U.S. exports (see Gruber et al., 1967; Keesing, 1967). U.S. exports also are more heavily dependent on R&D-intensive industries than are the exports of other industrial nations (Organisation for Economic Co-operation and Development, 1986b). Bartel and Lichtenberg (1987), among others, argue that this nation has specialized in the export of manufactured goods embodying advanced technologies, the development and initial production of which are relatively intensive in their use of skilled labor and scientific talent (for reasons noted in Chapter 2). U.S. export-intensive industries are large employers of skilled and professional labor when compared to all U.S. manufacturing industry (U.S. Congress, Office of Technology Assessment, 1986b; U.S. International Trade Commission, 1983). The Office of Technology Assessment (1986c) study of international trade in services corroborates this analysis for the nonmanufacturing sector; services exports tend to support high-wage, high-skill employment in comparison to overall U.S. nonmanufacturing employment.

During the 1960s and 1970s, the manufacturing workers displaced by increased imports of foreign goods were employed in relatively low-wage, low-skill jobs (Aho and Orr, 1981). As other nations continue to develop their technological and manufacturing capabilities, lower-skill, lower-wage U.S. manufacturing jobs will continue to be threatened. Moreover, the nonmanufacturing sector will feel the effects of increased import penetration as well; workers in that sector who are displaced because of increased imports are also likely to be employed in relatively low-skill, low-wage jobs.

A significant difference between the 1980s/1990s and the 1960s/1970s is that much low-wage foreign competition in manufacturing no longer is low-productivity competition. In part because of more rapid rates of technology transfer, as well as increased technological sophistication in many foreign economies, production and product technologies in some industries within many low-wage competitor nations now approach or exceed those of the United States in quality and product sophistication. This changing international environment is likely to increase the importance of investments by U.S. firms and public institutions in the skills of the labor force and in the R&D necessary to generate and adopt advanced technologies in both the manufacturing and nonmanufacturing sectors.

The Competitiveness of U.S. Industry

In view of the importance of international trade for U.S. employment and wages, recent signs of declining U.S. competitiveness are a cause for concern. International industrial competitiveness—that is, the ability of U.S. products to preserve or increase their share of international markets—subsumes a number of factors, among them product quality (including technological sophistication and design quality), product service, and price. As we noted in Chapter 1, a great many nontechnological factors also affect competitiveness, including the rate of domestic savings and capital formation, other nations' trade and financial policies, and the exchange rate of U.S. and foreign currencies. Because the appreciation of the U.S. dollar during 1980–1985 affected the price of U.S. goods in international trade, regardless of changes in their quality, at least some part of U.S. industry's competitiveness problems is related to the dollar's behavior during the first half of the 1980s.

Other evidence, however, suggests that declining competitiveness in some U.S. manufacturing industries predates the high dollar exchange rates of 1980–1985. Import penetration in 28 of 40 major U.S. manufacturing industries increased during 1972–1982, a decade that spanned a period of undervalued as well as overvalued U.S. dollars (President's Commission on Industrial Competitiveness, 1985). In addition, the U.S.

balance of trade in high-technology products, historically a U.S. export stronghold, has been deteriorating since the late 1970s; the 1986 balance of trade in these items yielded a deficit of $2.6 billion (based on unpublished 1986 data from the U.S. Department of Commerce, International Trade Administration). According to Finan et al. (1986), much of the deterioration in the U.S. high-technology trade balance reflects a combination of stagnant exports of U.S. goods and increases of more than 40 percent in imports in some sectors. In response to these trends, U.S. firms in several high-technology industries, especially electronics, have moved a larger share of their production to "offshore" locations:

This movement to offshore sourcing has developed especially rapidly with respect to Hong Kong, Taiwan, Korea, and Singapore—what we designate collectively here as the NICs [newly industrializing countries]. U.S. firms are sourcing subassemblies from low-labor-cost countries where usually the exchange rate has moved favorably—that is, where the dollar has remained relatively strong. As a result of U.S. firms' sourcing decisions, the trade balance with the NICs has deteriorated significantly. (p. 31)

Sanderson (1987) and others (e.g., Cyert, 1985), however, argue that widespread adoption of new computer-based manufacturing technologies within U.S. manufacturing, as well as the increasing competitive importance of shorter product development cycles, may reduce the attractiveness of offshore manufacturing for many U.S. firms in the future. The benefits of offshore manufacturing also should be reduced by declines in the foreign exchange value of the U.S. dollar from the levels it achieved in 1984 and 1985.[26]

Unit Labor Costs in U.S. and Foreign Manufacturing, 1950–1985

Technological change and productivity growth can accelerate output growth by enhancing the competitiveness of U.S. industry. As stated in Chapter 1, because productivity and output growth are linked in an open economy, growth in productivity within U.S. manufacturing, which reduces the labor costs of U.S. products, can reduce the price of U.S. manufactured goods in overseas markets. Reduced prices in turn lead to

---

[26]Caterpillar, Inc., which manufactures earthmoving equipment, increased offshore production from 19 percent of total sales in 1982 to 25 percent in 1986; it also increased its use of foreign sources of parts and components by a factor of four. The declining foreign exchange rate of the U.S. dollar sharply reduced the profitability of this strategy and contributed to the firm's loss of $148 million in the fourth quarter of 1986 (*The Economist*, April 4, 1987).

expanded U.S. exports of manufactured goods and reductions in U.S. imports. Conversely, if technological change and productivity growth in U.S. manufacturing industry fall sufficiently behind those of our trading partners, markets for U.S. products will shrink. Nevertheless, the higher productivity growth in U.S. manufacturing after 1979 largely failed to improve, and occurred simultaneously with dramatic declines in, U.S. trade performance. This section examines one explanation for the disjunction of U.S. productivity and trade performance after 1980.

Table 3-8 summarizes the price dimensions of international competitiveness and the contributions of productivity growth to the price competitiveness of U.S. manufacturing. The table shows changes in unit labor costs for the manufacturing sectors of other industrial nations relative to those of the United States. Unit labor costs measure the labor cost per unit of output of manufacturing industry; they grow with increases in the nominal wage of manufacturing labor. Productivity growth offsets the effect of wage increases on unit labor costs—as unit labor requirements decline, so will unit labor costs. If wage increases are comparable to growth in labor productivity and if exchange rates remain constant, unit labor costs will be unchanged.

The top panel of Table 3-8 shows the changes in foreign unit labor costs (measured in U.S. dollars) relative to U.S. unit labor costs for five intervals during 1950–1985; entries in the top panel are the sum of the entries in the three lower panels of the table. Negative entries indicate reductions in foreign unit labor costs relative to those of the United States. Because these costs are measured in U.S. dollars, they are affected by exchange rate movements as well as by movements in wages and labor productivity. Since 1979 unit labor costs in all of these foreign industrial nations except Canada have declined relative to those of the United States, the first period during which this has occurred since 1950–1957. As a result, the ability of U.S. manufacturing to compete in world markets declined significantly during 1979–1985, despite significant productivity growth in U.S. industry.

Technological change, which affects labor productivity growth, played a major role in the behavior of unit labor costs during this period. The second panel from the top in Table 3–8 shows foreign labor productivity growth rates relative to those of the United States. Negative entries indicate more rapid productivity growth in other nations' manufacturing industry; the table clearly shows that U.S. productivity growth has lagged behind that of other industrial nations throughout the postwar period. The 1979–1985 data, however, suggest that during this most recent period, U.S. labor productivity growth rates approached those of most industrial nations (with the exception of Japan). The relative productivity performance of U.S. manufacturing obviously improved during 1979–1985 to an

TABLE 3-8 International Comparisons of Unit Labor Costs, Productivity, and Compensation in Manufacturing in Selected Industrial Nations

Country	Annual Growth Rate of Foreign Unit Labor Costs (in U.S. dollars), Relative to the United States				
	1950–1957	1957–1966	1966–1973	1973–1979	1979–1985
West Germany	−2.0	3.0	6.9	3.3	−8.9
France	−0.6	0.0	2.1	3.2	−8.2
Italy	−2.8	1.9	5.0	1.8	−6.1
Japan	−3.8	1.7	5.3	2.5	−6.1
U.K.	2.0	1.9	−0.2	7.0	−5.4
Canada	1.2	−1.8	0.2	−1.0	0.2

	Annual Growth Rate of U.S. Productivity (output per hour), Relative to Foreign Manufacturing				
West Germany	−4.8	−3.3	−3.0	−2.8	−0.2
France	−2.2	−3.2	−3.6	−3.5	−0.9
Italy	−3.6	−3.6	−4.1	−1.9	−0.8
Japan	−7.5	−5.2	−8.3	−4.0	−2.5
U.K.	0.8	−0.5	−2.2	−0.2	−0.9
Canada	−1.4	−1.3	−2.2	−0.8	1.4

	Annual Growth Rate of Foreign Hourly Compensation (in domestic currency), Relative to the United States				
West Germany	2.7	5.8	4.1	0.0	−0.8
France	4.3	5.0	4.2	6.0	5.2
Italy	−0.7	5.6	8.1	9.7	8.5
Japan	3.8	7.0	9.5	3.0	−2.2
U.K.	1.2	2.5	3.9	9.7	3.7
Canada	0.8	0.8	1.3	2.5	1.4

	Annual Growth Rate of the Foreign Exchange Rate, Relative to the U.S. Dollar				
West Germany	0.0	0.5	5.9	6.2	−7.9
France	−2.6	−1.7	1.5	0.7	−12.5
Italy	0.0	0.0	1.0	−6.0	−13.9
Japan	0.0	−0.1	4.2	3.6	−1.5
U.K.	0.0	0.0	−1.9	−2.4	−8.2
Canada	1.9	−1.3	1.1	−2.6	−2.6

SOURCE: U.S. Bureau of Labor Statistics (1986c).

unprecedented extent. Moreover, measured in terms of their domestic currencies, hourly compensation for foreign manufacturing workers (the third panel from the top of Table 3-8) consistently has grown more rapidly than compensation for U.S. manufacturing workers. Prior to 1979, the impact of more rapid growth in labor costs on the competitiveness of these nations' manufactured exports was offset by productivity growth rates that also exceeded those of U.S. industry. During 1979–1985, however, increases in foreign worker compensation continued to exceed those of U.S. manufacturing workers, while the productivity gap between U.S. and foreign manufacturing narrowed. Yet, the growth of U.S. unit labor costs remained well above that of other industrial nations. Why?

The answer to this question is contained in the bottom panel of Table 3-8. Upward movement in the foreign exchange rate of the U.S. dollar during 1979–1985 more than offset declines in U.S. labor costs. The bottom panel of Table 3-8 shows that foreign unit labor costs (expressed in U.S. dollars) have declined, and this decline offset the effects of low growth in U.S. manufacturing compensation and high growth in U.S. manufacturing productivity.

Had the dollar not appreciated against foreign currencies during 1979–1985, U.S. unit labor costs would have *declined* relative to those of all of the industrial nations in Table 3-8 with the exceptions of West Germany and Japan. Even relative to these nations with higher productivity growth rates, the increase in U.S. unit labor costs would have been far smaller, thus making U.S. exports more competitive in world markets, reducing import penetration of U.S. markets, and reducing the incentives for U.S. firms to locate their production facilities offshore (Finan et al., 1986; Kravis and Lipsey, 1986). Indeed, in the absence of the surge in the foreign exchange rate of the U.S. dollar, U.S. employment growth during the past 7 years might have exhibited a rather different pattern, as productivity gains in U.S. manufacturing supported increases in exports and higher output growth, both of which could have led to growth or slower declines in manufacturing employment.[27]

---

[27]Data on changes in foreign hourly compensation and labor productivity trends through 1986 are not yet available to bring this comparative analysis of unit labor costs up to the end of 1986. Neef (1986) noted in his study that the decline in the foreign exchange value of the dollar from its peak in 1985 through October 1986 had not yet brought the dollar to its 1980 value vis-à-vis the currencies of Western European nations, although substantial depreciation had occurred against the Japanese yen. Moreover, the dollar's depreciation against many Latin American and East Asian currencies was minimal. The U.S. dollar also had not depreciated against the Canadian dollar, which accounted for 25 percent of U.S. manufactured exports. The declines in the foreign exchange value of the dollar since October 1986 are likely to reduce some but not all of the disparities that developed during 1980–1985 in U.S. and foreign nations' unit labor costs.

SUMMARY

This chapter has examined the determinants of labor supply and demand by focusing on the role technology plays in influencing aggregate employment and unemployment levels. The increase in aggregate unemployment since 1973, as well as the large number of experienced workers suffering permanent job losses in recent years, is disturbing. The direct contribution of technological change to these trends appears to be minor. As the growth rate of the labor supply declines during the next decade, at least one source of upward pressure on aggregate unemployment should diminish.

Differential rates of productivity growth in manufacturing and nonmanufacturing industry, combined with low rates of growth in the output of manufacturing industry, have contributed to higher rates of decline in manufacturing's share of total employment during 1979–1985. The decline in manufacturing's share of nonfarm employment does not represent a departure from longstanding patterns of economic growth and development in the United States, but the rate of decline has accelerated during the past 15 years.

Changes in the international economic environment during 1980–1985 have exacerbated and accelerated the reductions in manufacturing's share of total employment. The declines in the foreign exchange value of the dollar since late 1985 should improve the competitiveness of U.S. industry vis-à-vis a number of foreign competitors. Nonetheless, relying solely on this policy option to restore U.S. competitiveness will require severe (and in the view of this panel, unacceptable) declines in the purchasing power of U.S. workers and consumers. Technological change and productivity growth remain indispensable to the improvement of U.S. industrial competitiveness and real wages. In view of the fact that U.S. involvement in the international economy is likely to expand still further in the near future, the rapid generation and adoption of new technologies are essential to preserving and expanding U.S. employment and living standards during the next two decades.

4

Studies of the Impact of Technological Change on Employment, Skills, and Earnings: A Critical Review

This chapter reviews a number of studies that analyze the influence of new technologies on jobs, worker skills, and earnings. As in other areas of our inquiry, the extensive empirical literature covering these topics often is inconclusive and suffers from methodological weaknesses. Nonetheless, several important conclusions emerge from the discussion that follows. First, new technology will not bring massive unemployment; few studies predict large employment losses from such changes. Neither does it appear that, as a result of technological change, the skills required to get a job or to keep a job in the future will be substantially different from what they are today. Finally, technological change and productivity growth are associated with growth in real earnings. Although technological change in the U.S. economy has been cited by some as contributing to lower earnings growth and a more unequal distribution of income, there is little evidence to suggest that technology, as opposed to slow economic growth, has been responsible for these trends.

THE EMPLOYMENT EFFECTS OF TECHNOLOGICAL CHANGE

As we noted in Chapter 2, a number of factors interact to influence how technological change affects the level of employment in an industry or sector:

- the speed with which a product or process innovation is adopted;

86

- for a product innovation, the size and rate of growth of the domestic and international markets for the new product;
- for a process innovation, the size of any reductions in labor requirements per unit of output (i.e., increases in labor productivity);
- the magnitude of reductions in output prices resulting from labor productivity increases, movement down the "learning curve" (cost reductions associated with more extensive use of the new process technology), and subsequent refinements of the technology;
- the size of the increase in domestic and international demand for the product in response to price reductions resulting from the adoption of a new process technology;
- interindustry effects (e.g., expansion or contraction in another industry in response to changes in the cost of a key input); and
- the effects of technological change on wages in the industry or sector.

These variables exert offsetting influences on the demand for labor within sectors, and they operate with varying lags. A complete accounting of all of their effects is impossible. The studies considered below, in a survey that is meant to be illustrative rather than exhaustive, all ignore one or more of the variables in this list.[1] The range of influences considered within each study, as well as the level of aggregation at which each is conducted, varies considerably. As the number of sectors or technologies expands, however, the data requirements rapidly become overwhelming. To circumvent this difficulty, the studies cited here focus on the impacts of a single technology in many industries or on the effects of technological change within a single industry—with the exceptions of the U.S. Bureau of Labor Statistics (1986b) forecasts of employment and the policy-oriented studies by the Temporary National Economic Committee (1941) and the National Commission on Automation, Technology, and Economic Progress (1966).

Policy-Oriented Studies

A perception that technological change had played a role in the Great Depression led to the publication of studies of the economic effects of technological change by the Congress (U.S. House of Representatives, Committee on Labor, 1936), the National Resources Committee (1937), and the Temporary National Economic Committee (1941). Many of these

---

[1]For comprehensive surveys of this large and rapidly expanding literature, see Blair (1974), Brooks and Schneider (1985), Fechter (1974), Freeman and Soete (1985), and Kaplinsky (1987).

studies reached pessimistic conclusions. The following comments from the report of the Temporary National Economic Committee are representative:

. . . there is unmistakable evidence of a change in kind as well as severity of unemployment in the last depression. This change is characterized by the widespread use of electrical power and mass production methods which have shown a capacity to increase industrial activity on the upturn of the business cycle without a corresponding ability to absorb unemployed labor. (p. xvi)

With the return of full employment during World War II and sustained prosperity during the remainder of the 1940s, the conclusions of these studies had little discernible impact on policy or economic research. But high (by comparison with prior years) U.S. unemployment rates during the late 1950s and early 1960s,[2] coupled with rates of economic growth that fell behind those of Western European nations, fueled a resurgence of the debate over the employment consequences of automation. Pessimism and concern about the consequences of technological change were reflected in such work as Michael (1962), and this concern contributed to the formation of the National Commission on Technology, Automation, and Economic Progress in 1964 (see Critchlow, 1987). The tone of this commission's report, however, contrasted with the pessimistic views that had spurred its development.

The commission strongly endorsed the importance of technological change in raising living standards and improving the quality of worklife but acknowledged that its benefits were not costless. Moreover, despite its endorsement of the benefits of technology, the commission echoed the reports of the 1930s in expressing concern over a "glut of productivity." The historically unprecedented productivity growth rates of the postwar period were expected to continue, and the commission argued that increases in output per worker (i.e., labor productivity) would reduce the demand for labor if they were not offset by growth in the demand for output. Aggregate demand, the commission warned, had to be maintained at a level that ensured sufficient jobs for the growing work force.

Although it recommended additional assistance for the technologically displaced, the commission concluded that if macroeconomic policy were properly managed, the probability of massive technological unemployment was low because expanding aggregate demand could ensure more jobs, even in the face of an expanding work force and growing labor productivity. Such optimism rested on the apparent triumph in the early

---

[2]Annual unemployment averaged 5.8 percent during 1958–1962, well above the average rate of 4 percent that prevailed during 1950–1957 (President's Council of Economic Advisers, 1987, Table B-35).

1960s of policies for the management of aggregate demand. By the time the commission's report was released in 1966, however, the economic and political outlook had changed dramatically. Concern over the impacts of new technology had declined, in part because the U.S. unemployment rate was only 3.8 percent, having fallen from 5.2 percent in 1964 in response to an expansionary fiscal policy (President's Council of Economic Advisers, 1987). This improvement in the economic environment, as well as the escalating U.S. involvement in the Vietnam conflict, meant that the commission's policy recommendations were largely ignored by the Johnson administration. During the 1970s the employment consequences of technological change received little attention, but the subject returned to a position of prominence in public debate in the 1980s.

Studies of Individual Firms, Industries, or Occupations

A recent survey by Flynn (1985) analyzed almost 200 case studies of the employment effects of process innovations during 1940–1982. The technological advances considered by Flynn were evenly divided between those affecting the automation of production or distribution and those affecting office automation. Process innovations in skill-intensive manufacturing processes often eliminated high-skill jobs and generated low-skill jobs. The opposite was true, however, for the adoption of data- and word-processing technologies in offices, which eliminated low-skill jobs and created high-skill jobs. Flynn concluded that the net effect of process innovations on employment was indeterminate and depended heavily on conditions within individual industries or firms.

Hunt and Hunt (1986) surveyed the effects of technological change on clerical employment. The authors criticized several other studies of this topic for overlooking the often slow pace of technological change and diffusion, the output-expanding impacts of reductions in the price of such clerical or secretarial activities as text editing, and the effect of expanding aggregate demand. They argued that these flaws led the studies to overstate the job-displacing impact of technological change on clerical workers:

The forecasts of declining clerical employment are based on over-optimistic expectations of technological improvements or exaggerated productivity claims on behalf of existing technology. In our opinion, current office technology offers significant improvements in product quality and modest improvements in productivity. There is as yet no empirical evidence of an office productivity revolution that will displace significant numbers of clerical workers. (p. 65)

Osterman (1986) also studied the impact of information technologies on office and clerical employment in several industries and found that displacement was partly offset by an expansion in the demand for automated activities or functions. Although the adoption of computers initially reduced the employment of clerks and managers in these industries during 1972–1978, displacement typically was followed in a few years by increases in clerical and managerial employment.

The timing of the employment-displacing and employment-expanding effects of technological change in Osterman's study suggests the empirical problems that result from differences in the rates and timing of productivity growth, cost reduction, and output and employment growth. According to Osterman, the increases in employment that followed the introduction of computers generally were insufficient to overcome the employment losses. Over a longer period, however, the net employment losses might well have been smaller or nonexistent. Osterman also did not consider the employment effects of new jobs created elsewhere within the firms adopting computers. Nevertheless, differences in the timing of employment displacement and creation mean that the workers who are initially displaced may not be the individuals who are subsequently hired. Significant displacement problems thus may develop even in the face of expanding employment opportunities.

In their recent analysis of office automation, Roessner et al. (1985) present conclusions that contrast sharply with those of the National Research Council's Panel on Technology and Women's Employment. In its 1986 report the panel concluded that "massive job loss is unlikely to occur" (p. 125) within clerical and office occupations as a result of technological change. The Roessner team, on the other hand, projected that office automation could displace as much as 40 percent of 1980 clerical employment within the financial services and insurance industries by the year 2000. To reach this conclusion the authors surveyed experts on likely improvements in office automation technologies and applied these forecasts to a functional taxonomy of clerical tasks. They assumed that the functional composition of typical clerical tasks and duties would be unaffected by technological change during 1980–2000. They also assumed that technological change and diffusion would be rapid and minimized or dismissed the possibility that the enhanced productivity of clerical workers might increase the demand for clerical services. Finally, the study ignored the employment implications of product innovations that result from office automation technologies, even though executives within the financial services industry, among other sectors, have cited such innovations as important sources of employment growth.

Denny and Fuss (1983) investigated the effects of automation on occupational groups within Bell Canada, using data on four separate occupations and a direct measure of the rate of technological change (based on the share of direct distance dialing in total telephone traffic). Technological change in Bell Canada during 1952–1972 increased the amount of capital and reduced the amount of labor per unit of output, with the laborsaving effects felt most strongly in the least skilled occupations. The study found, however, that net employment growth within these occupations was positive because output growth more than offset the impact on employment of reductions in labor requirements per unit of output. The Denny-Fuss study did not deal with the potentially employment-creating effects of these innovations on other industries or on occupations within Bell Canada beyond the four considered.

Levy et al. (1984) analyzed the interactions among technological change, growth in productivity, and growth in output and employment in a number of industries. They assessed the effects on output growth and employment of labor productivity growth resulting from technological change and increases in production plant scale during 1960–1980 in five manufacturing and mining industries (steel, aluminum, automobiles, coal mining, and iron mining). Within all these industries, technological change led to the substitution of capital for labor and to increases in labor productivity (although steel exhibited a very low rate of technological change), a finding similar to that of Denny and Fuss. An important improvement in this analysis, however, is the Levy team's consideration of the effect of productivity growth on the demand for the output of these industries. By lowering prices and increasing the demand for industry output, labor productivity growth supported employment growth that offset much or all of the reduction in labor demand associated with the productivity-increasing impact of technological change. In three of the five industries (coal mining, iron mining, and aluminum production), the output-enhancing effect of technological change increased total employment; in the other two (steel, where technological change was minimal, and automobiles), demand growth was insufficient to offset the impact of reductions in the labor required per unit of output.

Studies by Ayres and Miller (1983) and Hunt and Hunt (1983) considered the impact of robots on manufacturing employment. Ayres and Miller concluded that current robotics technologies could displace 1.5 million jobs in current manufacturing and as many as 4 million by 2005. Hunt and Hunt, on the other hand, estimated that total employment displacement by 1990 would amount to only 68,000–134,000 jobs—well below levels of normal turnover within the manufacturing work force. (Turnover in U.S. manufacturing averages more than 20 percent per year, based on data from 1976–1980 cited in Levy et al., 1984.)

One reason for these divergent estimates is Ayres and Miller's assumption that diffusion and technological improvement within robotics would be rapid. Ayres and Miller's study focused on the technological "frontier" and considered the number of jobs that potentially could be performed by robots in 2005. The alternative approach, developing a model that incorporates adoption costs and diffusion rates, places greater emphasis on the length of time needed for investment in and adoption of the new technology. The Ayres-Miller study also surveyed a small and narrow sample of firms and industries (16 firms, almost all of which were in the automotive industry and therefore contained a high proportion of jobs that could be performed by currently available robots). The empirical basis for the less dramatic displacement estimates of Hunt and Hunt's 1983 work, which made explicit assumptions about rates of adoption of robotics technologies and employed a broader data base for estimates of employment effects, seems stronger than that for Ayres and Miller's predictions. Neither study considered the employment implications of the potential growth in output resulting from the positive effects of robots on manufacturing productivity growth, although Hunt and Hunt compared their displacement estimates with the BLS estimates of employment growth in affected occupations through 1995.

The contrasting results of these studies, like those of the studies by Roessner et al. (1985) and the National Research Council's Panel on Women's Employment and Technology (1986), illustrate the sensitivity of empirical estimates of the employment impacts of technological change to detailed assumptions concerning diffusion rates, technological improvement, and the organization of manufacturing and office production processes. Yet prediction of these variables, which is necessary for forecasts of employment impacts, is extremely difficult and frequently incorrect; therefore, the forecasts based on such assumptions are often unreliable.

An important collection of sectoral studies of employment and technological change in Great Britain recently has been completed by the Science Policy Research Unit of the University of Sussex. Known as the TEMPO (Technological Trends and Employment) project, these studies (Clark, 1985; Freeman, 1985a; Guy, 1984; Smith, 1986; Soete, 1985) analyzed recent trends in technological change, productivity growth, and employment in 17 British manufacturing and service industries. The project focused on sectoral studies because of the evidence that the impacts of technological change on productivity and employment growth varied greatly across sectors.[3]

The TEMPO studies also undertook forecasts of employment through the late 1990s. The analytic framework used by most of the studies (with the exceptions of Ray, 1985, and the studies of the services sector in

---

[3]"A broad macroeconomic approach was therefore deemed to be inadequate for assessing the specific employment effects of technological change. It was felt that only in-depth studies of each of the main sectors would encompass the full range and variety of technical change" (Guy, 1984, p. vii).

Smith, 1986) is discussed in Clark and Patel (1984); it relied on estimates of investment and the rate of growth of the capital stock to compute measures of growth in "best-practice" and "average" productivity for both labor and capital. ("Best-practice" productivity is the level attainable with the latest process technologies; "average" represents the actual level of measured productivity.) Estimation of these trends relied heavily on imperfect data on the value of the capital stock in industrial categories that are highly aggregated; the estimates also incorporated strong assumptions concerning the rate of growth in the productivity of new technologies. The methodology demands considerable data, and the absence of an aggregate analytic framework precludes the examination of interindustry effects of the type that are salient within input–output analysis (see below). Nonetheless, by emphasizing the roles of capital formation and diffusion in the growth of sectoral productivity and employment, this methodology makes an important contribution.

For many of the sectors in the TEMPO series, projected employment growth was low or even negative; these predictions were affected by the inability of the researchers to take into account interindustry linkages, by the low rate of growth of the British economy during the late 1970s and 1980s, and by the extensive penetration of many British markets by imports. Many of the studies examined capital productivity trends and reached conclusions resembling those of Baily (1986); in a number of British industries during the 1970s and early 1980s, the measured productivity gains from additional investments in physical capital appear to have declined somewhat for reasons that are not well understood. Freeman (1985b), for example, suggested that the radical nature of many new technologies made it difficult for British firms to exploit their productive potential rapidly.[4]

As this survey of the empirical literature suggests, few case studies are able to consider the complex effects of technological change on employment beyond the confines of a single firm, industry, or occupation. A study of the effects of robotics on assembly line workers, for example, may estimate the worker displacement that occurs due to one aspect of this technological change, but it cannot assess all the employment impacts of the new technology. Such an assessment requires additional information on the number of jobs created in designing, manufacturing, and servicing robotics machinery, as well as data on the effects on prices,

---

[4]Freeman (1985b) stressed the ". . . tendency to diminishing returns with incremental innovations and economies of scale in the older electro-mechanical plant and equipment of the 1960s . . . ," and the ". . . failure to exploit the full productivity potential of the revolutionary new technologies, based on computerisation, because of the piecemeal pattern of implementation and the lack of necessary skills" (p. 77).

demand (how much will demand for the product increase if the price is reduced?), and, consequently, employment in all industries affected by the robotics technology. A broad analytic perspective is needed to capture interactions among firms, industries, and occupations, as well as changes over time in these effects. Despite their value as descriptions of potential employment impacts, sectoral studies cannot incorporate these complex interactions and should not be relied on for forecasts of the aggregate employment impacts of technological change.

Aggregate Analyses

Input–output analysis can incorporate the interactions among industries that are essential to determining the total employment effects of technological change. The expanded scope of such an analysis, however, creates extensive data requirements. Input–output analysis requires the estimation of "input–output coefficients," which describe the amount of labor and each industry's output needed to produce the outputs of all other industries in the analysis.[5] The effect of technological change on these coefficients must be estimated, and final demand for each good must be projected in forecasts of the employment impact of new technologies. The input–output coefficients in many cases are invariant with respect to price: doubling the cost of an input need not affect the amount of that input consumed by an industry. Thus, most forms of input–output analysis can account only for changes in interindustry relationships that are based on the technologically driven substitution of one input (e.g., capital) for another (e.g., labor).

Recent applications of input–output methodology to the analysis of the employment effects of new technologies largely ignore changes in final demand and in the demand for inputs that result from changes in price. This means that there is no link between growth in labor productivity and growth in demand within a specific industry. Because input–output analysis typically projects the existing matrix of output and input requirements forward in time, predictions based on this methodology also have difficulty incorporating the employment effects of product innovation.

Howell (1985) used an input–output framework to forecast the employment effects of industrial robots. His methodology required projections of the use of robots in each of 86 industrial sectors in 1990, as well as estimates of input–output coefficients that measure the robotics industry's consumption of the output of other industries in the production of robots. Howell considered the employment consequences of six different

---

[5]Leontief and Duchin (1985) used an 89-industry input–output table.

estimates of the number of installed robots in 1990, ranging from 72,000 to 285,000.[6] Howell's analysis did not consider the increases in employment that might result from reductions in price and increases in demand associated with the diffusion of robotics technology. For example, the introduction of robots within an industry might lower prices and increase demand for the industry's output, but Howell's methodology largely ignores the employment effects of such potential growth in output.

Using a methodology that may overstate the potential employment displacement due to robots, Howell concluded that the net number of jobs displaced by robots by 1990 would range from 168,000 (assuming slow diffusion of robotics) to 718,000 (for the most rapid assumed diffusion rate). The latter figure is only 0.7 percent of total U.S. employment and 3.7 percent of manufacturing employment in 1986; it accounts for an even smaller share of total projected 1990 employment.

Leontief and Duchin (1985) undertook the most extensive input–output study of the effects of computer technology on employment. Their study concluded that the widespread use of this technology would reduce employment in the year 2000 to approximately 8–12 percent below the levels that would be needed to produce this output with an unchanged technology. The Leontief-Duchin study illuminates the serious limitations of aggregate studies of technological change. The study's assumptions concerning the quantity of labor displaced as a result of computer diffusion were based on limited evidence from case studies. Rates of diffusion and technological change were assumed to be rapid, but the authors did not allow for any output- and employment-expanding effects of reductions in the costs of clerical and other functions as a result of technological change and productivity growth.

A more serious defect of the Leontief-Duchin study is that it combined an economy-wide analysis of employment impacts with the assumption that advances would occur in only one technology. For example, as a result of assuming that no technological change beyond that in computers would occur within the agricultural sector and that demand for total output would grow, the authors projected employment gains in farming by the year 2000. Such an outcome is open to considerable question. The Leontief-Duchin projections of reduced employment by the year 2000 were criticized by the National Research Council's Panel on Technology and Women's Employment (1986), which concluded that "there is insufficient evidence to support the . . . negative outlook of the Leontief-Duchin study" (p. 111). This panel concurs in that assessment.

---

[6]In 1986, according to the Robotic Industries Association (1986), the U.S. stock of industrial robots was slightly more than 25,000.

The most recent aggregate projections of employment that incorporate the effects of technological change were prepared by BLS for 378 industries and 562 occupations in 1995. In the past the BLS projections have proved quite accurate in tracking changes in employment, although they tend to understate employment growth in the fastest growing occupations and employment decreases in declining occupations (Carey, 1980; Carey and Kasunic, 1982; Rumberger and Levin, 1984). For its 1986 forecasts, the bureau used a system of five interconnected economic models to project growth in the labor force, the level of aggregate economic activity, each industry's output of goods and services, and each industry's demand for labor. The industry demand projections were based on historical relationships between growth in GNP and growth in the output of individual industries.[7]

In recent years the bureau has disclosed much of its methodology for measuring and incorporating technological change within these projections, and further disclosure and discussion of these methods are highly desirable. Technological change was incorporated into the BLS projections through assumptions about the rates of development and diffusion of new technologies and their direct impacts on occupational structure and input–output coefficients. BLS also allowed for changes in output demand resulting from productivity increases and changes in production processes within industries. The bureau was conservative in making technology adjustments in these models. Nevertheless, hundreds of adjustments were made in the most recent revision of the projections (Hansen, 1984).

The 1995 employment projections issued by BLS forecast growth in virtually all of its more than 350 occupations with at least 25,000 workers. Some categories, however, were projected to decline in absolute terms as a result of technological change. Information technologies affected a number of the 11 occupations posting absolute declines in projected employment as a result of technological change (Table 4-1). The declining occupations fall into four groups: office workers involved primarily in data-entry tasks; communications workers who are displaced by declines in the service requirements of telecommunications equipment; truck and tractor operators affected by increases in warehouse automation; and

---

[7]The moderate-growth scenario used by BLS as the basis for industrial and occupational employment projections assumes strong productivity and investment growth, a declining unemployment rate (6 percent in 1995), and a real annual rate of GNP growth of 2.9 percent between 1984 and 1995; using those assumptions, the bureau forecast that employment in the U.S. economy will increase by 16 million. For a detailed discussion of these assumptions and those underlying the alternative low- and high-growth scenarios, see U.S. Bureau of Labor Statistics (1986b).

TABLE 4-1   Occupations with 25,000 or More Workers Forecast by the U.S. Bureau of Labor Statistics to Experience Net Employment Declines Due in Part to Technological Change: Moderate Growth Scenario, 1984–1995

Occupation	1984 Employment (000)	Net Employment Decline (000), 1984–1995	Percentage Share of Decline
Stenographers	239	−96	40
Industrial truck and tractor operators	389	−46	12
Postal service clerks	317	−27	9
Station installers and repairers, telephone	111	−19	17
Stock clerks	788	−16	2
Statistical clerks	93	−12	13
Payroll and timekeeping clerks	207	−11	5
Central office telephone operators	77	−9	11
Order filers, wholesale and retail sales	226	−7	3
Service station attendants	303	−6	2
Directory assistance telephone operators	32	−2	7
Total decline		−251	

SOURCE: U.S. Bureau of Labor Statistics (1986b).

service station attendants displaced by the use of information technology in self-service gas stations. In total, BLS predicts that there will be 251,000 fewer employment opportunities in these occupations by 1995. This is equivalent to 1.6 percent of total projected employment growth during 1984–1995.

A recent retrospective analysis of the employment effects of technological change used input–output methodology to decompose the growth in employment during 1972–1984 into changes resulting from growth in final demand and those resulting from technological advance in 79 industries (Young and Lawson, 1986). The authors computed the changes in employment that would have resulted if the 1984 output had been produced with 1972 technology. This calculation yields the change in employment that is attributable solely to growth in demand. The "constant technology" employment change is subtracted from the actual 1972–1984 employment change. The difference provides an estimate of the effect of technological change on employment during 1972–1984.

The Young-Lawson methodology did not require the forecasts of rates of diffusion and technological progress that were so salient in the BLS, Roessner et al., and Leontief-Duchin studies. Like the Roessner and Leontief-Duchin studies, however, the Young-Lawson study was unable to determine the employment impact of output growth that resulted from price reductions stemming from productivity growth. As a result, Young and Lawson attributed many of the employment-increasing effects of technological change to changes in final demand rather than to the expansionary impact of new technology. Technology-related effects on employment in this analysis incorporate only the labor-displacing effects of changes in process technology, a procedure that ignores Levy et al.'s (1984) "output enhancement" effect. In addition, Young and Lawson could not isolate the reductions in industry demand for domestic inputs that resulted from increases in imports of foreign inputs. This effect, which had negative employment implications, was categorized by Young and Lawson as technology based, although ironically it may reflect the absence of technological change within U.S. industry.

Young and Lawson found that technological change during 1972–1984 reduced labor requirements per unit of output in 65 of 79 industries. Changes in final demand during this same period affected some or all of the decline in labor demand in 73 of the 79 industries.[8] In 44 of the 79 industries, the laborsaving effects of new technologies were more than offset by growth in final demand; that is, total employment expanded. Even this assessment of the employment effects of technological change, which overstates the job displacement consequences of it, suggests that sectoral employment displacement often is more than offset by output growth.

Summary

Process and product innovations affect prices, wages, incomes, and international trade flows. Unfortunately for analysts, all of these forces operate simultaneously and interact. Forecasting methodologies for the assessment of the sectoral or aggregate employment impacts of technological change remain primitive, and therefore any results must be viewed with skepticism and caution.

Although this brief survey of recent empirical studies should lessen concerns about massive technological unemployment, technological displacement remains a potentially serious problem for some workers in the

---

[8]Sixty-one of the 65 industries in which technological change had a laborsaving impact also experienced increases in labor demand as a result of changes in final demand.

American economy of the 1980s and 1990s. Differences in the timing of the labor-displacing and labor-enhancing effects of technological change, coupled with the fact that jobs may be lost in industries, regions, or occupations that are very different from the ones in which job creation occurs, make it difficult for those workers and managers who must change their occupations and learn new skills. Indeed, the entire issue of skills—those a worker needs to get a job and those necessary to do a job—is central to the debate about the effect of technological change on employment.

SKILL REQUIREMENTS AND TECHNOLOGICAL CHANGE

Recent poll data (Cambridge Reports, Inc., 1986) confirm that the public remains concerned that technological change will make the skills of the average worker obsolete and will raise the level of skill required for good jobs (defined in terms of wages or advancement prospects) beyond the reach of those workers entering the labor force or changing jobs. Two types of worker skills are relevant to our discussion of the effects of technological change on skill requirements. *Basic skills* typically are acquired by workers prior to entering the labor force. They consist of literacy, problem-solving, numerical reasoning, and written communications competencies. Within this economy, workers acquire basic skills through the public and adult educational systems rather than through employers. U.S. employers, however, historically have been willing to provide the specific occupational or *job-related skills* required by their employees—that is, those skills necessary to perform a specific job or function.

Basic cognitive skills and job-related skills appear to be complementary; the real contribution of basic skills to productivity lies in helping workers learn what they need to do their current and future jobs (Bishop, 1984; COSEPUP Panel on Secondary School Education for the Changing Workplace, 1984). Most empirical studies of the impact of technological change on skills focus on job-related skills, which in many instances are acquired through on-the-job training (see Chapter 7).[9]

A substantial body of literature on the skill impacts of technological change has reached few consistent conclusions. There are a number of

---

[9]Computer skills are one example of job-related skills. Goldstein and Fraser (1985) studied the sources of computer training and concluded that most workers were able to obtain such training on the job. The amount of training required for computer users was modest; no more than 5 percent of computer users actually required extensive computer training.

reasons for this, many of which also apply to the literature on the employment impacts of technological change:

- The methodologies and data used in studies of technological change and skills are weak and imprecise.
- There is little agreement on the definition (and therefore the measurement) of job-related skills. Analysts often disagree as to whether skills are an attribute of individuals—in which case they would be related to educational attainment and would be portable among jobs—or whether skills are highly specific to firms or occupations and only loosely related to educational attainment.
- To study skills, it is also necessary to study occupations; but data on the U.S. occupational structure are unreliable for comparisons over time because of extensive revisions in the classifications in successive published dictionaries of occupational titles and categories (see Spenner, 1985, for a detailed discussion).
- Case studies of the impacts on skills of specific technologies or of technological change within a specific industry rarely consider a lengthy period of time; thus, they are unable to trace changes in skill requirements as a technology, industry, or production process passes through different stages of its development or diffusion (see Chapter 2).
- The skill effects of technological change are sensitive to the ways in which new technologies are implemented in the workplace. Managers have considerable discretion in such implementation, which may affect skill requirements (Adler, 1984). Thus, identical innovations introduced in different firms can alter skill requirements in different ways (Spenner, 1985).

The literature on technology and skills includes aggregate studies, which examine changes in skills within a large number of occupations and industries, and case studies, which focus on a single occupation, firm, or industry. Aggregate studies obtain greater coverage but at the cost of overlooking certain types of skill change. They generally report greater stability in skill requirements because they aggregate industry- or firm-specific variations. Spenner's review of 11 aggregate studies (1986) is consistent with this description; he found no evidence to support claims of significant upgrading or downgrading in aggregate skill requirements as a result of technological change. Levin and Rumberger (1986) used educational attainment as a proxy for skill requirements in their analysis of the overall skill implications of the BLS employment forecast for 1982 through 1995 and reached similar conclusions. Indeed, these scholars found that the educational requirements of projected 1995 jobs were virtually identical to those needed for 1982 jobs.

Case Studies of Manufacturing

Case studies sacrifice the breadth of the aggregate approach but offer a detailed understanding of skill changes within a single occupation, firm, or industry. These studies generally show more change and volatility in skill requirements (Spenner, 1985). Flynn's 1985 survey of process automation, which was discussed earlier, also considered the impacts of technological change on skill requirements. According to Flynn, the automation of high-skill jobs shifted their content from the direct operation of a machine to monitoring the operations of a different machine that was more nearly self-controlling.

Do these changes in job content represent a reduction of work skills or a shift from higher-level mechanical to higher-level mental skills? Flynn argued that the changes resulting from new technology reduced skill requirements; although process automation often increased the level of worker responsibility, the use of technologically sophisticated equipment made operator positions less demanding. Hirschhorn (1984) reviewed similar evidence on changes in job content but reached the opposite conclusion, arguing that the shift toward increased responsibility required higher-order mental skills to ensure quick and appropriate responses to mechanical breakdowns. (The Three Mile Island and Bhopal accidents are examples of breakdowns in complex systems in which initial operator responses aggravated the problem.) These conflicting interpretations reflect the problems of defining and measuring skills.

Flynn found that in addition to transforming the content of many jobs, automation created new jobs at both ends of the skill spectrum. New, lower-skill jobs required less judgment, skill, and discretion than the previous higher-level craft and operative positions. The adoption of computerized process control systems, on the other hand, created new jobs for computer programmers and systems analysts. These systems also required more advanced technical knowledge for supervisory, maintenance, and technician tasks. The evidence summarized by Flynn, however, does not include estimates of the proportion of high- and low-skill jobs created as a result of technological change.

Complementing Flynn's work is the recent report by the National Research Council's Committee on the Effective Implementation of Advanced Manufacturing Technology (1986). The committee found that the introduction of automated manufacturing technologies reduced the number of job classifications while broadening the scope of activities within each classification. The new groupings typically involved a broader range of skills, reflecting greater numbers of machines, an expansion of the range of operations for which a worker was responsible, or the rotation of workers through different jobs. Finally, Baran (1986) notes that the effects of product innovation and redesign (e.g., substituting microelectronics for electromechanical components in office equipment) on skills are also considerable.

Case Studies of Office Automation

Numerous case studies of office automation have analyzed the impact of a single group of technologies—information and computer technologies—on skill requirements. A review of these studies suggests that the impact of these technologies on job skill requirements has changed as the technologies have developed, a phenomenon consistent with the discussion in Chapter 2 of the skill-intensive characteristics of new technologies in the early stages of their development. As a result of this characteristic of technological development, successive studies of these technologies have reached different conclusions.

Studies of office automation in the 1950s and 1960s (summarized in Flynn, 1985) found that office and "back-office" (transactions processing, recordkeeping, data entry, and other functions involving little or no customer contact) automation created new employment opportunities for skilled computer programmers, systems analysts, computer maintenance engineers, and other administrative and managerial personnel. At the same time, back-office automation eliminated low-skill clerical positions but created positions for low-skill data-entry workers. Many of these early case studies reported "job enlargement" for clerical positions as the personnel occupying them became less specialized and absorbed new, computer-related tasks. As computer technology developed, however, the number of higher-skill opportunities for clericals appeared to decline. Many case studies during the 1970s (see Baran, 1986) reported that automation fragmented and standardized clerical work, requiring lower-level and narrower skills.

The most recent set of case studies suggests that a new wave of computer technology, supporting the movement of office automation out of the back office and into desktop and distributed data processing, may be reversing these tendencies toward reductions in skill requirements. Baran (1986) reports that the introduction of minicomputers, personal computers, and higher-level programming languages has restructured office work. The insurance clerical worker of the future, for example, is likely to have a computerized workstation. Because of increased desktop computing power, this worker will be responsible for a wider range of tasks including rating, underwriting, issuing new policies, and policy updating and renewal. Continued advances in data-processing and office automation technologies have also changed the skills required for many of the support personnel employed in data-processing departments. Consistent with the argument that skill requirements change over the life cycle of a technology, many of the operating tasks assigned to engineers in the 1950s shifted to technicians in the 1960s; in the 1980s, they appear to be shifting to clerical employees (Flynn, 1985).

Like the literature and evidence on the employment impacts of technological change, the empirical evidence of technology's effects on skills is too fragmentary and mixed to support confident predictions of aggregate skill impacts. Despite this uncertainty, however, the evidence suggests that the skill requirements for entry into future jobs will not be radically upgraded from those of current jobs. Many of the computer-based technologies examined by this panel are now being developed with more powerful software and user-friendly interfaces, which should reduce the device-specific skills needed to operate them. As more such "intelligence" is embedded in hardware or software, users will require less training for particular equipment. Consequently, the workplace of the future will place a greater premium on a strong foundation in basic skills for career advancement and for changing jobs but should not require massive investments in computer literacy for all entrants or employees.

Even more than in the analysis of the employment impacts of technological change, the evidence on skill impacts has led us to stress the considerable uncertainties that pervade the issue. In examining educational and other policy responses to the challenges of technological change, it behooves policymakers and others to avoid planning based on inflexible commitments to a single (and almost certainly flawed) vision of the skill and vocational requirements of the workplace of the future. Nonetheless, education and training that improve the basic and job-related skills of American workers are important contributors to U.S. competitiveness and living standards. Continued investment in the training of professional scientists and engineers to sustain the development and adoption of new technologies is also critical.

THE EFFECTS OF TECHNOLOGICAL CHANGE ON THE LEVEL OF EARNINGS

Technological change and its effects on earnings have long been topics of debate among economists and other analysts. Poll data (Cambridge Reports, Inc., 1986) suggest that a large segment of the U.S. public views technological change as a force that may erode wages, leading (among other things) to a polarized wage and income distribution. This section reviews the evidence on the impact of technological change on the level of wages and considers the relationship between technological change and the distribution of earnings (i.e., salaries and wages) and income within the United States.

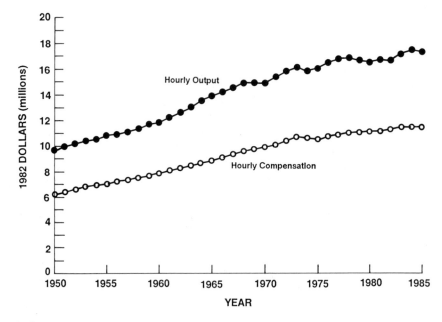

FIGURE 4-1 Real output per hour and real employee compensation, 1950–1985. SOURCE: U.S. Bureau of Labor Statistics, Office of Productivity and Technology. Developed by the bureau from U.S. Department of Commerce, Bureau of Economic Analysis, national income and product account data.

Growth in Real Earnings During the Postwar Period

A widely accepted measure of real earnings growth is average real compensation (wages and salaries plus employee benefits) per hour in the nonfarm business sector. Figure 4-1 plots trends in this quantity and in labor productivity over time, revealing a close relationship between the two.[10] The share of labor in total output has remained fairly stable throughout the postwar period in the U.S. economy, in contrast to its behavior in Western European economies in which, according to Bruno and Sachs (1985), this share fluctuates. Increases in U.S. real compensation therefore depend on growth in labor productivity; far from supporting erosion in real earnings, technological change, by increasing labor productivity, is associated with increases in them. The stagnation in U.S. real

---

[10]Figure 4-1 plots real nonfarm output per hour and real compensation per hour. Both series are deflated (converted into constant dollars) by the implicit nonfarm output deflator.

earnings that has occurred since 1973 reflects lagging labor productivity growth. Improvements in real earnings within this economy depend on renewed productivity growth, which in turn requires more rapid generation and adoption of new technologies.

The Impact on Compensation of Worker Movement Among Sectors

The growth rate of average compensation within the overall economy can be broken down into a weighted average of the growth rates of earnings within each sector and a composition effect, reflecting the impact on average compensation of shifts in the shares of total employment accounted for by sectors with different levels of average earnings. Costrell (1987) broke down growth in real hourly compensation into compositional effects and changes in real compensation growth within sectors (the 12 sectors of Table 3-7) and obtained striking results. The effect on real compensation growth of changes in employment shares was modest and, if anything, positive (approximately 1–2 percent) prior to 1979. During 1979–1985, however, the impact on average compensation of changes in employment shares became negative and increased in size (to more than 10 percent), consistent with the findings of Bluestone and Harrison (1986) for 1979–1984. Yet real compensation growth within sectors remained positive during 1979–1985, increasing by almost 7 percent. Costrell identified the decline in the share of durables manufacturing employment and growth in the share of services employment during 1979–1985 as the major contributors to the negative compensation impact of intersectoral employment shifts. This finding is qualified, however, by the small number of workers that have actually moved from the manufacturing to the nonmanufacturing sector; absolute levels of manufacturing employment have not fallen below the levels of the 1960s.

Although these estimates are based on aggregate data and represent average compensation losses, they are broadly consistent with survey data on earnings losses among displaced manufacturing workers (Podgursky, 1987). Relatively well-paid, unionized, blue-collar workers in durables manufacturing have made disproportionate contributions to the displaced worker population, as was noted in Chapter 3, and many (but not all) of these workers have found new jobs outside of manufacturing that pay substantially lower wages than their previous jobs.[11]

---

[11]More than 40 percent of the displaced workers formerly employed in durables manufacturing and more than 30 percent of those previously employed in nondurables manufacturing found jobs in wholesale and retail trade or services, according to data from the 1984 survey of displaced workers summarized in Podgursky (1987).

This evidence suggests that recent structural change in the U.S. economy—that is, changes in the employment shares of different sectors—has contributed to lower earnings growth. Domestic technological change, however, is not the primary factor affecting the displacement of manufacturing workers. In addition, the role of technological change in supporting productivity growth and competitiveness in many U.S. manufacturing industries means that new technologies may aid in the stabilization, rather than any erosion, of high-wage manufacturing employment. We must also distinguish the impact on average earnings of movements of workers among different industries from the impacts of changes in the occupational structure of the economy. The potential reductions in average U.S. wages caused by employment growth in lower-wage industries have thus far been largely offset by growth in employment in higher-wage occupations. Nevertheless, the wage reductions associated with movement of displaced workers from manufacturing (especially those from durables manufacturing) to nonmanufacturing employment contribute to the high social and individual costs of displacement.

TECHNOLOGICAL CHANGE AND THE DISTRIBUTION OF EARNINGS AND INCOME

Trends in the distribution of income and earnings within the United States recently have received considerable attention (Blackburn and Bloom, 1985, 1986, 1987; Bluestone and Harrison, 1986; Harrison et al., 1986; Henle and Ryscavage, 1980; Kuttner, 1983; Lawrence, 1984; Levy, 1987; Levy and Michael, 1983, 1985; Medoff, 1984; Rosenthal, 1985). Some analysts have attributed increased inequality in the distribution of income and wages to the growth of service sector employment and the development of "two-tiered" occupational structures within high-technology and service industries, both of which are widely perceived to result from technological change (Industrial Union Department, 1984). This section briefly reviews the evidence concerning changes in household income[12] and earnings[13] distributions and discusses explanations for these distributional shifts. It is important to note at the outset that the distribution of income may shift with no corresponding change in the distribution of earnings as a result of changes in household structure. Moreover, the distribution of annual earnings also

---

[12]Household income is defined as all income received by a household, which in turn is defined to be a housing unit occupied by related or unrelated individuals.

[13]Earnings are typically defined as employment-related wages and salaries, commissions, and tips received by an individual. Both hourly and annual measures of earnings have been used in analyses of the distribution of earnings.

may change with no corresponding shift in hourly earnings as a result of changes in the shares of full- and part-time employment within the work force.

The Distribution of Earnings and Income

Nearly all of the analyses to date (most of which examine data from the CPS compiled by BLS) agree that household income inequality— however it is measured—has increased during the past two decades. This tendency reverses a previous trend of increasing equality, which appears to have peaked in the late 1960s. The current level of inequality in the U.S. household income distribution is slightly less pronounced than in 1947 (Levy and Michael, 1983).

Researchers have used several measures of household income to reach these conclusions. Blackburn and Bloom (1987) analyzed changes in the distribution of total household income (including income derived from sources not related to the occupations of household members—e.g., interest income) and the distribution of household earnings during 1967–1984.[14] Analyzing changes in the number of households in each quintile of this distribution, Blackburn and Bloom found that the distributions of both household income and household earnings exhibited increasing inequality during this period. In the case of total household income, increased inequality reflected increases in the number of households classified as "upper middle" or "upper" class, at the expense of middle class households. The distribution of household earnings displayed a similar trend while also exhibiting growth in the number of households whose total earnings placed them in the "lower" class. Levy and Michael (1983) adjusted household income for taxes paid and food stamps received and found increasing inequality in the distribution of this category of household income. Thurow (1987) used data from the U.S. Bureau of the Census to trace declines during 1969–1985 in the share of total income received by the poorest 60 percent of the population. During this period, the income share of the top 20 percent of all U.S. families increased.

---

[14]Blackburn and Bloom divided the distribution into five categories, or quintiles. "Lower class" households received incomes of less than or equal to 60 percent of the median income; "lower middle class" households received incomes greater than 60 percent but less than or equal to 100 percent of the median income. "Middle class" households received incomes greater than 100 percent but less than or equal to 160 percent of the median income; "upper middle class" households received incomes greater than 160 percent of the median income but less than or equal to 225 percent of the median; and "upper class" households received incomes greater than 225 percent of the median income.

The evidence on trends toward polarization in the distribution of earnings in the U.S. economy is much weaker than it is for the distribution of income during the past two decades. Blackburn and Bloom (1986) found "no evidence of any trend in the dispersion [i.e., polarization] of annual individual earnings over time" (p. 7) during 1967–1983, based on analyses of data for the "principal earners" in each household. Kosters and Ross (1987) found that the dispersion of average hourly earnings (a measure of the inequality of the distribution of earnings—i.e., greater dispersion implies a more unequal distribution) for full-time workers has declined since 1973.

Other researchers, however, have detected some tendency toward increased inequality in the earnings distribution. Henle and Ryscavage (1980) detected a modest tendency toward increased inequality in the annual earnings of all workers during 1958–1977, although this polarizing trend peaked during 1968–1973, well before technological or other forms of employment displacement were a major concern.[15] Moreover, Henle and Ryscavage found growing earnings inequality only among part-time workers, a group that largely excludes the "principal earners" analyzed by Blackburn and Bloom. (Interestingly, the distribution of the earnings of women does not exhibit increasing inequality during or after this period.) Blackburn and Bloom (1987), however, suggest that during 1967–1984, the inequality of the annual earnings distribution may have increased among both full- and part-time male workers (although the inequality of the earnings distribution among women declined during this period). Tilly et al. (1987) also found increases in the inequality of annual earnings among male workers during 1979–1984, although their results are influenced by declines in labor force participation among older male workers and by the poor performance of the economy during this period. As in the case of Bluestone and Harrison (1986), the magnitude of the increases in earnings in equality found by Tilly et al. (1987) therefore may be sensitive to the choice of years for analysis. Without additional data and analysis, it is difficult to determine the significance or durability of any trend toward greater inequality in the earnings distribution.

Explaining the Trends

The trends in the distribution of household income reflect changes in the structure of the American family and increased participation by

---

[15]The results of the Henle-Ryscavage analysis conflict with the findings of Harrison et al. (1986), who detected no trend toward increased earnings inequality prior to the late 1970s. Harrison et al. found increasing inequality in the earnings distribution beginning in the late 1970s.

women in the labor force, all of which affect household income rather than individual wages. The number of single-parent, low-income households has grown since the 1970s, fattening the lower "tail" of the family income distribution. The number of two-earner households also has grown, which has led to some expansion in the upper reaches of the income distribution. According to Levy and Michael (1983), changes in federal tax and income support policies during the early 1980s also increased household income inequality. Reductions in transfer payment programs benefiting low-income households, combined with large tax reductions in the uppermost income brackets, increased the polarization of the distribution of after-tax income.

What factors might account for any observed increases in the dispersion of earnings? Among the least likely causes are movements of workers from manufacturing into service sector occupations or a change in the structure of the work force within high-technology industry. The current share of manufacturing within total U.S. employment is sufficiently small, and the size of the middle-income share of the manufacturing work force sufficiently resembles that of nonmanufacturing, that movements of labor out of manufacturing have little effect on recent earnings trends (Lawrence, 1984).[17] Moreover, the characteristic form of structural change within this economy does not involve a large net outflow of labor from manufacturing into nonmanufacturing employment; rather, it reflects more rapid employment growth in the nonmanufacturing sector than in manufacturing industry. During the past seven decades, employment has been growing in industries in which average wages currently are lower than in manufacturing. At the same time, however, the occupational structure of the U.S. economy has shifted in an opposite direction, with faster growth in higher-skill, higher-wage occupations (Leon, 1982; Singelmann and Tienda, 1985). Partly for this reason the gap in average wages between manufacturing and rapidly growing nonmanufacturing sectors such as business services (which include computer services and consulting) has been shrinking during the past decade (Howe, 1986). Many declining manufacturing industries—for example, textiles, apparel, and leather products—now pay wages that are low in comparison with those paid by much of the services sector.

There is little evidence to suggest that newer high-technology manufacturing industries have occupational structures that support increases in the inequality of the earnings distribution. Data from the 1980 census

---

[17]Blackburn and Bloom (1987) concluded that the impact on the earnings distribution of shifts in the sectoral distribution of employment during 1967–1984 was small.

(Lawrence, 1984) suggest that high-technology industries "have smaller shares of lower-class jobs than manufacturing in general has, and almost all of them have larger shares of middle-class jobs" (p. 4). Assertions that technological change will produce a "two-tiered" work force, reducing the skills (and earnings) of a large share of jobs while producing a much smaller number of highly paid jobs for scientists, managers, and engineers thus receive little support from either this evidence on occupational structure in high-technology industries or the evidence on skill requirements discussed above.

Demographic trends and slow economic growth, rather than technological change, appear to be the primary causes of any tendency toward earnings polarization. Dooley and Gottschalk (1984) found that increases in the inequality of the distribution of weekly and annual earnings for males were attributable to the "baby boom and bust" since World War II, which brought large numbers of workers into the labor force during the late 1970s and early 1980s. This surge in the labor supply, along with low productivity growth and continued growth in the real wages of established workers covered by cost-of-living clauses in labor contracts, resulted in entry-level wages that were lower and that grew more slowly than the wages of older workers. Slow growth in earnings, which contributes to such increases in earnings inequality as are detectable, appears to be concentrated among workers between the ages of 25 and 34 (Lawrence, 1984). Because of low productivity growth, these new entrants have not experienced the rapid increases in earnings that had characterized previous cohorts.

The lower end of the earnings distribution thus appears to have expanded as a result of demographic and productivity trends rather than because of technological or structural changes (Levy and Michael, 1985). BLS projections of future employment growth do not suggest that the jobs of the future will produce additional polarization in earnings. Indeed, Rosenthal (1985) maintains that these projections "show an increasing proportion of employment in higher than average earnings occupations and a declining proportion in occupations with lower than average earnings, rather than a trend toward bipolarization" (p. 6).

Completion of the absorption of the large baby boom cohort into the labor force should reduce earnings inequality somewhat, whereas the expansion of income transfer and entitlement programs could offset trends toward increased inequality in the distribution of income. A resumption of productivity growth also appears to be a major component of the solution to the problem of earnings dispersion; because technological change supports such growth, it may help to reverse any trends toward the polarization of earnings in the U.S. economy.

The evidence suggests that reports of a vanishing middle class due to technological change are exaggerated. The existing and very disturbing tendencies toward increased inequality in the distribution of income reflect changes in government policy, family structure, and labor force participation rather than the effects of technological change. Earnings, rather than household incomes, is the variable that should be most responsive to technologically induced changes in employment opportunities; but the hypothesis that the distribution of earnings has become more unequal receives limited support from the data. The data on the earnings distribution (e.g., Henle and Ryscavage, 1980) also suggest that much of the growth in earnings inequality predates the recent period of concern over technological and structural change in the U.S. economy. Trends in the distribution of earnings also appear to be influenced more by demographic than by technological factors, as well as by slow growth in productivity and in the overall economy.

There is certainly cause for concern in the apparent inability of the young workers of the 1980s to experience the earnings growth and employment expansion that was the lot of their predecessors in the 1950s and 1960s. To ascribe this circumstance solely to the effects of technological change, however, would be incorrect. The panel believes that the answer to this problem is to be found in policies that will support a resumption of productivity and output growth at the levels of the 1950s and 1960s. We further believe that the increased use of new technologies, in conjunction with policies to facilitate adjustment to them, is indispensable to the achievement of this goal.

5

Differential Technology Impacts: Black Workers, Female Workers, and Labor Force Entrants

Technological change may differentially affect workers from various demographic or ethnic groups. In this chapter, we briefly examine the effects of new technology on three such groups: black workers,[1] female workers, and labor force entrants. The evidence, limited as it is, indicates that the direct effects of technological change on these groups will be minor. Nevertheless, concerns have long been expressed (see Harrington, 1962; the National Commission on Technology, Automation, and Economic Progress, 1966) that employment opportunities for young and minority workers in the future U.S. economy may be reduced as a result of technological change. Those concerns have not diminished since the 1960s—unemployment rates among minorities in the United States, especially rates for black youths, have shown a disturbing pattern of increase relative to those for whites. What are the likely impacts of technological change on the employment prospects of minorities and labor force entrants, as well as for women?

BLACK WORKERS

Technological change may affect the employment prospects of black workers in at least three ways:

---

[1] The results of a less detailed analysis of the employment effects of technology for Hispanic workers are reported later in this chapter.

113

1. They may be concentrated in occupations and industries that are particularly vulnerable to technological change.

2. Once displaced by technological change, black workers may face particular difficulties in obtaining new jobs.

3. The economic welfare of black workers also may be affected by the impact of technological change on the skills required for employment. If technological change increases the skill requirements of jobs and black workers are not well prepared educationally to deal with such changes, they may be detrimentally affected by the introduction of new technology. Some scholars (e.g., Kasarda, 1986) have suggested that the concentration of minority populations in central cities in which high-skill jobs are being created may restrict employment opportunities for blacks and Hispanics.

Each of these possibilities is discussed more fully below.

Occupational forecasts by the U.S. Bureau of Labor Statistics (1986b) can be combined with data on the racial composition of occupations from the 1980 Census of Population of the Bureau of the Census to reveal the race (black or white) and gender of workers in occupations identified by BLS as likely to experience absolute employment declines due to technological change in the United States. These data provide rough estimates of the potential negative effect of technological change on black employment opportunities. Eleven occupations (out of more than 350 occupations with at least 25,000 workers for which BLS prepares 1995 forecasts) are projected to experience absolute declines through 1995 as a result of technological change (see Table 5-1, later in this chapter). The 11 occupations (discussed in Chapter 4) include several clerical and administrative support groups; within these groups, historical patterns of job growth, skill requirements, and discrimination have contributed to an overrepresentation of blacks. Blacks account for 12 percent of the workers in these declining occupations, a slightly higher proportion than their 11 percent share of the 1986 labor force.

Assuming that the current racial composition of employment in declining occupations remains unchanged through 1995, black employment opportunities in these occupations could be reduced by 30,000 jobs, admittedly a small fraction (at most 0.3 percent) of projected employment growth through 1995 (10 million–21 million jobs).[2] The BLS forecasts have often underestimated the magnitude of declines in specific occupations, but even assuming that the magnitude of these declines is twice as

---

[2]The U.S. Bureau of Labor Statistics (1986b) published three estimates of employment growth for 1984–1995. The bounds on the 10 million–21 million range correspond to the low and high BLS projections.

large as that forecast by BLS still yields a very small impact on employment (60,000 jobs). If the racial composition of these occupations changes so that the share of blacks in these positions increases above their 1980 levels, the displacement consequences of technological change could be more severe than these projections suggest. Barring such increases, however, the prospective negative impacts of technological change on black employment appear to be small.[3] Moreover, some evidence suggests that the overrepresentation of blacks in these occupations has been declining rather than growing during the past two decades. The U.S. Equal Employment Opportunity Commission's (1985) analysis of employment trends for minority and female workers is too highly aggregated to support strong conclusions, but it suggests that during 1967–1983 the overrepresentation of blacks in most of these occupational categories has declined; the one exception to this trend is the share of black women in clerical employment, which increased. If this decline in overrepresentation continues, the adjustment of blacks to technological change should be further eased.

Once displaced by technological change or other causes, however, black workers do not fare as well as white workers with similar backgrounds. As we noted in Chapter 3, Podgursky's (1987) analysis of factors influencing the duration of displacement, which controlled for the educational attainment and other attributes of displaced workers, found that the influence of race on the duration of unemployment outweighed that of any other variable (including tenure in a job prior to displacement). Although blacks account for nearly 13 percent of the total population of displaced male, blue-collar workers, their share of the population of workers unemployed for 52 weeks or more is 18 percent. The black–white gap is even greater in the duration of unemployment for black service workers and black women displaced from manufacturing and nonmanufacturing industries.

Although the BLS forecasts suggest relatively stable employment opportunities for blacks, Kasarda (1986) has argued that the geographic implications of technological change may reduce employment opportunities for urban minority populations. He contends that information technology has increased job opportunities in relatively high-skill occupations located in central cities while reducing employment opportunities in other sectors. According to Kasarda, members of urban minority populations with limited educational backgrounds are less likely to obtain these high-skill jobs. At the

---

[3]A similar analysis for Hispanic workers found that they were underrepresented in all of the 11 occupations projected by BLS to decline as a result of technological change. Total projected employment declines for Hispanics in these occupations amount to 0.1 percent of the 1986 Hispanic labor force in the United States.

same time, lower-skill manufacturing jobs are moving out of central cities, reducing the accessibility of such jobs to minority workers.

Kasarda's argument rests on several assumptions about the skill requirements of new technologies that were discussed in Chapter 4. Contrary to his assumptions, technological change does not appear to result in dramatic increases in the skills required for entry-level jobs. Most workers are able to obtain computer and other "new technology" skills through on-the-job training and experience. Technological change does, however, appear to increase the importance of basic skills for individuals seeking employment at any point during their careers. To the extent that black or other minority job seekers do not have strong basic skills, they will face difficulties in both the urban and suburban job markets.

The geographic component of Kasarda's hypothesis also is largely untested. Recent empirical work (Ellwood, 1986) has questioned the significance of geographic proximity, as opposed to race, in an analysis of the effect of distance and travel time on the employment opportunities of men in Chicago. Race appeared to be more significant than proximity to employment in explaining differences in the employment rates of otherwise comparable young white and black workers. This and other evidence (e.g., on the duration of unemployment for displaced black workers) suggests that a significant share of the difficulties faced by blacks in adjusting to technological change, whether they are displaced workers or entrants seeking employment, is due to racial discrimination. Policies to combat discrimination should reduce the difficulties faced by minority workers in adjusting to technological change.

As is generally the case in considering the employment impacts of technological change, the state of the overall economy plays a major role in the way new technology affects minority employment prospects. Full employment is especially beneficial for minority workers. The effect of a full-employment economy on job opportunities for blacks, and especially for young blacks, is illustrated by analyses of minority unemployment in New England, where the unemployment rate fell to 4.4 percent in 1985. Although unemployment among blacks (7.7 percent) remained nearly twice as high as that among whites (4.3 percent), the unemployment rate for blacks in New England was about half that for blacks nationwide (15.1 percent). The unemployment rate for black teenagers in New England, although still very high (20.9 percent), was far lower than the national rate of 40.2 percent. In addition, the gap between the unemployment rates of white teens and black teens narrowed to 9.6 percentage points in New England, far lower than the national gap of 24.5 points (Harrington and Sum, 1986).

Technological change should not greatly affect the employment prospects of black workers. Nonetheless, for blacks as well as whites who lack basic skills, such prospects are dim, and they would remain so for the foreseeable future even if technological change were somehow to stop tomorrow. Policies that reduce occupational segregation and discrimination in the labor market will aid the adjustment of minority groups to technological change and will benefit society as a whole; a more robust economy will greatly improve minority employment opportunities. Yet, limited access by urban minority populations to quality education in basic skills impairs the ability of these groups to adapt to the requirements of a technologically advanced workplace. The data in Chapter 3 suggest that black and Hispanic workers continue to lag behind white workers in educational attainment, although the gap is steadily shrinking. Continued efforts to close this gap, combined with improved access to basic skills training for employed or displaced workers, are crucial in easing the burden of adjustment to technological change for black and Hispanic workers.

FEMALE WORKERS

There is insufficient evidence to make even a cautious estimate of the long-term effects of technological change on employment for women. The National Research Council's Panel on Technology and Women's Employment (1986) reviewed trends for 37 clerical occupations representing approximately 29 percent of women's employment and concluded that there was little likelihood of "massive technologically induced unemployment" (p. 125). Still, the panel noted that the introduction of advanced information and computer technologies thus far had resulted in relative, and in some cases absolute, declines in back-office clerical jobs while supporting increases in positions requiring greater contact with customers. Minority women are particularly affected by this shift; they are more highly concentrated in occupations (i.e., clerical and administrative support occupations such as those of postal clerk, file clerk, data-entry operator, and telephone operator) in which employment is projected either to grow slowly or decline (U.S. Bureau of Labor Statistics, 1986b).

BLS's 1995 occupational projections also suggest that technological change will reduce growth in a number of occupations in which women historically have been heavily represented. Five of the 11 occupations that BLS predicts will experience an absolute employment decline as a result of technological change have work forces in which 75 percent or more of the workers are women (Table 5-1). Assuming that the current gender composition of these occupations is unchanged by 1995,[4] these

---

[4]The National Research Council's Committee on Women's Employment and Related Social Issues (1986) projected that declines in occupational segregation by sex would continue through the 1980s and 1990s but would occur more slowly than they had in the 1960s and 1970s.

TABLE 5-1 Selected Characteristics of Occupations with 25,000 or More Workers Forecast by the Bureau of Labor Statistics to Experience Net Employment Declines Due in Part to Technological Change: Moderate Growth Scenario, 1984–1995

Occupation	Forecast Decline 1984–1995 (000)	%	Gender or Racial Composition Women Total %	Black Women %	Black Total %	Projected Decline Women Total (000)	Black Women (000)	Black Total (000)
Stenographers	-96	-40	91	9	9	-87	-9	-9
Industrial truck and tractor operators	-46	-12	2	0	13	-1	0	-6
Postal service clerks	-27	-9	36	12	25	-10	-3	-7
Station installers and repairers, telephone	-19	-17	11	2	7	-2	0	-1
Stock clerks	-16	-2	35	4	13	-6	-1	-2
Statistical clerks	-12	-13	75	10	13	-9	-1	-2
Payroll timekeeping clerks	-11	-5	83	7	8	-9	-1	-2
Central office telephone operators	-9	-11	91	13	14	-8	-1	-1
Order filers, wholesale and retail sales	-7	-3	35	4	13	-2	0	-1
Service station attendants	-6	-2	8	0	8	0	0	0
Directory assistance telephone operators	-2	-7	91	13	14	-2	0	0
Total decline	-251					-136	-16	-30

SOURCE: U.S. Bureau of Labor Statistics (1986b). Gender and race estimates based on the 1980 U.S. Census of Population (U.S. Bureau of the Census, 1984).

employment declines could reduce job openings for women in these occupations by approximately 115,000 jobs. Combined with losses in other declining occupations, total reductions in job openings for women due to technological change could reach 136,000. The total reduction in job openings is approximately 0.2 percent of the projected 1995 female labor force and roughly 0.6–1.4 percent of the projected growth in jobs through 1995; an employment reduction of this magnitude should not pose a serious adjustment problem (U.S. Bureau of Labor Statistics, 1986b). The more pessimistic forecasts of reduced clerical employment discussed in Chapter 4 (see Leontief and Duchin, 1985, and Roessner et al., 1985) rely on weak assumptions and methodologies and are not endorsed by this panel.

Like minority workers, displaced female workers experience longer spells of unemployment than white male workers. Podgursky (1987) found that in both blue-collar and white-collar occupations, displaced women had a higher incidence of long-term unemployment than men. Among displaced blue-collar workers, 37 percent of women experienced unemployment spells of 53 weeks or more versus 30 percent of men. Among white-collar workers, 26 percent of the displaced women experienced more than 53 weeks of unemployment versus 15 percent of displaced men.

Female workers do not appear to face differentially severe employment losses as a result of technological change. The women's job losses that are forecast by reliable analysts are modest in size and will be offset many times over by growth in employment opportunities for women. The secondary educational attainment of female workers exceeds that of male workers, which suggests that women in fact may be better prepared to deal with the workplace of the future. Employment prospects for women will be further improved by continued enforcement of such policies as affirmative action, which discourage sexual discrimination and occupational segregation. Even with economic growth and reduced discrimination, however, gaining and retaining a job will be difficult for the 7 million women workers 18 years and older (14 percent of the 1986 female labor force) whose failure to complete high school implies weaknesses in their basic skills (U.S. Bureau of Labor Statistics, Office of Employment and Unemployment Statistics, 1986).

LABOR FORCE ENTRANTS

Typically, individuals first enter the labor force between the ages of 16 and 24.[5] For most, the early years of work are characterized by spells of

---

[5]The impact of technological change on the employment prospects for women over 16–24 years of age who enter the labor force is discussed in the previous section.

TABLE 5-2   Occupational Distribution of Labor Force Entrants in 1983 and Total Projected Growth, by Category, 1984–1995

Occupation	1983 Employment Ages 16–24 (%)	1984–1995 BLS Forecast Employment Change (%)
Executive, administrative, and managerial workers	3.5	22.1
Professional workers	5.3	21.7
Technicians and related support workers	2.9	28.7
Sales workers	14.2	19.9
Administrative support workers, including clerical	17.6	9.5
Private household workers	1.7	−18.3
Service workers, except private household	19.2	21.3
Precision production, craft, and repair workers	8.9	11.7
Operators, fabricators, and laborers	18.3	7.3
Farming, forestry, and fishing workers	3.2	−3.0
Active duty military	5.3	n.a.

SOURCES: The figures for 1983 employment are based on unpublished data from the BLS January 1983 Current Population Survey and unpublished (1987) information from the Defense Manpower Center, Arlington, Virginia. The 1984–1995 BLS forecast data are from the U.S. Bureau of Labor Statistics (1986b).

voluntary part-time or short-term employment during schooling. On leaving school, they enter a career path that over their lifetimes will involve working for an average of 10 employers (Hall, 1982). Most of the jobs first held by entrants to the labor force are concentrated in service, sales, and administrative support occupations (Table 5-2); less than 10 percent are in professional or executive categories. Over time, as entrants gain work experience and move into craft, technical, executive, and professional occupations, the occupational distribution of a particular cohort of entrants comes to resemble that of the overall labor force.

How will labor force entrants be affected by technology-induced changes in the structure of their employment opportunities? According to BLS forecasts, only two of the entry-level occupational groups listed in Table 5-2 (farming, forestry, and fishery workers and private household workers) will decrease in size during the next decade for any reason, including technological change. Steady economic growth, together with a projected decline in the rate of growth of the labor force (see Chapter 3) from roughly 2.3 percent per year during 1970–1986 to a projected level of roughly 1.2 percent per year during 1984–1995 (U.S. Bureau of Labor Statistics, 1986b), should offer entrants with basic skills reasonable prospects for entry-level employment through the next decade. Indeed, employers who rely on this labor pool to fill vacancies, such as the military, are likely to encounter increased competition for these entrants.

For those entrants who lack basic skills, however, the future will be less promising, according to COSEPUP's Panel on Secondary School Education for the Changing Workplace (1984). Even the full-employment economy of New England currently displays unemployment rates for teenagers in excess of 10 percent. Many (though by no means all) of these individuals lack the basic skills necessary to take advantage of existing job opportunities. A full-employment economy can help many, but for entrants with basic educational deficiencies, even a full-employment economy may be insufficient.

6

Technological Change and the Work Environment

The impacts of technological change on employment within the U.S. economy extend well beyond the availability of jobs and the wages associated with those jobs. Technology also affects the organization of work and the structure of the firm; as we discussed in Chapter 2, the adoption of new technology in many industries and firms requires significant changes in the organization of the work process to realize the potential productivity gains of innovations. In addition, labor relations and human resources policies are affected. Cooperation between labor and management is essential to address worker concerns about employment security and to plan the large-scale adoption of new technology and the development of new systems for job classification and compensation. New technologies also may have important effects on health and safety in the workplace, imposing new demands on private and public policies and organizations charged with responsibility for regulating workplace hazards.

THE IMPACT OF TECHNOLOGICAL CHANGE ON ORGANIZATIONAL STRUCTURE

Evidence of the effects of technological change on organizational structure can be found in three bodies of work: case studies of individual firms, studies of changes in the occupational structure of sectors or the entire economy, and studies of changes in the occupational and organizational structure of individual industries. As in the case of the employ-

122

ment impacts of technological change, this evidence is mixed in its quality and conclusions because of several major shortcomings. As we suggested in Chapters 2 and 5, the skill requirements and job characteristics of many of the occupational categories for the overall U.S. economy can change significantly over time. Occupational categories also have undergone considerable redefinition in successive published tabulations of occupational data (see the 1980 report of the National Research Council's Committee on Occupational Classification and Analysis), which makes longitudinal comparisons extremely difficult. This analytic approach also is hampered by the fact that the impact of technology on changes in firm and workplace structure frequently cannot be disentangled from that of other influences, such as increased international competition. Finally, as was discussed in Chapter 2, the relationship between technology and the structure of the firm and workplace is interactive—technology influences but does not "cause" a particular structure. Organizational factors and managerial decisions often influence the effects of a given technology on workplace structure and worker skills. Separating the influence of technology on organizational structure from that of other factors and assigning a causal role to this factor are very difficult tasks.

In view of these limitations, the following discussion of changes in the structure of the firm draws heavily on a limited number of case studies and examples, rather than on comprehensive evidence. These studies suggest that the adoption of new technologies will transform the content of many jobs in both the manufacturing and nonmanufacturing sectors. The new jobs that result will involve a wider range of functions or duties, training for these more numerous tasks, and (as discussed in Chapter 4) more emphasis on mental acuity than on physical strength. Moreover, despite contentions and anecdotal evidence to the contrary, we do not expect that the adoption of these technologies will reduce opportunities for intrafirm advancement and thereby produce a "two-tiered" labor force.

The Structure of the Firm

We can better understand the effects of new technologies on manufacturing and service sector firms by considering the technological origins of the structure of the U.S. firm and its production organization. The organizational structure of the modern U.S. manufacturing firm arose during the late nineteenth century in response to innovations in production processes that favored the development of continuous-flow, mass-production technologies for the manufacture of goods. The development of low-cost, reliable, and rapid modes of communication and transportation also influenced the structure of the firm. Reductions in the costs of managing the flow of goods and information within a single organization increased the payoffs from centralizing the management of a growing number of production plants and a broadening range of activities within the firm (Chandler, 1976). These changes resulted in an expansion of the geographic area that could be served by a single production plant, as well as an increase in the number of production establishments that could be managed by one organization.

Within many manufacturing and nonmanufacturing establishments, the work process was organized along lines pioneered by Henry Ford and Frederick Taylor in the early twentieth century. Tasks were broken down into a series of relatively unskilled, repetitive activities, the performance of which relied on specialized capital equipment. The production assembly line had an analogue in the large keypunching and data-entry "back-room" operations of the central management staff of manufacturing and nonmanufacturing firms.

Although controlling the pace of work and the structure of jobs was the exclusive province of management within this work environment, unions sought to establish internal employment regulations based on seniority and job classifications. Narrow job classifications for production workers allowed management to rely on lower-level managers, rather than workers, to make decisions and also lowered the firm's costs for training replacements for workers leaving the firm. From the union's viewpoint, narrow job classifications increased the number of workers on the payroll while protecting senior workers from displacement. Although these practices benefited both labor and management, they also contributed to the development of an adversarial relationship between these groups in many industries and workplaces.

The technologies of product design and manufacture within this environment relied on long production runs of standardized goods, a system that was developed to defray the high costs of specialized capital equipment. "Hard" automation—for example, automatic drill presses— is representative of the manufacturing process technologies associated with this production structure; machinery was specialized, the pace and characteristics of tasks generally were beyond the control of the individual worker, and changes in product design were time-consuming and expensive. Management's control of production processes, as well as the growth in nonmanufacturing functions within the large firm (e.g., marketing and product distribution), meant that middle management employment expanded considerably within U.S. manufacturing firms. These middle managers exhibited considerable specialization by function; research, product development, and design often were carried out separately from production engineering.

In many firms this organizational structure is now changing in ways that have been facilitated, if not always caused, by new manufacturing and information technologies. For example, information technologies have lowered the costs of managing information, which in some instances has reduced the advantages of intrafirm management and performance of such activities as marketing or research. The advantages of the large firm, which were rooted for many years in the low costs of intrafirm communications, are being eroded in some industries by the rapid decline in the costs of interfirm communication, in addition to other factors. Together with intensified international competition, this development has led U.S. firms in some industries to rely on external sources for administrative and support services, which often results in "spinning off" portions of these activities to other organizations. Consequently, the number of employees in some large U.S. manufacturing firms is growing very slowly or is shrinking. Simultaneously, growth in the business services sector generally, and in the temporary worker industry in particular, has been very rapid (Carey and Hazelbaker, 1986; Howe, 1986). Similar trends are apparent in other industrial nations. (See Pearson, 1986, for a discussion of this phenomenon in Great Britain.)

The case of the Benetton Group of Italy illustrates one pattern of change in firm structure (see Belussi, 1986). Sales of Benetton, an international producer of woolen goods, have increased from 55 billion lira in 1978 (at current exchange rates, roughly $42 million), when the firm consisted of roughly 1,000 employees, to more than 623 billion lira (nearly $480 million) in 1984 with only 1,600 employees. Through extensive reliance on subcontractors and franchisees, the firm has grown rapidly in domestic and international markets while expanding its management staff very little (total headquarters employment at Benetton in early 1986 amounted to fewer than 250 people). To accomplish this feat, Benetton maintains communications with retailers and minimizes inventories through technologies that support an intensive, two-way flow of information between the firm's far-flung retailing operations (a thousand stores in at least seven industrial nations) and the northern Italian headquarters of the firm in Ponzano.

The future growth of middle management in large manufacturing and nonmanufacturing firms may well be much slower or even nonexistent because of the restructuring of these firms. Much of the work control function formerly performed by supervisors and middle managers is now superfluous—increasingly, control and monitoring activities are embodied in hardware and software installed on a production line or at a desktop computer or workstation. The displacement (or reduced employment growth) of middle managers within individual firms, however, must not be confused with reductions in the total employment of white-collar workers within the U.S. economy. There will continue to be ample employment opportunities for individuals with white-collar managerial qualifications— BLS projections for white-collar and professional occupations (U.S. Bureau of Labor Statistics, 1986b) forecast growth through 1995—but these opportunities may be located less frequently within a large firm.

Another organizational change that is being encouraged in some sectors by the conjunction of advances in information technology, higher research costs, and greater international competition is increased interfirm collaboration in product development and manufacture. International collaboration in the development of commercial aircraft, engines, and other products relies heavily on the rapid digital transmission of design and test data through satellite links, as well as on the exchange of design, engineering, and test data and specifications on computer tapes (Brooks and Guile, 1987; Mowery, 1987). Domestic and international technology transfer among firms in many manufacturing industries will increase considerably as a result of collaboration among firms in product research and development.

Within firms, as noted in Chapter 2, the successful exploitation of CIM technologies, as well as computer-aided design and manufacturing, frequently requires that firms reduce organizational barriers to cooperation among different functional areas.[1] Compton and Gjostein (1986) argue that "the computer will undoubtedly assist in reducing the time required to complete a design and bring it into production. The key to such reductions is the transformation of design from a serial process to a simultaneous one . . ." (p. 94). In addition, more rapid rates of international technology transfer, as well as intensified international competition, mean that U.S. firms must move new products from laboratory to market more rapidly; in some U.S. firms, this development has contributed to the more extensive use of project teams combining research, design, production engineering, and marketing personnel for product development efforts. New product development periods often can be shortened significantly by increased collaboration between product design and production engineering staffs. In addition, in some U.S. industries, the imperative for more rapid development of new designs and the modification of existing ones, combined with lower direct labor costs resulting from the use of computer-aided manufacturing technologies, may reduce the attractiveness of offshore assembly and fabrication (Cyert, 1985; Sanderson, 1987).

---

[1]As is true of other changes wrought by the adoption of computer-based technologies, however, the development of project teams does not depend solely on the adoption of computer-integrated or other computer-based manufacturing technologies. Japanese manufacturing firms, for instance, used multifunction project management teams for a number of years prior to their adoption of computer-based manufacturing technologies (Abegglen and Stalk, 1986).

The Structure of the Workplace

The adoption of information and computer-based manufacturing technologies will place new demands on individual workers. As was noted previously, the adoption of these technologies in many industries means that functions formerly performed by middle management will move downward within the organizational structure—to the teller, clerk, or machine operator. The breadth of the tasks performed by workers in many cases also will expand. As the National Research Council's Committee on Effective Implementation of Advanced Manufacturing Technology (1986) has noted, many jobs in the CIM establishment ". . . include more planning and diagnosis, and both operating and maintenance duties, in recognition that traditional distinctions between such tasks are blurring" (p. 3). Tasks that formerly were separate can be integrated in a single workstation by the worker with a computer.

This expansion in the range of tasks performed by a worker is likely to increase the requirements for employers to provide training in job-related skills, although the job-related skill requirements for entry into a job should not be affected, as noted in Chapter 4. Management has a number of incentives to encourage the acquisition by workers of the capabilities to perform more tasks, or "multiskilling." Coordination is easier when workers can perform a greater variety of activities. Workers also perform better (productivity increases, as does attention to product quality) when they can see the relationship between their job and other jobs, a relationship that becomes clearer when the worker is trained to perform more than one job.

From a worker's point of view, multiskilling can lead to higher wages or the retention of current wages. Most workers also find multiskilled jobs to be more interesting and challenging than single-skill jobs. Serious disincentives to investment by firms in such training arise from its costs, which may be particularly burdensome for small firms, and the fact that it may be difficult for firms to recover the fruits of their investments in training (see Chapter 7).

As we noted in Chapter 4, the increased use of advanced manufacturing technologies means that worker productivity will depend more on mental ability than on physical effort. Diagnostic skills will be necessary to recognize a potential problem before a machine, a production cell, or an entire plant shut down and cause expensive production delays. These changes in the duties of workers will force changes in the criteria for selecting, promoting, and rewarding workers in the CIM or office workplace. Moreover, the steady evolution of the technologies used within the office or factory, as well as the greater responsibility of workers for controlling production quality and speed in many industries, means that training and retraining in these industries may have to be continuous rather than sporadic. The knowledge requirements and responsibilities of production workers may well come to resemble those of engineers, who have long recognized the need for constant upgrade and "brush-up" training to keep up with changes in their fields. On the one hand, employers and other institutions will have to provide training on a continuous basis; on the other, the work force will have to adapt to these changing requirements.

A number of researchers (Appelbaum, 1984; Baran, 1986; U.S. Congress, Office of Technology Assessment, 1986b) have expressed concern about the effects of computer-based technologies on opportunities for internal promotion within service and manufacturing firms. Will upward mobility within the workplace be reduced as a consequence of reductions in the skill requirements for entry-level jobs and increases in the educational qualifications for high-level management positions? These misgivings were echoed in the widespread belief voiced by respondents to the Cambridge Reports (1986) poll that information and computer technologies were moving the U.S. work force toward a two-tiered structure, characterized by a technological elite and a large group of low-skill workers engaged in data entry and hamburger turning. This two-level characterization of the future workplace, however, rests on assertions concerning skills that we contested in Chapter 4; it also predicts changes in the distribution of earnings and income that disagree with the data presented in that chapter.

The evidence gathered by this panel on trends in the occupational structure of the U.S. work force does not support the hypothesis that technological change leads to a polarized aggregate occupational structure. Singelmann and Tienda (1985) analyzed data on occupational trends within industries, concluding that during 1970–1980, occupational upgrading, rather than polarization, characterized the U.S. economy. Much of this upgrading reflected changes in the occupational mix within industries, rather than shifts in the relative importance of sectors with contrasting occupational mixes: "This turn-around of the relative importance of intra-industry occupational shifts on total occupational change is—if continued—of major importance, because it implies possibilities for future occupational upgrading even after the industrial transformation towards a service economy has been completed" (Singelmann and Tienda, 1985, p. 64).[2] Technological change thus does not appear to be systematically "deskilling" workers or creating a two-tiered work force, although additional evidence on occupational trends and continued monitoring are needed.

---

[2]Similar evidence on changes in the U.S. occupational structure is found in the work by Rosenthal (1985) and Lawrence (1984) discussed in Chapter 4.

LABOR–MANAGEMENT RELATIONS AND THE IMPLEMENTATION OF TECHNOLOGICAL CHANGE

Many of the previous innovations of the post-1945 period could be accommodated without great changes in the structure of the firm and workplace. Information and computer-based technologies, however, pose fundamental challenges to the existing organization of many firms (as discussed previously) and therefore place great demands on the relationships between labor and management in the manufacturing and office workplace. Thus far, U.S. labor and management have been slow to develop creative and cooperative responses to these demands, although there are important and heartening exceptions to this generalization. Nonetheless, we are concerned that managers and workers may not appreciate the need to change many of the management practices and divisions of responsibility that historically have governed their activities.

The changes in the structure of the firm and the workplace offered by new technologies in many cases lead to more satisfying, stimulating work. Both labor and management stand to gain from the smooth, rapid adoption of these innovations. Yet such adoption has proceeded slowly within many sectors of the U.S. economy. Moreover, the full productivity gains from the adoption of computer-based manufacturing processes have been realized only slowly, if at all, in many production establishments. In this section, we discuss strategies for managing the adoption of new technologies, drawing on the study by the National Research Council's Committee on the Effective Implementation of Advanced Manufacturing Technology (1986) and on other case study evidence.

Human Resources Challenges and Strategies

Successful implementation of new technologies often requires considerable modification of the tasks performed by individuals in the workplace and the skills required to fill those jobs. Many of these changes apply to both management and labor—if workers are to exercise greater control over the pace and character of work, the duties of supervisors and middle management also must be modified.

Our examination of the evidence, which is largely anecdotal, has led to the conclusion that "best-practice" (i.e., most effective, equitable, and productive for management and labor) strategies for meeting these challenges involve several elements. First, successful adoption of new technology requires strong assurances from management to the work force concerning job security. These assurances enable management to retain the loyalty and commitment of the work force and may reduce turnover rates among workers who have been retrained at considerable cost to the employer. Fundamental components of any adoption strategy thus include job security provisions and extensive retraining programs for managers and workers. Such a strategy appears to yield considerable payoffs for both management and labor, producing a more highly skilled, motivated work force with lower turnover rates.

Job classification, seniority, and pay structures may require considerable modification to realize the potential payoffs from the adoption of new technologies. The incentive for both labor and management to implement these changes is great; labor can gain greater job security and skills enhancement, while managers obtain greater control over the structure of tasks within manufacturing and office establishments. The role of supervisors also may be altered, as many of their duties—for example, setting production schedules and hours—may be delegated wholly or partly to a work team.

The complexity and amount of planning and reorganization that underpin a successful adoption strategy make it imperative that management begin planning, retraining, and job reclassification, as well as notification of and consultation with the work force, well in advance of the introduction of new technologies. Advance announcement of the adoption of major new technologies and consultation with the work force are central components of a successful strategy. In many cases, the adoption of these technologies, combined with reorganization of the production process, will increase worker responsibility for product quality and production rates. This in turn means that worker involvement in planning the adoption of the production technology can enhance the performance of the new process. In cases in which the characteristics and performance of new technologies are not well understood by managers prior to adoption, worker input into the design and purchase of this equipment can contribute significantly to the productivity of the new technology.

Adoption Strategies in the Unionized Workplace

There is a long history in this country of union–management bargaining over the effects of technological change. In some industries, this bargaining has resulted in "red-circling" jobs that have had their skills downgraded by technology, a practice that enables the occupant of such a job to retain the same wage for a specified period of time. Firms in such industries as printing also have provided attractive retirement packages to workers faced with displacement. A growing number of union contracts have provisions dealing with these issues. One analysis of 400 such contracts (Bureau of National Affairs, 1986) found that 25 percent had clauses covering the introduction of new technology, a considerable increase from less than 10 percent within a similar sample of 1961 agreements. Fifteen percent of these agreements provided for discussions with or notification of the union prior to the introduction of new technologies; in roughly 6 percent, retraining was required for any displaced worker.

Union and worker concerns over the impact of new technologies, job classifications, and work rules on the integrity of the bargaining unit (the union local's size and coverage of the establishment work force) have been addressed in many contracts through retraining and employment security provisions. These provisions stipulate that union members will be retrained to perform the jobs created by technological change that replace jobs previously held by union members. Training programs funded by employers or jointly by union and employer contributions have been adopted in a number of recent contracts. The United Automobile Workers (UAW) contract with General Motors provided for advance notice to the union of the adoption of new technology and created a special union–company committee to deal with technology-related lay-offs. In addition, workers whose jobs are eliminated as a result of technological change are guaranteed employment with full pay and benefits as long as they are willing to retrain (Pascoe and Collins, 1985). A similar scheme has been established under the terms of the 1986 contract between the Communications Workers of America and the American Telephone and Telegraph Corporation, as well as in agreements between the union and various regional operating telephone companies. Comparable guarantees, however, do not exist in other industries in which employment issues are increasingly salient.

Katz (1985) and others have noted that collective bargaining between industrial unions and employers over employment security, job reclassification, and other issues related to technology adoption is introducing differences in the financial and other provisions of contracts between a single union and different firms (and different plants operated by a single firm) within an industry. As a result of technological change and increased competitive pressure on workers and management, "pattern bargaining," in which a settlement with one firm largely determined the terms of contracts with all or most other firms in an industry, has declined in importance (Freedman and Fulmer, 1982). Its demise will increase demands on industrial union leaders faced with differences in the financial treatment of members at different firms, as well as pressure from firms to gain contractual agreements no less favorable than those of their competitors (Schlesinger, 1987).

Impediments to Best-Practice Adoption Strategies

The elements of best-practice adoption strategies seem sufficiently prosaic and profitable for both labor and management that serious questions arise as to why these policies are not pursued more widely. A number of large manufacturing firms, many of which have unionized work forces, recently have adopted some or all of the elements of such strategies. Many firms have not, however, and we believe that the reasons for this failure extend beyond a lack of information.

The pursuit of best-practice adoption strategies requires mutual accommodation and trust between labor and management. Where labor–management relations historically have been adversarial in tone and character, the use of these strategies is less likely. In such a situation, the conditions that engender mistrust must be addressed before the adoption of new technologies can be discussed. This may require that labor and management complement intermittent bargaining over wages and job classifications with continuous joint problem-solving sessions that address general workplace topics. Firms that have used labor–management committees to deal with such issues as worklife quality or workplace safety often have laid the groundwork for dealing with the introduction of new technologies.

Even in those workplaces in which labor and management historically have not been in conflict, serious misconceptions on both sides may impede the pursuit of best-practice policies. The manager of the General Electric household appliances plant in Louisville, Kentucky, a model of labor–management cooperation in the adoption of new production technologies that have improved product quality, was amazed at the level of worker interest in the new production and marketing strategies that were an important part of the reorganization of plant operations:

We [General Electric-Louisville plant management] set up a series of meetings with foremen which we followed every time with a meeting with all the union stewards in the building. We began by showing a lot of market and business information we had never disclosed to them in the past, partly because it had not occurred to us that they would be interested. But they were! We included information about what was going on elsewhere in the world with respect to the modernization of factories. . . . They watched and listened with great interest. In the end we *all* believed that unless we took a major leap ahead in productivity and quality we were going to be overrun. (Stevens, 1983, p. 35; emphasis in original)

The need for consultation with the work force, as well as the loss of managerial powers and responsibilities that may result from many adoption strategies, often conflicts with the goals of middle management. For example, middle managers may resist transferring a portion of their power to workers who seek greater involvement in production decisions, as was noted in a recent discussion of participative management:

Information is power, and access to it remains a clear badge of rank to managers. Even though many companies are forcing managers to put out information on the number of units produced, costs, and other sensitive issues, the idea still doesn't sit right.

Fearing a loss of power, many middle managers torpedoed early participative programs. . . . (Saporito, 1986, p. 60)

Many firms have found that when senior managers communicate clearly their commitment to new forms of production organization and are willing to alter internal incentives and evaluation criteria, middle managers and supervisors are able to overcome their natural reluctance to implement novel procedures. There also may be resistance to restructuring job classification and compensation schemes, however, within the leadership of union locals and within the work force in nonunion plants and offices. Managers in nonunion workplaces may resist the development of formal labor–management consultation mechanisms because these mechanisms may imply recognition of a collective organization representing workers.

Another significant impediment to the widespread use of these technology adoption strategies is their high cost. The ambitious retraining, screening, and reclassification efforts that are an integral element of the success of these strategies are expensive and may be particularly difficult for small firms to sustain. It may also be difficult for firms, no matter what their size, to justify the costs of the strategies relative to their measured benefits. Conventional accounting methods often are unable to measure the productivity and product quality payoffs from the reorganization of the work process, which impedes the adoption of other new manufacturing technologies such as robots (Kaplan, 1986). The savings from lower work force absenteeism and turnover, for example, or higher product quality and shorter product development cycles are not easily captured within conventional accounting methods, which look at individual operations or processing steps and may not account fully for all components of overhead or fixed costs.

We are concerned by the slow adoption of new process technologies in some manufacturing industries and the frequent inability of U.S. firms to develop organizational structures that can accommodate and fully exploit the productive potential of these innovations. These problems stem in part from the lack of proficiency of many U.S. managers in evaluating the overall costs, consequences, and benefits of new technologies, as well as the difficulties workers and managers often experience in developing a more fruitful, cooperative relationship within the workplace. Both of these problems must be addressed by workers, managers, and the organizations that train them if the benefits of technological change are to be realized more rapidly and distributed equitably within the U.S. economy.

TECHNOLOGICAL CHANGE AND WORKPLACE HEALTH AND SAFETY

Ensuring human health and safety during new technology adoption and application is one of the most significant challenges of technological change. The topic, however, is far too complex to address in a single section of this report. Instead, we note and briefly discuss areas in which more study and research are needed. These areas range from the effects on workers of workplace design to the potential use of new methods to try to determine the susceptibility of workers to health effects from exposure to substances in the workplace. We have grouped the issues into three broad categories: (1) new workplace health and safety hazards resulting from technological change; (2) opportunities for greater workplace safety made possible by technological change; and (3) challenges to existing health and safety regulations that arise from the novel environments within which many of these technologies will be applied.

Workplace Hazards Created by Technological Change

Many of the workplace hazards produced by new technologies are not novel in themselves. For example, the substances to which workers in the microelectronics industry are exposed, such as arsenic compounds, have been present in other manufacturing occupations for years. In the case of the microelectronics industry, it is the novel environment within which exposure is occurring rather than the exposure per se that may require new control strategies. Other worrisome issues include worker exposure to new materials and solvents for which few toxicological data have been compiled.

The extended use of video display terminals has highlighted the issue of workplace stress. Workplace stress is not new; fast-paced, high-pressure assembly and clerical occupations in which worker productivity was carefully monitored have characterized many American workplaces throughout this century. Proper design of equipment and the workplace, as well as training, also can minimize the symptoms of eyestrain, back strain, and wrist strain that occur among clerical employees using computer terminals and other electronic displays for extended periods.

Technology's Potential for Reducing Workplace Hazards

Information and computer-based manufacturing technologies have significant promise for reducing workplace hazards. Robotics and automatic materials transfer, for example, can reduce lifting and other strenuous, injury-producing tasks; they can also reduce worker handling of hazardous substances (e.g., through the use of robot painting and welding operations in automobile production). Advanced computer-based technologies for monitoring and correcting chemical and other production processes can reduce the emission of toxic or hazardous substances and enable workers to control such processes from more remote and consequently safer locations.

Technological change also has improved our ability to monitor worker exposure to various substances through such techniques as the analysis of chemicals or their metabolic products in blood, urine, or exhaled air. Enhanced monitoring technologies allow greater precision in controlling and restricting worker exposure to toxic and other substances. In addition, information technologies have enhanced the ability of researchers to conduct large-scale exposure and epidemiological studies of health and safety effects. These developments will expand our knowledge of workplace hazards and aid in our choice of more effective control strategies and safer production technologies.

Changes in the Work Environment

In conjunction with other forces, technological change is altering the structure of the workplace in the United States. As we noted in the first section of this chapter, such change may favor the growth of smaller firms. This phenomenon in turn could affect the level of worker protection from hazards provided by federal regulation. The current enforcement strategy of the federal Occupational Safety and Health Administration, as well as state agencies, relies on a limited number of inspections of larger plants. To the extent that the share of total employment accounted for by larger manufacturing plants declines, an increasing share of the U.S. work force will be located in firms that typically receive limited enforcement attention.

In addition, new technologies increasingly will be found in offices rather than on assembly lines; they will also be found in establishments with work forces that include larger shares of women. Employment growth is likely to be most rapid in sectors that historically have not had extensive union representation, which means that internal pressures for monitoring workplace health and safety may be less intense within some firms. Finally, the work force in many firms is likely to include more individuals with a limited understanding of English; additional resources may be required to provide these workers with information about hazards and the training in workplace safety now mandated by law. The environment within which new technologies are applied thus will depart in a number of ways from the workplace that existing federal and state regulatory structures have been designed to monitor.

This brief survey is intended to highlight important emerging issues in the area of workplace safety and health. Rather than developing specific findings, we wish to ensure that the potential hazards created by these technologies are investigated promptly and then carefully monitored, that efforts are undertaken to exploit the potential of these technologies for reducing workplace safety and health hazards, and that the effectiveness of existing regulatory structures for the workplace of the future receive appropriate consideration.

7

Current Policies for Worker Adjustment

In this chapter, we survey the structure and adequacy of the public and private policies that deal with the needs of entrants to the labor force and workers displaced by technological change. We include in this discussion a consideration of human resources policies, including training for entrants to the labor market, job search assistance, training and retraining for workers who have been or may be displaced by technological change, and income support for those displaced workers. The primary emphasis of this chapter is on public policies; Chapter 6 discusses private sector policies that encourage cooperation between managers and labor. Because of the complexity of the adjustment problem, however, we also address here the human resources policies that can be used by firms to deal with worker displacement—policies such as advance notice of plant closings or large permanent layoffs, severance pay, and employer-provided training. There are important deficiencies in current policies in all of these areas. Many of our recommendations in Chapter 10 follow from this analysis.

As noted in previous chapters, technological change will create unemployment in some occupations, industries, or regions, and it appears likely that it will increase the demands on the existing system through which workers retrain and acquire job-related skills. Indeed, the broader issue of worker training and skills requires attention. Where do workers currently receive their job-related training? How is the employer investment in training allocated between blue-collar and white-collar employees? Can the U.S. training system respond to surges in the demand for new skills—for example, can it train robot technicians or software engineers in response to increased demand for these specialists? Building on the discussion in Chapters 3 and 5, we also discuss briefly the skills needed by labor force entrants and the ability of training institutions to provide them. Finally, we consider displaced workers and the public and private programs for dealing with displacement.

JOB-RELATED TRAINING

Some evidence from other nations supports the hypothesis that job-related training contributes to international competitiveness, although these data are qualitative rather than quantitative. Japan, Sweden, and West Germany each have unique systems for job-related skills training, and all of them appear to provide higher levels of such training to the blue-collar work force than does the U.S. system.[1] These nations also appear to be adopting some advanced manufacturing technologies more rapidly than the United States (see Chapter 2). There is no direct evidence of a link between these phenomena, nor do we have internationally comparable data on investments in job-related skills training within the United States and other countries. Nonetheless, the work of Nelson et al. (1967) and Bartel and Lichtenberg (1987), discussed in Chapter 2, suggests that such investments may play a role in the more rapid adoption of new technologies within these foreign economies.

Where Do Workers Receive Their Training?

In the United States, occupational training is provided by a large, decentralized "system" that defies neat description. A. P. Carnevale of the American Society for Training and Development has explored some of the system's proportions; as he states in a 1986 article in the *Training*

---

[1]Detailed descriptions of the national training systems in these countries can be found in such sources as the International Labour Office (1985), the Organisation for Economic Co-operation and Development (1973), and the U.S. Congress's Office of Technology Assessment (1986b). The West German system relies heavily on apprenticeship programs for its labor force entrants; 50 percent of the individuals completing compulsory education entered such programs in 1977. The Japanese system, which since the 1950s has been characterized by long-term employment commitments to workers from large corporations, features heavy investment by such corporations in training employees through formal and informal means and job rotation. Public funding in Japan also supports upgrade training for employed workers. In Sweden, large public investments (retraining and labor adjustment programs account for 2–3 percent of Swedish GNP) in training and retraining of the employed work force are combined with an elaborate system of vocational and technical education for labor force entrants and the unemployed.

and Development Journal: "Workplace training and development is roughly equivalent in size to the entire elementary, secondary, and higher education systems" (p. 18). Carnevale estimated that the annual costs of the "total learning enterprise"[2] in the United States were over $450 billion in 1985; of this total, he estimated that about $210 billion (or 47 percent) goes for formal and informal employee training.

The most important source of skill improvement training, which is acquired once a worker is employed, is the employer (Table 7-1). More than 70 percent of skill improvement courses ("Formal Company Programs" and "Informal On-the-Job Training," in Table 7-1) are conducted at a worker's place of employment[3] (Carnevale and Goldstein, 1983). The dominant role of employers in funding or providing such training also affects its distribution between white-collar and blue-collar workers; white-collar workers receive much more employer-provided training. College graduates are twice as likely as the average worker to receive employer-provided adult education, whereas those with less than a high school education are only one-fourth as likely to receive such education. Employer-provided adult education thus tends to increase any differences in the educational attainment of workers that are already present when they enter the labor force. These conclusions about the skewed distribution of employer-provided adult education were confirmed by Tierney (1983), who found that those workers with some graduate training were seven times as likely to have received employer-provided training as those with less than a high school education. This divergence also means that whites are almost twice as likely to receive employer-provided training as nonwhites. According to Tierney, "formal education and training programs appear to be directed toward those workers who already have substantial levels of educational achievement" (p. 16).

Employees in large firms also receive more employer-provided training than employees in small firms. Lusterman (1977) reports that firms with 10,000 or more employees spent an average of $86 per worker on

---

[2]Carnevale defines the "enterprise" as comprising all public and private expenditures on elementary, secondary, and postsecondary education; informal and formal employee training; and government training for civilians. Although the U.S. military is a major investor in training in a wide range of basic and job-related skills (it spent $18 billion in fiscal year 1987 for formal training alone), the impact of this investment on the civilian work force appears to be small, as Marcus (1987) has noted.

[3]The duration of training differs in school-based and workplace programs. In 1983 over 70 percent of the workers in formal company programs trained for less than 12 weeks; two-thirds of the workers in school-based training (an unknown portion of which is employer financed) trained for over 12 weeks, with approximately 38 percent in programs lasting more than a year (Carey and Eck, 1985, Tables 32 and 41).

TABLE 7-1   Sources of Skill Improvement Training by Occupation (1983)

Occupational Group	Workers Who Took Training	School	Formal Company Programs	Informal On-the-Job Training	Other
Executive, administrative, and managerial	5,098 (47)	1,916 (18)	1,884 (17)	1,688 (16)	836 (8)
Professional specialty	7,802 (61)	4,352 (34)	1,936 (15)	1,756 (14)	1,408 (11)
Technicians and related support	1,588 (52)	600 (20)	550 (18)	585 (19)	166 (5)
Sales	3,578 (32)	769 (7)	1,411 (13)	1,642 (15)	487 (4)
Administrative support, including clerical	5,152 (32)	1,547 (10)	1,565 (10)	2,423 (15)	392 (2)
Private household	33 (3)	10 (1)	7 (1)	14 (1)	10 (1)
Service workers, except private household	3,151 (25)	814 (7)	955 (8)	1,528 (12)	360 (3)
Farming, forestry, and fishing	500 (16)	164 (5)	51 (2)	203 (7)	142 (5)
Precision production, craft, and repair	4,133 (35)	863 (7)	1,654 (14)	1,860 (16)	353 (3)
Machine operators, assemblers, and inspectors	1,639 (22)	228 (3)	286 (4)	1,151 (16)	78 (1)
Transportation and material moving	706 (18)	84 (2)	235 (6)	376 (9)	50 (1)
Handlers, equipment cleaners, helpers, and laborers	520 (14)	57 (2)	92 (2)	381 (10)	19 (<0.5)
Total	33,901 (35)	11,404 (12)	10,625 (11)	13,606 (14)	4,301 (4)

NOTE: All employment figures are in thousands. Percentages, which are calculated on the basis of total employment in each occupational group, appear in parentheses. Many workers reported more than one source of training, so percentages may not sum to 100. An unknown fraction of skill improvement training in school is employer financed.

SOURCE: Carey and Eck (1985).

training annually. Smaller firms (500–999 employees) invested an average of $27 per worker annually. Of particular relevance to this study is the fact that, according to Lillard and Tan (1986), reliance on employer-provided training is even greater in technologically dynamic industries.

In sum, employers provide the bulk of skill improvement training in the United States, and such training tends to reinforce, rather than offset, inequalities in preemployment educational attainment within the work force. Inasmuch as technological change is likely to inflict the most serious dislocations (measured, for example, in terms of duration of unemployment) on the least educated workers, this tendency of employer-provided training to reinforce inequality in the educational attainment of employees is likely to exacerbate the severity of technological displacement for low-skill, poorly educated workers.

Why do U.S. blue-collar workers (as used here, a category that includes white-collar female clerical employees) receive less employer-provided training than U.S. white-collar workers and less than blue-collar workers in some other industrial nations? One tentative explanation for U.S.–Japanese differences in such training investments focuses on the contrasting structures of U.S. and Japanese labor markets (Hashimoto, 1979; Hashimoto and Raisian, 1987). U.S. markets for blue-collar labor tend to display relatively inflexible nominal wages, and the supply of and demand for labor are equated through cyclical layoffs. Japanese labor markets, on the other hand, historically have exhibited greater nominal wage flexibility. A large share of the annual earnings of Japanese production workers consists of bonuses, the amount of which is tied to corporate performance, and Japanese labor markets also rely on longer-term employment relationships.[4] Both employer and employee therefore face less uncertainty about turnovers and layoffs and can share the costs of training in job-related skills more efficiently. For example, employees can contribute a share of these costs by accepting starting wages that are lower than would be the case in the absence of the training investment by the employer.

In the United States, where blue-collar employee turnover is relatively high (Levy et al., 1984, estimated that average annual turnover rates in manufacturing were more than 20 percent) and layoffs are more common, sharing training costs between employer and employee is more difficult; there is, among other things, greater uncertainty about the probability of layoffs and a firm's ability to retain the returns from its investment in job-related skills training. Thus, the levels of investment in such training appear to be lower, although better data are needed to support more strongly or reject the predictions of this heuristic model. Interestingly, some recent union contracts in the United States contain provisions resembling those of Japanese labor contracts. Several recent collective bargaining contracts in the U.S. aerospace and automotive industries, for example, combine annual bonuses or profit sharing for workers with corporate commitments to greater employment security and larger investments in worker retraining.

---

[4]Although this contrast has characterized U.S. and Japanese labor markets since the early 1950s, recent structural changes in the Japanese economy, which have resulted in some large layoffs, may alter the structure of Japanese labor markets and labor contracts in the future.

The Adequacy of the Training System

Can the U.S. system we have described respond to changes in the demands for specific job-related skills? Based on the evidence reviewed by this panel, the U.S. training system for job-related skills appears to be responsive to the demands of employers. This measure of adequacy does not address the issue of the distribution of such education, nor does it confront the adequacy of worker preparation in basic skills. Nevertheless, a serious "structural" mismatch between the supply of and demand for skills in the American economy should be revealed in recurrent skill shortages or in the unemployment of workers with particular skills in low demand. In fact, there is little evidence of significant skill shortages for any extended period, although unemployment within the population receiving little job-related or basic skills training (the disadvantaged and unskilled) has been a persistent problem for much of the post-1945 period.

The formal training system (comprising elementary, secondary, and higher education) for labor market entrants (16–24 years old) also appears to respond rapidly to changes in the skills demanded by employers (Berryman, 1985). Especially within higher education, perceptions of oversupply or excess demand in specific fields heavily influence students' intended fields of study, their actual fields of study, and the level of completed degrees. Comparable data for employer-provided training almost certainly would reveal similar flexibility. Operating in conjunction with the enormous size of the decentralized U.S. training system, this flexibility offers considerable opportunities to alter rapidly the mix of job-related skills in the U.S. work force. About 6 million students completed programs of study at the secondary and postsecondary levels during the 1980–1981 academic year; the annual output from these formal channels was approximately 5.7 percent of the work force. As Berryman puts it, "the sheer number of these completions per year represents a remarkable opportunity to rapidly re-configure the skill profile of the American labor force" (p. iii).

This evidence suggests that the enormous system that trains workers in job-specific skills can respond to changes in the demand for skills of different types resulting from the adoption of new technology or structural change in the economy. In fact, in some instances the supply mechanism may respond too rapidly to anticipated changes in demand—as in the rush to secure robotics technician training in 1982–1983, when there was one student enrolled in an introductory robotics course for every robot likely to be purchased (Hunt and Hunt, 1983). Consequently, we see little if any need for additional investments in forecasting skill requirements or training needs, especially since the reliability of these forecasts—reflecting their high levels of uncertainty and the weak methodologies they use—has been low. (See Binkin, 1987, for a critical assessment of the U.S. military's experience in forecasting occupational trends and training requirements.)

TRAINING IN BASIC SKILLS FOR LABOR FORCE ENTRANTS[5]

Labor force entrants acquire basic skills largely within the U.S. public educational system, and educational attainment is a rough index of a worker's level of preparation in these skills. As we noted earlier, basic skills currently are important for obtaining entry-level jobs and will be even more important in the future for obtaining better-paying jobs and for climbing the economic ladder toward higher earnings. As indicated by the evidence in Chapter 3 on growth during the past decade in the returns to higher levels of educational attainment, the distribution of educational attainment within the U.S. population will have a great influence on the distribution of the economic fruits of technological change. Although educational attainment is improving within the labor force entrant population, the large remaining gaps in attainment among whites, blacks, and Hispanics are a cause for concern. More limited evidence, noted in Chapter 3, suggests that the quality of basic skills training for U.S. labor force entrants is lower than that provided to the labor force entrants of other nations (e.g., Japan). Significant deficiencies in the quality of such training for U.S. labor force entrants relative to other nations will impede the ability of this nation to generate and adopt new technologies with sufficient speed and effectiveness to remain competitive in the world economy.

DISPLACED WORKERS

Although we believe that employment displacement resulting from technological change will not be widespread, there will be transitional, regional, and occupational dislocation. As we noted in Chapter 3, the BLS estimates that the number of experienced workers suffering permanent job loss from all causes is roughly 1 million persons per year. Currently, there are no analyses of the number or characteristics of the smaller population of workers who have been displaced by technological change. Such data are important because the needs of these workers may differ substantially from those of the larger displaced worker population.

---

[5]The data on educational attainment in Chapters 3 and 5 underlie this assessment of the adequacy of basic skills training for labor force entrants.

Lacking this information, in the discussion later in this section we do not try to differentiate among workers according to cause of displacement. As we note in Chapter 10, there are also strong arguments against making such distinctions in the design and implementation of adjustment assistance programs for displaced workers.

Workers displaced by technological change receive greater attention than firms suffering dislocations from the same cause because of the greater adjustment problems of workers. Over a working career a worker accumulates a stock of skills and "human capital" that may be highly specific to a single occupation within a firm. When technological change or other forces transform or result in the loss of that job, the value of a worker's skill-based assets may suddenly vanish. A firm facing the loss of markets for its products generally can redeploy its assets and working capital more easily than an individual worker. Machinery and inventories can be sold (albeit at a discount), allowing a firm to realize some return on these assets and enabling it to adjust. Adjustment to technological or structural change is difficult for both workers and firms, but the unique problems faced by workers have drawn attention to their needs.

Much of the following discussion of programs for displaced workers focuses on training in both basic and job-related skills. Although we believe that additional resources should be devoted to retraining displaced workers, we must stress that retraining is not a panacea. The ability of retraining to restore the earning power of some displaced workers, especially those previously employed in durables manufacturing (e.g., basic steel), may be limited. Furthermore, many displaced workers may not participate in retraining programs; they are interested primarily in rapid reemployment, rather than retraining. The most important function of public adjustment programs often is to provide job search assistance and information, rather than retraining, for individuals who may not have changed jobs for 20 years.

Characteristics

To assess the adequacy of policies that address their needs, reliable information on the characteristics of displaced workers is essential. The description in Chapter 3 of the displaced worker population noted the following characteristics:

- Younger workers are more likely to be displaced, but the duration of unemployment after displacement is greater for older workers.
- Both the duration of unemployment and the magnitude of earnings losses associated with reemployment after displacement are higher in regions with relatively high unemployment.

• A large fraction of this population either is ineligible for unemployment compensation or exhausts these benefits prior to reemployment.

• Many displaced workers, especially those from durables manufacturing, experience serious financial losses as a result of displacement and receive lower wages in their new jobs.

• A large portion of the displaced worker population suffers from serious basic skill deficiencies.

Displaced workers are a heterogeneous population made up of groups with different histories of employment and earnings and consequently different needs for retraining and employment assistance. This fact complicates the design of programs to serve them, as illustrated by a discussion of two particular groups.

During the early 1980s, permanent job loss affected a segment of the U.S. work force that previously had experienced limited long-term unemployment—that is, unionized, high-wage workers in durables manufacturing. By 1984 more than 800,000 of the 5.1 million experienced workers identified by BLS as displaced during the previous 5 years came from the nonelectrical machinery, automobile, and primary metals (largely steel) manufacturing industries. Displacement of workers in these industries has been a particular concern for policymakers and the public alike, due to the unprecedented (by post-1945 standards) scope of long-term unemployment within this group, as well as the financial hardships associated with job loss in these industries.

Displaced workers from this sector generally are well-paid men with years of steady employment in the same plant (Flaim and Sehgal, 1985). Retraining in job-related skills is not likely to restore the previous earnings of many members of this group, and most programs to aid them focus on the transition between jobs. Job transition needs are addressed by union contract provisions in many of these industries, provisions whose aims are to reduce the short-term financial hardships of displacement. Despite such transitional help, however, a substantial portion of this group of displaced workers may face difficulties in finding new employment because they lack the basic skills that ease the search for new jobs.

Designing policies to aid this group is complicated by the difficulty of determining whether their displacement is permanent. The high wages these workers were able to secure in their original jobs, the likelihood that alternative employment will mean a substantial cut in these wages, and the availability of supplemental unemployment benefits (SUB) in many of these industries all encourage these workers to avoid any action that might divert them from reemployment in their former occupation. Many of these workers choose to avoid the costs of retraining and searching for a new job, in hopes of being recalled to work.

Another group within the displaced worker population comprises individuals who are poorly educated, female, black or Hispanic, and nonunion. According to the January 1984 displaced worker survey, nearly 900,000 of the 5.1 million experienced workers displaced during 1979–1983 were black or Hispanic; these workers experienced significantly longer unemployment than did white workers (Flaim and Sehgal, 1985; Podgursky, 1987). The characteristics just noted (low education, female, nonwhite, and nonunion) often are associated with lower-wage employment; for these individuals, the acquisition of basic or job-related skills may enhance their prospects for reemployment and also lead to jobs at higher wages. Thus, this group is more likely to benefit from retraining or training.

These two groups of displaced workers have different needs. The effectiveness of retraining in job-related skills to restore the earning power of a displaced steelworker or autoworker may well be limited, although training in basic skills is essential to some of these individuals in finding new employment and job search counseling and assistance also may be beneficial. For members of the second group, a combination of basic skills training, job-related retraining, and job search counseling and assistance could be of substantial help.

Federal Training and Income Support Programs

Since 1945, federal programs to aid displaced workers have consisted of the Manpower Development and Training Act (MDTA) of 1962, superseded in 1973 by the Comprehensive Employment and Training Act; Title III of the Job Training Partnership Act (JTPA) of 1982; Trade Adjustment Assistance (TAA), passed in 1962; unemployment insurance, which provides short-term income support to unemployed workers; and the Perkins Vocational Education Act of 1984.[6]

MDTA was passed on the wave of public concern over technological change and unemployment that gave rise to the National Commission on Technology, Automation, and Economic Progress. The law was intended to help technologically displaced workers with 3 or more years of work experience by retraining these individuals for occupations believed to be

---

[6]Numerous sectoral federal adjustment programs have been developed during the past century, ranging from the Interstate Commerce Act of 1887 to the Redwood National Park legislation of 1978. These programs typically provided income support and retraining to workers in industries affected by legislative or other governmental actions. All of them were very narrowly focused.

in high demand. After 1964, however, declining aggregate unemployment resulted in a reorientation of the program toward disadvantaged rather than displaced workers; it was eventually replaced by the Comprehensive Employment and Training Act (CETA), which focused primarily on disadvantaged workers. In 1982 CETA was replaced by the JTPA.

THE JOB TRAINING PARTNERSHIP ACT

After the reorientation of MDTA in the early 1960s, no federal programs other than TAA addressed the problems of displaced workers until the passage in 1982 of JTPA. JTPA's Title III, Employment and Training Assistance for Dislocated Workers, provides federal funds to the states for training and related employment services for workers who have been laid off or have received notice of layoff and who are unlikely to return to their previous industry or occupation. Workers who have been laid off or who are about to be laid off because of a permanent plant closing and the long-term unemployed are also covered.

Although the actual services available to workers under Title III vary by state, they generally emphasize job search assistance. Support for job-related retraining is modest, and there is little training offered in basic skills. The U.S. General Accounting Office's recent survey of JTPA Title III programs (1987a) found that in 1985 only 6 percent of program participants received basic skills training (with a median duration of only 2 weeks), whereas 42 percent received some form of job-related training through classroom or on-the-job learning. Eighty-four percent of Title III program participants, on the other hand, received job counseling, and 66 percent received job search assistance. Overall, the General Accounting Office has estimated that Title III serves only 6–7 percent of the annual flow of displaced workers.

TRADE ADJUSTMENT ASSISTANCE

Trade adjustment assistance was first provided under the Trade Expansion Act of 1962 to assist workers displaced as a result of the bill's reduction of trade barriers. As originally enacted, workers were eligible for the income support and training benefits offered by TAA only when tariff reduction—and the import penetration of U.S. markets that often followed—was the single most important cause of displacement. The Trade Act of 1974 broadened participation in the program by extending benefits to any worker for whom imports "contributed importantly" to his or her displacement. ("Contributed importantly" meant that import penetration was an important cause of job loss but not necessarily more important than any other cause.) As a result of this change in eligibility criteria, as well as surging auto imports, the program grew from approximately 14,000 workers and $15 million in benefits in fiscal year 1973 to a peak in fiscal year 1980 of 532,000 workers and approximately $1.6 billion in benefits, much of which went to displaced auto workers.

In 1981, Congress redefined and limited TAA income support payments. In fiscal year 1986, TAA served an estimated 42,000 workers at a cost of approximately $148 million. Projected outlays for fiscal year 1987 are approximately $206 million. The President's budget for fiscal year 1988 has proposed that the program be replaced with a broader displaced worker program (Aho and Bayard, 1984; U.S. House of Representatives, Committee on Ways and Means, 1987; unpublished 1987 data obtained from the U.S. Office of Trade Adjustment Assistance).

Despite the program's stated goal of providing both income support and retraining, TAA has emphasized retraining only since 1985. Of the more than $4 billion in program outlays since the passage of the Trade Act of 1974, less than 5 percent has been allocated to retraining (U.S. House of Representatives, Committee on Ways and Means, 1987). One reason for the minor role accorded to retraining stems from the design of TAA. Throughout its life, the program has been hampered by the requirement to determine the contribution of import competition to a worker's displacement. According to one evaluation, during the mid-1970s, this requirement so slowed the delivery of TAA services that the first payment of TAA funds was received by a worker *on average 14 months after layoff* (Corson et al., 1979). Such delays meant that in many cases workers received payments well after they had found new jobs and largely precluded any meaningful role for retraining within TAA.

UNEMPLOYMENT INSURANCE

The unemployment insurance system is the only public income support program for which most displaced workers are eligible. Previous employment can qualify workers for a maximum of 26 weeks of benefits.[7] Benefit levels vary across states, with the highest weekly benefits ranging

---

[7]Washington and Massachusetts have a 30-week maximum benefit period. In addition, Massachusetts provides up to 13 weeks of supplemental reemployment assistance benefits to workers unemployed as a result of a large layoff or plant closing who did not receive at least 90 days' advance notice and/or separation pay (Commonwealth of Massachusetts, Division of Employment Security, 1987). Federal law provides for a 13-week extension of benefits during periods of very high unemployment. As of January 1987, only Alaska and Puerto Rico qualified for this extension.

between 50 and 70 percent of the average weekly wage. Because those workers with above-average wages receive a lower proportion of their former salary in unemployment benefits, the national average weekly benefit was only 36 percent of the average wage in fiscal year 1986. Average total benefits for fiscal year 1986 were $1,956; maximum total 1987 benefits range among the states from $3,120 to $9,900 (U.S. House of Representatives, Committee on Ways and Means, 1987). For a worker undertaking retraining, these benefits could provide as much as 26 weeks of income support; but many states prohibit or otherwise discourage individuals from receiving unemployment insurance payments while enrolled in retraining (Barton, 1986) in order to minimize the time an unemployed worker is drawing unemployment compensation.[8]

FEDERAL ASSISTANCE FOR "UPGRADE" TRAINING FOR EMPLOYED WORKERS

The Perkins Vocational Education Act of 1984, the most recent revision to legislation authorizing federal support for state-level programs in vocational education, mandated that more than $90 million of the roughly $882 million in federal support for vocational education be spent by states on "adult" education, including "upgrade" training for employed workers and education in basic skills for adults. In 1986 the U.S. Department of Education began a large-scale evaluation of the Perkins Act; when its results are available, they should inform the development of other federal policies to improve the job-related and basic skills of the U.S. work force (U.S. Department of Education, 1986). Indeed, rigorous program evaluation is critical to all efforts to design new programs to help displaced workers.

Evaluation of Federal Displaced Worker Programs

Have federal displaced worker programs improved the reemployment prospects of participants? Unfortunately, research on the effectiveness of adjustment assistance, including job training for experienced adult workers, suffers from methodological problems and a shortage of data and funding. The evaluations of MDTA (Ashenfelter, 1978; Bloom,

---

[8]California, through the California Training Benefit Program, provides an additional 26 weeks of state-funded unemployment benefits for displaced workers undertaking training in an occupation for which there is demand in their geographical area (California Employment Development Department, 1986a, 1986b). Displaced workers enrolled in training or other adjustment assistance programs supported by funds from Title III of the JTPA also are permitted to collect unemployment compensation throughout the United States.

1982; Sommers, 1968) do not provide sufficient evidence to support broad statements about the effectiveness of these programs. Only three recent evaluations of displaced worker programs—the Downriver Community Conference Economic Adjustment Program (Kulik et al., 1984), the Buffalo Dislocated Worker Demonstration Program (Corson et al., 1985), and that sponsored by the Texas Department of Community Affairs (Kulik and Bloom, 1986)—have yielded reliable evidence on their effectiveness.[9] This small number of rigorous evaluations is disturbing, considering that over $500 million has been spent on JTPA Title III programs.

Two of these evaluations, supported by the U.S. Department of Labor, examined demonstration and experimental programs that had been undertaken immediately prior to the implementation of JTPA. The third was supported by the Texas Department of Community Affairs, which used a portion of its JTPA Title III program funds to sponsor and evaluate several demonstration programs. These evaluations found that most workers who received services from the programs were unemployed for shorter periods and had higher wages in jobs found immediately after completing the program than was true of workers in the control group (Bowman, 1986). Additional evaluations of workers over longer periods of time, however, are necessary to determine whether these gains in wages persist over the long run.

Despite their positive general findings, these evaluations provide much less information on the effects of the specific services provided by the programs. All three evaluations had design and implementation problems that do not allow definitive conclusions about the relative merits of different services within adjustment programs for displaced workers. For example, the effect of job training, as opposed to job search assistance, cannot be ascertained. The conclusions of these studies also may not be applicable to displaced worker populations that are significantly different from those of the study populations. Finally, although case study evidence suggests that a large percentage of displaced workers suffer from basic skill deficiencies, none of these programs offered this type of training; thus, we have minimal evidence on the design and effectiveness of programs providing basic skills training to displaced workers.

Clearer insights into the effectiveness of displaced worker programs and the appropriate design of such programs must await the results of further evaluations, one of which currently is being planned by the U.S.

---

[9]We exclude evaluation of TAA from this discussion because of the program's design and certification requirements. The results of a large-scale evaluation of TAA are reported in Corson et al. (1979); Aho and Bayard (1984) provide an overview and summary of a number of evaluations of TAA.

Department of Labor. Yet present levels of support for evaluation are insufficient. The magnitude of projected expenditures on displaced worker programs (as proposed in the President's fiscal year 1988 budget, as much as $980 million annually), the paucity of evidence concerning the most effective mix of services, and the significant differences in the costs of various services all suggest that greater investments in program evaluation are needed (see Chapters 8 and 10 for further discussion).

Although additional evaluations are needed to measure the effectiveness of various program services, the bias in the existing JTPA Title III program mix toward job search and placement services suggests that workers with basic skill deficiencies may be underserved. Generally speaking, we believe that there is too little emphasis on basic skills training within Title III. It is difficult to accept the proposition that the needs of workers with basic skills deficiencies can be addressed in 2 weeks of training, the average amount provided by Title III programs (U.S. General Accounting Office, 1987a). In addition, Title III programs, by virtue of the design of their contracts with service providers (contracts that are based on performance in placing participants in jobs), tend to process and train only those displaced workers who are easy to place. Workers with basic skills deficiencies thus may be excluded. The absence of income support within most Title III programs (beyond any unemployment compensation for which displaced workers are eligible) means that any training must generally be completed in 26 weeks or less to avoid exhausting their unemployment insurance benefits. This reduces the attractiveness and efficacy of retraining and may make it completely infeasible for the many displaced workers who do not receive unemployment compensation.

State Programs: The California Employment Training Panel

Most state-administered displaced worker training programs rely in part on JTPA Title III funds. The California Employment Training Panel (ETP), however, a training and employment assistance program, is funded entirely with state monies. (ETP is also of interest because of its size and innovative design.) The program was established in 1982; it receives an annual allocation of approximately $55 million from a small state payroll tax imposed on employers who pay unemployment insurance.[10] ETP provides training for both displaced workers and employed

---

[10]Imposition of the ETP tax was made less onerous by an offsetting reduction in the state unemployment insurance tax, a move made possible by the large surplus in California's unemployment insurance fund.

workers threatened with layoff. Unlike JTPA, however, the worker need not have received notice of an impending layoff to qualify for training assistance.

By investing in training for workers before they are laid off, ETP supporters argue that the program reduces the costs of personnel turnover for employers and reduces outlays from the state unemployment insurance fund. The state's support of retraining for employed workers also is based on the belief that such retraining improves the competitiveness of the state's industry by encouraging the adoption of new technologies; ETP's goal is to avoid immediate job losses while strengthening long-term employment opportunities (California Employment Training Panel, 1985). A preliminary study of 1,200 ETP project participants who completed training and were placed in jobs during 1983–1985 suggests that these goals have been met: the average number of weeks of unemployment for participants declined by more than 60 percent after ETP training, and average earnings rose by more than 50 percent (Moore, 1986). This evidence, however, is preliminary rather than definitive; it was not compiled from a rigorous experimental design that included a control group, nor were the workers graduating from ETP training tracked over an extended period of time.

Without question, ETP represents an imaginative response to the impediments to greater investment by firms in training their blue-collar work force. The program's effectiveness in delivering retraining to the displaced worker population, however, is limited. Basic skills training for employed and displaced workers alike is not supported by the program as a matter of policy. Moreover, ETP's performance requirement (in its contractual agreements with training providers, the program requires that displaced workers be placed in jobs for 90 days prior to payment for the training provided) discourages many potential external providers of training for displaced workers (e.g., community colleges) from participating. Although it was initially intended to provide retraining for experienced workers who were actually unemployed as well as threatened with unemployment, ETP increasingly appears to be financing the training by firms of their employed work force. Thus, the program may in some cases substitute public funds for training investments that would have been made in the absence of the program, which means that there is no net increase in the delivery of training services to workers threatened with displacement.

ETP and other state-level programs that fund training for the employed work force offer a rich set of policy experiments for analysis and evaluation. (See Stevens, 1987, for a descriptive survey of such programs.) Federally supported evaluations of a sample of state programs could yield useful information about the design and effectiveness of these programs for decision making at both the state and federal levels.

Displaced Workers and Adult Education

The majority of federal and state programs for displaced workers rely on the existing adult and community college educational infrastructure to deliver basic skills and job-related training. These postsecondary educational institutions have compiled a mixed record of success in meeting such demands. A recent study by Bruno (1986) noted that many community colleges historically have served college-age students rather than more mature displaced or employed workers. Historically, many of these institutions have not pursued curriculum development and staffing policies to meet the needs of displaced workers for training in basic or job-related skills. This pattern of development has hampered the ability of many of these institutions to meet the needs of displaced workers. As Bruno observes:

. . . the community colleges and vocational-technical schools must reexamine their philosophy and policies if they are to meet the growing need for training created by dislocated workers. Unlike traditional college students, they have neither the time nor financial resources after being laid-off to enroll in a one- or two-year certificate program. They are in a state of crisis that must be addressed quickly. (p. 59)

The very technologies whose development has created concern over worker displacement have great potential for the innovative delivery of training in basic and job-specific skills. For example, one of the greatest impediments to participation in adult education programs is the reluctance of displaced workers to subject themselves to a classroom environment. Advanced teaching technologies, such as self-paced instructional workstations, can support individualized learning outside the classroom, thereby enhancing the attractiveness and effectiveness of basic skills and job-related skills training.

Although the existing educational system exhibits a number of deficiencies in meeting the needs of displaced workers, many innovative community colleges have shown themselves capable of doing so when offered financial incentives. Better financing of worker access to this system through income support and other financial assistance for retraining can motivate community colleges and other adult education institutions to address the special needs of displaced workers. Careful program oversight and evaluation, however, also are necessary.

Private Adjustment Programs

In recent years, federal and state income support and retraining programs have been supplemented by a growing number of privately funded, joint union–management programs. In a number of manufacturing industries, unions have negotiated supplements to regular unemployment benefits. These benefits are coordinated with regular unemployment insurance and provide higher benefit levels—as much as 95 percent of take-home pay—for up to 1 year (Jacobson, 1986). Through collective bargaining, a number of firms have also established early retirement programs. (Such plans, however, typically require giving up the right to be recalled to work.) In some unionized industries (e.g., steel), workers who are displaced can qualify for severance pay or pension supplements based on a combination of years of service and age. Severance pay is not widely available, mainly because workers do not want to give up recall rights, and it is often offered as part of a plant closing settlement. Moreover, recent events (e.g., the bankruptcy of the LTV Corporation, a major steel producer, in 1986) suggest that these payments are not completely reliable. Firm bankruptcies can jeopardize these supplemental or severance benefits.

An analysis of data from a recent survey by the U.S. General Accounting Office (1987b) of layoffs and plant shutdowns involving establishments with more that 100 workers[11] found that severance pay was one of the most common forms of private adjustment assistance—37 percent of the respondents provided severance pay to their blue-collar employees, and 57 percent provided such compensation to white-collar employees. Another common form of assistance was employer continuation of health insurance coverage. Thirty-eight percent of firms provided this benefit for blue-collar employees, and 48 percent did so for white-collar employees (the published survey data do not specify the length of the period of health insurance continuation). Other common forms of employer-provided adjustment assistance include the continuation of life insurance coverage (22 percent of the firms provided this benefit for blue-collar employees and 30 percent did so for white-collar workers) and job search assistance (provided by 26 percent of firms to blue-collar employees and by 35 percent to white-collar employees). The survey does not provide a breakdown of the benefits coverage of unionized and nonunionized workers. Nevertheless, this evidence suggests that white-collar employees receive somewhat more generous adjustment assistance from employers after plant shutdowns or layoffs.

A number of programs have been established recently through collec-

---

[11]GAO mailed survey forms to 500 establishments chosen from an initial sample of 2,400. Data incorporating responses from 60 percent of the firms surveyed are published in its 1986 report (U.S. General Accounting Office, 1986); data incorporating responses from 80 percent of the firms are published in a 1987 report (U.S. General Accounting Office, 1987b). Brown (1987) presents data from the GAO survey that includes responses from 80 percent of the firms.

tive bargaining to assist displaced workers and provide training services. The best-known examples of these programs are the United Auto Workers (UAW)-Ford and UAW-GM "nickel" and "dime" funds. The UAW-Ford program, which began with the 1982 contract, provides services to displaced hourly employees that are similar to those provided under JTPA; job search assistance, counseling, tuition assistance for education and retraining, and, beginning in 1984, relocation assistance in the form of loans. Between 1982 and 1985, approximately 12,600 laid-off Ford workers took part in one or more of the programs. Based on industry and union estimates that at some point during this period approximately 100,000 Ford hourly workers were laid off, this yields a participation rate of 13 percent. Although these programs are primarily funded by employer contributions, they also receive JTPA funds (Pascoe and Collins, 1985).

Advance Notice of Plant Shutdowns or Permanent Layoffs as a Mechanism for Adjustment

The best time to undertake programs of job search assistance, counseling, and retraining for workers is prior to their displacement. In most cases, this can occur only with the cooperation of the employer—cooperation that includes advance notice to workers of impending plant shutdowns or large permanent layoffs. The efficacy of predischarge help reflects the tendency of workers to disperse after layoff, the greater effectiveness of programs that have the cooperation of management and workers, and the greater willingness of workers to enroll in such programs when they are available prior to layoff.[12]

Data on the operation of several adjustment assistance programs for displaced workers confirm that pre-layoff assistance is used more intensively by workers. According to the Downriver Community Conference, 50 percent of workers participated in adjustment programs that were available prior to plant closure, 35 percent participated in programs made available up to 1 year later, and only 17 percent participated in programs offered after 2 years (U.S. Congress, Office of Technology Assessment, 1986a). The Philadelphia Area Labor–Management Committee found that employee participation in worker assistance workshops ranged between 70 and 80 percent when these workshops were provided prior to layoff;

---

[12]There exists no consensus on the "optimal" period of advance notice, but discussions of best-practice methods for plant shutdowns (Driever and Baumgardner, 1984) suggest that 1–6 months' notice is helpful. Section 283 of the Trade Act of 1974 urges firms moving production facilities to other countries to provide 60 days' notice to employees (cited in U.S. Congress, Office of Technology Assessment, 1986a).

when the workshops were offered after layoff, participation dropped to less than 20 percent (Berenbeim, 1986).

Statistical evidence on the effects of advance notice suggests in addition that advance notice of shutdowns or layoffs is associated with shorter spells of unemployment after these events. A study by Folbre et al. (1984) of the impact of advance notice in Maine found, on average, that unemployment in local labor markets in which plant closings were announced in advance was lower than unemployment in regions that experienced plant shutdowns without advance notice. The study also found that providing at least 1 month's advance notice reduced the average duration of unemployment per worker from 5 to 4 months. Addison and Portugal (1987), who applied a model of unemployment duration associated with advance notice to national data from the BLS 1984 displaced worker survey, confirmed Folbre et al.'s results, concluding that advance notice reduced the average spell of unemployment after layoff by roughly 27 percent, or 4 weeks. Data in Flaim and Sehgal (1985) suggest that advance notice of layoffs did not have a substantial impact on the probability that a worker displaced during 1979–1983 was employed as of January 1984. The data on which their analysis was based, however, were flawed. They were drawn from the BLS 1984 survey of displaced workers, which did not specify the period of advance notice. In addition, because the survey asked whether workers received advance notice or "expected" that layoffs were imminent, the methodology may have introduced significant recall bias.

Because this evidence suggests that advance notice of plant closures and large-scale layoffs increases the effectiveness of publicly supported programs of worker adjustment assistance and reduces the average duration of unemployment after layoff, advance notice may reduce the costs to taxpayers of such actions. Plant shutdowns and large-scale layoffs that occur without advance notice appear to impose substantial additional costs on both workers and the public sector, by comparison with situations in which notice is given. Such costs are "externalities," costs imposed on individuals and society that are not borne by the firms closing the plant or laying off the workers. In other areas (e.g., health and safety regulation, pollution controls), public regulations have been developed to ensure that a portion of these costs are also borne by the organizations that contribute to them.

In addition to externalities, plant closures and layoffs in which workers do not receive information available to managers concerning the imminence of displacement may cause workers to make career decisions based on defective or incomplete information. Hamermesh (1987) estimated that plant shutdowns without advance notice impose an average cost on workers (measured as the difference in the level of worker investments in job-related skills for a specific employer in a situation in which notice is provided and a situation in which it is not provided) of $4,500–$15,000.[13] Competitive markets function most efficiently when all of the actors in them have equal access to information concerning their environment and the consequences of their actions. The incentives for participants in markets to disclose freely all information, however, often are minimal— strategic use or selective disclosure of information (as in the many recent "insider trading" cases in securities markets) can prove extremely profitable. The disclosure of relevant information to all parties to a transaction or contract is one of the primary motivations for statutory and regulatory control of securities markets, health and safety regulations, and consumer protection regulations and laws.

Employers are often concerned about employee behavior and productivity after advance notice. Do employees facing permanent layoffs react by sabotaging products or otherwise lowering productivity substantially? There is widespread agreement among business and union leaders (Berenbeim, 1986, p. 14; Driever and Baumgardner, 1984, p. 14; the Secretary of Labor's Task Force on Economic Adjustment and Worker Dislocation, 1986, p. 23; U.S. Congress, Office of Technology Assessment, 1986b, quoting business and union participants in a workshop, p. 22) that advance notice does not lower worker productivity after the announcement. Indeed, the recent study by Ronald Berenbeim for the Conference Board reported that "all industrial plants studied [five] noted improvements in quality and productivity in the final phase of the facility's operations" (1986, p. 14). These results corroborate those of an earlier study by Weber and Taylor (1963) of 32 plant shutdowns. The productivity and quality improvements that occur appear to reflect the reaction of employees to the evidence that management is concerned about their welfare, the operation of counseling and job search programs that begin prior to layoff, the resolution of anxieties and uncertainties, and the desire of workers concerned about reemployment to demonstrate to new employers that the quality of the work force in the closed plant was high.

The evidence on the benefits of advance notice for worker adjustment and the distribution of social costs, combined with evidence on its productivity effects, has led a large number of employer organizations, labor–management task forces, and public commissions to endorse voluntary advance notice. Private sector groups endorsing advance notice include the Business Roundtable (1983), the National Association

---

[13]This cost measures only the loss in the value of workers' investments in such training and ignores the loss of earnings associated with unemployment and the possibility that reemployment will involve reductions in wages.

of Manufacturers (1987), the National Alliance of Business (1987), and the National Center on Occupational Readjustment (1984). Recent public commissions, study groups, and officials endorsing advance notice include the President's Commission on Industrial Competitiveness (1985), the Secretary of Labor's Task Force on Economic Adjustment and Worker Dislocation (1986), and the Assistant Secretary of Labor for Employment and Training (Semerad, 1987).

Despite this support for advance notice, however, many of these groups oppose or have failed to endorse public actions to mandate advance notice of plant closures and permanent, large-scale layoffs, citing as justification the high costs and counterproductive employment effects of mandatory regulations. The costs of mandatory advance notice cited by these analysts include the additional burdens that these regulations place on small firms, the impracticality of advance notice under all circumstances in an economic environment characterized by uncertainty and change, the need to preserve managerial discretion in decision making, and the possibility that such regulations will raise the costs of operating production establishments within the United States, further encouraging the movement of production to offshore locations and discouraging domestic job creation. As an example of the negative effects of mandatory advance notice, analysts point to Western Europe, where advance notice regulations are relatively common. Opponents of mandatory advance notice cite these regulations as contributing to low rates of job creation, due to their tendency to raise the costs of operating a business. (See the National Alliance of Business, 1987, and Semerad, 1987; Balassa, 1984, presents related evidence on European job creation and regulatory costs.)

There is little or no evidence that would allow a systematic estimation of the magnitude or significance of these costs. Federal legislative proposals to require advance notice of plant shutdowns and permanent layoffs have accommodated several of these objections, typically exempting small firms (those with fewer than 50–100 employees) and allowing exemptions for "unforeseen circumstances." Although a number of Western European nations enforce mandatory advance notice regulations, in many nations these are combined with requirements for substantial severance payments to displaced workers, making a precise comparison with the impacts of notification alone very difficult.[14]

---

[14]The report of the Subcommittee on the Foreign Experience of the Secretary of Labor's Task Force on Economic Adjustment and Worker Dislocation (1986) has disputed the argument that social regulations have contributed to low rates of job creation in Western Europe, arguing that macroeconomic policies and inefficient nationalized industries, among other factors, are more significant.

The primary issue in the debate over advance notice does not concern its merits—there appears to be widespread agreement that such notice aids worker adjustment—but the most effective way of ensuring its widespread application at reasonable cost. A number of U.S. employers (both union and nonunion firms) currently provide voluntary advance notice of plant closures and layoffs to their employees. Evidence from a recent national survey administered by the U.S. General Accounting Office (1986, 1987b), however, strongly suggests that voluntary advance notice is not functioning effectively—few workers are receiving even 30 days' advance notice. The GAO survey data, which appear in Brown (1987), suggest that 31 percent of the respondents provided no specific notice of plant closure or layoff (i.e., informing workers in advance of a specific date of layoff), 34 percent provided 1–14 days' notice, 15 percent provided 15–30 days' notice, and 20 percent provided 31 or more days' notice. On average, blue-collar workers received 7 days' notice and white-collar workers received 14 days' notice.[15] In unionized establishments, blue-collar workers received an average of 2 weeks' specific notice; *blue-collar workers in establishments without unions received an average of only 2 days' advance notice of plant closure or layoff* (U.S. Congress, Office of Technology Assessment, 1986a; U.S. General Accounting Office, 1986, 1987b).

---

[15]The first set of survey results published by the General Accounting Office (1986) found that 76 percent of establishments provided "general" advance notice, defined as notice to groups of workers that some or all of them might be laid off in the future. "Specific" advance notice was defined as telling individual workers of the date of their impending layoff. A more restrictive definition of general advance notice was used by Brown (1987) who defined it as notification of individual workers that layoffs or a plant closing were likely. Drawing on data from the BLS Permanent Mass Layoff and Plant Closing Program (Secretary of Labor's Task Force, 1986, Appendix C), which defined general advance notice as notification to individual employees that they would be laid off, Brown found from a survey of establishments employing 50 or more workers that only 36 percent of the establishments provided general notice. The most recent tabulation of a more complete set of responses to the GAO survey (U.S. General Accounting Office, 1987b) has eliminated any analysis of "general" advance notice.

8

The Quality of Data on Technological Change, Its Employment Effects, and Adjustment Mechanisms

An important part of the charge to this panel called for a review of the adequacy of the available data on the impacts of technological advances on employment, productivity, and economic growth in the United States. For many of the questions of concern to this panel, the data are sufficient to support informed conclusions. In a number of other areas, however, especially areas of interest for further research or policymaking, these data are seriously deficient. The problems with the evidence are both conceptual and empirical. In many areas the only measures of technological change (e.g., productivity trends) are indirect, responding to many influences other than technology, or they are direct measures that capture only a part of the processes of innovation and adoption (e.g., patents). In other areas, insufficient public investment in data collection and analysis means that the relevant data are of poor quality.

This chapter surveys the deficiencies in the public data on technological change and its economic impacts (in terms of employment, productivity, and output growth) and suggests a research strategy to illuminate the effects of new technology on the worker, the firm, and the workplace. In addition, we briefly discuss potential improvements in the evaluation of programs to aid worker adjustment to technological change. The broader issue is an important one; although data do not drive the policy formation process, their absence surely leaves this process less informed, less effective, and potentially counterproductive.

160

DATA ON TECHNOLOGY AND ECONOMIC PERFORMANCE

Elsewhere in this report, we have criticized the use of case studies and other methodologies to predict the employment and skill impacts of technological change. Although these methodologies do offer important insights into the processes and effects of such change, the consumer of the findings of such studies must be wary of treating them as applicable to the entire economy or even to a sector of the economy. Moreover, the large bands of uncertainty that underlie virtually all estimates of impacts must be acknowledged, both by researchers and by those who would apply these findings.

A key reason for caution in interpreting and generalizing the results of sectoral or case studies is the disjunction between the aggregate and detailed levels of analysis of the employment and economic effects of technology. Virtually all of the data on the effects of technological change have been compiled at the individual industry, firm, or even production establishment level; statements or conclusions about overall trends, impacts, and rates of change, however, require aggregate data. Unfortunately, sectoral and industry studies do not aggregate well, and the transition from the detailed or sectoral to the aggregate level of analysis cannot be made with most data. Data on the aggregate economic impact of technological change in manufacturing are sparse, and their quality may be declining, due in part to reductions in federal programs of data collection and analysis.

Spending under the fiscal year 1987 budget for several key federal statistical agencies has been stagnant or has declined in real terms since fiscal year 1980 (Slater, 1986).[1] Budget cutbacks have produced significant deterioration in data on innovation and economic change in several specific programs. The line-of-business data of the Federal Trade Commission have been an important source of information about R&D and other measures of economic performance (e.g., sales and net revenues) at the level of individual product lines within large U.S. businesses. These data allow a researcher to account explicitly for the multiproduct character of the modern manufacturing and service sector firm. For example,

---

[1]Measured in 1982 dollars, appropriations for Census Bureau programs excluding the Survey of Income and Program Participation (which analyzes household participation in federal assistance programs, including Social Security, Medicaid, and food stamps) have declined from $62 million in fiscal year 1980 to $58.6 million in fiscal year 1987; appropriations for the Bureau of Economic Analysis have remained constant, at $18.6 million, and appropriations for the BLS (excluding the project charged with revising the consumer price index) have declined from $121.1 million in fiscal year 1980 to $119.9 million in fiscal year 1987.

the line-of-business data allow one to take into account the fact that a firm like General Electric produces a vast array of goods and services (e.g., financial services), instead of assuming that its products are only those of the electrical equipment industry. Unfortunately, these data are no longer being collected, and research on the existing data base has been sharply reduced.

Still another significant data collection effort within the federal government has been abandoned recently. In the 1970s a unit of the Patent Office, the Office of Technology Assessment and Forecasting, began to compile and analyze machine-readable time series data on U.S. patenting activity, assessing overall trends and analyzing patenting activity in specific economic sectors and technologies. Although they are an imperfect measure of innovation, patents capture an important part of the overall innovation process. This unit, however, has been disbanded; its data analysis and dissemination activities have been reduced considerably.

Any analysis of the impact of technological change is also hampered by the incompatibility of many of the data bases supported by federal agencies. As Courtenay Slater (1986), former chief economist of the U.S. Department of Commerce, has noted, the lack of a central statistical agency in the federal government has encouraged the proliferation of incompatible statistical series and surveys. For example, the organizational and analytic categories used by the Census Bureau are only partly compatible with the data structure developed by the BLS, which in turn is compatible with only a few of the data bases of the Bureau of Economic Analysis of the Commerce Department. There are potentially great returns to better coordination among these publicly funded data collection and organization efforts. Slater has recommended that statistical agencies (mainly the Bureaus of Labor Statistics, the Census, and Economic Analysis) be allowed and encouraged to exchange—with appropriate safeguards to ensure privacy—confidential information about businesses and individuals. Such a policy also might require coordination and agreement among federal statistical agencies on the specific topics of interest in a coordinated data collection and publication effort.

Another deficiency in our knowledge stems from the fact that data on technological change within the United States cover only the generation of new technology. As we noted in Chapter 2, adoption (i.e., diffusion) is crucial to a technology's economic impact; but virtually no data on adoption are collected by public statistical agencies. Developing statistical series on the diffusion of innovations within the manufacturing and services sectors would be a useful investment of public funds.

A final area of concern is the poor quality of the data on the economic behavior and performance of the nonmanufacturing sector, a large and still growing portion of the U.S. economy that now employs more than 70 percent of the U.S. work force (President's Council of Economic Advisers, 1987). As Representative David Obey and Senator Paul Sarbanes (1986) noted:

A review of our national data collection efforts with regard to the American labor force and American businesses would lead one to believe that we are still a society of blue collar workers primarily engaged in manufacturing. While we continue carefully to count the number of people employed in the textile industry who are engaged in sewing on snaps as opposed to those who stitch sleeves, we have no information on how many Americans now work in computer sales. We do not know how many people make a living writing software or how much they make. We have no definite information on whether the Nation's movement toward a "service economy" has helped or hurt family income or what kinds of specific skills are required in growth industries. We don't even have detailed information on what the growth industries are or how fast they are growing. (p. 2)

The deficiencies in the data on service sector output, employment, and productivity—to say nothing of technological change in this sector of the economy (see National Research Council, Committee on National Statistics, 1986)—are such that there is genuine uncertainty as to whether the apparent productivity slowdown of the past decade is significant or whether it reflects increasing problems in measuring service sector productivity growth outside of manufacturing. Neither can one distinguish with precision among productivity, trade output, or employment trends in different service industries because of the high levels of aggregation within these data. For instance, despite rapid growth in international trade in the services sector, the categories of primary interest, such as earnings from the foreign sale of U.S. financial, insurance, and consulting services, are lumped together into a "miscellaneous" grouping that is the largest single category of U.S. services exports.

The industrial classification scheme used for service sector data collection and analysis is in need of major revisions; such revisions would allow disaggregation of the data and analyses of the trends in more economically meaningful components of the nonmanufacturing sector. Whatever specific actions are taken, however, we feel that the quality of these data are a cause for concern. Continued neglect of the nonmanufacturing sector data base is dangerous in view of the growing importance of this sector to the national economy and to economic policy decisions.

A STRATEGY FOR SURVEYS OF THE IMPACT
OF TECHNOLOGY ON THE WORKPLACE

As we noted in Chapter 4 and the previous section of this chapter, researchers need representative data bases that combine data on the rate of technological change and diffusion with data on the changing level and distribution of employment and investment within firms, allowing aggregate trends to be monitored with greater precision. In addition, they require better data on the quality and character of the work environment and on workers' reactions to new technology. In this section we briefly discuss strategies for collecting such data.

Surveys of Firms

Hunt and Hunt (1985) noted in their survey of data sources for the analysis of technological change that the Bureaus of Labor Statistics and the Census have already collected much of the data needed to analyze aggregate trends in employment and technology. Currently, however, there is no way to link these data either with one another or with data on investment and technology. As these researchers put it: "We have occupational data, but it cannot be linked to specific technologies in use. We have demographic data, but it does not possess sufficient occupational or technological content. In the area of the technology itself, we lack even the most rudimentary data with which to address policy concerns" (p. 42). Another crucial data deficiency stems from the fact that technological change in most cases involves substituting capital for labor. To analyze such change, compatible data must be gathered on the evolving demand of firms for inputs of capital and labor. Currently, no such data exist at the firm or establishment level.

Responding to these gaps, Hunt and Hunt (1985) proposed that a "Current Firm Survey" of manufacturing and nonmanufacturing firms be undertaken to complement BLS's Current Population Survey. Like the population survey, the firm survey would be constructed as a sample of various groups within the relevant population—in the case of the establishment survey, firms would be chosen from various industries. The survey would be designed to elicit detailed data on the characteristics of new capital investment in the lines of business of respondent firms; those data in turn would enable researchers to develop an accurate profile of the rates of adoption of new technologies. Similarly detailed data would be obtained on the characteristics of the firm's work force.

Firm surveys have problems that are well known to anyone who has ever tried to conduct empirical studies of the behavior of companies over time. The product lines of large modern firms are extremely diverse, which makes the development of a balanced cross-industry sample of firms extremely difficult. Moreover, companies vanish and are born with considerable frequency, although an appropriate sampling technique could reduce problems from such changes in the population. Resolving these difficulties would be well worth the time and effort involved, however, because this type of survey could provide valuable product-line data on investment, technological change, and occupational requirements. Without such data, it is unlikely that significant progress can be made in the study of technology and employment. If the costs of such a survey are judged to be excessive, a less expensive alternative is an expansion of the range of questions asked of firms in the Census of Manufactures administered by the Census Bureau. In addition, as in the population census, a sample of these firms could be asked to provide more detailed and extensive data.

A Survey of Workers and Working Conditions

A detailed study of the effects of technological change is also constrained by a dearth of reliable data. One survey-based study of U.S. firms and workers (Mueller et al., 1969) was published 18 years ago, and serves as a model for the proposal outlined below. The survey of workers we propose would be more rigorous than that in the Mueller team's study; it would attempt to resurvey respondents at regular intervals to track changes in the workplace resulting from the use of new technologies and to trace the employment and skill effects of technological change on individuals. The survey also would include a matched sample of employers and workers for a subset of the worker population, an addition that allows tests for biases in the survey responses and supports further analyses of technology's impacts on workers.

The proposed survey would include monitoring and research studies at 5-year intervals in which respondents would be asked about their current job and the job they had 5 years earlier (the employer would be asked about the changing mix of jobs over the 5 years). The basic sample would be drawn from adults of working age (16–75 years old). In addition, through a sample of establishments, employers could be asked to provide workplace data for a sample of employees in each establishment, allowing information to be compiled both on individuals and on their interaction with a changing workplace. Follow-up interviews would concentrate on individuals and their experience. The two samples would include some overlap—for example, interviewing workers in the first sample who work for employers interviewed in the second sample.

How might such a survey be undertaken? One option is to supplement the regular BLS CPS questionnaire with these inquiries every 5 years. Such a procedure, however, does not allow for tracking particular workers. The alternative is a large-scale study in which a sample of workers is followed over a number of decades; such a study would resemble the large panel studies of family income and economic status that have been developed during the past 20 years. Combined with results from the detailed survey of firms proposed earlier, these data would permit an analysis of the effects of technological change on both employers and employees.

A similar survey was proposed in a recent report to the U.S. Department of Labor by a Social Science Research Council (1986) advisory group. This group proposed collecting information from both employees and employers. The quality of worklife was the main concern of this proposed research, but the advisory group's proposed survey could easily be modified to cover the impact of technology on both employment and the nature of work.

INFORMATION ON THE EFFECTIVENESS OF WORKER ADJUSTMENT PROGRAMS

The panel's charge called for an evaluation of adjustment assistance programs for workers displaced by technological change. Such an evaluation is difficult, however, in view of the embryonic state of research and knowledge concerning program design and effectiveness in retraining for displaced workers. As we discussed in Chapter 7, there have been few rigorous evaluations of displaced worker programs of the type being supported by Title III of the JTPA. Those that have been conducted offer limited evidence on the design of successful programs for improving the long-term employment and income prospects of displaced workers.

We are encouraged by the U.S. Department of Labor's recent support of rigorous evaluations of displaced worker adjustment programs. Without additional evaluative research and related policy experiments, the knowledge base from which to develop effective programs cannot be assembled. Evaluations are needed that will provide information on the effectiveness of adjustment program designs that combine job search assistance, basic skills training, and job-related training in different quantities and use varied delivery approaches. Evaluation of these programs also should incorporate analyses of their effectiveness in assisting displaced workers with different characteristics.

The requirement for additional research need not and should not preclude the development of new initiatives to aid displaced workers. A pluralistic policy is required that will encourage the development and evaluation of different approaches to worker adjustment, including retraining in job-related and basic skills. In this regard, we concur with the report of the U.S. Department of Labor's Advisory Panel on Job Training

Longitudinal Survey Research (1985), which recommended that more experimental programs be conducted using randomly selected experimental and control populations.

A useful principle to guide the evaluation of worker adjustment assistance programs would be for the federal or state agency charged with the administration of the program to share responsibility for its evaluation with another agency or advisory group. For example, the evaluation of federal adjustment programs might be shared by the Department of Labor with another agency or outside advisory panel, and a similar procedure could be used by the Department of Education in evaluating the Perkins Act. The Advisory Panel on Job Training Longitudinal Survey Research recommended that the "research process should be monitored by a firm or group with no ax to grind in order to assure adherence to DOL's [the Department of Labor's] policy needs and maintain a quality level that will inspire public confidence in the final research products" (1985, p. 32). An expert panel could be established under the auspices of the National Research Council or another group to oversee the design and implementation of evaluations. Whatever actions are taken in this area should proceed simultaneously with the development of additional innovative programs for worker adjustment.

Finally, evaluations are needed of state-level programs in skills improvement for the employed work force to determine whether this strategy is effective in improving the productivity and technological performance of U.S. firms. To what extent, for example, are these programs simply providing public funds to support training activities that otherwise would have been supported by private firms? Answers to this and other questions are difficult to obtain, but they are essential for determining the returns on investment in such training. As noted in Chapter 7, the number and heterogeneity of these state efforts provide an opportunity for comparisons and evaluations of programs that serve similar populations but use different designs. Such evaluations could also inform modifications of the federal vocational education assistance legislation (the Perkins Act) that allows for state support of employer-provided training to employed workers.

9

Findings

Our principal finding on the employment-related effects of technology states that:

Technological change is an essential component of a dynamic, expanding economy. The modern U.S. economic system, in which international trade plays an increasingly important role, must generate and adopt advanced technologies rapidly, in both the manufacturing and nonmanufacturing sectors, if growth in employment and wages is to be maintained. Recent and prospective levels of technological change will not produce significant increases in total unemployment, although individuals will face painful and costly adjustments. Rather than producing mass unemployment, technological change will make its maximum contribution to higher living standards, wages, and employment levels if appropriate public and private policies are adopted to support the adjustment to new technologies.

The panel's other central findings, which cover a number of dimensions of the employment impact of technological change and form the basis for the policy recommendations in Chapter 10, are listed below. This listing is followed by subsidiary findings from each chapter.

CENTRAL FINDINGS

Employment and Wage Impacts of Technological Change in an Open Economy

● *Historically, technological change and productivity growth have been associated with expanding rather than contracting total employ-*

ment and rising earnings. The future will see little change in this pattern. As in the past, however, there will be declines in specific industries and growth in others, and some individuals will be displaced. Technological change in the U.S. economy is not the sole or even the most important cause of these dislocations (see Chapters 2 and 3).

• *The adoption of new technologies generally is gradual rather than sudden.* The employment impacts of new technologies are realized through the diffusion and adoption of technology, which typically take a considerable amount of time. The employment impacts of new technologies therefore are likely to be felt more gradually than the employment impacts of other factors, such as changes in exchange rates. The gradual pace of technological change should simplify somewhat the development and implementation of adjustment policies to help affected workers (see Chapter 2).

• *Within today's international economic environment, slow adoption by U.S. firms (relative to other industrial nations) of productivity-increasing technologies is likely to cause more job displacement than the rapid adoption of such technologies.* Much of the job displacement of the past 7 years does not reflect a sudden increase in the adoption of labor-saving innovations but instead is due in part to increased U.S. imports and sluggish exports, which in turn reflect macroeconomic forces (the large U.S. budget deficit and the high foreign exchange value of the dollar during 1980–1985), slow adoption of some technologies in U.S. manufacturing, and other factors (see Chapters 2 and 3).

• *The rate of technology transfer across national boundaries has grown; for the United States, this transfer increasingly incorporates significant inflows of technology from foreign sources, as well as outflows of U.S. research findings and innovations.* In many technologies, the United States no longer commands a significant lead over industrial competitor nations. Moreover, technology "gaps" (the time it takes another country to become competitive with U.S. industry or for U.S. firms to absorb foreign technologies) are likely to be shorter in the future (see Chapter 3).

Technology and the Characteristics of Tomorrow's Jobs

• *New technologies by themselves are not likely to change the level of job-related skills required for the labor force as a whole.* We do not project a uniform upgrading or downgrading of job skill requirements in the U.S. economy as a result of technological change. This does not deny the need, however, for continued investment and improvement in the job-related skills of the U.S. work force to support the rapid adoption of new technologies that will contribute to U.S. competitiveness (see Chapter 4).

• *Technological change will not limit employment opportunities for individuals entering the labor force with strong basic skills.* The most reliable projections of future job growth suggest that the number of jobs in the broad occupational categories accounting for the majority of entrant employment will continue to expand. Combined with a projected lower rate of growth in the entrant pool, this conclusion suggests that labor force entrants with strong basic skills (numerical reasoning, problem solving, literacy, and written communication) will fare well in the job markets of the future (see Chapter 5).

Technology and Work Force Adjustment

• *A substantial portion—from 20 to 30 percent—of displaced workers with job experience lack basic skills.* These workers often remain unemployed longer and have difficulty finding new jobs without incurring significant wage reductions. In view of the fact that technological and structural change in this economy will place increasing demands on the ability of workers to adjust, experienced workers who lack basic skills will face even greater difficulties in future job markets (see Chapter 3).

• *The evidence suggests that displaced workers who receive substantial advance notice of permanent job loss experience shorter periods of unemployment than workers who do not receive such notice.* Substantial advance notice (several months) of permanent layoffs or plant shutdowns appears to reduce the severity of worker displacement. Moreover, such a policy can improve the effectiveness of job search assistance, counseling, and retraining programs, thereby reducing the public costs of unemployment (see Chapter 7).

• *The primary federal program for displaced workers, Title III of the Job Training Partnership Act (JTPA), emphasizes the rapid placement of workers in new jobs. It does not appear to serve the needs of many displaced workers.* JTPA provides little training for the substantial number of displaced workers who need better basic skills; it also provides little extended training in job-related skills for other workers (see Chapter 7).

• *Displaced worker adjustment assistance programs reduce the duration of unemployment after displacement and result in higher wages in new jobs obtained immediately after participation in such programs.* There is limited evidence on the contribution of retraining in basic and job-related skills (a component of many such programs) to the employment and earnings prospects of displaced workers. Nevertheless, it would be wrong to conclude from this that retraining is ineffective or that it has a negative impact on earnings or reemployment prospects. Too little is known about the components of effective adjustment programs for displaced worker populations with different characteristics because of the paucity of rigorous evaluations of such programs. Additional policy experiments and evaluations are badly needed to improve these programs (see Chapters 7 and 8).

CHAPTER FINDINGS

Chapter 2: The Sources and Rate of Technological Change in the U.S. Economy

• *Nontechnological, managerial, and organizational factors powerfully influence the adoption of new technologies and the impact of their adoption on product quality, labor productivity, and the skill requirements of labor.* Indeed, the recent experience of some U.S. adopters of advanced manufacturing technologies suggests that changes in the structure of management and production organization are as important as the technologies themselves in improving productivity and product quality.

• *A work force that is well trained in job-related skills, and therefore capable of adopting new technologies more rapidly, can improve the ability of U.S. firms to remain at the technological frontier and to compete more effectively in international markets.* The evidence on job-specific training and the adoption of new technologies in other nations, such as Japan, Sweden, and West Germany, is qualitative rather than quantitative, but it suggests that investments in improving the job-related skills of the blue-collar work force can contribute to more rapid adoption and effective utilization of new technologies.

• *The rate of technological change in the United States does not appear to have increased in recent years.* Acceleration in the rate at which new technologies are developed and adopted within this economy should be revealed in increases in labor productivity growth within the overall economy. Such growth during the past decade has been well below its postwar average. Within the manufacturing sector, labor productivity growth recently has increased, although it does not significantly exceed levels of the 1950s or early 1960s. In the nonmanufacturing sector, labor productivity growth remains low, well below the postwar average (although this may reflect measurement problems).

Chapter 3: Labor Supply and Demand Within the U.S. Economy

• *An average of more than 1 million experienced workers (those with at least 3 years' tenure in their jobs) were displaced each year during 1979–1983.* The annual flow of displaced workers accounted for 10–13 percent of the unemployed population during 1979–1983, although the share of total unemployment during this period for all displaced workers ranged between 20 and 31 percent. Data covering 1983 and 1984 suggest that the rate of displacement of experienced workers has not declined significantly.

• *Workers with higher levels of training in job-related skills experience shorter spells of unemployment after layoffs than workers without such training.* These workers are also more likely to find better-paying jobs than their less skilled colleagues. Blue-collar workers' adjustment to new technologies and structural change may be impaired as a result of the tendency for these workers to receive less employer-financed training than white-collar employees, as Chapter 7 discusses in greater detail.

• *The rate of growth in the U.S. labor force is projected to be considerably lower during the next decade than it was during 1975–1985.* This slower rate of growth should reduce somewhat the supply of labor relative to demand and should ease worker adjustment to technological change. Projected low rates of labor force growth during 1987–1995 also mean that the gender composition and ethnic makeup of the 1995 labor force will closely resemble those of the 1987 labor force.

• *The economic returns from higher educational attainment within the U.S. labor force have increased substantially since the 1970s.* Measured as the difference in median annual income, the economic returns to completing high school have increased significantly since 1973. Such increases reflect the importance of basic skills for quality jobs and career advancement within the modern economy.

• *Serious gaps persist in the level of secondary educational attainment of whites, blacks, and Hispanics within the U.S. work force, although these gaps have narrowed in recent years.* As the data on the economic returns from educational attainment suggest, workers with lower levels of educational attainment have more trouble obtaining quality jobs as entrants or displaced workers. The persistence of these educational gaps therefore will contribute to racial and ethnic economic inequality.

• *The dynamic character of U.S. labor markets, combined with the gradual pace of technological change, should ease worker adjustment to such change.* Although the U.S. labor market is characterized by high rates of job creation and loss, this fluidity is not caused by technological change; rather, it reflects changes in the structure of the economy and the growth of individual firms. For many U.S. workers, the costs of displacement are high, but the duration of unemployment after displacement is shorter than for displaced workers in Western Europe.

• *The level of demand for U.S. labor, especially in manufacturing, has been affected by declines in the international competitiveness of many U.S. industries.* The recent realignment of foreign exchange rates will aid U.S. exports and reduce import penetration of many U.S. markets. Yet this realignment has not solved and will not solve the nation's competitiveness problem without improved U.S. performance in technological and other areas (e.g., rates of capital formation).

• *The rate of decline in the manufacturing sector's share of total employment has accelerated during the past 7 years. In addition, the wage losses incurred by the small stream of workers moving involuntarily from manufacturing to nonmanufacturing industry have increased.* Technological change is but one of a number of influences affecting this decline—and by no means the most important one. The foreign exchange rate of the U.S. dollar and slow rates of economic growth in nations buying a large share of U.S. exports appear to be even more significant factors.

Chapter 4: Studies of the Impact of Technological Change on Employment, Skills, and Earnings: A Critical Review

• *Forecasting the sectoral or occupational impacts of technological change is extremely difficult.* Numerous factors, such as the length of time required for the widespread diffusion of an innovation, affect the employment impacts of technological change. These factors operate with varying lags and exert offsetting influences on the demand for labor. In addition, the data available to measure these factors often are deficient in quantity and quality. The results of most forecasts in this area therefore should be viewed with considerable skepticism.

• *Technological change does not appear to be responsible for growth in the inequality of the distribution of household incomes during the past two decades.* Increasing inequality in the before-tax household income distribution reflects changes in the composition of the U.S. work force and the structure of the family, rather than the impact of technological change. Changes in the structure of federal entitlement programs and tax policies since 1981 appear to have contributed to increased inequality in the after-tax household income distribution.

• *Assessing the effect of technological change on occupational structure and entry-level job skill requirements beyond basic skills is fraught with uncertainty.* Such uncertainty derives from the dynamic character of the U.S. economy, the unpredictable direction and impacts of future technological change, and the fact that the effects of new technologies on skill requirements often are affected heavily by managerial decisions concerning the organization of work. This uncertainty reinforces the arguments favoring a "generalist" approach to the education of entrants to the labor force, emphasizing basic skills, rather than a large investment of resources in training for a specific set of vocations.

Chapter 5: Differential Technology Impacts: Black Workers, Female Workers, and Labor Force Entrants

• *The negative employment impact of technological change within specific occupations will have little if any effect on the future employment prospects of black workers.* Nevertheless, reductions in barriers to minority employment in all occupations would improve the ability of blacks to adjust to technological change.

• *As in the case of blacks, the employment-reducing impacts of technological change within specific occupations, which are small in the aggregate, will have little effect on the employment prospects of women.* Reducing barriers that impede the entry of women into other occupations would expand their employment options and thus improve their ability to adjust to such change.

• *Labor force entrants from minority groups often have low levels of educational attainment that imply weak basic skills and that impair the adjustment of these groups to technological change.* Continued efforts to raise the quality of entrants' basic skills preparation, narrowing the gap in educational attainment between black and white as well as Hispanic and white youth, will aid such adjustment.

Chapter 6: Technological Change and the Work Environment

• *A "two-tiered" work force, which might develop as a result of decreases in career mobility within the workplace and reductions in the skill requirements for some jobs, does not appear to be an inevitable result of technological change.* The evidence is limited on the effects of technological change on career mobility within the workplace. These effects are not determined solely by technological factors but are also influenced by managerial decisions on the design and implementation of new technologies. Case studies, which provide some indication of these impacts, do not suggest a uniform reduction in such mobility. Although future developments may change this judgment, our review of the evidence suggests that new technologies will not reduce upward mobility within the workplace.

• *Management policies (including retraining for other jobs within the firm, advance notification of the introduction of new technologies, or labor–management consultation on the introduction of technology) that help workers adjust to technological change often benefit both management and labor by allowing more rapid introduction of new technologies without significant production losses or other disruptions.* Worker involvement and responsibility in planning the adoption of technology often can improve the performance of new process technologies. Greater cooperation between management and labor (both union and nonunion) can improve U.S. productivity and competitiveness, thereby enhancing job security and supporting growth in real wages.

• *The direct and indirect impacts of technological change may pose significant challenges to the structure of health and safety regulation, while also contributing to the reduction of workplace hazards.* For example, information and computer-aided manufacturing technologies could reduce workplace hazards by contributing to safer production processes. Increases in the share of employment accounted for by small firms, however, may create problems for the enforcement of federal and state workplace safety and health regulations.

Chapter 7: Current Policies for Worker Adjustment

• *Some federal policies for dealing with displaced workers, such as Trade Adjustment Assistance (TAA), have differentiated among these workers by the cause of their displacement. This program design has resulted in the inequitable treatment of different groups of displaced workers and frequently has introduced long delays in the delivery of assistance.* Because of the need to certify the causes of worker displacement under the provisions of TAA, assistance was delayed in some cases as long as 14 months, which hampered the use of program funds for retraining displaced workers.

• *Existing unemployment compensation policies provide income support during temporary layoffs, but they do not deal effectively with the problems of long-term displacement.* Moreover, in many states, workers undertaking retraining are ineligible for unemployment compensation.

• *The training system as a whole appears to be highly responsive to the changing demands of employers for new job-related skills.* There are serious questions, however, about the ability of displaced workers to finance their access to this system.

• *Forecasts of detailed skill requirements for the U.S. economy historically have been inaccurate and of marginal value.* In view of this fact, as well as the evidence on the high degree of flexibility and responsiveness of the training system to changing employer and worker demands, we see little need for additional investments in forecasting detailed skill or training requirements.

Chapter 8: The Quality of Data on Technological Change, Its Employment Effects, and Adjustment Mechanisms

• *The quality of data on many detailed aspects of technological change and its economic consequences is poor.* In areas ranging from productivity growth in nonmanufacturing industries to the rates of diffusion of technologies in both manufacturing and nonmanufacturing industry to the effectiveness of worker adjustment programs, knowledge and understanding are impaired by a dearth of reliable quantitative measures. Deficiencies in the available data hinder detailed analyses of the impact of technology on employment and the design of policies to address the problems created by technological and structural change.

10

Policy Options and Recommendations

Our discussion of policy options and recommendations is based on the conclusions that technological change is essential to growth in U.S. employment and living standards and that an appropriate policy structure can facilitate such change. In devising these policies, policymakers are aided by the nature of technological change, which tends to be gradual in its effects on employment and the work environment. We have developed recommendations that emphasize three broad initiatives in public and private sector policies: (1) public policies to aid worker adjustment to technological change; (2) public policies to support the development and application of advanced technologies; and (3) improvements in labor–management cooperation in the adoption of new technologies, as well as improvements in private managers' expertise in evaluating and implementing new technologies.

Although the overall U.S. standard of living and average real wages increase as a result of the productivity advances associated with technological change, individuals also suffer losses. Many of our public policy recommendations stem from the belief that a portion of the affluence created by technological change should be used to assist those suffering losses as a result of it. In addition, public policies that deal with the equitable distribution of gains and losses from technological change can facilitate such change by reducing the resistance of potential losers to new technologies in the workplace. Just as management policies to support adoption of new technologies within the firm must address worker concerns about adjustment and employment security (see Chapter 7),

177

public policies that aid adjustment can reduce potential resistance to technology and support its more rapid adoption. On balance, if policies are developed that ease the burden of adjustment for those individuals faced with job loss, thereby facilitating the adoption of new technologies, all members of our society can benefit.

RECOMMENDATIONS FOR THE PUBLIC SECTOR

Policies for Worker Adjustment

Our review of the evidence on the employment effects of technological change has identified two groups of workers that may be adversely affected: experienced workers, who may lose their jobs as a result of the adoption of technology, and labor force entrants, who may find that job opportunities are reduced by technological change. Our public policy recommendations also address the impacts of technological change on female and minority workers. The evaluation of policies affecting the educational attainment and basic skills preparation of labor force entrants is beyond the scope of this report. We therefore make no specific recommendations in this area beyond noting the severity and urgency of the problem and recommending that additional research and actions based on that research be undertaken. We do propose several steps to improve and expand programs serving technologically displaced workers. These recommendations are necessarily tentative—the available data and program evaluations provide limited information about the needs of these workers, the effectiveness and costs of various adjustment strategies, and the rates of participation by technologically displaced workers in retraining programs that offer income support. Nevertheless, the costs of inaction are great, as are the potential benefits from improvements in the adjustment assistance policies of this nation.

AIDING WORKER ADJUSTMENT TO TECHNOLOGICAL CHANGE

The panel's charge called for an identification and analysis of the efficacy of existing and alternative policies for dealing with the employment-related effects of technological change. Two existing federal programs offer adjustment assistance to technologically displaced workers. One program is Title III of the Job Training Partnership Act (JTPA), which provides assistance to all displaced workers, including those displaced by new technology; the other is Trade Adjustment Assistance (TAA). Eligibility for TAA, however, is restricted to those workers in goods-producing industries who can demonstrate that their displacement was caused by imports. Certifying the causes of displacement for this program is time-consuming and reduces its ability to provide job search assistance, retraining, and other adjustment services rapidly following displacements.[1] We have therefore chosen to focus our recommendations and options for changes in publicly financed worker adjustment assistance programs on Title III of JTPA.

The fact that Title III does not differentiate among displaced workers by the cause of their displacement is an important positive feature of this program, one that strengthens its ability to deal with technological displacement. This assessment of JTPA reflects the severe administrative difficulties and service delivery problems of programs that attempt to distinguish among workers according to the causes of their displacement. Although the charge to the panel focused on the employment effects of technological change, our judgment, based on our review of the evidence, is that a program of adjustment assistance for technologically displaced workers enforcing a strict requirement that the cause of such displacement be certified is unworkable.

Determining the precise causes of worker displacement is extraordinarily difficult, in part because of the complexity and number of channels through which the impact of technological change on the economy is realized. For example, when a worker is displaced by the closure of a U.S. plant supplying basic steel, the usual explanation is the absence of technological change in the U.S. steel industry. The lack of such change makes costs higher and quality lower than otherwise could be the case. In fact, however, much of the worker displacement in the steel industry reflects the slow growth of markets for steel products as a result of technological change in materials. How are we to determine the relative importance to steel industry worker displacement of materials substitution due to technological change, increasingly severe foreign competition as a result of technological change in steelmaking overseas, predatory pricing by foreign producers, and competition from domestic steel producers? Such distinctions are virtually impossible.

Moreover, the requirement that such a determination be made introduces severe delays and uncertainties into the delivery of services to displaced workers. One of the essential attributes of successful worker adjustment programs is rapid response—as we noted in Chapter 7 and discuss below, workers benefit most from adjustment assistance that is offered prior to or immediately after displacement, rather than after a lag of several months. The TAA requirement that the causes of displacement be determined has delayed the delivery of assistance to workers by as

---

[1]A portion of import-related displacement, as we have noted previously, reflects more rapid adoption of new technologies by foreign firms. This share, however, cannot be estimated with the available data.

much as 14 months. The severe uncertainties among workers and service providers concerning their eventual eligibility for assistance under TAA (or any other program with such a determination requirement) further reduce the effectiveness of the program.

Options for Adjustment Assistance for Displaced Workers

We recommend that action be taken to improve existing JTPA Title III job search and placement assistance programs and programs for training in both basic and job-related skills for displaced workers. We recommend that some or all of the following options be implemented:

- *broadening the range of employment services provided to displaced workers and those facing imminent displacement, including job counseling, skills diagnosis, job search assistance, and placement services;*
- *increasing the share of Title III funds devoted to training in basic and job-related skills;*
- *broadening income support for displaced workers engaged in training;*
- *instituting a program of federally provided direct loans or loan guarantees, administered by state or local authorities, to workers displaced by technological change, plant shutdowns, or large-scale layoffs (these loans could be used by displaced workers to finance retraining or relocation or to establish new businesses); and*
- *establishing a program for demonstrations and experiments with rigorous evaluation requirements to test and compare specific program designs.*

In addition to these modifications to JTPA, we recommend revising state unemployment compensation laws to guarantee explicitly that displaced workers who are eligible for unemployment compensation can continue to receive benefits while undertaking retraining.

Expanded job search assistance, counseling, and skills diagnosis services for displaced workers could be provided by existing JTPA Title III service providers and state programs. The state agency or organization providing these services might also act as a provider or referral agent for basic skills and job-related training for displaced workers. Income support for displaced workers undertaking retraining could take the form of a federally financed 26-week extension of unemployment compensation (for those eligible for unemployment compensation) or a training stipend of comparable duration for individuals enrolled in retraining or basic skills training. To encourage early enrollment in training by recipients of unemployment compensation, benefit extensions of up to 26 weeks could be made available only to those who enrolled during the early weeks of receiving regular unemployment compensation (e.g., during the first 6–10 weeks). Extended unemployment assistance could be offered on a "matching" basis, with incremental extensions of unemployment compensation beyond the conventional benefits for each week the recipient is enrolled in training with the support of regular unemployment compensation. Individuals not eligible for unemployment compensation could receive the training stipend if they satisfied an attendance or performance requirement.

As Chapters 3 and 7 noted, some displaced workers require more financial support for retraining and other forms of adjustment assistance than that provided by unemployment compensation. To meet these needs, we recommend that consideration be given to making other funds available (possibly on a trial basis or as part of a large-scale program experiment) through mechanisms similar to those used for individuals suffering dislocation due to natural disasters. Both state and federal governments alike provide extensive emergency assistance to victims of natural disasters. Federal financial assistance in these cases often takes the form of direct loans or guarantees for loans to individuals in business or to homeowners. The dislocations induced by permanent layoffs or plant closures often are no less severe than those caused by hurricanes or floods. The direct provision of loans from federal sources or the extension of federal guarantees to cover loans made by private institutions are important potential sources of income support for workers interested in relocating, establishing independent businesses, or pursuing retraining.

Although the evidence on the benefits of adjustment programs for displaced workers is limited, it is generally positive. Unfortunately, this evidence does not provide clear guidelines for the design of effective displaced worker adjustment programs. There are few data on the ideal mix of job counseling, job search assistance, skills diagnosis, or training in basic or job-related skills within these programs. Therefore, estimates of participation rates, training costs and duration, and overall program effectiveness for the economic adjustment program detailed here are subject to uncertainty. As evaluation data accumulate, however, the program's design can be modified and improved. It is important that any adjustment assistance initiatives incorporate carefully designed, rigorous evaluations.

Operation and Costs of Program Options

We have concluded that the federal government should be the primary source of funding for the abovementioned policy options. Federal financing is preferable to state funding because of the inequities created by differences in the level of state resources for such programs. Indeed, states experiencing severe economic dislocations are likely to face serious problems in funding worker adjustment assistance programs. In view of the fact that one of the central motives for these programs is the equitable distribution of the employment-related costs and benefits of new technology among the U.S. population, the avoidance of regional inequities is an important consideration. One option for financing the economic adjustment loans, like the arrangements for other federal loan programs, would use the Federal Financing Bank and therefore would not require federal funds from general revenues.

Estimates of the costs of the adjustment assistance options for workers displaced by technology depend on estimates of this population. There are no reliable estimates, however, of the number of U.S. workers displaced by the adoption of technology within this and foreign economies. The lack of such data reflects the difficulties of determining the precise causes of worker displacement within a complex economy, as was noted previously.

Our estimates of the potential costs of these adjustment assistance options are based on estimates of the annual flow of workers displaced by all causes. In view of the fact that JTPA Title III currently does not restrict eligibility according to the cause of displacement, this basis for our cost estimates also is the most realistic alternative. In Chapter 3, we note that estimates of the number of workers displaced annually by all causes range from 1 million, if displaced workers are defined as individuals with 3 years of employment in their jobs prior to layoff, up to 2.3 million when all displaced workers are included. Cost estimates also depend on assumptions about the rates of worker participation in the program, an area in which reliable data are scarce. Existing programs that combine income support with retraining for displaced workers, such as the UAW-Ford program, have enrolled 10–15 percent of the eligible population (see Chapter 7). Although we lack conclusive evidence on this point, it may be that participation rates would be higher in programs involving displaced workers from industries that pay lower wages than the automotive industry.[2]

We have made estimates of the costs to the federal government of job search assistance, training, and extended unemployment compensation for two values of the annual flow of displaced workers: 1 million workers and 2.3 million. As estimated rates of participation in these adjustment assistance programs are increased from 5 to 30 percent of the displaced worker population, the estimated costs of these policy options range from $131 million (5 percent participation rate) to $786 million (30 percent) for

---

[2]Participation rates also will be affected by the policies and guidelines adopted by states in administering any system of training, job assistance, and income support.

an annual flow of 1 million displaced workers.[3] It is important to note that the highest estimated participation rate exceeds any observed thus far in a displaced worker training program in the United States. If we assume that the flow of eligible displaced workers is 2.3 million annually, the estimated costs of the program range from $301 million (5 percent participation rate) to approximately $1.8 billion (30 percent).[4]

How could these policy options be financed? The panel discussed revenue alternatives and found no single method that was preferable to all others on equity and other grounds. In the absence of evidence suggesting that one alternative is superior to all others, the decision on funding sources and budgetary reallocations is properly political, involving considerations that extend well beyond this panel's charge.

Advance Notice of Plant Closures and Large Permanent Layoffs[5]

Although the options discussed above will improve JTPA's ability to deal with the problems of workers displaced by technological change and for other causes, a substantial body of evidence (summarized in Chapter 7) suggests that these programs are more effective when they are instituted prior to the dismissal of workers. This is especially true of large-scale layoffs or plant closings because public and private groups providing adjustment assistance may require additional time to assist a relatively large number of workers. We therefore view advance notification of these events as an indispensable component of JTPA Title III improvements.

We have concluded that substantial (a minimum of 2–3 months) advance notice of permanent plant shutdowns and large permanent layoffs offers significant benefits to the workers who are displaced and to the nation by reducing the average duration of the workers' unemployment and lessening the public costs of such unemployment. The current system of voluntary advance notice, however, fails to provide sufficient advance notice to many U.S. workers. We therefore recommend that federal action be taken to ensure that substantial advance notice is provided to all workers. Although the panel agreed on the need for federal action to broaden the coverage of advance notice within the U.S. work force, panel members were not unanimous in their support of a specific legislative or administrative mechanism to achieve this goal. The panel

---

[3]If the annual flow of displaced workers is estimated to amount to 1.2 million workers (the estimate used by the Secretary of Labor's Task Force on Economic Change and Dislocation, 1986), the estimated costs of these options range from $157 million to $943 million.

[4]JTPA Title III outlays for fiscal year 1987 are roughly $200 million, although a significant expansion in this program has been proposed in the President's budget for fiscal year 1988.

[5]Panel member Anne O. Krueger dissents from this recommendation. Her statement appears in Appendix D.

believes that the following alternatives are viable options to achieve broader advance notice, with appropriate provisions to reduce the burden on small business and provide for unforeseen circumstances:

- *federal action to require employers to provide substantial advance notice of permanent plant shutdowns and large permanent layoffs; or*
- *federal action to provide tax incentives for employers to give such notice.*

The current system of voluntary advance notice does not provide workers with the "best-practice" amount of advance notice (a minimum of 2–3 months)—as Chapter 7 notes, too few workers are notified in advance of permanent plant closures or large permanent layoffs, thus hampering their adjustment. When workers receive sufficient advance notice, the evidence suggests that they adjust more rapidly and more successfully to job loss, which reduces the costs of displacement to them and to the public sector. We believe that the benefits of advance notice more than outweigh the costs of such a policy—costs that exist, but that are distributed differently, when no advance notice is provided. When advance notice is given, the costs of worker displacement are shared by taxpayers, by the displaced workers, and by the firms closing plants or permanently discharging workers, rather than being borne primarily by taxpayers and the workers being laid off.

Through its public policies, this society has made a judgment that the costs of many regulations (e.g., those covering health and safety, consumer protection, or securities markets) that enhance the flow of information to workers and consumers and distribute costs more equitably among workers, consumers, and firms are more than offset by the benefits of such policies. We believe that advance notice falls into the same category of public policy.

The policy options to achieve greater coverage of U.S. workers by advance notice all emphasize the need for such a policy to be national in scope and design, rather than being left to the discretion of states and cities. This feature of our policy recommendation is based in large part on the panel's conclusion that all of the U.S. work force should be covered by these policies, an outcome that is feasible only if federal action is taken. Moreover, leaving the development of advance notice policies to the discretion of the states and cities is likely to produce a patchwork of conflicting policies with which managers would have to contend, increasing their costs of doing business while reducing the coverage of the U.S. work force.

Both of the policy options offered above for extending the coverage of advance notice have advantages and disadvantages. We do not endorse any specific piece of legislation in listing these options but wish to contribute to the debate and formulation of policy in this area. The first option, requiring advance notice of all firms above a specific size and exempting those firms encountering unforeseen business circumstances, has the advantage of directly affecting corporate behavior and thereby yielding benefits to workers. This goal is achieved, however, at the cost of restricting managerial discretion to respond to the changing business environment.

The second alternative also could exempt firms below a specified size threshold and those encountering unforeseen business circumstances. Its implementation could include a combination of credits on the corporate income tax for firms that pledge to provide advance notice and/or surcharges on federal unemployment insurance taxes for firms choosing not to make such a commitment. This alternative "internalizes" the social costs of plant closures and large layoffs without advance notice (in other words, firms will make such decisions based on a more complete accounting of the social and private costs), while preserving managerial discretion—firms choosing to close plants and lay off large numbers of workers without providing advance notice are able to do so while incurring higher costs. If a large number of firms decide to incur the higher taxes and/or forego the tax credits associated with providing advance notice, however, the second alternative may benefit a smaller share of the U.S. work force.

Choosing among these and other options is a political function and must be carried out through public, congressional, and executive branch debate. The choice of enforcement mechanisms for either policy option is particularly important for the effectiveness of advance notice policies. We strongly urge that action be taken by the federal government to aid worker adjustment to technological and other types of economic change by extending advance notice of plant closures and layoffs to as many workers as possible.

TRAINING FOR LABOR MARKET ENTRANTS

We share the concerns of other studies, set forth in the reports of the COSEPUP Panel on Secondary School Education for the Changing Workplace ("High Schools and the Changing Workplace: The Employers' View," 1984), the Task Force on Teaching as a Profession, of the Carnegie Forum on Education and the Economy ("A Nation Prepared: Teachers for the 21st Century," 1986), and the U.S. Department of Education ("A Nation at Risk: The Imperative for Educational Reform," 1983), regarding the amount and quality of basic skills preparation provided to labor force entrants by U.S. public schools. Improvement in the basic literacy, problem-solving, numerical reasoning, and written communication skills of labor force entrants is essential. We endorse additional public support for research on strategies to achieve this goal, as well as financial support for the implementation of programs that improve the basic skills of labor force entrants and of those already in the labor force who lack these skills.

Although technological change is not likely to impose significant demands on labor market entrants for additional job-related skills, the basic skills of this group are often weak and must be strengthened. U.S. elementary and secondary school systems, as well as providers of adult education, must improve basic skills training. In addition, the gap between white, black, and Hispanic educational attainment must be closed if all members of our society are to deal successfully with the demands of the workplace of the future.

EQUAL EMPLOYMENT OPPORTUNITY

We recommend more vigorous enforcement of policies to combat racial and sexual discrimination in the labor market as a means of improving the ability of minority and female workers, as well as minority and female labor force entrants, to adjust to the demands of technological change.

It appears that technological change will not induce large-scale unemployment in the occupations historically accounting for a large proportion of minority and female employment. Nevertheless, policies to reduce discrimination within the job market broaden the employment prospects for minority and female labor force entrants as well as experienced minority workers and women, thus improving the ability of these groups to adjust to workplace changes triggered by the adoption of new technologies.

Science and Technology Policy to Support the Adoption of New Technologies

We support continued high levels of investment by industry and the federal government in basic and applied research—this is the essential "seed corn" of innovation, and such investments play a significant role in the education of scientists and engineers. Federal support for nondefense R&D is particularly important, in view of the limited commercial payoffs from the high historical levels of defense R&D in this nation (there are important but limited exceptions to this generalization, as noted in Chapter 2). The foreseeable contribution of defense R&D to the civilian U.S. technology base appears to be limited at best.

In addition to a strong research base, however, public policies to support more rapid adoption of new technologies within this economy deserve consideration. The historic focus of post-World War II science and technology policy on the generation rather than the adoption of new civilian technologies (once again, a generalization with several important exceptions) contrasts with the orientation of public science and technology policy in several other industrial nations (e.g., Japan, Sweden, and West Germany) and may have contributed to more rapid adoption of manufacturing process innovations and more rapid commercialization of new product technologies in these nations. We therefore support the development and evaluation of additional public policies to encourage the more rapid adoption of new technologies within the United States.

We recommend increased federal support for activities and research to encourage more rapid adoption of new technologies. Although the achievement of this goal requires actions in a number of areas not considered by this panel, our review of policies leads us to recommend the following options for consideration:

• *Strengthen research on technical standards by public agencies (primarily the National Bureau of Standards) to support, where appropriate, private standard-setting efforts.*

Although standards are important to the adoption of many innovations, they play a particularly significant role in the adoption of computer-based manufacturing and information technologies. In many cases, the establishment of product standards requires extensive and diversified research efforts, which may not profit any single firm. Public agencies can play an important role in providing technical support for standard setting as well as in supporting research on alternatives to current standards. Because research by the National Bureau of Standards in these areas is financed by U.S. taxpayers, the results of its research could be licensed to U.S. firms on a royalty-free basis and licensed to foreign enterprises in return for the payment of royalties.

• *Strengthen research programs supporting cooperative research between industry and the federal government in the development and application of technologies.*

Research in the "gray areas" lying between fundamental research and development plays a major role in validating design concepts and demonstrating technological feasibility. The President's Office of Science and Technology Policy (1982) clearly recognized the importance and appropriateness of federal support of such research in its report on the aeronautics research program of the National Aeronautics and Space Administration. The success of this program in supporting high rates of technological change and adoption within an internationally competitive U.S. industry merits cautious emulation in other sectors.

We also believe that stronger research linkages between industry and the fundamental research performed on the nation's campuses can support more rapid adoption and commercialization of a number of advanced technologies; thus, we support recent federal efforts, led by the National Science Foundation, to provide seed money for university–industry research collaboration. Besides strengthening the financial foundations of higher education within the United States, such collaboration allows U.S. firms to monitor the development of new technology in a wide range of areas, attract high-quality graduate students, and join with other firms and academic researchers in precommercial research.

• *Increase support for federal programs to improve U.S. firms' access to foreign science and engineering developments and innovations.*

Chapter 2 noted that an important change in the economic environment during the past two decades is the increased technological and scientific capabilities of foreign nations and firms. The panel believes that U.S. firms on average do too little to gain access to foreign scientific and engineering research, despite the importance of these "offshore" sources of commercial technologies. Options to increase such access include continued expansion of public support for translations of foreign scientific and engineering journals (e.g., broadening and expanding P.L. 99-382, the Japanese Technical Literature Act) or strengthening the links between U.S. science attachés stationed overseas and the U.S. industrial community. These and other steps could improve the transfer of technologies from foreign sources to U.S. firms.

The Adequacy of the Data

We recommend that the post-fiscal year 1980 reductions in key federal data collection and analysis budgets be reversed and that (at a minimum) these budgets be stabilized in real terms for the next decade in recognition of the important "infrastructural" role data bases play within research and policymaking. We urge that a portion of these budgets be devoted to improvements in the collection and analysis of employment, productivity, and output data on the nonmanufacturing sector of this economy.

We recommend that a new panel study or a supplement and follow-up to the Current Population Survey be undertaken by the Bureau of Labor Statistics to examine the effects of technological change on the skill requirements, employment, and working conditions of individuals of working age. We also support the development by the Census Bureau of better data on technology adoption by firms.

In the course of this study, the panel has found that the data available from public sources are barely sufficient to analyze the impacts of technology on employment. In some cases these data problems reflect the rapid expansion of new sectors of the economy, such as services, for which federal agencies have been hard-pressed to monitor and collect data comparable in quality and quantity to those available for manufacturing. In other cases the data have declined in quality during the past decade as a result of reductions in collection budgets and efforts.

We recommend that the Bureau of Labor Statistics expand its survey of displaced workers (the special supplement to the Current Population Survey) to allow annual data collection and that this survey improve its question on the nature and effect of advance notice of layoffs.

We recommend that any expansion of adjustment assistance services for displaced workers be accompanied by rigorous evaluations of these programs to provide information on the long-term effectiveness of different program designs and strategies.

To reduce the potential for conflicts of interest that may arise when an organization charged with operating adjustment assistance programs has sole responsibility for the design and administration of evaluations of these programs, we recommend that federal and state agencies responsible for the operation of such programs share with other agencies the responsibility for evaluating them, or conduct such evaluations with the advice of independent expert panels.

We recommend that evaluations be undertaken of the implementation of the provisions of the Perkins Vocational Education Act of 1984 that allow federal and state funds to be used for improving the skills of the employed work force. In addition, a federally sponsored evaluation of a sample of state-level programs in upgrade training should be undertaken to determine the overall effectiveness of such programs and the specific design features that contribute to success.

Better data on the needs of displaced workers and better evaluations of the effectiveness of adjustment assistance programs for them, including retraining and advance notice of plant closures and large-scale layoffs, are urgently needed. To promote the development of the most appropriate evaluation designs and techniques, it may be useful to divide the responsibility for the evaluation of worker adjustment programs between the agencies in charge of program administration (at the federal level, the Departments of Labor and Education) and another federal agency, in a fashion similar to that recommended by the U.S. Department of Labor's Advisory Panel on Job Training Longitudinal Survey Research (1985). Such an assignment of evaluation responsibility would ensure a critical and rigorous evaluation of the numerous experiments that we believe are necessary in this area. Another alternative would be for the departments to carry out their evaluations in cooperation with an expert standing panel, organized by their secretaries, the National Research Council, or another independent group. One model for such a panel is the Panel on Decennial Census Methodology of the National Research Council's Committee on Behavioral and Social Sciences and Education, which works closely with the Bureau of the Census.

Health and Safety Impacts of Technological Change

We recommend a major interdisciplinary study of the consequences of technological change for workplace health and safety and the regulatory structure designed to ensure that worker health and safety are protected. These areas also should be monitored carefully by federal and state agencies.

The impacts of technological change on workplace health and safety raise important issues in areas ranging from engineering and toxicology to employee rights. Many of the workplace hazards associated with new technologies are not themselves novel, but they may raise issues for the enforcement of health and safety regulations as a result of changes in the structure of the workplace and the composition of the work force. On the other hand, significant opportunities for improving health and safety should be created by applications of information and computer-based manufacturing technologies. In view of the importance of this issue for the welfare of the American population, we feel that a major study should be undertaken of worker health and safety in the workplace of the future.

RECOMMENDATIONS FOR THE PRIVATE SECTOR

Labor–Management Collaboration in Technology Adoption

Rates of adoption of new technologies, as well as the exploitation of computer-based manufacturing and office automation technologies to increase worker productivity, satisfaction, and safety, are affected significantly by the management of the adoption process. If the process proceeds smoothly, both workers and management can benefit from these technologies, which have the potential to enrich work as well as enhance its efficiency. The potential payoffs from cooperation between labor and management in technology adoption are high, but such cooperation has been lacking in some U.S. industries. Our recommendations in this area highlight some key components of successful adoption strategies.

ELEMENTS OF "BEST-PRACTICE" STRATEGIES FOR TECHNOLOGY ADOPTION

We recommend that management give advance notice of and consult with workers about job redesign and technological change.

The adoption of new technology carries with it multiple requirements for work reorganization, retraining of workers, and job redesign and reclassification. Managers must plan the process well in advance and should consult with workers in such planning because these technologies often place greater responsibility on workers for maintenance and quality assurance. Considering the inevitable uncertainties surrounding the characteristics and potentials of new technologies, input from workers in job redesign and technology adoption can be extremely valuable.

We recommend that the adoption of new workplace technologies be accompanied by employment policies that strengthen employment security; such policies include retraining of affected workers for other jobs and reliance on attrition rather than on permanent layoffs wherever possible. At the same time, workers and unions must recognize their stake in a more productive workplace and consider modifications of work rules and job classifications in exchange for such employment security policies.

Employment security is a central concern of workers in organizations that are adopting new technologies. Management can address these concerns directly through a combination of retraining and assurances of employment security for workers. The fact that the adoption and "debugging" of new technologies often take considerable time means that work force reductions, when necessary, often can be accomplished through attrition rather than by permanent layoffs. In some cases, unions can agree to revisions in job classifications in exchange for employment security guarantees by management. Retraining and employment security programs similar to the UAW-Ford and UAW-GM training and job security programs, as well as the new training programs established by the agreements between the Communications Workers of America and Pacific Telesis and the American Telephone and Telegraph Company, have considerable promise for application in other industries.

PROTECTION FROM THE COSTS OF DISPLACEMENT

We recommend that management and labor explore the use of severance payments for permanent layoffs of experienced workers. To preserve such benefits in the event of a firm's bankruptcy, we also recommend that employers and workers consider establishing a joint insurance fund.

As noted in Chapter 7, the needs of middle-aged displaced workers from high-wage, unionized manufacturing industries differ from those of other groups of displaced workers. Middle-aged displaced workers face significant financial losses as a result of displacement and may require income support as much or more than retraining. In industries such as steel and automobiles, these workers have been covered by employer-funded supplements to unemployment benefits, by early retirement pensions, and by other forms of severance payments that have reduced the financial hardships of permanent layoffs. Such privately funded plans appear to address the needs of the high-wage, experienced worker who has been displaced, regardless of the cause of displacement. Supplemented by our proposed system of loans (discussed earlier in this chapter), these union–management agreements protect the interests of an important portion of the displaced worker population and provide a partial cushion against the financial consequences of job loss. These plans may require some form of insurance or guarantee, however, to guard against the consequences of bankruptcy of the firms providing the benefits.

Education for Managers

We recommend that the current efforts to strengthen the quality of managerial education in the management, adoption, and evaluation of advanced manufacturing and service production processes be continued, both within business schools and through other institutions. Additional research on this topic is needed and could be funded through university–industry research collaboration, among other possibilities. Education for those currently employed as managers also must be strengthened to incorporate instruction in the adoption of new technologies and in strategies for helping the work force to adjust to technological change.

Many observers ascribe the slow rates of adoption of new technologies in some sectors of U.S. manufacturing and the often disappointing productivity and quality gains resulting from the use of these technologies to failings in U.S. management. What is not widely appreciated is that new technologies impose requirements on managers for reorganization of the entire work process and, frequently, the redesign of products. All of these demands can impede the adoption process if managers are not well trained in evaluation techniques and methods for the adoption of new technologies. In some cases, for example, outmoded management accounting systems are unable to take into account the payoffs from the adoption of advanced manufacturing or office automation technologies. As a result, actual productivity and quality gains may not be incorporated in management analyses of new technologies.

Continued efforts to revise these accounting and project evaluation techniques and to instruct both students and managers in their application could contribute to more rapid and effective adoption of new technologies in U.S. industry. Further research and managerial education in the management of the relationships among research, product design, and the adoption of new production technologies also could improve the performance of some sectors of U.S. industry.

References

Abegglen, J. C., and G. Stalk. 1986. *Kaisha: The Japanese Corporation*. New York: Basic Books.

Abramovitz, M. 1956. Resource and Output Trends in the United States Since 1870. *American Economic Review Papers and Proceedings* 46(2):5–23.

Abramovitz, M. A. 1986. Catching Up, Forging Ahead, and Falling Behind. *Journal of Economic History* 46:385–406.

Abramovitz, M. A., and P. A. David. 1973. Economic Growth in America: Historical Parables and Realities. *De Economist* 121(3):253–272.

Addison, J. T., and P. Portugal. 1987. "The Effect of Advance Notification of Plant Closings on Unemployment." Department of Economics, University of South Carolina.

Adler, P. 1984. "Rethinking the Skill Requirements of New Technologies" (Working Paper 9-784-027). Graduate School of Business Administration, Harvard University, Cambridge, Mass.

Aho, C. M., and T. O. Bayard. 1984. Costs and Benefits of Trade Adjustment Assistance. In: *The Structure and Evolution of Recent U.S. Trade Policy* (pp. 153–193). Robert E. Baldwin and Anne O. Krueger, eds. Chicago: University of Chicago Press.

Aho, C. M., and J. Orr. 1981. Trade-Sensitive Employment: Who Are the Affected Workers? *Monthly Labor Review* 104(2):29–35.

Appelbaum, E. 1984. "Technology and the Redesign of Work in the Insurance Industry" (Rep. No. 84-A22). Institute for Research on Educational Finance and Governance, Stanford University.

Ashenfelter, O. 1978. Estimating the Effects of Training Programs on Earnings. *Review of Economics and Statistics* 60:47–57.

Ayres, R. U., and S. M. Miller. 1983. *Robotics: Applications and Social Impacts*. Cambridge, Mass.: Ballinger.

Baily, M. N. 1986. "An Analysis of the Productivity Decline." Paper prepared for the Panel on Technology and Employment.

Balassa, B. 1984. The Economic Consequences of Social Policies in the Industrial Countries. *Weltwirtschaftliches Archiv* 120:213–227.

194

Baran, B. 1987. The Technological Transformation of White-Collar Work: A Case Study of the Insurance Industry. In: *Computer Chips and Paper Clips: Technology and Women's Employment. Vol. 2, Case Studies and Policy Perspectives* (pp. 25–62), H. Hartman, ed. Washington, D.C.: National Academy Press.

Barnow, B. S. 1985. "The Education, Training and Work Experience of the Adult Labor Force from 1984 to 1995" (Res. Rep. 85-10). National Commission on Employment Policy. June.

Bartel, A. P., and F. R. Lichtenberg. 1987. The Comparative Advantage of Educated Workers in Implementing New Technology: Some Empirical Evidence. *Review of Economics and Statistics* 59:1–11.

Barton, P. E. 1986. "A Better Fit Between Unemployment Insurance and Retraining." National Institute for Work and Learning, Washington, D.C.

Baumol, W. J. 1986. Productivity Growth, Convergence, and Welfare: What the Long-Run Data Show. *American Economic Review* 76:1072–1085.

Belussi, F. 1986. "The Diffusion of Innovations in Traditional Sectors: The Case of Benetton." Science Policy Research Unit, University of Sussex.

Bendick, M. 1982. "The Role of Public Programs and Private Markets in Reemploying Workers Dislocated by Economic Change." Urban Institute project report.

Bendick, M., and J. R. Devine. 1981. Workers Dislocated by Economic Change: Do They Need Federal Employment and Training Assistance? In: *Seventh Annual Report: The Federal Interest in Employment and Training* (pp. 175–226). The National Commission for Employment Policy. Washington, D.C.: U.S. Government Printing Office.

Bendick, M., and M. L. Egan. 1982. "Recycling America's Workers: Public and Private Approaches to Midcareer Training." Urban Institute project report.

Berenbeim, R. E. 1986. *Company Programs to Ease the Impact of Shutdowns.* New York: The Conference Board.

Berryman, S. 1985. "The Adjustments of Youth and Educational Institutions to Technologically-Generated Changes in Skill Requirements" (Res. Rep. 85-08). Report prepared for the National Commission on Employment Policy, Washington, D.C.

Binkin, M. 1987. "Technology and Skills: Lessons from the Military." Paper prepared for the Panel on Technology and Employment.

Birch, D. 1979. "The Job Generation Process." Massachusetts Institute of Technology, Center for Regional and Neighborhood Studies, Cambridge, Mass.

Bishop, J. 1984. "Academic Education and Occupational Training." Paper presented at the Planning Conference for the National Assessment of Vocational Education, Washington, D.C., September 11–12.

Blackburn, M. L., and D. E. Bloom. 1985. What Is Happening to the Middle Class? *American Demographics* 7:18–25.

Blackburn, M. L., and D. E. Bloom. 1986. "Family Income Inequality in the United States: 1967–84." Paper presented at the 1986 meetings of the Industrial Relations Research Association, New Orleans.

Blackburn, M. L., and D. E. Bloom. 1987. "The Effects of Technological Change on the U.S. Distribution of Earnings and Income." Paper prepared for the Panel on Technology and Employment.

Blair, L. M. 1974. "Technological Impact in the Labor Market: Conceptual Issues" (Vol. 1, Pt. 1 and 2). Human Resources Institute, University of Utah.

Bloom, H. S. 1982. "Estimating the Long-Run Effects of Job Training Using Longitudinal Earnings Data: Ashenfelter's Findings Reconsidered." John F. Kennedy School of Government, Harvard University.

Bluestone, B., and B. Harrison. 1986. "The Great American Job Machine: The Proliferation of Low Wage Employment in the U.S. Economy." Paper prepared for the U.S. Congress, Joint Economic Committee.

Bowman, W. R. 1986. "Do Dislocated Worker Programs Work?" Report prepared for the U.S. Department of Labor, Employment and Training Administration. July 22.

Braun, E., and S. MacDonald. 1978. *Revolution in Miniature: The History and Impact of Semiconductor Electronics.* Cambridge, England: Cambridge University Press.

Brooks, H. 1985. "Returns on Federal Investments: The Physical Sciences." Paper presented at the Committee on Science, Engineering, and Public Policy Workshop on the Federal Role in Research and Development, National Academy of Sciences, November.

Brooks, H., and B. Guile. 1987. Overview. In: *Technology and Global Industry* (pp. 1–15). B. Guile and H. Brooks, eds. Washington, D.C.: National Academy Press.

Brooks, H., and L. Schneider. 1985. "Potential Impact of New Manufacturing Technology on Employment and Work in Industrial and Developing Countries." John F. Kennedy School of Government, Harvard University.

Brown, S. 1987. How Often Do Workers Receive Advance Notice of Layoffs? *Monthly Labor Review* 110(6):15–19.

Brueckner, L., and M. Borrus. 1984. "Assessing the Commercial Impact of the VHSIC Program." Berkeley Roundtable on the International Economy Working Paper No. 5. University of California, Berkeley.

Bruno, L. A. 1986. "Operating Effective Reemployment Strategies for Displaced Workers." Paper prepared for the U.S. Department of Labor, Division of Management and Program Evaluation, Employment and Training Administration. CRS Incorporated, Washington, D.C.

Bruno, M., and J. Sachs. 1985. *Economics of Worldwide Stagflation.* Cambridge, Mass.: Harvard University Press.

Bureau of National Affairs, Inc. 1986. *Collective Bargaining Negotiations and Contracts. Basic Patterns in Union Contracts. Vol. 2: Management and Union Rights.* Washington, D.C.: BNA, Inc.

Business Roundtable. 1983. *Plant Closings: A Position Paper.* New York: Business Roundtable.

California Employment Development Department. 1986a. "Looking for Tomorrow's Jobs with Yesterday's Skills?" Sacramento, Calif.

California Employment Development Department. 1986b. "Retraining Benefits Program, 1985–1986: Annual Report to the Legislature." Sacramento, Calif.

California Employment Training Panel. 1985. "Employment Training Panel: Annual Report 1985." Sacramento, Calif.

Cambridge Reports, Inc. 1986. *Cambridge Report: First Quarter 1986.* Cambridge, Mass.: Cambridge Reports, Inc.

Carey, M. L. 1980. Evaluating the 1975 Projections of Occupational Employment. *Monthly Labor Review* 103(6):10–21.

Carey, M. L., and A. Eck. 1985. *How Workers Get Their Training.* U.S. Department of Labor, Bureau of Labor Statistics Bulletin 2226. Washington, D.C.: U.S. Government Printing Office.

Carey, M. L., and K. L. Hazelbaker. 1986. Employment Growth in the Temporary Help Industry. *Monthly Labor Review* 109(4):37–44.

Carey, M. L., and K. Kasunic. 1982. Evaluating the 1980 Projections of Occupational Employment. *Monthly Labor Review* 105(7):22–30.

Carnegie Forum on Education and the Economy, Task Force on Teaching As a Profession. 1986. *A Nation Prepared: Teachers for the 21st Century.* New York: Carnegie Corporation.

Carnevale, A. P. 1986. The Learning Enterprise: A Report on the Size and Scope of Training. *Training and Development Journal* 40:18–26.

Carnevale, A. P., and H. Goldstein. 1983. *Employee Training: Its Changing Role and An Analysis of New Data*. National Issues Series. Washington, D.C.: American Society for Training and Development.

Ceruzzi, P. 1986. An Unforeseen Revolution: Computers and Expectations, 1935–1985. In: *Imagining Tomorrow*. J. J. Corn, ed. Cambridge, Mass.: MIT Press.

Chandler, A. D., Jr. 1976. *The Visible Hand*. Cambridge, Mass.: Harvard University Press.

Chaudhari, P. 1986. Electronic and Magnetic Materials. *Scientific American* 255(10):136–145.

Clark, J., ed. 1985. *Technological Trends and Employment 2: Basic Process Industries*. Brookfield, Vt.: Gower.

Clark, J., and P. Patel. 1984. A Model of Technical Change and Employment. In: *Technological Trends and Employment 1: Basic Consumer Goods* (pp. 223–234). K. Guy, ed. Brookfield, Vt.: Gower.

Cole, R., Y. C. Chen, J. A. Barquin-Stolleman, E. Dulberger, N. Helvacian, and J. H. Hodge. 1986. Quality-Adjusted Price Indexes for Computer Processors and Selected Peripheral Equipment. *Survey of Current Business* 66(1):41–50.

Commonwealth of Massachusetts, Division of Employment Security. 1987. "A Report to the Legislature on Worker Assistance Programs Under the Mature Industries Law."

Compton, W. D., and N. A. Gjostein. 1986. Materials for Ground Transportation. *Scientific American* 255(10):92–101.

Congressional Budget Office. 1986. *Trends in Educational Achievement*. Washington, D.C.: U.S. Government Printing Office.

Cordes, J. J. 1986. "The Impact of Tax Policy on the Creation of New Technical Knowledge: An Assessment of the Evidence." Paper prepared for the Panel on Technology and Employment.

Corson, W. S., S. Long, and R. Maynard. 1985. "An Impact Evaluation of the Buffalo Dislocated Worker Demonstration Program." Mathematica Policy Research, Inc., Princeton, N.J.

Corson, W. S., W. Nicholson, D. Richardson, and A. Vayda. 1979. *Final Report: Survey of Trade Adjustment Assistance Recipients*. Princeton, N.J.: Mathematica Policy Research, Inc.

COSEPUP (Committee on Science, Engineering, and Public Policy) Panel on Secondary School Education for the Changing Workplace. 1984. *High Schools and the Changing Workplace: The Employers' View*. Washington, D.C.: National Academy Press.

COSEPUP Panel on the Impact of National Security Controls on International Technology Transfer. 1987. *Balancing the National Interest: U.S. National Security Export Controls and Global Economic Competition*. Washington, D.C.: National Academy Press.

Costrell, R. M. 1987. "The Impact of Technical Progress on Productivity, Wages, and the Distribution of Employment: Theory and Postwar Experience in the U.S." Paper prepared for the Panel on Technology and Employment.

Critchlow, D. T. 1987. "The Politics of Technology and Employment: The 1965 National Commission on Technology, Automation, and Economic Progress." Paper prepared for the Panel on Technology and Employment.

Cyert, R. M. 1985. The Plight of Manufacturing. *Issues in Science and Technology* 1:87–100.

David, P. A. 1985. Clio and the Economics of QWERTY. *American Economic Review* 75(2):332–337.

Davis, L. A. 1986. Contribution of Exports to U.S. Employment. In: *United States Trade: Performance in 1985 and Outlook* (pp. 92–94). U.S. Department of Commerce, International Trade Administration. Washington, D.C.: U.S. Government Printing Office.

Denison, E. F. 1962. *The Sources of Economic Growth and the Alternatives Before Us*. New York: Committee for Economic Development.

Denny, M., and M. Fuss. 1983. The Effect of Factor Prices and Technological Change on the

Occupational Demand for Labor: Evidence from Canadian Telecommunications. *Journal of Human Resources* 18:161–176.

Dooley, M. D., and P. Gottschalk. 1984. Earnings Inequality Among Males in the United States: Trends and the Effect of Labor Force Growth. *Journal of Political Economy* 92:59–89.

Driever, L. S., and C. R. Baumgardner. 1984. Internal Company Preparation. In: *Managing Plant Closings and Occupational Readjustment: An Employer's Guidebook* (pp. 5–17). R. P. Swigart, ed. Washington, D.C.: National Center on Occupational Readjustment.

Ellwood, D. T. 1986. The Spatial Mismatch Hypothesis: Are There Teenage Jobs Missing in the Ghetto? In: *The Black Youth Employment Crisis* (pp. 147–185). R. B. Freeman and H. J. Holzor, eds. National Bureau of Economic Research Project Report. Chicago: University of Chicago Press.

Enos, J. L. 1962. *Petroleum Progress and Profit: History of Process Innovation.* Cambridge, Mass.: MIT Press.

Ergas, H. 1987. Does Technology Policy Matter? In: *Technology and Global Industry* (pp. 191–245). B. Guile and H. Brooks, eds. Washington, D.C.: National Academy Press.

Ettlie, J. E. 1985. "The Implementation of Programmable Manufacturing Innovations." Working paper. Center for Social and Economic Issues, Industrial Technology Institute, Ann Arbor, Mich.

Ettlie, J. E. 1986. "Management Issues for Computer-Based Process Technologies in Manufacturing." Paper prepared for the Panel on Technology and Employment.

Fechter, A. 1974. "Forecasting the Impact of Technological Change on Manpower Utilization and Displacement: An Analytic Study." Urban Institute working paper. Washington, D.C.

Fieleke, N. S. 1984. The Budget Deficit: Are the International Consequences Unfavorable? *New England Economic Review* May/June:5–10.

Finan, W. F., P. D. Quick, and K. M. Sandberg. 1986. "The U.S. Trade Position in High Technology: 1980–86." Report prepared for the U.S. Congress, Joint Economic Committee.

Flaim, P. O., and E. Sehgal. 1985. Displaced Workers of 1979–83: How Well Have They Fared? *Monthly Labor Review* 108(6):3–16.

Flamm, K. 1986. "The Changing Pattern of Industrial Robot Use." Paper prepared for the Panel on Technology and Employment.

Flynn, P. M. 1985. "The Impact of Technological Change on Jobs and Workers." Paper prepared for the U.S. Department of Labor, Employment Training Administration.

Folbre, N. R., J. L. Leighton, and M. R. Roderick. 1984. Plant Closings and Their Regulation in Maine, 1971–1982. *Industrial and Labor Relations Review* 37:185–196.

Freedman, A., and W. E. Fulmer. 1982. Last Rites for Pattern Bargaining. *Harvard Business Review* 61(2):30–48.

Freeman, C., ed. 1985a. *Technological Trends and Employment 4: Engineering and Vehicles.* Brookfield, Vt.: Gower.

Freeman, C. 1985b. The Engineering Industry. In: *Technological Trends and Employment 4: Engineering and Vehicles* (pp. 1–127). C. Freeman, ed. Brookfield, Vt.: Gower.

Freeman, C., and L. Soete. 1985. *Information Technology and Employment: An Assessment.* Brighton, England: Science Policy Research Unit, University of Sussex.

Goldstein, H., and Bryna S. Fraser. 1985. "Training for Work in the Computer Age: How Workers Who Use Computers Get Their Training" (Res. Rep. No. 85-09). National Commission for Employment Policy, Washington, D.C.

Griliches, Z. 1957. Hybrid Corn: An Exploration in the Economics of Technological Change. *Econometrica* 25:501–522.

Griliches, Z. 1960. Hybrid Corn and the Economics of Innovation. *Science* 132:275–280.

Griliches, Z. 1985. "Productivity, R&D, and Basic Research at the Firm Level in the 1970s" (NBER Working Paper No. 1547). National Bureau of Economic Research, Cambridge, Mass. January.

Gruber, W., D. Mehta, and R. Vernon. 1967. The R&D Factor in International Trade and International Investment of United States Industries. *Journal of Political Economy* 75:20–37.

Gullickson, W., and M. J. Harper. 1986. "Multifactor Productivity Measurement for Two-Digit Manufacturing Industries." Paper presented at meetings of the Western Economic Association, San Francisco, July 1–5.

Guy, K., ed. 1984. *Technological Trends and Employment 1: Basic Consumer Goods.* Brookfield, Vt.: Gower.

Hall, R. E. 1982. The Importance of Lifetime Jobs in the U.S. Economy. *American Economic Review* 72:716–724.

Hamermesh, D. S. 1987. The Costs of Worker Displacement. *Quarterly Journal of Economics* 102(1):51–75.

Hansen, J. A. 1984. "Bureau of Labor Statistics Methodology for Occupational Forecasts: Incorporating Technological Change." Paper prepared for the U.S. Congress, Office of Technology Assessment.

Harrington, M. 1962. *The Other America.* New York: Penguin.

Harrington, P. E., and A. M. Sum. 1986. "The Impact of a Near Full Employment Economy on the Structure of Unemployment and Poverty Problems in New England." Center for Labor Market Studies, Northeastern University. January.

Harris, Louis, and Associates. 1983. *The Road After 1984: The Impact of Technology on Society.* Poll conducted for Southern New England Telephone for presentation at the Eighth International Smithsonian Symposium. December.

Harrison, B., C. Tilly, and B. Bluestone. 1986. "The Great U-Turn: Increasing Inequality in Wage and Salary Income in the U.S." Paper prepared for the Fortieth Anniversary Symposium of the Congressional Joint Economic Committee, Washington, D.C., January 16–17.

Hashimoto, M. 1979. Bonus Payments, On-the-Job Training and Lifetime Employment in Japan. *Journal of Political Economy* 87:1086–1104.

Hashimoto, M., and J. Raisian. 1987. Wage Flexibility in the United States and Japan. In: *Labor Market Adjustments in the Pacific Basin* (pp. 33–59). P. T. Chinloy and E. W. Stromsdorfer, eds. Boston: Kluwer-Nijhoff.

Henle, P., and P. Ryscavage. 1980. The Distribution of Income Among Men and Women, 1958–77. *Monthly Labor Review* 103:3–10.

Hight, J. E. 1986. "Measuring Sources of Employment Change in U.S. Mining and Manufacturing, 1978–84: The Income Accounting Approach." Paper prepared for the Panel on Technology and Employment.

Hirschhorn, L. 1984. *Beyond Mechanization: Work and Technology in a Postindustrial Age.* Cambridge, Mass.: MIT Press.

Howe, W. J. 1986. The Business Services Industry Sets Pace in Employment Growth. *Monthly Labor Review* 109(4):29–36.

Howell, D. R. 1985. The Future Employment Impacts of Industrial Robots: An Input–Output Approach. *Technological Forecasting and Social Change* 28:297–310.

Hunt, H. A., and T. Hunt. 1983. *Human Resource Implications of Robotics.* Kalamazoo, Mich.: W.E. Upjohn Institute for Employment Research.

Hunt, H. A., and T. Hunt. 1985. An Assessment of Data Sources to Study the Employment Effects of Technological Change. In: *Technology and Employment Effects: Interim Report* (pp. 1–116). The Panel on Technology and Women's Employment, Committee on Women's Employment and Related Social Issues, National Research Council. Washington, D.C.: National Academy Press.

Hunt, H. A., and T. Hunt. 1986. "Clerical Employment and Technological Change: A Review of Recent Trends and Projections" (Res. Rep. 86–14). National Commission for Employment Policy. February.

Industrial Union Department. 1984. *Deindustrialization and the Two Tier Society: Challenges for an Industrial Policy.* Washington, D.C.: The Department.

International Labour Office. 1985. *World Labour Report 2.* Geneva: ILO.

Jacobson, L. 1986. "Policies to Reduce the Cost to Workers of Structural Change." Memorandum prepared for the Panel on Technology and Employment.

Jaikumar, R. 1986. Postindustrial Manufacturing. *Harvard Business Review* 64(6):69–76.

Jordan, W. A. 1970. *Airline Regulation in America.* Baltimore, Md.: Johns Hopkins University Press.

Kaplan, R. S. 1986. Must CIM Be Justified by Faith Alone? *Harvard Business Review* 64(2):87–95.

Kaplinsky, R. 1987. *Micro-Electronics and Employment Revisited: A Review.* Geneva: International Labour Office.

Kasarda, J. D. 1986. "The Regional and Urban Redistribution of People and Jobs in the U.S." Paper presented at the National Research Council's Urban Policy Workshop, Washington, D.C., July 16–17.

Katz, H. 1985. *Shifting Gears: Changing Labor Relations in the U.S. Automobile Industry.* Cambridge, Mass.: MIT Press.

Keesing, D. B. 1967. The Impact of Research and Development on United States Trade. *Journal of Political Economy* 75:38–48.

Kendrick, J. W. 1986. Outputs, Inputs, and Productivity in the Service Industries. In: *Statistics About Service Industries* (pp. 60–89). The National Research Council, Committee on National Statistics. Washington, D.C.: National Academy Press.

Kline, S. J., and N. Rosenberg. 1986. An Overview of Innovation. In: *The Positive Sum Strategy* (pp. 273–305). R. Landau and N. Rosenberg, eds. Washington, D.C.: National Academy Press.

Kosters, M. H., and M. N. Ross. 1987. The Influence of Employment Shifts and Job Opportunities on the Growth and Distribution of Real Wages. In: *Contemporary Economic Problems: 1987* (pp. 209–242). P. M. Cagan, ed. Washington, D.C.: American Enterprise Institute.

Kravis, I. B., and R. E. Lipsey. 1986. "The Competitiveness and Comparative Advantage of U.S. Multinationals, 1957–83." National Bureau of Economic Research Working Paper 2051.

Kulik, J., and H. Bloom. 1986. *The Worker Adjustment Demonstration Evaluation: Preliminary Impact Report.* Cambridge, Mass.: Abt Associates, Inc. March 11.

Kulik, J., D. Smith, and E. Stromsdorfer. 1984. *The Downriver Community Conference Economic Readjustment Program: Final Evaluation Report.* Cambridge, Mass.: Abt Associates, Inc. September 30.

Kuttner, R. 1983. The Declining Middle. *The Atlantic* 252(1):60–72.

Lawrence, R. Z. 1984. Sectoral Shifts and the Size of the Middle Class. *The Brookings Review* 3:3–11.

Lee, S. Y., V. Ichikawa, and H. W. Stevenson. 1987. "Beliefs and Achievement in Mathematics and Reading: A Cross-national Study of Chinese, Japanese, and American Children and Their Brothers." Paper presented at the Symposium on International Comparisons of Mathematics Education, National Academy of Sciences, Washington, D.C., January 15–16.

Lehnerd, A. P. 1987. Revitalizing the Manufacture and Design of Mature Global Products. In: *Technology and Global Industry* (pp. 49–63). B. Guile and H. Brooks, eds. Washington, D.C.: National Academy Press.

Leon, C. B. 1982. Occupational Winners and Losers: Who They Were During 1972–80. *Monthly Labor Review* 105(6):18–28.

Leonard, J. S. 1986. "Technological Change and the Extent of Frictional and Structural Unemployment." Paper prepared for the Panel on Technology and Employment.

Leontief, W., and F. Duchin. 1985. *The Future Impact of Automation on Workers*. New York: Oxford University Press.

Levin, H., and Rumberger, R. 1986. "Educational Requirements for New Technologies: Visions, Possibilities, and Current Realities" (Working Paper 86-SEPI-2). Stanford Education Policy Institute.

Levy, F. 1987. *Dollars and Dreams: The Changing American Income Distribution*. New York: Basic Books.

Levy, F., and R. C. Michael. 1983. "The Way We'll Be in 1984: Recent Changes in the Level and Distribution of Disposable Income." Urban Institute discussion paper.

Levy, F., and R. C. Michael. 1985. "The Economic Future of the Baby Boom." Urban Institute discussion paper.

Levy, R. A., M. Bowes, and J. M. Jondrow. 1984. Technical Advance and Other Sources of Employment Change in Basic Industry. In: *American Jobs and the Changing Industrial Base* (pp. 77–95). E. L. Collins and L. D. Tanner, eds. Cambridge, Mass.: Ballinger.

Lichtenberg, F. R. 1985. "Assessing the Impact of Federal Industrial Research and Development Expenditure on Private Research and Development Activity." Paper presented at the COSEPUP Workshop on the Federal Role in Research and Development, National Academy of Sciences, Washington, D.C., November.

Lillard, L. A., and H. W. Tan. 1986. *Private Sector Training: Who Gets It and What Are Its Effects?* (R-3331-DOL/RC). Santa Monica, Calif.: The Rand Corporation.

Lusterman, S. 1977. *Education and Industry*. New York: The Conference Board.

Lynn, F. 1966. An Investigation of the Rate of Development and Diffusion of Technology in Our Modern Industrial Society. In: *The Employment Impact of Technological Change* (Appendix Vol. 2; pp. 31–91). The National Commission on Technology, Automation, and Economic Progress. Washington, D.C.: U.S. Government Printing Office.

Mansfield, E. 1961. Technical Change and the Rate of Innovation. *Econometrica* 29:741–766.

Mansfield, E. 1963a. Size of Firm, Market Structure, and Innovation. *Journal of Political Economy* 71:556–576.

Mansfield, E. 1963b. The Speed of Response of Firms to New Techniques. *Quarterly Journal of Economics* 77:290–311.

Mansfield, E. 1966. Technological Change: Measurement, Determinants, and Diffusion. In: *The Employment Impact of Technological Change* (Appendix Vol. 2; pp. 97–125). The National Commission on Technology, Automation, and Economic Progress. Washington, D.C.: U.S. Government Printing Office.

Mansfield, E. 1972. Contribution of R&D to Economic Growth in the United States. *Science* 175:477–486.

Mansfield, E. 1980a. Basic Research and Productivity Increase in Manufacturing. *American Economic Review* 70:863–873.

Mansfield, E. 1980b. Research and Development, Productivity, and Inflation. *Science* 209:1091–1093.

Mansfield, E. 1984. R&D and Innovation: Some Empirical Findings. In: *R&D, Patents, and Productivity* (pp. 127–148). Z. Griliches, ed. Chicago: University of Chicago Press.

Mansfield, E., and A. Romeo. 1980. Technology Transfer to Overseas Subsidiaries by U.S.-based Firms. *Quarterly Journal of Economics* 94:737–750.

Marcus, A. J. 1987. "Military Training and the Civilian Economy." Paper prepared for the Panel on Technology and Employment.

Marimont, M. L., and C. M. Slater. 1986. Overview of Statistics for Service Industries. In: *Statistics about Service Industries* (pp. 20–36). The National Research Council, Committee on National Statistics. Washington, D.C.: National Academy Press.

McKnight, C. C., F. J. Crosswhite, J. A. Dossey, E. Kifer, J. O. Swafford, K. J. Travers, and T. J. Cooney. 1987. *The Underachieving Curriculum: Assessing U.S. School Mathematics from an International Perspective.* Champaign, Ill.: Stipes.

McMahon, P. J., and J. H. Tschetter. 1986. The Declining Middle Class: A Further Analysis. *Monthly Labor Review* 109(9):22–27.

Medoff, J. L. 1984. "The Structure of Hourly Earnings Among U.S. Private Sector Employees: 1973–1984." Harvard University and the National Bureau of Economic Research.

Michael, D. N. 1962. *Cybernation: The Silent Conquest.* Santa Barbara, Calif.: Center for the Study of Democratic Institutions.

Miller, H. I., and F. E. Young. 1987. Isn't It About Time We Dispensed with "Biotechnology" and "Genetic Engineering"? *Bio/Technology* 5:184.

Moore, P. W. 1986. "ETP Participants' Earning and Unemployment Records: A Preliminary Analysis." Training Research Corporation, Santa Monica, Calif.

Mowery, D. C. 1983. Innovation, Market Structure and Government Policy in the American Semi-Conductor Electronics Industry: A Survey. *Research Policy* 12(4):183–197.

Mowery, D. C. 1984. Testimony before the Economic Stabilization Subcommittee, House Committee on Banking, Finance, and Urban Affairs, March 25.

Mowery, D. C. 1985. "Federal Funding of Research and Development in Transportation: The Case of Aviation." Paper presented at the COSEPUP Workshop on the Federal Role in Research and Development, National Academy of Sciences, Washington, D.C., November.

Mowery, D. C. 1986. "The Diffusion of New Manufacturing Technologies." Paper prepared for the Panel on Technology and Employment.

Mowery, D. C. 1987. *Alliance Politics and Economics: Multinational Joint Ventures in the Commercial Aircraft Industry.* Cambridge, Mass.: Ballinger.

Mueller, E. L., J. Hybels, J. W. Schmiedeskamp, J. A. Sonquist, and C. Staelin. 1969. *Technological Advance in an Expanding Economy: Its Impact on a Cross-section of the Labor Force.* Ann Arbor, Mich.: Survey Research Center.

Nag, A. 1986. Auto Makers Discover "Factory of the Future" is Headache Just Now. *Wall Street Journal*, May 13.

National Alliance of Business. 1987. "Testimony of the National Alliance of Business Before a Joint Hearing of the Subcommittee on Employment and Productivity and Committee on Labor and Human Resources, United States Senate, on Economic Adjustment Assistance for Dislocated Workers." Submitted by John L. Clendinen, Chairman of the National Alliance of Business, March 26.

National Association of Manufacturers. 1987. "N.A.M. Encourages Voluntary Corporate Plant Closing Programs, Opposes Government Mandates." Press release regarding testimony of John S. Irving on behalf of the National Association of Manufacturers before the Senate Subcommittees on Labor, and Employment and Productivity, March 26.

National Center on Occupational Readjustment. 1984. *Managing Plant Closings and Occupational Readjustment: An Employer's Guidebook.* R. P. Swigart, ed. Washington, D.C.: The Center.

National Commission for Employment Policy. 1981. *Seventh Annual Report: The Federal Interest in Employment and Training.* Washington, D.C.: U.S. Government Printing Office.

National Commission on Technology, Automation, and Economic Progress. 1966. *Technol-*

ogy and the American Economy. Washington, D.C.: U.S. Government Printing Office. February.

National Research Council, Board on Agriculture. 1987. *Agricultural Biotechnology: Strategies for National Competitiveness*. Washington, D.C.: National Academy Press.

National Research Council, Committee on the Effective Implementation of Advanced Manufacturing Technology. 1986. *Human Resource Practices for Implementing Advanced Manufacturing Technology*. Washington, D.C.: National Academy Press.

National Research Council, Committee on National Statistics. 1986. *Statistics About Service Industries: Report of a Conference*. Washington, D.C.: National Academy Press.

National Research Council, Committee on Occupational Classification and Analysis. 1980. *Work, Jobs, and Occupations: A Critical Review of the Dictionary of Occupational Titles*. Washington, D.C.: National Academy Press.

National Research Council, Committee on Women's Employment and Related Social Issues. 1986. *Women's Work, Men's Work: Sex Segregation on the Job*. Washington, D.C.: National Academy Press.

National Research Council, Panel on Engineering Labor Markets. 1986. *The Impact of Defense Spending on Nondefense Engineering Labor Markets—A Report to the National Academy of Engineering*. Washington, D.C.: National Academy Press.

National Research Council, Panel on Technology and Women's Employment. 1986. *Computer Chips and Paper Clips: Technology and Women's Employment*. Washington, D.C.: National Academy Press.

National Resources Committee. 1937. *Technological Trends and National Policy*. Report to the Subcommittee on Technology of the National Resources Committee. Washington, D.C.: U.S. Government Printing Office. (Reprint, New York: Arno Press, 1972.)

National Science Foundation. 1985. *Science Indicators: 1985*. Washington, D.C.: U.S. Government Printing Office.

National Science Foundation. 1986a. *International Science and Technology Data Update: 1986*. Washington, D.C.: National Science Foundation.

National Science Foundation. 1986b. *National Patterns of Science and Technology Resources*. Washington, D.C.: National Science Foundation.

National Science Foundation. 1987. "FY 1988 Budget Briefing to the Scientific and Engineering Research and Education Community." Symposium conducted for the National Academy of Sciences, Washington, D.C., January 28.

Neef, A. 1986. International Trends in Productivity and Unit Labor Costs in Manufacturing. *Monthly Labor Review* 109(12):12–17.

Nelson, R. R. 1962. The Link Between Science and Innovation: The Case of the Transistor. In: *The Rate and Direction of Inventive Activity* (pp. 549–583). R. R. Nelson, ed. Princeton, N.J.: Princeton University Press.

Nelson, R. R., and R. Langlois. 1983. Industrial Innovation Policy: Lessons from American History. *Science* 219:814–818.

Nelson, R. R., M. J. Peck, and E. D. Kalachek. 1967. *Technology, Economic Growth and Public Policy*. Washington, D.C.: Brookings Institution.

Nelson, R. R., and E. S. Phelps. 1966. Investment in Humans, Technological Diffusion and Economic Growth. *American Economic Review* 56(2):69–75.

Norwood, J. L. 1983. Labor Market Contrasts: United States and Europe. *Monthly Labor Review* 106(8):3–7.

Obey, D., and P. Sarbanes. 1986. "Obey, Sarbanes Offer Plan to Upgrade Nation's Information Base." U.S. Congress, Joint Economic Committee, press release. Washington, D.C. June 20.

Organisation for Economic Co-operation and Development. 1973. *Manpower Policy in Japan*. Paris: OECD.

Organisation for Economic Co-operation and Development. 1979. *The Impact of the Newly Industrializing Countries on Production and Trade in Manufactures.* Paris: OECD.

Organisation for Economic Co-operation and Development. 1984. *Educational Trends in the 1970's: A Quantitative Analysis.* Paris: OECD.

Organisation for Economic Co-operation and Development. 1985. *Education and Training After Basic Schooling.* Paris: OECD.

Organisation for Economic Co-operation and Development. 1986a. *Labour Market Flexibility.* Paris: OECD.

Organisation for Economic Co-operation and Development. 1986b. *OECD Science and Technology Indicators. No. 2, R&D, Invention, and Competitiveness.* Paris: OECD.

Osterman, P. 1986. The Impact of Computers on the Employment of Clerks and Managers. *Industrial and Labor Relations Review* 39:175–186.

Pascoe, T. J., and R. J. Collins. 1985. UAW–Ford Employee Development and Training Program: Overview of Operation and Structure. *Labor Law Journal* 36:519–526.

Pearson, R. 1986. Occupational Trends in Britain to 1990. *Nature* 323:94.

Podgursky, M. 1984. Sources of Secular Increases in the Unemployment Rate. *Monthly Labor Review* 107(7):19–25.

Podgursky, M. 1987. "Job Displacement and Labor Market Adjustment: Evidence from the Displaced Worker Survey." Paper prepared for the Panel on Technology and Employment.

Pollock, S. H., and C. Almon. 1986. "Technical Change, Imports, and Final Demand: Their Impacts on Employment, 1961–85." Paper presented at the meetings of the American Economics Association, December 30.

President's Commission on Industrial Competitiveness. 1985. *Global Competition: The New Reality.* Washington, D.C.: U.S. Government Printing Office.

President's Council of Economic Advisers. 1986. *Economic Report of the President: 1986.* Washington, D.C.: U.S. Government Printing Office.

President's Council of Economic Advisers. 1987. *Economic Report of the President: 1987.* Washington, D.C.: U.S. Government Printing Office.

President's Office of Science and Technology Policy. 1982. *Aeronautics Research and Technology. Vol. 2: Final Report.* Washington, D.C.: Executive Office of the President.

Ravenscraft, D., and F. M. Scherer. 1982. The Lag Structure of Returns to R&D. *Applied Economics* 14:603–620.

Ray, G. 1985. Energy. In: *Technological Trends and Employment 2: Basic Process Industries* (pp. 1–69). J. Clark, ed. Brookfield, Vt.: Gower.

Rissman, E. R. 1986. What Is the Natural Rate of Unemployment? *Economic Perspectives: Federal Reserve Bank of Chicago* 3–17.

Robotic Industries Association. 1986. *RIA Quarterly Statistical Report—End of Year 1986.* Ann Arbor, Mich.: RIA.

Roessner, J. D., R. M. Mason, A. L. Porter, F. A. Rossini, A. P. Schwartz, and K. R. Nelms. 1985. *The Impact of Office Automation on Clerical Employment, 1985–2000.* Westport, Conn.: Quorum.

Rogers, E. M. 1983. *Diffusion of Innovations* (3d ed.). New York: Free Press.

Rosenberg, N. 1976. *Perspectives on Technology.* New York: Cambridge University Press.

Rosenberg, N. 1983. How Exogenous is Science? In: *Inside the Black Box: Technology in Economics* (pp. 141–159). N. Rosenberg, ed. New York: Cambridge University Press.

Rosenberg, N. 1986. "Civilian 'Spillovers' from Military R&D Spending: The American Experience Since World War II." Paper presented at the Conference on Technical Cooperation and International Competitiveness, Lucca, Italy, April 2–4.

Rosenthal, N. H. 1985. The Shrinking Middle Class: Myth or Reality. *Monthly Labor Review* 108(3):3–10.

Rumberger, R. W., and H. M. Levin. 1984. "Forecasting the Impact of New Technologies on the Future Job Market" (Project Rep. No. 84-A4). Institute for Research on Educational Finance and Governance, School of Education, Stanford University.

Sanderson, S. W. 1987. "Implications of New Manufacturing Technologies in International Markets." Paper presented at the meetings of the American Association for the Advancement of Science, Chicago, Illinois, February 14.

Saporito, B. 1986. The Revolt Against "Working Smarter." *Fortune* Magazine, July 2, pp. 58–65.

Schlesinger, J. M. 1987. Plant-Level Talks Rise Quickly in Importance; Big Issue: Work Rules. *Wall Street Journal*, March 16.

Schmookler, J. 1957. Inventors Past and Present. *Review of Economics and Statistics* 39:321–333.

Schwartzman, D. 1976. *Innovation in the Pharmaceutical Industry.* Baltimore, Md.: Johns Hopkins University Press.

Secretary of Labor's Task Force on Economic Adjustment and Worker Dislocation. 1986. *Economic Adjustment and Worker Dislocation in a Competitive Society.* Washington, D.C.: U.S. Government Printing Office.

Semerad, R. 1987. Testimony before joint hearings of the Subcommittees on Labor and Employment and Productivity, Committee on Labor and Human Resources. U.S. Senate, March 10.

Singlemann, J., and M. Tienda. 1985. The Process of Occupational Change in a Service Society: The Case of the United States, 1960–80. In: *New Approaches to Economic Life* (pp. 48–67). B. Rober, R. Finnegan, and D. Gallie, eds. Manchester, N. H.: Manchester University Press.

Slater, C. 1986. "Opportunities for Improving Economic Statistics." Paper prepared for the U.S. Congress, Joint Economic Committee.

Smith, A. D. 1986. *Technological Trends and Employment 5: Commercial Service Industries.* Brookfield, Vt.: Gower.

Social Science Research Council, Advisory Group on 1986 Quality of Employment Survey. 1986. *America at Work: National Surveys of Employees and Employers.* New York: SSRC.

Soete, L., ed. 1985. *Technological Trends and Employment 3: Electronics and Communications.* Brookfield, Vt.: Gower.

Solow, R. M. 1957. Technical Change and the Aggregate Production Function. *Review of Economics and Statistics* 3:312–320.

Sommers, G. G. 1968. *Retraining the Unemployed.* Madison: University of Wisconsin Press.

Spenner, K. I. 1985. The Upgrading and Downgrading of Occupations: Issues, Evidence, and Implications for Education. *Review of Education Research* 55:125–154.

Stevens, D. W. 1987. "State Industry-Specific Training Programs: 1987." University of Missouri, Columbia.

Stevens, J. 1983. Forging the Focused Factory. *Appliance* 40(6):34–39.

Stoneman, P. 1976. *The Economic Consequences of the Computer Revolution.* New York: Cambridge University Press.

Summers, L. H. 1986. Why Is the Unemployment Rate So Very High Near Full Employment? In: *Brookings Papers on Economic Activity 2* (pp. 339–383). W. C. Brainard and G. L. Perry, eds. Washington, D.C.: The Brookings Institution.

Technology Management Center. 1985. "The Use of Advanced Manufacturing Technology in Industries Impacted by Import Competition: An Analysis of Three Pennsylvania Industries." Philadelphia.

Temin, P. 1975. *Causal Factors in American Economic Growth in the Nineteenth Century.* London: Macmillan.

Temporary National Economic Committee. 1941. *Technology in Our Economy* (Monograph 22). Washington, D.C.

Thurow, L. C. 1987. A Surge in Inequality. *Scientific American* 256(May):30–37.

Tierney, M. L. 1983. Employer Provided Education and Training in 1981. In: *Training's Benchmarks: A Statistical Sketch of Employer-Provided Training and Education: 1969–1981*. Task I report: *The Impact of Public Policy on Education and Training in the Private Sector*. R. Zemesky, ed. Submitted to the National Institute of Education, Philadelphia, by the Higher Education Finance Research Institute, University of Pennsylvania.

Tilly, C., B. Bluestone, and B. Harrison. 1987. "The Reasons for Increasing Wage and Salary Inequality, 1978–84." John W. McCormack Institute of Public Affairs, University of Massachusetts, Boston.

Tilton, J. E. 1971. *International Diffusion of Technology: The Case of Semiconductors*. Washington, D.C.: The Brookings Institution.

U.S. Bureau of the Census. 1975. *Money Income in 1973 of Families and Persons in the United States* (Current Population Reports, Ser. P-60, No. 97). Washington, D.C.: U.S. Government Printing Office.

U.S. Bureau of the Census. 1980. *Classified Index of Industries and Occupations: 1980 Census of Population*. Washington, D.C.: U.S. Government Printing Office.

U.S. Bureau of the Census. 1982a. *Census of Manufactures : Industry Series*. Washington, D.C.: U.S. Government Printing Office.

U.S. Bureau of the Census. 1982b. *Census of Manufactures: Office Computing and Accounting Machines*. Washington, D.C.: U.S. Government Printing Office.

U.S. Bureau of the Census. 1984. *1980 Census of Population*. Washington, D.C.: U.S. Government Printing Office.

U.S. Bureau of the Census. 1985a. *Current Industrial Reports: Computers and Office and Accounting Machines*. Washington, D.C.: U.S. Government Printing Office.

U.S. Bureau of the Census. 1985b. *Current Industrial Reports: Semi-Conductors, Painted Circuit Boards, and Other Electronic Components*. Washington, D.C.: U.S. Government Printing Office.

U.S. Bureau of the Census. 1986. *Money Income of Households, Families, and Persons in the United States: 1984* (Current Population Reports, Ser. P-60, No. 151). Washington, D.C.: U.S. Government Printing Office.

U.S. Bureau of the Census. 1987. *Statistical Abstract of the United States*. Washington, D.C.: U.S. Government Printing Office.

U.S. Bureau of Labor Statistics. 1985a. *Employment, Hours, and Earnings*. United States, 1909–84, vol. 1 (Bulletin 1312-12). Washington, D.C.: U.S. Government Printing Office.

U.S. Bureau of Labor Statistics. 1985b. *Handbook of Labor Statistics*. (Bulletin 2217.) Washington, D.C.: U.S. Government Printing Office.

U.S. Bureau of Labor Statistics. 1986a. *Employment and Earnings*. Washington, D.C.: U.S. Government Printing Office.

U.S. Bureau of Labor Statistics. 1986b. *Employment Projections for 1995: Data and Methods*. Washington, D.C.: U.S. Government Printing Office.

U.S. Bureau of Labor Statistics. 1986c. "International Comparisons of Manufacturing Productivity and Labor Cost Trends in 1985." News release, June 18.

U.S. Bureau of Labor Statistics. 1986d. "Reemployment Increases Among Displaced Workers." News release, October 14.

U.S. Bureau of Labor Statistics, Office of Employment and Unemployment Statistics. 1985. "Educational Attainment of Workers."

U.S. Bureau of Labor Statistics, Office of Employment and Unemployment Statistics. 1986. "Educational Attainment of Workers."

U.S. Congress, Office of Technology Assessment. 1984. *Commercial Biotechnology: An International Analysis.* Washington, D.C.: U.S. Government Printing Office.

U.S. Congress, Office of Technology Assessment. 1985a. *Demographic Trends and the Scientific and Engineering Workforce—A Technical Memorandum* (OTA-TM-SET-35). Washington, D.C.: U.S. Government Printing Office.

U.S. Congress, Office of Technology Assessment. 1985b. *Information Technology R&D: Critical Trends and Issues.* Washington, D.C.: U.S. Government Printing Office.

U.S. Congress, Office of Technology Assessment. 1986a. *Plant Closing: Advance Notice and Rapid Response.* Washington, D.C.: U.S. Government Printing Office.

U.S. Congress, Office of Technology Assessment. 1986b. *Technology and Structural Unemployment: Reemploying Displaced Adults.* Washington, D.C.: U.S. Government Printing Office.

U.S. Congress, Office of Technology Assessment. 1986c. *Trade in Services: Exports and Foreign Revenues—Special Report* (OTA-ITE-316). Washington, D.C.: U.S. Government Printing Office.

U.S. Department of Commerce, Bureau of Economic Analysis. 1985. An Advance Overview of the Comprehensive Revision of the National Income and Product Accounts. *Survey of Current Business* 65(10):19–28.

U.S. Department of Commerce, International Trade Administration. 1983. *Domestic Employment Generated by U.S. Exports.* Washington, D.C.: U.S. Government Printing Office.

U.S. Department of Commerce, International Trade Administration. 1986. "The Contribution of Exports to U.S. Employment." Washington, D.C.

U.S. Department of Commerce, International Trade Administration. 1987. *1987 Industrial Outlook.* Washington, D.C.: U.S. Government Printing Office.

U.S. Department of Education. 1986. "Study Plan for the National Assessment of Vocational Education." Washington, D.C.

U.S. Department of Labor, Advisory Panel on Job Training Longitudinal Survey Research. 1985. "Recommendations of the Job Training Longitudinal Survey Research Advisory Panel." Washington, D.C.

U.S. Equal Employment Opportunity Commission. 1985. *The Changing National Employment Patterns of Minorities and Women in Private Industry, 1967–83* (Rep. No. 85-103). Washington, D.C.: The Commission.

U.S. General Accounting Office. 1986. *Dislocated Workers: Extent of Business Closures, Layoffs and the Public and Private Response.* Washington, D.C.: U.S. Government Printing Office.

U.S. General Accounting Office. 1987a. *Dislocated Workers: Local Programs and Outcomes Under the Job Training Partnership Act* (GAO/HRD-87-41). Washington, D.C.: U.S. Government Printing Office.

U.S. General Accounting Office. 1987b. *Plant Closings: Information on Advance Notice and Assistance to Dislocated Workers.* Washington, D.C.: U.S. Government Printing Office.

U.S. House of Representatives, Committee on Labor. 1936. *Investigation of Unemployment Caused by Labor-Saving Devices.* Washington, D.C.: U.S. Government Printing Office.

U.S. House of Representatives, Committee on Ways and Means. 1987. *Background Material and Data on Programs Within the Jurisdiction of the Committee on Ways and Means.* 100th Cong., 1st Sess. Committee print.

U.S. International Trade Commission. 1983. *U.S. Trade-Related Employment.* Washington, D.C.: U.S. Government Printing Office.

Weber, A. R., and D. P. Taylor. 1963. Procedure for Employee Displacement: Advance Notification of Plant Shutdown. *Journal of Business* 36:302–315.

Wolff, E. N. 1985. The Magnitude and Causes of the Recent Productivity Slowdown in the United States: A Survey of Recent Studies. In: *Productivity Growth and U.S. Competitiveness* (pp. 29–57). W. J. Baumol and K. McLennan, eds. New York: Oxford University Press.

Womack, J. P. In press. Multinational Joint Ventures in the Motor Vehicle Sector. In: *International Joint Ventures and Multifirm Collaboration in U.S. Manufacturing*. D. C. Mowery, ed. Cambridge, Mass.: Ballinger.

Young, A. McD. 1980. Trends in Educational Attainment Among Workers in the 1970s. *Monthly Labor Review* 101(7):44–55.

Young, K., and C. Lawson. 1986. "What Fuels U.S. Job Growth? Changes in Technology and Demand on Employment Growth Across Industries, 1972–84." Paper prepared for the Panel on Technology and Employment.

A

COSEPUP Charge to the Panel

"On the basis of present knowledge, the panel shall:

(1) report on the probable effect of current and future technological changes* on employment, focusing on the prospects for full employment and changes in the distribution of employment across occupations, social groups, and regions;

(2) report on the probable effect of current and future technological changes on the working environment, including probable impacts on labor–management relations, occupational safety and health, job skill content, and the length of the working day;

(3) report on the probable effect of current and future technological changes on existing and new employment opportunities, including probable impacts on wages, opportunities for advancement, and job security;

(4) identify economic sectors in which it is probable that the rapidity of technological change will cause significant transient effects for individuals and communities;

(5) report on the probable effect of current and future technological changes on the demand for employment-related training and education, including areas such as retraining of workers displaced by new technology, the continuing educational needs of professionals, and vocational education;

---

*Wherever "technological change(s)" appears in the charge, it is to be understood that the term includes consideration of rates of diffusion.

(6) identify and analyze the efficacy of existing and alternative public policies to manage the probable employment-related effects of current and future technological changes.

The panel shall also review the state of technological and economic forecasting methodologies and report on their potential for contributing unique insights into the employment-related consequences of technological change.

For those areas in which present knowledge is found to be insufficient to support a conclusion, the panel shall propose an agenda for research and other related activities.''

B

Consultants to and Briefers of the Panel

ROBERT U. AYRES, Professor, Department of Engineering and Public Policy, Carnegie-Mellon University

LOUIS BLAIR, Consultant, Falls Church, Virginia

ROBERT M. COSTRELL, Associate Professor, Department of Economics, University of Massachusetts, Amherst

PAUL F. GLASER, Vice President and Chairman, Corporate Technology Committee, Citicorp

JEFFREY A. HART, Associate Professor, Department of Political Science, Indiana University

H. ALLAN HUNT, Manager of Research, Upjohn Institute for Employment Research

LOUIS JACOBSON, Senior Staff Research Economist, Upjohn Institute for Employment Research

BARRY LEVY, Professor and Director, Occupational Health Program, Department of Family and Community Medicine, University of Massachusetts Medical Center

MICHAEL PODGURSKY, Associate Professor, Department of Economics, University of Massachusetts, Amherst

LAWRENCE PULLEY, Associate Professor, School of Business Administration, College of William and Mary

DUVVURU SRIRAM, Assistant Professor, Department of Civil Engineering, Massachusetts Institute of Technology

GERALD I. SUSMAN, Professor, College of Business Administration, and Director, Center for the Management of Technological and Organizational Change, Pennsylvania State University

DAVID E. WILLIAMS, Vice President, Cambridge Reports, Inc.

HILLIARD L. WILLIAMS, Director, Central Research Laboratories, Monsanto Company

C

Papers Commissioned by the Panel

C. Michael Aho, Council on Foreign Relations: A survey of the problems for U.S. trade policy created by the increased importance of technology in international trade, including an evaluation of policy responses.

Martin Neil Baily, The Brookings Institution: An analysis of the decline in productivity during the past decade, including discussion of the role of innovation, diffusion, and investment. Evidence is provided from specific studies of the textile, electronics, chemical, financial services, automobile, and apparel industries.

Martin Binkin, The Brookings Institution: A description and evaluation of military efforts to assess the training and skill requirements of new technology, including a review of specific military assessments of manpower and skill requirements associated with the use and maintenance of computer-based weapons systems.

David E. Bloom and McKinley L. Blackburn, Harvard University: A review of the literature on the impact of technological change on the distribution of income, including an evaluation of new evidence on the distributions of income and earnings and on changes in those distributions over the past two decades.

Joseph Cordes, George Washington University: A survey of the empirical evidence on the impacts of tax policy on investment in the creation of technological knowledge (through R&D), as well as the impact of tax

213

policy on the adoption of new technologies (primarily through investment incentives). The paper also incorporates a brief comparison of the treatment of these issues in industrial competitor nations.

Robert M. Costrell, University of Massachusetts: Analysis of a multisector model with supporting statistical evidence on the process of technical change and the shift of employment from goods production to services. The model incorporates the foreign sector and considers its implications for wages as well as employment.

Donald Critchlow, University of Notre Dame: An analysis and critique of the report of the 1966 National Commission on Technology, Automation, and Economic Progress with particular reference to its impact on policy.

Steven Deutsch, University of Oregon: A survey of the literature analyzing and evaluating public and private programs for retraining and job placement for displaced workers in manufacturing. The paper incorporates discussion of similar programs in Europe and Canada.

Kenneth Flamm, The Brookings Institution and The World Bank: An analysis of the economics of robot use. The paper also examines the adoption and utilization of robots based on recently collected U.S. and Japanese data.

Jeffrey Hart, Indiana University, and Jeanne Schaaf, Telenet Corporation: A discussion of the U.S. employment impacts of current and prospective growth in international trade in services, considering the role of new technologies in supporting such trade.

Joseph Hight, U.S. Department of Labor: An analysis apportioning sectoral changes in employment levels during 1972–1985 into demand effects, productivity effects, and import effects.

Larry Hirschhorn, University of Pennsylvania: A summary of the extensive literature on management and human resources problems associated with the adoption of information technologies in the services sector, examining the evidence on labor displacement and skill impacts and considering the effects of information technologies on the organization of work and firms in the services sector.

Jonathan Leonard, University of California, Berkeley, and National Bureau of Economic Research: An analysis of microdata on job creation and loss as well as the dynamics of employment and unemployment trends during 1978–1984.

Alan Jay Marcus, Center for Naval Analyses: A description of the military's experience with providing training for technology-based occupations. The paper includes a profile of those receiving such training and compares their postservice employment experiences with those of graduates of comparable civilian training.

Michael Morgan, University of Washington: Examination of the challenges to the existing occupational safety and health regulatory apparatus that are raised by microelectronics-based and information technologies in manufacturing and services.

David C. Mowery, Carnegie-Mellon University: An assessment of the scope and speed of diffusion of technological innovations.

Walter Oi, University of Rochester: A report on the impacts of technological change on wages, hours, and conditions of work in retail and wholesale trade.

Michael Podgursky, University of Massachusetts: A statistical analysis of the wage, benefit, and employment experience of displaced workers.

Kenneth I. Spenner, Duke University: An analysis of the effect of information technologies on the demand for skills and the implications for training and education.

Kan Young and Carol Lawson, Department of Commerce: An input–output model based on investigation of the effects of technological change on employment at the industry level over the period 1977–1984.

D

Statement of Anne O. Krueger

Advance notification of layoffs is undoubtedly beneficial to those workers who will lose their jobs. If there were no negative side effects associated with advance notification, it would clearly be beneficial to all.

There will be several side effects, however, if notification is mandatory. First, the necessary enforcement apparatus would increase the cost of doing business. Second, for all firms, but especially for risky ones, knowledge that layoffs could not be made on short notice would increase incentives to use capital and hire fewer workers. To the extent that fewer jobs would be created, the proposed requirement would hurt the employment prospects of those the proposal is designed to assist. That mandatory periods prior to layoffs can result in smaller levels of employment has been well documented in a number of developing countries. Third, requirements of advance notification reduce the flexibility of firms already in difficulty. The requirement is, in effect, the same as a tax for these firms.

I conclude that advance notification is desirable, and efforts to educate employers of its value to employees should be encouraged. With respect to mandatory notification, however, I believe that the evidence is far from sufficient to warrant such a step.

Index

217